A Date with a Prince

Alex stepped closer and brushed some of the hair away from my face. My breath caught as he leaned down and pressed a soft kiss to my cheek. "It's been . . . an honor to meet you, Samantha."

I looked at him sharply to see if he was joking, mocking what I had said when we first met, but it brought our faces nose-to-nose. There was an amused glint in his eyes, but underneath that was something much warmer. We stood there, neither moving, only our breaths tangling in the cold air between our lips. Part of me demanded to move closer, to press my hungry mouth to his, while another part of me screamed to run for the hills. He shifted closer and I tilted my head up as his hand moved to cup my cheek.

By Nichole Chase

SUDDENLY *Royal*

NICHOLE CHASE

AVON

An Imprint of HarperCollinsPublishers

AVON BOOKS
An Imprint of HarperCollins*Publishers*
10 East 53rd Street
New York, New York 10022-5299

Copyright © 2013 by Nichole Chase
Excerpt from *Recklessly Royal* copyright © 2014 by Nichole Chase
ISBN 978-0-06-231745-2
www.avonromance.com

First Avon Books mass market printing: December 2013

Avon Trademark Reg. U.S. Pat. Off. and in Other Countries, Marca Registrada, Hecho en U.S.A.
HarperCollins® is a registered trademark of HarperCollins Publishers.

Printed in the U.S.A.

10 9 8 7 6 5 4 3 2 1

For Daniele, Ben, Andrew, and Lily

SUDDENLY
Royal

ONE

Royal Donors Cause Congestion on Campus
—*COLLEGE DAILY*

To say my day was not going well, would be like saying the French Revolution had been a bit troublesome for Marie Antoinette. My truck had coughed and sputtered all the way to school. I couldn't find my gloves, so my fingers had turned into frozen sticks by the time I reached my classroom. Only half of the students in my first class showed up, and then I couldn't find the tests I had spent the entire weekend grading. My entire day was turning into a bad country song. By the time lunch rolled around I had been more than ready for a break. I snagged a sandwich and ate it on my way to the library. The server for our building was down and I needed to do some research.

Crossing campus, I had to wade through a crowd of people. It was like the entire student body had gathered in the middle of the school for a pep rally. Hordes of giggling freshmen were pushing their way to the front and one of them elbowed me, making me drop the notebook I was carrying. The fraternities and sororities had painted signs and hung them on trees to welcome someone. I grimaced when I realized one of them was actually a sheet that didn't look very clean. I looked from the signs to the crowd and realized I would never be able to make it up the stairs to the library. Standing in the middle of the steps was a group of people, but my eyes focused on the tall blond man. I couldn't pull my eyes away from him. He was joking with a girl while she batted her eyes and twirled a lock of hair around her finger.

I tried to see exactly why everyone was so excited, but none of it made sense. Donors came to the school all the time and most of the self-absorbed student body never noticed. The man on the steps was attractive enough to be a movie star and that had to be what had brought the mob out.

"Do you see him, Sam? The prince?" One of the girls in my first class pulled on my arm.

"Prince? Yeah, I see him." A prince? A real-life prince with a crown and throne? No wonder the masses were out in the snow. A royal donor would bring out everyone. Movie stars were one thing, but a prince? That wasn't something you saw every day. I wondered why royalty would be donating to our school, but standing out in the cold watching some guy flirt was not part of my plans. I only had a little longer before I had to be at the research center and a lot to get done in the meantime.

"He's gorgeous," the girl gushed while her friends made noises of agreement.

"Yeah, I guess." I rolled my eyes.

"Even you have to admit he's hot." She laughed at me. What the hell did that mean? I wasn't blind. Of course I noticed he was hot. What the hell kind of good would that do me? I'd never see him again. He was a freaking prince!

Spinning on my heel, I headed for a side entrance, only to see it was blocked by police. Gritting my teeth, I stomped through the snow to the back entrance. It took forever, because I was dodging mobs of people. I almost tripped on a cord and the news reporter hollered at me. I gave him my best eat-shit-and-die look, but he wasn't fazed. By the time I reached the back steps I was ready to murder someone.

There was a group of cops standing at the door, but I didn't care. I marched up and went straight for the entrance.

"You can't go in there, miss."

"Why not? I pay tuition so I can use this library."

"It's closed right now. Should be open again in an hour or so."

"I'll be busy in an hour." I gave him my best imitation of puppy eyes. "I just need to use the Internet and check out some books. Please? I'll be good. One of you guys can come in with me."

"Sorry."

I took a deep breath, the cold air stinging my lungs, and turned back toward the parking lot. My angry breath caused plumes of fog as I stomped across the pavement. I went straight to my truck, cranked it up, and headed for the center. The stars had not aligned and I wouldn't be doing what I had needed to, so I might as well throw myself into the other part of my work.

I weaved through the campus traffic, careful to not run over any of the people that seemed to see vehicles on icy roads as anything but dangerous. Thankfully, the closer I got to the wildlife center, the fewer people were out to annoy me. My old truck slid into a parking spot, coughing noisily. Ready to move on to the favorite part of my day, I hurried inside and immediately felt better. Working with the birds brightened my mood. After checking through the cages to make sure there were no problems, I moved to weighing and measuring the birds. When I got to Dover, an owl who had been hit by a car, I cooed softly. She had lost an eye, so tended to be nervous when people approached her mew.

"Hi, sweetheart. Time for some food." I unlocked the cage door and stepped in slowly. I untied the string that held her to her perch and gave her a good look-over.

Once I had her in the office, I weighed her, careful to note the exact amount in our logs before getting her food.

"Eat up. You know you want it." I lifted the mouse to her beak but she turned away. "Aw, c'mon, Dover. It's yummy mouse guts. Your favorite."

She ruffled her feathers and sighed. Dover was beautiful, but getting her to eat was always a frustrating process. I lifted the mouse to her beak again, making sure she could see the food out of her good eye. Delicately, as if she was doing me a favor, she took a small bite.

"That's it," I hummed. "Eat up."

Slowly she lifted her claw and grasped the mouse. I sighed in relief. She needed to eat to keep her weight up. It was also how we administered her medicine. Dover was a smart bird and I suspected she knew we were putting something in her food.

Once she was done, I took a few measurements and took her back to her mew. I checked the cage quickly and then cleaned up any mess she had made. I checked all our logbooks to make sure nothing had been missed, made a few notes about a Harris hawk with an injured wing, and closed up shop.

I felt much better by the time I was ready to leave. The annoyances from earlier didn't seem like such a big deal and I was looking forward to getting home. After double-checking the medicines and the food for the next day, I flipped the lights and headed out the door. I fished out my keys to lock the gate as I neared the entrance. No one else would be in until the morning.

"Samantha Rousseau?"

I looked up at the man standing just outside the gate to my research center. Dark pants met with a black blazer and an equally boring tie. The only thing remarkable about him was the expensive pair of sunglasses sitting on his nose and the little gizmo tucked into his ear, complete with a curly cord running down into his shirt collar.

"Yeah?" I finished locking the bottom of the gate and stood up. He wasn't a very tall man, possibly my father's age, but he radiated power. Since I tend to have issues with authority, I immediately disliked the guy. He hadn't really given me a reason to not like him, but people that think they're better than you or know more than you make me itch.

"Are you Samantha Rousseau?" he asked again. He didn't introduce himself or make an attempt to appear friendly. No offer to shake hands.

"Who wants to know?" I slung my bag over my shoulder as I headed toward the old pickup I drive. Authority dude followed close behind, making my hackles rise even farther.

"If you are Samantha, I need to speak with you privately."

I threw my bag into the back of my truck and turned around to look at him. I didn't bother to keep the annoyance off my face when I realized how close he was standing to me. "Well, if I was Samantha, you're in luck. There isn't anyone else around." I motioned toward the unoccupied parking lot. We were the only two people.

His frosty expression seemed to crack a little and he

gave me something that could almost pass as a smile. "Miss Rousseau, I would like to ask you to accompany me. I have someone who would like to speak to you downtown."

"Uh, yeah. That's not going to happen, Mr. Uptight. Look, if you're here about my father's medical bills, I made a payment today. If he could make any more payments, then we would, but since he can't work I doubt that's going to happen anytime soon." I yanked open the door to my truck and started to climb in. A hand landed on my shoulder and I reacted without thinking. Grabbing his fingers, I twisted as I turned and swung my other arm around in an attempt to clock him. Unfortunately he seemed to be expecting this move and countered smoothly. Taking his hand back, he ducked under my swing and danced out of the way.

"Who the hell do you think you are?" Brushing some of my brown hair out of my eyes, I glared at him. The fact that his weird smile had grown made me even more irritated.

"Nicely executed, Miss Rousseau. You almost had me." The FBI wannabe nodded his head at me. I clenched my fists at my sides to keep from trying to cream him. What a snide little—

"Here is my card. My name is Duvall. It would please my boss a great deal if you could meet us for dinner tonight. She is staying at the Parallel and has dinner reservations set for eight-thirty at the restaurant downstairs." I looked at his card and then back to his face. What on earth could this be about? The Parallel was the nicest hotel in town. I looked back at his card and noticed the odd crest at the top. A small bird rested on a branch that wrapped around a blue shield. Who was this weird little dude wearing an earpiece?

"Who's your boss?"

"The Duchess Rose Sverelle of Dollange."

I looked at him for a moment to see if he was joking. Nope, his face was still set in that frosty, serious expression. I blinked slowly and looked back at his card before returning my eyes to his face.

"I think you have the wrong Samantha. There is no reason a duchess would be looking for me." I climbed into the driver's seat and he closed the door once my leg was in, attempting a smile. It looked weird on his face, as if he wasn't used to doing it very often. I rolled down the window and tried to hand him back his business card, but he waved a hand to signal I should keep it.

"You are Samantha Rousseau, wildlife biologist specializing in raptors? Graduate student, daughter of Martha Rousseau?"

"Uh, yeah, but—" I shook my head when he stepped a little closer to the window.

"I am very good at my job, Miss Rousseau. I was told to find Samantha Rousseau, and I have. The duchess's reasons are her own." He shrugged. "Of course, falconry is a large sport in our country. Perhaps it has something to do with that."

"And what country is that?" I looked back at his card as if it might offer some answers.

"Lilaria." He stepped away from the car and nodded to me. I looked at him for a moment in confusion. Eventually I threw the business card onto the pickup bench next to me and stuck my key in the ignition.

"Okay, Duvall. I might be there, but I'm a pretty busy person. Got to check the calendar first." With that, I threw the truck into reverse and backed up.

"Of course." He nodded at me as I switched to drive and pulled out of the parking lot. From the way he smirked at me, I was pretty sure he knew I was lying about being busy.

I watched him get into his black sedan, noticing for the first time the little flags on the hood. What on Earth would a duchess want with me? How had I ended up on some royal's radar? I hit the switch for the radio and leaned back into the old driver's seat. My mind worked through reasons that someone from a country I barely knew existed could possibly want to speak to me. Maybe she was interested in the research center. But why would she come to me? Wouldn't it make more sense for her to contact Dr. Geller? He would be the one to handle donations or any sort of involvement on her part. He was out of town; maybe he forgot to tell me this lady was coming.

The truck coughed as it switched gears and I entered the on-ramp for the highway. The clock on the dashboard said it was almost five-thirty. Dr. Geller would still be in the field, so there was no point in calling him to find out what was going on. I'd just have to wing it. I snorted and sped the truck up. I didn't have much time to change and make it back downtown.

It wasn't like I had anything else to do and she might be able to help the research center. The staff was making do with half the supplies they really needed to rehabilitate the injured raptors in their care. The cages were much smaller than they needed to be, and medical supplies were expensive. We're always cutting out things from the budget to afford more medicines or training equipment.

When I pulled up to the little house I shared with Jess, I sighed and parked at the curb. Her boyfriend was parked in my spot again, not that it mattered since I was leaving soon. Yanking the key out of the ignition, I hopped out and grabbed my bag from the truck bed. When I opened the front door, the smell of fresh chili wafted to my nose and I groaned. It smelled delish. I dropped my bag and kicked off my boots before walking to the kitchen.

Bert was wearing a flowered apron and stirring the chili with a large wooden spoon while Jess sat on the counter next to him. He held up the spoon for her to taste and she laughed when some of it dropped onto her legs. The little TV was on and there was some type of news show playing, which surprised me. Jess liked to watch all the pregame shows.

"We made chili! Ready for the game?" When she saw me she smiled and waved me over.

"I forgot about the game." I looked over Bert's shoulder at the chili and my stomach growled. "I made plans."

"Sam!" Jess groaned. "What could be more important than this game? It's the most important game of the year."

"Every game is the most important game of the year to you." I rolled my eyes and looked back at the TV. "What are you watching?"

"Don't," Bert whispered. But it was too late.

"Some idiot prince and duchess are in town and all the news stations are acting like it's some kind of big deal." Jess glared at the old television set. "It's not like they're from an important country or anything. I mean, I'm missing the stats from the other games!"

"Oh." I looked back at the TV, interested. There on the steps of the university's new museum was the good-looking guy and an older, dignified woman. She used a gold pair of scissors to cut a red ribbon and waved at the people around her. The prince was speaking to a blond coed near the front door. He was definitely not a frumpy prince. Nope, not frumpy at all. Short blond hair, long legs, and broad shoulders. Even without the royal credentials, he would probably have snagged all the female's attention. And from the cocky grin, it was obvious he knew it. I really hoped he wouldn't be at dinner. Mainly because I didn't want to stare at him like a dumbass. I was already nervous about meeting royalty.

"So?" Jess's voice cut through my thoughts and I tore my eyes from the screen.

"What?"

"I asked what your big plans were." Jess frowned. "Quit staring at Prince Yummy and pay attention."

"Prince Yummy?" Bert pulled off the apron and frowned at Jess. I tried not to laugh.

"That's what the undergrads were calling him. It's annoying, but it stuck in my head." Jess hopped down and wrapped her arms around Bert's neck. She wasn't a short girl, but she looked petite next to her boyfriend. I started to leave to avoid their PDA, but she wasn't ready to let me escape. She leaned back and frowned at me. "You didn't answer!"

"I'm going to dinner with Prince Yummy's dear old relative." I smiled at her shocked expression and made my way to my tiny bedroom.

I started flicking through the clothes in my closet as Jess banged in after me. She was looking at me like I was crazy, so I just shrugged.

"You're serious."

"Yeah. I've got to be at the Parallel in less than three hours."

"Oh my God. You're going to have dinner with a duchess? Is Prince Yummy going to be there too?" Her eyes were huge and I frowned. It would be much better if someone like Jess went to this dinner. She was gorgeous and people tended to like her immediately. I, on the other hand, rarely dressed up and couldn't remember the last time I painted my fingernails. What was the point if I was going to be scraping dirt out from under my nails in a few hours?

"I don't know about Prince Yummy." I shook my head. I needed to find out his name so I didn't accidentally refer to him that way.

"Why?" She sat down on my bed and watched as I pulled out the few dresses I owned. I held up a bright summer print and she shook her head.

"I don't know. Some guy showed up at work and said the duchess wanted to have dinner with me. I guess Dr. Geller forgot to tell me she was coming." I looked at the dresses in my hands and put the blue back. Black was probably the safest option. That way if I spilled anything on myself, it wouldn't be overly obvious.

"Some guy said she wanted to have dinner with you. Why do you think this has anything to do with Dr. Geller?" Jess crossed her legs and I realized she wasn't leaving. "Seems pretty fishy. Are you sure he is who he says he is?" Jess was pretty practical when things boiled down to it.

"I think so. And if not, then I'll have only wasted one night." I shrugged. "Why else would a duchess want to talk to me? And she was at the school earlier. Maybe she's a donor or something." I laid the dress out on the bed and thought about jewelry. "I have no idea how to talk to her. I mean, do I address her as Duchess? My lady? Your Highness?" This wasn't something I'd grown up knowing. It wasn't like I was from England.

"The Internet is our friend!" Jess grabbed my laptop off the bedside table and popped it open. She typed for a moment and then looked up at me. "They are from Lilaria, right? Says here they're big into birds, so I guess it makes sense."

"Okay. What about their royalty?" I turned to look back at my closet, realizing I didn't have an appropriate jacket.

"Just the usual stuff. A prince is addressed as His

Royal Highness." Jess skimmed through the link she was reading. "Address the duchess as Duchess Whatever. But it says you should adopt their type of formality."

"So, I shouldn't call him Prince Dude or her Royal Lady?"

"I think you nailed that one on the head." Jess closed the computer. "You'll be fine. Just be the charming person I know you can be."

"Note to self: Don't eat with fingers or burp in their faces. Got it." I smiled at Jess and she laughed.

"We'll save you some chili." Jess got up and looked at me. "Text me when you get there and let me know it's legit."

"Sure." I smiled at her over my shoulder as I headed for my bathroom. Time to make myself presentable. Thank God, I had time to shower.

TWO

Royals in Rags
—*CHICAGO GAZETTE*

My truck sounded like it was on its last leg as I pulled up to the hotel. The traffic had been terrible, so I didn't have time to park the thing myself and avoid the embarrassment of valet. Cursing under my breath, I tried to stuff some of the garbage from the bench under the seat before the attendant opened my door. Looking up I smiled at the young guy.

"Sorry, the Bentley is being detailed."

"Looks to me like you traded up, ma'am. This is a classic." He held his hand out and helped me out of the car. I smiled gratefully at him because I had let Jess talk me into wearing heels tonight. He handed me my ticket and I gave him my keys.

I tried to not cringe as my truck made a coughing noise before it pulled away. The hostess was watching me through the glass doors, so I took a deep breath and held my head high, all the time quietly praying I wouldn't end up busting my ass in the damn shoes. The doorman opened the door for me, but even he had a look of disdain as he studied me.

Chili was already sounding much better. Hopefully the food would be decent. And not overly expensive. I'd just sent three hundred dollars to the hospital for my dad's monthly payment. To say I was scraping the bottom of the barrel would be putting it nicely. I smiled at the hostess, hoping that being polite would smooth over the truck fiasco.

"Hi. I'm meeting Duchess Sverelle for dinner."

"Does she know you're coming?" The blond woman's voice grated on my ears. It was high and nasally. Why would they want that for their first impression? There are lots of blond, modelesque women who would love a job like this. Her eyes narrowed and ran over me in disgust.

"Since she's the one who invited me, I would assume so." Operation Nice was over.

"Uh-huh. And what's your name?" The woman looked down at the list in front of her with so much seriousness you would think it was full of people waiting for a heart transplant.

"Samantha Rousseau." I watched her as she looked at the list and then back to me. "I'm from the university."

"I see. Just a moment." She walked away, her hair swishing behind her like she was walking in a wind tunnel for a photo shoot and I found myself wondering how she did that.

She returned a moment later, accompanied by a man with a bored look. He was tall, thin, and older, and reminded me of Alfred from the Batman movies. But without any of the humor or intelligence. His eyes traveled over my big winter coat and glimmered with disgust. He lived here, didn't he? How could he think it was weird to wear a big winter coat?

"Miss . . ." He looked at me expectantly.

"Rousseau. Samantha Rousseau."

"Miss Rousseau, your name isn't on the list."

"I'm sure it was a simple mistake." I narrowed my eyes at the man. "Perhaps you could go check with the duchess."

"I'm sure the duchess would have informed me had she been expecting someone else for dinner." He smiled at me and I had to take a deep breath before answering.

"Well, as close as you apparently are with the duchess, it must've slipped her mind." I leaned forward. "Look, I'm just trying to keep an appointment here. Can't you go ask her if she was expecting me?"

"I'm afraid it is against policy to bother guests while they are dining."

"You've got to be kidding me." I brushed the hair out of my eyes and glared at mini-Alfred. "Just go ask her."

"Miss Rousseau, this is a very respectable restaurant. I suggest you leave and not cause a scene. I will call security if I need to."

"I suggest you go ask the duchess if she's expecting me, or go ahead and call security and you can expect a scene. Then when she sees you escorting me out of the restaurant, you can explain why you sent me away."

"I'll go. This once." He eyed me for a long moment before sighing heavily. "If it turns out you are not an invited member of their party, I will be returning with security."

"And you can apologize when you get back with your tail between your legs." Operation Pissed was coming into play. I had a hard time holding my tongue when I got into that mode.

The man sniffed again and I was tempted to offer him a tissue but bit the inside of my cheek instead. "We'll see."

He walked away from the little podium and the

blond hostess took his place. She ignored me as if I wasn't there, and that was just fine by me. I slid closer and looked at the sheet in front of her. Just before she covered it with her arm, my eyes landed on my name.

"Oh, now that's just rude." I turned away and quickly followed the old man to a table in the center of the room. Those petty jerks were trying to keep me out because they thought I didn't belong? Because of my truck or my clothes?

My furious stride made quick work of the space between the door and the table Alfred was standing next to. I caught up to him in time to hear the last of his words.

"She looks rather questionable."

"The 'rather questionable' woman is standing right behind you." *You stupid little dildo.* I glared at his head, barely registering the people at the table until they stood up.

"I was told the Parallel, and I would assume its restaurant, was used to hosting dignitaries and royalty." The woman's voice was calm and cool. "Your tone would be embarrassing no matter who you thought Lady Rousseau was."

My eyes jerked to the woman and I wondered if the duchess was losing her mind. Perhaps it was appropriate to address people by Lady or Sir in their country. Her mouth twitched in amusement as she watched the man grovel and I decided she must be teaching him a lesson. She might be my hero.

"I'm so sorry, I had no idea. . . ." The Alfred wannabe was sputtering apologies and it took all my willpower to keep from rolling my eyes.

"No, don't apologize to me. Apologize to Lady Rousseau." Her eyes twinkled when she looked at me.

"My apologies, Miss—I mean, Lady Rousseau."

I bowed my head a little. "Accepted. Perhaps you shouldn't be so quick to judge next time."

"Yes, my lady. May I take your coat?"

I shrugged out of my coat and that's when I felt his eyes on me. Looking up, I realized Prince Yummy had indeed come for the dinner. Jess and the undergrads had been wrong. He wasn't yummy, he was delicious; a feast to be savored. Dark blond hair hung a smidge too long, eyes so blue it was like looking into the heart of a glacier. Built like the statue of David; the contours of his suit hugging every delicious muscle. Laugh lines around his mouth and eyes brought him into the realm of humanity, and gave him a personality. As his eyes ran over my face and down my body slowly, heat washed over my skin. When I handed the jacket to the maître d' I felt naked. There was something about his bright blue eyes that left me feeling exposed.

"Thank you, Alfred." I mumbled the words, feeling completely off guard by the look I'd just received. The man left without a word, and I really hoped he didn't do anything nasty to my jacket.

"Alfred?" The prince's mouth quirked on one side, revealing a dimple, and I wondered if a dimple could kill a person. It was possible I was having a heart attack right now. "Is that his name?"

"Oh, you know. He looks a bit like Batman's butler, but without the wicked sense of humor." I winced. I was speaking to a prince, a real live prince, and my first interaction was describing a comic-book character. At least I wasn't a slobbering mess looking at him.

"I vaguely recall something about Batman and his butler." The prince's eyes glittered mischievously. I felt my mouth twist a little, relieved he had gotten my ill-timed sense of humor. "I would have pegged him more as Jarvis. Slow, annoyed voice."

"Samantha, it's a pleasure to meet you." The duchess held her hand out for me, and for a brief moment I panicked, not sure if I was supposed to bow over it or shake it. I decided if she was in America I was just going to shake it. Her fingers were dry and warm, her grip surprisingly tight. "I'm Rose."

"It's nice to meet you." Jesus. I should have read that article myself. I had no idea what to say or how to act.

"This is my nephew, Alex." I turned toward the outstretched hand and hoped my palms weren't sweaty.

"An honor to meet you." As soon as the words had left my mouth, I regretted them. Why had I said that? Why didn't I just say it was nice to meet him? Surely it hadn't sounded like a come-on. I was just being paranoid. How had I lost control of this evening already? Who was I kidding? I'd lost control as soon as that weirdo Duvall had approached me.

"The honor is mine. Trust me." Instead of shaking, he lifted my hand to his mouth and his lips brushed across my knuckles gently. They were warm and full, and my body tingled at the contact. I stopped breathing for a moment and had to remind myself that oxygen was important. When he lowered my hand, his thumb ran over my knuckles. He knew how to affect a woman, that was for sure. Stepping around me, he pulled my chair out. I don't think anyone has ever pulled a chair out for me. It was weird. What did I do with my feet? The stupid heels caught on the floor and almost came off, so I just lifted them up until he was done.

He moved around to his aunt and helped her into her chair as well. She was watching me with bright, intelligent eyes and I wondered what she was thinking. I felt a bit like she was measuring me. She motioned to the waitress standing off to the side and I was offered a glass of wine. I took it, but only to be courteous. I was already feeling out of my element.

"I apologize for that terribly inappropriate behavior, Samantha." Rose frowned.

"It's okay, Duchess. I'm sure he was just trying to keep people from bothering you." I was being generous. I was mentally debating egging the hotel.

"Please, call me Rose." She smiled at me and I smiled back.

"Thank you, Rose."

"Are you ready to order?" The waitress was back, her white button-up shirt was undone a bit and she stood close to the prince. The question had been addressed to him and only him. Rose looked at me and winked as if amused, but when I noted his uncomfortable expression I couldn't help but feel bad for him. His face had transformed from friendly and thoughtful to stony.

"Actually, I haven't had a chance to look at the selection." I cleared my throat and picked up the large red menu.

"I'll give you a little more time."

"Could you turn the heat up a little?" The waitress started to turn, but his voice stopped her. His blue eyes locked on mine and for a minute I wondered if my clothes had caught on fire. Or maybe his accent had managed to make it hotter without turning up the heat. "I noticed your hands were cold."

"No, no. I'm fine really." It was cold in the restaurant, not that I noticed right this minute. Or maybe that was just the dress I was wearing. It wasn't exactly designed for winter wear, but it was the nicest dress I owned. When my mother passed, it was one of the things I had made sure didn't disappear. I wasn't much of a fashionista, but I loved the vintage Chanel.

He looked at the waitress and smiled. "The heat, please."

"Of course, Your Highness." At her use of his title, the corners of his mouth twitched down briefly and he looked back at his menu.

"Thank you, but I really was fine." I looked at him and narrowed my eyes. I didn't care for men that ordered food for their women and picked out their clothing. Even if he was hot as hell.

"No reason to be uncomfortable." He smiled, his eyes moving back to my face. I felt heat creep into my cheeks and I looked away. Squinting, I stared at my menu, not really seeing the words, and tried to crush the odd effect he seemed to have on me. This was a business meeting and it needed to stay professional.

I could feel his gaze like a hot touch. It had been a while since I had been with a man, but that was fixable. They made toys to replace men. However, I had a feeling Prince Alex could do things that would make my toy wholly inadequate.

"Have you been here before, Samantha?" Rose's voice drifted to my ears and I was glad for the distraction.

"No, this is the first time I've eaten at the Parallel, but I've heard the food is wonderful." I smiled over my menu at her. Sometimes there's a feeling when you meet someone, a sense of understanding and connection. I felt it with Rose. "Dr. Geller comes here occasionally for business lunches. Speaking of Dr. Geller, I wasn't able to get in touch with him before coming to dinner, so please forgive me for being unprepared. I'm not sure what exactly we're discussing tonight."

Rose smiled at me for a minute as if amused. I looked over at Prince Yummy—dang it, Alex—and frowned. His eyes were moving back and forth between me and his aunt, a small smile playing along his delicious lips. They both looked like they were hiding something.

"Let's order and then we'll talk about it. I'm starving." Rose set her menu down, so I quickly looked through and picked something to eat. Something weird was going on here and I was going to figure it out. I looked for the waitress and smiled, hoping that would bring her to the table a little faster so we could get down to business.

She glared at me as she sauntered back to us and I wondered why the staff here seemed to hate me so much. What on Earth had I done? Shown up to dinner with the duchess and the prince— Oh. The prince. She was glaring at me because I was eating dinner with Prince Yummy. Sheesh. It wasn't like we were alone. Who brings their aunt on a date?

The thought brought heat to my cheeks—again. I was never going on a date with Alex. We were from different worlds. He wore expensive suits and probably never got his hands dirty. I wore blue jeans and flannel shirts. My hands were always dirty. Okay, not always dirty. I washed them, but I never met a bird that hadn't at least thought about pooping on me.

"You're ready?" The waitress once again turned her body and ample cleavage toward Alex and leered.

"Ladies first." Alex leaned forward so he could look around the waitress. "Samantha, what would you like?" My name spoken in that accent made it sound much sexier, but it was the glint in his blue eyes that made my skin burn.

"I'll take the chicken, please." There were no prices on the menu, but I was certain that had to be the cheapest thing on there. Chicken would certainly fall under lamb or duck. I hoped.

"Got it." If the waitress had been chewing gum she would have popped it in her mouth at me. I was torn between laughter and being offended. She smiled at Rose, though. A disgustingly sweet expression that made her look sick. Or maybe it just made me nauseated. "And for you, Duchess?"

"I'll have the same thing Lady Rousseau is having." Rose pushed her menu toward the waitress, but the girl didn't notice. She was looking at me with a worried expression. I shrugged, not sure what to say. A deep chuckle made me sit up straighter in my seat and look at Alex. He was watching me, an amused gleam in his eyes as if he was in on a secret.

"I'd like the rib eye, please. Rare." He handed his menu to the waitress without looking at her and leaned forward, his hands clasped in front of him, and smiled at me. "Samantha. Are you from here?"

"I'm a transplant. My family moved here ten years ago for a job. Thankfully, the college I wanted was nearby."

"Is that so?" Alex leaned forward and looked at me intently. "I would think most people going off to college would want to get as far away from home as possible."

"My mother passed away and I didn't want to leave my father." I didn't like where this conversation was going. He seemed almost too interested. Like in my private life there were secrets that he had to know.

"How is your stepfather? I understand he's been sick." Rose's eyebrows drew together. "I can't say I care very much for the way that health care is handled in the States."

"He's handling everything very well, thank you." I guess my outburst with her lackey earlier hadn't gone unreported. "But we're not here to discuss my family. What kind of questions do you have about the center and our program?"

Rose leaned forward. "Actually, your family is exactly why I am here."

THREE

How to Lose a Royal
—PERRY TALKS

"**M**Y FAMILY?" I felt my eyebrows rise and tried to control my expression. What the hell was going on?

"Why did you decide to keep your mother's maiden name when she married your father?" Rose folded her hands in front of her and her eyes bored into mine.

"I'm not sure why that would be any of your business." I looked at Alex, but his face gave nothing away. "I thought I was here to discuss the raptor program for Dr. Geller."

"Yes, I realized that earlier. However, I was hoping to discuss something else." Rose leaned back as the waitress and several helpers delivered their food to the table. "I was hoping to discuss you."

"I can't imagine why." Shaking my head, I leaned back so the waitress could set my plate in front of me. "Thank you."

"Do you know much about Lilaria?" Rose took a sip from her glass before picking up her fork and knife. "We're a small but proud country."

"No, I can't say I know much about your homeland."

"Let me tell you a bit about it. We control a rather large portion of Europe's oil resources, which brings a great deal of wealth to our citizens, but it also brings trouble. In the late eighteen hundreds, a royal family of the name Malatar felt it was time for a change; however, they didn't want an outright war. You see, they didn't have many supporters. The country was flourishing and the people were happy." Rose looked at the waitress, who seemed to be taking longer than needed to deliver Alex's plate. With annoyance, I realized she was buttering his roll while pushing her cleavage into his face. I don't know why I cared, but it bothered me. Here we were trying to have an important conversation and this chick was acting like a dog in heat. He didn't look exactly happy about it, but also looked like he wasn't sure how to stop it without a fuss.

When the waitress stood up with a smile on her face, I pushed my dinner roll in her direction. "What exceptional service the Parallel offers. Thank you." The waitress's eyebrows pulled together, but there wasn't much she could do. Taking the butter knife off my dish, she generously slathered the roll with butter and set it back on the plate.

"I haven't seen bread buttered that well in a long time." I smiled at her sweetly and heard Alex chuckle. The waitress turned around and stormed away. Narrowing my eyes at Alex, I frowned. "Don't take this the wrong way, but maybe you should practice telling people to leave you alone. I thought she was going to maul you."

"Occupational hazard. If I'm rude, there's a story in the paper about me mistreating the staff. If I do nothing, it could go either way." He raised an eyebrow. I was obviously not cut out for diplomacy. "But thank you for stepping in. I was afraid to breathe or I might fall into her shirt."

"No problem." I shook my head, amazed by how people behave, and looked back at Rose, who was watching us. "You were telling me about the family trying to take over."

"Yes. Well, they didn't have much support, so began going after the royal families they thought would put up the most resistance. Several royal families died in bizarre accidents and that's when everyone became nervous. There was a lot of anger and finger-pointing, but no hard evidence. Our family was left with no way to legally arrest the traitors." Her sigh was laced with frustration. It was obviously something that had caused her relatives a great deal of stress, although how something that happened over one hundred years ago had bearing on this conversation about me was still a mystery. "Eventually, some of the families felt threatened enough to leave the country. At times with no notice, leaving everything behind like they would be back any day." Rose leaned forward, her keen eyes brightening. "One of the largest families to leave was that of Duke Rousseau."

I was glad I didn't have anything in my mouth, because I was pretty sure I would have spit it out on the table. "You think I'm part of his family?"

"I know you are part of his family." Rose's grin was victorious. "My sister, the queen, has been searching for all the families for years in hopes of bringing them home. We've traced your family all the way back to the day they set sail from the French coast for America."

I sat there for a minute, completely unable to form a coherent thought. Images of my mother passed before my eyes. Snippets of conversation repeated themselves. I knew that at one point my family had come from money, but my great-grandfather had gambled most of it away. Now there was the fact that my family had supposedly run. Run away and deserted our homeland.

"Why? Why are you telling me this?" I looked up from the plate of food I was no longer interested in.

"We want to reinstate your title and lands, Samantha. They are yours and have been kept in trust until we could find you." Rose watched me, apparently not sure of my reaction.

"It's true, Samantha. My mother has been searching for the missing families for years. If my aunt says you're from the Rousseau line, then you are." Alex reached out and touched my hand, the one that was clutching the fork so tightly my knuckles had turned white. Heat washed up my arm and I met his eyes.

"Why? Why would she want to find the people who abandoned their country?" I couldn't wrap my brain around this being about my family.

"Samantha, in our country, the most important thing to us is family. Not just among the royals, but all our citizens. Our work laws are geared to protecting families. Duke Rousseau did what he did to protect his family. There was no legal way of safeguarding themselves, and he knew they would be targets." Alex squeezed my fingers and I looked down at our hands. His was much larger than mine, and somehow, even though I had just met him, I found his touch comforting.

"What does this have to do with me? What do you want?" I thought I'd come here tonight to discuss a donation for the raptor program.

"As I said, the queen wants to reinstate your lands, Samantha." Rose calmly folded her hands in her lap. "She wants to reinstate your title."

"Title?" My mind was mush. I couldn't make sense of what they were telling me.

"Yes. By all rights, you are the Duchess of Rousseau. You are the legal heir."

I stared at her and tried to wrap my brain around

what she was telling me. "That can't be right. There must've been a mistake. I'm not a duchess. I'm a grad student." I gently pulled my hand out from under Alex's.

"Samantha, ask yourself this: Why did your mother keep her maiden name? Why did she not take your stepfather's last name for you and herself?" Rose sat patiently, her face blank as she waited for me to think about it.

Unbidden, my mother's voice filled my mind. *There are two things you must never forget. One, you are a Rousseau and you should always be proud of that. Two, family always comes first. Always.* She had told me those things a hundred times, but I'd always thought she was telling me to be proud of who I was, it didn't matter that I didn't know my father. And we were a family until we met Dean, my stepfather. And then he too became family. The saying never changed. Family comes first.

"Did she know?" I looked at Rose and hoped she didn't notice the tears in my eyes. Mom had been gone for five years, but it still hurt when I heard her voice in my head like that. And now, to find out this, I wasn't sure what to do. What to think.

"I'm not sure. It's likely she knew a little, but I don't believe she knew everything." Rose frowned. "I'm sorry we didn't find you sooner. I would have liked to have met your mother. I understand she was a brilliant biologist."

"She was." My eyes slid around the room as I tried to regain my composure. How could she not tell me? Did she know the truth? Part of the truth? And what about my dad? My feet started to itch and I wanted to run out of there and demand an answer.

"I'm leaving in a couple of days to head home. I'd like it very much if you would return with me." Rose leaned forward. "The Rousseau family was a very important one and my sister is extremely excited to meet you."

"In a few days?" This was insane. "I can't. I have school. Projects. I can't just leave." I shook my head. "What would I do?"

"Aunt, surely we can give her more time to consider everything." Alex looked at Rose, his bright blue eyes serious. "That's a lot to put on her all at once."

"True." Rose picked up her fork and knife and cut her chicken. "But the world has a way of throwing us curve balls. We have to decide whether to swing or strike out. This is your moment, Samantha. You're up to bat."

I snorted. I couldn't help it. The duchess had just made a baseball analogy about my life. I picked up the glass of wine, deciding I needed a sip or maybe a whole bottle to help calm my jangling nerves. "How long would I be away?"

"That would depend on you. There is a ceremony to be performed. Legalities to be followed through with. Of course, once you take control of the estate and become the family head, it would be pertinent for you to stay in the country as much as possible. You would be your family's voice on the council to the queen."

"You've got to be kidding me." I looked at her, my mouth hanging open. "Holy shit. You're serious." Rose's mouth twitched and I realized I had just cursed in the presence of royalty. "Sorry. A seat on the council to the queen? You guys know nothing about me!"

"That's not true. You've made the dean's list at your school every year. You were the top student to be chosen for your graduate program. You are dutiful to your family and take good care of your stepfather. You are a remarkable young woman our country would be proud to have."

I knew my mouth was still agape. I didn't care. Rose

had just outlined my life, but instead of making it sound boring, she had made it sound like I was a saint.

"I can't just leave school. My degree is very important to me." I'd worked so hard to get to where I was. The scholarships alone had taken countless hours of work.

"Raptors are incredibly important in our country. Each of the noble houses has one as their symbol. Your family is the merlin. As you know, a small but fierce bird. There are several well-known schools and programs that would be pleased to have you. And you would have the added benefits of our medical system for your father." Rose looked up from her food. "There are many treatments available overseas your government has not allowed here."

More than anything she could have said tonight, that was the one thing that would make me seriously consider this craziness. From the look in her eyes, she knew it too. I was being maneuvered. I didn't like it, but at the same time, she made a good case. And I knew about merlins. They were amazing birds.

"I need to think about this." I picked up my fork and pushed the potatoes on my plate.

"Of course." Rose smiled and I caught a hint of victory in it. "Like I said, I will be here for a few more days. And if you decide to come, we can push it back a little so you can accomplish any tasks you'd need to do first. I'm sure you will want to speak with your father, as well."

"Thank you, but I'm not sure I'll be going." I took another sip of wine. And then another. Oh good God. What would Dad say?

"I hope he will be able to come for the ceremony." Rose sipped from her wine. "If you decide to take up the mantle, of course."

If I decided, of course. I had a feeling it wouldn't be that easy to say no.

"If you come out, you'll have to go hunting with me." Alex nodded toward me.

"I'm not much of a hunter." I racked my brain, wondering why he would think I would want to go hunting, but found it a little difficult to get past the fact he had asked me to do something with him at all. "I've only shot a gun a few times."

He chuckled, and the sound sent a wave of goose bumps down my arms. "No, I meant with birds. I own several hawks that are excellent hunters."

"Oh." That made much more sense. I scooped some of the food into my mouth, enjoying the flavors. Despite the crappy—or inappropriate?—service, the Parallel's food had lived up to the hype. "I've been a few times, but don't have a bird of my own."

"I'd be happy to lend you one of my birds. I've been away for a while, so it would be good to have help exercising them." The corners of my mouth pulled up a little. He was being nice. There was no way he didn't have a gamekeeper to help him take care of the birds while he was away.

"What do you have?" I pulled apart some of the bread I had asked the waitress to butter.

"Three Harris hawks."

"Alex is a bird advocate, as was his father." Rose tilted her glass toward her nephew. "He presented his first bill to the Lilarian council when he was twelve. He called for stricter punishments for the purposeful deaths of raptors and endangered birds."

I looked over at Alex and felt my first true smile of the night. "That's a pretty big proposal. Good for you."

"Didn't do it for me." Alex sipped from his glass and grinned.

FOUR

Playboy Prince on the Prowl
—L.A. CHATTER

WHEN I ASKED for the bill, Rose waved it off. "You're our guest. We will take care of the bill."

"Thank you." I didn't want to offend her by insisting, even though it made me uncomfortable.

"I hope to hear from you soon, Samantha." Rose looked over her shoulder and Duvall appeared from the shadows of the room. I tried to keep my face from registering my distaste. The man gave me the willies. He handed Rose a card and a pen. She wrote something on the back and handed it to me. "Call me if you have any questions. That's my direct line."

"Thank you." I tucked the card into the small purse I was carrying. I was sure Rose didn't give out that number very often, so I didn't want to risk losing it.

"Off to bed then, for me. I'm not as young as I used to be. But don't let that stop you and Alex. I've heard there are many interesting places in town for young people." Rose held her hand out to me and pulled me close once. Softly she kissed my cheek and smiled. "It's been a pleasure, my dear. A pleasure."

"Very much so." I kissed her cheek and tried to suppress the queasy feeling that surfaced when she suggested I spend more time with Alex. What the hell was I going to do with a prince? Good grief, even the voice in my head squeaked when I thought the word *prince*.

I watched quietly as Alex kissed his aunt good-bye before Duvall ushered her through the restaurant. I looked up into Alex's amused eyes when he cleared his throat.

"Would you like to get a drink? The bartender seems rather knowledgeable." His eyes slid over my body in a lazy perusal. "Or if you'd prefer, we could try somewhere else."

"I probably shouldn't." The most attractive man I had ever met just asked me for a drink and I tell him no? I'm insane. "I drove, so no more drinks for me tonight."

"Ah." He looked down at me and I felt small. Not in the personal sense, but literally small. The man was tall. "Well then, let me walk you to your car."

"Thank you." As we moved toward the entrance, he placed a hand on the small of my back. The warmth from his palm seeped through the thin material of my dress and made me shiver.

"I thought you weren't cold." He dipped his head so his breath tickled my ear.

"I'm not." My voice sounded a little breathy and I swallowed to wet my throat. "I mean, it's cooler closer to the door."

"Hm." As we neared the door, he dropped his hand from my back and smiled at the hostess. "Our coats, please."

"Of course." She batted her eyes and I had to fight to not roll mine. When she brought our coats back, she practically threw mine at me and I had to scramble not to drop it. Alex swooped down and grabbed the coat before it could touch the floor and held it open for me. Carefully I shrugged into the ugly jacket and let him help shift the shoulders so it sat correctly. Why did I have to wear a puffy coat? After pulling on his jacket, he led me outside and motioned for the attendants. The young man who had given me my ticket earlier waved at me before running off toward the parking garage.

"Samantha, I hope you don't mind my saying this, but I hope you consider what my aunt has offered. Our country would benefit from another forward-thinking member on the council. And our health care rivals the best. Your father would be well seen to." Alex stepped close to me, buffering the strong winter wind.

"I'm going to have to think about it. This is so out of left field." I shook my head—his eyes were almost hypnotizing. And he smelled scrumptious, like clean, delicious man. The longer I spent time with him, the harder it was to ignore how attractive he was.

"Of course." He looked away from me for a minute, his eyes trailing over the traffic before turning back to me. "I know what it's like to have your life turned upside down. Especially when you've worked as hard as you have at your education."

"I have no idea how to be a royal. I can't even speak Lilarian." Thinking about it was overwhelming. "It's a lot of responsibility. I don't even know what a duchess does."

"We wouldn't throw you to the wolves." He dipped his head down so that he was looking me in the eye. "*I* wouldn't throw you to the wolves."

Not sure how to respond to that, I just nodded my head. His eyes stared down into mine and I felt entranced. There was some kind of emotion swirling behind those ice blue eyes that I didn't understand. I had the feeling he wouldn't have promised to help just anyone.

"Miss!" The parking attendant jogged toward us, my keys in his hand. I groaned when I realized what that meant. "I'm sorry, ma'am, but I can't get her to start."

"Not again." I closed my eyes for a brief moment. "Okay. Where is it parked?"

"It's on the third deck. I can take you to it, but I popped the lid and checked the battery and I don't think a jump will do it." The young man held the keys out to me and I took them from his hand.

"It's probably the starter." Turning toward Alex, I smiled ruefully. "Thank you for dinner. I'll be in touch with your aunt about what we discussed."

"How are you going to get home?" Alex stepped closer and touched my shoulder when I started to turn.

"Well, I'm going to go check to see what's wrong, and I guess I'll call a cab." I winced slightly at the thought. A cab home from downtown would cost a small fortune.

"Let me call a car for you and I'll have someone take care of your truck in the morning." Without waiting for my response he looked at the attendant. "Will the vehicle be fine where it is for now?"

"Yes, sir."

"Very well. Please call us a car."

"No, thank you, but I can take care of my own business." I contemplated his expression. He was definitely used to being in charge. Too bad I wasn't used to people making my decisions for me.

"Samantha, I'm not going to let you run off into a dark parking garage to take care of a broken vehicle." He shook his head. "What kind of man would I be?"

"One from the twenty-first century."

Alex threw his head back and laughed. The sound drew the eyes of pedestrians and other people waiting on their cars. "Samantha, the century doesn't dictate chivalry."

"Of course it does. Women have proven to be just as capable as men."

"Oh, I have no doubt you are quite capable." His eyes raked over my body in a way that made me hot all over. "But I'm still not going to let you walk into a dark parking garage in the freezing weather when we know your car is already refusing to start. Let me see you home, and we'll get your car to you tomorrow."

"For the love of . . . Fine. I can take a cab." My mind went over the contents of my purse. Maybe I could take a cab a couple of blocks to a coffee shop and call Jess and Bert.

"Samantha, I'm seeing you home. I want to make sure you get there safely." His mouth pulled up into a cocky grin that was both irritating and sexy. "Besides, I can see the wheels spinning in your head. You'd likely take the taxi around the block and come back to work on your truck."

"I wouldn't . . ." An exasperated burst of laughter flew out of my mouth and I looked away from Alex and bit my lip. "Okay, you got me. I'll let you take me home."

"Thank you." Alex reached down and captured my hand with a quick squeeze. "My chivalrous heart appreciates it."

"I'd hate for you to lose sleep over my safety." His thumb ran across my knuckles and I felt my heart rate increase.

"Agreed." He leaned closer to me, the heat from his body warming my arm. "There are much more enjoyable ways of losing sleep." He winked and looked toward the curb. "Our ride."

The black limo pulled up to the hotel and the attendant opened the door for us. Alex led me to the car and I tried to not focus on the fact that he was still holding my fingers. I felt foolish sliding into the luxury car. The last time I had been in a limo was prom, a thousand years ago. My date had been drunk and thrown up on my dress. Not exactly good memories.

Alex slid into the seat and looked at me. I started to shift uncomfortably. "What?"

"Your address?" He smiled and I found myself flushing again.

"Oh." I rattled off the street address and watched as Alex nodded at the driver. Once we pulled away from the curb, the driver closed the window between the front and back. I leaned into my seat and watched as the lights of the city flew by.

"Do you have a roommate? Or do you still live with your father?" Alex shifted in his seat. I found it odd that we were in this huge car and yet both sat on the smallest bench in the very rear. Should I have scooted around once I climbed in? Was there limo etiquette?

"Yes. Jess and I have lived together since our freshman year." I pursed my lips. "And her boyfriend, Bert, he practically lives with us."

"And your boyfriend?" Alex watched my face carefully.

"Did you really just ask if I had a boyfriend?" I laughed.

"Apparently not very smoothly." He laughed. "Are you ducking the question?"

"No boyfriend. I don't have time for that type of stuff." Boyfriends required time and patience. Not to mention energy, and lately all that was spent on my degree or taking care of my father.

He hm'd to himself for a minute and I felt one of my eyebrows rise in amusement.

"What?" I asked.

"Well, if the only thing holding you here is school and your father, then there's hope you will come home with us. No bothersome boyfriend to worry about." He leaned back comfortably, his eyes trained on my face. "Besides, you'll be on all the men's radar when you get there. Beautiful, American, intelligent, and funny. Not to mention your comic-book knowledge. I might have some competition."

"Oh." Had he just called me attractive? Competition for me? I should know better. He was just being flirty, trying to convince me to go. Alex couldn't be interested in someone like me. I was light-years from the type of women he was probably used to. I wasn't sophisticated or fashionable. Hell, I hadn't even known what fork to use at dinner tonight.

"Why does it matter to you?" I hoped he didn't hear the irritation in my voice. I was mainly upset with myself for caring. "Is there something in it for you if I go to Lilaria?"

He ran a hand across his jaw, taking his time before answering. "I'm not sure. You're intriguing."

"What does that mean?" Intriguing? As in a possible pawn he could use? "Look, if I go to Lilaria and take a seat on the council, I'm not going to side with you on things just because you told me I was from a long-lost line of royalty. So if you're planning on using me for some political maneuvering, you'd be sorely disappointed."

"And that's exactly why we need you." Alex chuckled. "Lord, you're a feisty woman."

I snorted and started to respond but was interrupted by my beeping cell phone. I pulled it out of the little clutch I was carrying and checked the text message. Jess was making sure I was okay, so I sent her a quick message letting her know I was on my way home. She replied that I shouldn't text and drive. Little did she know I was in a limo.

Before I could put the phone back in my purse, Alex held his hand out. "May I?"

"Uh, sure." Not sure if he needed to use the phone or if he was being nosy, I watched as he unlocked the screen and typed something quickly. He held the phone to his ear and nodded.

"Now you have my number." He turned it off and handed it back to me. "If you need anything or have any questions, let me know. Anything at all."

The limo pulled off the expressway and turned toward my neighborhood. "Thanks."

As we pulled up to my little house, I grew nervous. I berated myself, because it wasn't like this was a date. He wasn't going to be looking for a good-night kiss.

"Well, this is me." I nodded toward my little house and watched his reaction. Would he think my house was sad? Or would he think it funny that a long-lost line of royalty lived in such an old home? I liked our little place. It was ours. Well, not really ours. We rented it but had been there for three years. It was home.

"Lovely place." Alex opened the door to the limo and held his hand out for me. His warm fingers wrapped around mine to help me before moving to the small of my back as we walked through the snow-covered grass. I knew it was a gentlemanly thing to do, to assist a woman walking through the snow, but it amused me. I didn't need help walking through my own yard. In fact, I was the last person who had cut the grass.

"It does look pretty cozy all covered in snow." When we got to the front stoop I turned to look at Alex and smiled. I pulled the keys out of my purse and looked for the door key. "Thank you for making sure I got home safely."

"Thank you for letting me keep my dignity." Alex stepped closer and brushed some of the hair away from my face. My breath caught as he leaned down and pressed a soft kiss to my cheek. "It's been . . . an honor to meet you, Samantha."

I looked at him sharply to see if he was joking, mocking what I had said when we first met, but it brought our faces nose-to-nose. There was an amused glint in his eyes, but underneath that was something much warmer. We stood there, neither moving, only our breaths tangling in the cold air between our lips. Part of me demanded to move closer, to press my hungry mouth to his, while another part of me screamed to run for the hills. He shifted closer and I tilted my head up as his hand moved to cup my cheek.

The front door was pulled open in a rush of warm air, and I almost stumbled off the top step. Alex's warm fingers closed around my elbow to help steady me. I turned to look into Jess's wide eyes and smiled weakly.

"Sorry, I thought you were having trouble with your key again." Jess swung her gaze from Alex to me and back. "I didn't mean to interrupt."

"You didn't. Alex brought me home when my truck wouldn't start." I cleared my throat and turned to smile at the prince standing on my tiny front porch.

"My pleasure." Alex winked at me before tipping his head to Jess. "You must be Jess." Holding his hand out, I watched as my roommate looked at it like it was something unreal before slowly leaning out of the front door to shake it.

"Yes. Jess. I am. I mean, I am Jess. Um, nice to meet you." Jess looked at me and then back at Alex. She yanked her hand away from him. "Sorry. I didn't mean to hold your hand like some kind of crazy stalker. Boyfriend! Bert! My boyfriend is in the living room."

My eyes grew wider with each word out of Jess's mouth and I had to fight to not laugh out loud. I looked over Jess's shoulder to see Bert staring at us with the same look of hilarity.

"Right. This is my roommate, the not-stalker, and that's her boyfriend, Bert, back there." Bert raised his hand in greeting.

"Nice to meet you both." Alex looked back at me, and I could see the amusement rippling in the blues of his eyes. "I'll be in touch, Samantha."

"Sure." I nodded my head, trying to make everything seem very businesslike. "I look forward to it." My heart stopped. Had I really just added that? What was wrong with me?

"As do I." His eyes held mine before he bowed his head and backed down the steps. I didn't move as I watched him walk across the lawn and climb through the limo door, which the driver was holding open. I gave a small wave of my fingers as they drove off before going inside. Turning, I shooed Jess back into the house and closed the door behind me. I leaned against the heavy wood and kicked the heels off my feet.

Jess stood there staring at me, her eyes the size of saucers. I sighed and shrugged out of my coat. "Go ahead and get it out of your system."

"Prince Yummy brought you home." Jess pointed a finger at me like I was in trouble. This was going to be bad.

"His Royal Highness, Prince Alex, brought me home." I frowned at her. "You have to stop calling him that. It was stuck in my head all night."

"His Royal Highness, Prince Alex of the Yummy, brought you home. In a limo." Jess took a deep breath. "And you were about to kiss him. Right there. On our porch!"

"What? No. No I wasn't." I shook my head and dropped my coat on the rack before walking to the kitchen.

"I'm not blind, Sam. You were, like, this far apart!" She held her finger and thumb up so I could see the sliver of space between them. "You were going to kiss him!"

"Don't be ridiculous. He's European. They kiss cheeks. That's all." I fixed a glass of water before hauling myself up onto the counter.

Bert followed us into the kitchen and leaned against the door frame, his arms across his chest. I didn't like the look in his eyes. Jess could jump to conclusions. She was brilliant, but I also knew that me being involved with Alex would be the stuff of her daydreams. Bert, however, was a practical guy with an eye for detail.

"Look, I met with the duchess and she brought Alex. When it was time to leave, the parking attendant said my car wouldn't start, so Alex insisted on seeing me home." I took a sip of water, trying to calm my nerves. I could still smell him—it was like he had permeated all my senses. "Some kind of princely chivalry. That's all."

"I'm not stupid, Sam. I know what I saw." Jess smiled. "Prince Yummy likes you."

I shook my head and hopped down from the counter. I needed to derail that thought process before it got out of hand.

"Even if he did, which he doesn't, I'm not interested. You know me, Jess. A guy like that is nothing like what I want."

"We usually need exactly what we think we don't want." Bert's quiet voice filled the tiny kitchen and Jess nodded her head like a madwoman.

"Give me a break. Save your psycho mumbo-jumbo for someone else."

"What did they want to see you about, anyway?"

Bert cocked his head to the side. "Are they donating money to the program?"

"No." I let that rattle around in their heads for a minute. "Apparently I'm royalty." You could've heard a pin drop because I was pretty sure they had both stopped breathing. "Go figure, right?" I refilled my water glass and squeezed past Bert's giant frame before heading for my room.

"You know what the best part of my night was, though?" I stopped at my door and turned to look at Jess and Bert, who were both standing in the doorway staring at me with open mouths. "It was seeing Jess meet Prince Yummy in her giant college football jersey and fuzzy socks."

"Oh my God." Jess's voice followed me as I walked into my room and I couldn't help but snicker.

FIVE

A Royal Hidden Among Us
—*MINNESOTA DAILY*

SOMETHING BEEPED IN my room and I groaned. I rolled over, thinking it was probably just the e-mail notification on my phone, but it beeped again. Without opening my eyes, I felt along the bedside table and grabbed my phone. Cracking open one eye, I read the messages.

> 651–555–1212: Don't go outside.
> 651–555–1212: I'm sending someone to help.

Sitting up in bed, I rubbed the crusty mess out of my eyes and glared at the phone. Who the hell was telling me not to go outside? Who was sending someone to the house for me? I looked at the number again and my brain kicked into gear. I checked my outgoing calls, and sure enough, it was the same number. My heart rate picked up as I realized Alex was contacting me.

I swung my feet over the edge of my bed and gasped when my warm toes touched the cold hardwood. I slid into my slippers and opened my door. Sounds of the TV drifted to me from the living room, so I padded out to see who was awake. Jess was sitting on the couch, curled up under a blanket and staring at the TV with large eyes.

"What got you out of bed so early?" I sat down next to her and tugged some of the blanket over to cover my legs.

Jess just pointed at the TV. I looked at the bright screen through slitted eyes and gasped. "Why is there a picture of our house on the news?" A sinking feeling filled my gut. The next picture flashed onto the screen answered my question. It was me and Alex outside the Parallel, his hand on my shoulder. That was followed by a picture of him helping me put on my oversized coat. "Oh no. Oh no."

"My mom texted me at five this morning." Jess looked at me with large eyes. "I didn't want to wake you up—I figured you'd need your sleep to deal with it."

"Alex texted me." I held up my phone for her to see.

"He's sending someone here? That's good."

"Why is that good?"

"How do you think the news station got a picture of our house?" Jess cocked her head to the side.

"You're kidding." I turned and looked at the closed blinds. "They're really sitting out there still?"

"Three news stations." Jess nodded. "Bert checked earlier."

"Three news stations?" Part of me wanted to go peek out the window, but the saner part of me just wanted to crawl back into bed and pull the covers over my head. "Where is Bert?"

"Back in bed. He has a class in a couple of hours."

I groaned. I had classes to teach today and Dr. Geller wasn't going to be back until tomorrow. "Oh, today is going to suck."

"What are you going to tell Prince Yumm—"

"Don't call him that!" I slapped her arm. "What if you see him again and that accidentally slips out?"

"Well, he's already seen me in my nightshirt—it can't get much more embarrassing." I glared at her and she rolled her eyes. "Fine. What are you going to tell Prince Alex? He saved you from opening the door to some media-type person while still in your bathrobe."

"It's his fault I'm in this mess."

"No it isn't—it's his aunt's. Or more importantly, it's whoever sold those pictures fault." Jess scooted down into the couch cushions and glared at me. "You should blame them. He was just watching out for you."

"You're right. I'm going back to that restaurant and tearing the hostess a new one. It had to have been her. Lousy tramp." I glared at the headline scrolling under the pictures. "You've got to be kidding. 'A Royal Hidden Among Us'? That's the best they could do? Why does it even matter?"

"Um, hello? Because nothing cool happens here and Alex is a serious hottie. He's only the most eligible bachelor in the world." There was no arguing about Alex's hottie status, so I focused on something else.

"Why are they acting like I knew I was a royal? Do they just report whatever they want without checking facts?"

"It's like a big game of telephone. One station reports something with a tiny fact wrong. Then the next station just reports what they reported. The next one reports what the second station reported, but draws conclusions that aren't right, and so on and so on." Jess shrugged, the blanket falling off her shoulders.

"That's terrible. And scary." I looked back at the TV. "Not to mention it pisses me off."

Jess stared at me. "You know, you haven't said much about it. About being royal."

"That's because I came home, went to sleep, and woke up to people watching my house like Elvis had come back from the dead." Jess just stared at me. I leaned my head back against the cushion and sighed. "Fine, I don't know what to say. I mean, I have no proof, really. It's not like I can ask my mom." My throat tightened and I had to pause. "They seemed pretty convinced and I can't imagine they would have come to me if they weren't sure. It's . . . a lot to take in. They want me to go back with them."

"Go back with them?" Jess sat up a little. "Wow."

"I don't know if I'm going to do it."

"Are you crazy? Of course you're going! You have to!" Jess stared at me like I was losing my mind. "You need to know more about your family. And imagine what all you could do as a royal."

"I have school and my dad." I shook my head. "I have a life here, and they want me to just drop it and become someone else."

"That's stupid. You'd still be Sam! Take your dad with you. I've always heard they have great health care over there. I mean, it's not perfect, but Lilaria is one of the leaders in new health care treatments."

I sighed. Did everyone know about their health care but me? "Yeah, they told me. I need to talk to Dad. I don't know if he's even up for that trip."

"How did your family end up in the States? I mean, you had no idea you were royalty."

"Apparently we defected when there was an uprising. Our family was a target, so they left in the middle of the night with no word and went into hiding." I shrugged. "They left everything, not wanting to draw attention to themselves. You know my great-grandfather was a gambler, so I guess it's no surprise we have no money left.

What upsets me the most is the fact that Mom never told me."

"Maybe she didn't know."

"I'll never find out." I looked back at the TV and grimaced. They were using my school ID photo. Oh, bad-hair days. "I guess I need to get dressed if someone is on their way here."

"You better text Prince Charming back too."

"Would you stop with the nicknames?" I stood up and stretched.

"No way. I'm having too much fun."

I flipped her the bird on my way back to my room but she just laughed. We'd known each other for too long for it to be anything other than a joke. When I closed my door, I looked at the phone in my hand. Quickly, before I overthought it, I texted him.

ME: Thank you for the heads-up. I probably would have walked right out into a reporter.

Immediately my phone dinged back.

651–555–1212: I should have been ready for this, I'm sorry. Duvall is on his way with your truck. Please be careful today.

I frowned. Why would I need to be careful? And I couldn't imagine having to second-guess my every move, trying to figure out how it would be perceived by everyone. I set the phone down on the dresser and grabbed some clothes out of my closet. I hesitated for a minute, wondering if I should worry about what I was wearing, but decided to stick with my normal stuff. It would be stupid to get all dressed up when I would most likely be cleaning cages later. Besides, maybe if I acted like there was nothing different, people would leave me alone.

I grabbed my favorite jeans and a plaid shirt and pulled my hair up into a ponytail before taking a minute to text my dad and let him know I would be over after school to talk about something. I'd call, but he often slept late. Grabbing my bag and shoes, I headed for the living room. Bert was sitting on the couch, eating a bowl of cereal.

"Hey. Would you mind giving me a ride to school? I'm not sure if my truck is up for it."

"Sure." Bert looked away from the television. "Are you worried about people giving you a hard time?"

"Nah. I guess they might ask questions, but it's not really a big deal."

"You don't think it's a big deal?"

I shrugged and sat down next to him. As I was lacing up my work boots I heard a knock on our front door. I started to go for it, but Bert stopped me.

"Let me get it." Bert walked over to the door and peered out the curved window at the top before opening it a little ways. "Can I help you?"

"I'm Duvall. His Highness sent me for Lady Rousseau."

Bert turned to look over his shoulder at me. "Were you expecting a Duvall, Lady Rousseau?"

I rolled my eyes. "Please see him in, Sir Bert."

Bert stepped back and Duvall entered our tiny home. He was wearing his black suit and the little earpiece again. He walked directly toward me and produced my keys and two file folders.

"Good morning, Lady Rousseau. The duchess sent this for you to look through. She thought you might have more questions about your family. And Prince Alex sent the other folder."

"Good morning." I murmured the words as I immediately thumbed through the smaller folder from Alex. It was articles about the health care in their country, reports about chemo and cancer drugs that weren't available in the States. Had he put this together himself? Or had he asked someone else to do it? Did it even matter? No matter how you cut it, he had sent me information he knew would make me want to go.

Everyone was watching me as I flipped through the folder, so I cleared my throat and closed the file. "Thank you for bringing these and my truck. I guess I'll get it fixed later."

"I believe the starter was broken. His Highness had it towed to a shop last night and fixed early this morning."

"Oh." I would have fixed it myself—paying for a garage was out of the question. I'd have to borrow money to pay it off. "Who should I pay for the repairs?"

"Prince Alex has already handled all the repairs, my lady."

"What? And stop calling me that." I frowned at him. "Please. I'm just Samantha."

"As you wish." Duvall nodded his head. "When is your first class?"

"Um, in an hour. Why?" I could feel my eyebrows drawing together. Could I have a moment to breathe? I was still processing the fact that Alex had paid for the repairs.

"I wanted to let the team know when we were leaving." Duvall walked a couple of steps away and spoke into his shirtsleeve. Literally, into the cuff of his shirtsleeve the way the Secret Service does.

"Excuse me?" I stood up. "What do you mean *we*?"

"The duchess has sent a detail to stay with you. She's worried you will run into problems with the way your media has attacked this story." Duvall folded his hands in front of him. "I have a team of six if you include me, and three cars."

"What story? There is no story!" Three cars? Just for me to go to school? I put my hands on my hips and saw Bert trying to edge out of the room. "Bert! You're a psych major. Don't you agree that if I act like there is nothing going on, other people will behave that way too?"

"Well," he said. His face looked a bit panicked. "I'm not sure this is the same thing as pretending like you're fine after a breakup. This could have repercussions for your safety."

"What are you talking about? I work with birds. They don't give a crap if I'm royalty!" Too much change, happening too fast. I hadn't even talked to my dad yet. Oh God—Dad.

"That's not true, Sam. You teach a lecture hall full of people who will know their teaching assistant is in the headlines. Not to mention the people who make the drops at the center." Bert frowned and shrugged his shoulders. "I can't blame you for wanting it all to just fade away, but right now it isn't going to."

"Samantha, we will be as unobtrusive as possible." Duvall's calm voice did not make me feel any less frustrated.

"I don't like this." The thought was so loud in my head it escaped my mouth. I pointed at Duvall and frowned. "You do as I say. Stay out of the way and try to not be conspicuous."

"Of course." Duvall spoke into his shirtsleeve again and I fought the urge to laugh. There was no way Duvall could be inconspicuous. "I have a car waiting at the curb, but you should be prepared that the number of reporters and journalists outside has grown since I arrived."

"How many?" I could hear voices from outside and felt my heart rate pick up.

"They're still coming."

I groaned and looked around the room for my coat before shoving the files into my bag. "Then let's get this over with now, before even more arrive. I guess I don't need that ride after all, Bert."

"Call me if you need me." He saluted me with his spoon and I smiled at him.

"Samantha, they may shout questions at you. It's up to you if you want to answer them, but I would suggest that you not. If you do, they will push for more and more." Duvall looked at me seriously.

"Keep your head down and smile. Nothing too big, just a small smile," Bert said from his seat. "You don't want to frown, because you're probably going to be photographed."

"Oh God." I tightened my hand on the strap to my bag.

"Ready?" Duvall put his hand on the doorknob.

I nodded my head and forced a smile. Cold air blew into the house and I followed Duvall out into the craziness.

SIX

Press Denied Access to Campus
—WXCV, DALE GORDON

THE LIGHTS FROM video equipment and the flashing of cameras blinded me. Duvall put his hand on my elbow as we walked down the stairs. People hollered my name, screamed questions, and waved their hands to try to draw my attention. I kept my gaze down, not wanting to make eye contact, and forced myself to continue smiling.

As soon as I saw the car come into my line of down-turned vision, I was relieved. The trek from the front of my house to the car had been the longest walk of my life. Duvall opened the back door for me, letting me slide into the car before he took the front passenger seat.

"They are likely to follow us, my lady. I wouldn't do anything you wouldn't want them to see until we are ahead of them." Duvall looked back at me with serious eyes. He had put on sunglasses, and for some reason it made me want to giggle.

"Okay." I pulled on my seat belt and slid my bag next to me. "I thought you were going to call me Sam."

"In private. In public we must maintain courtesy." He turned back to the front and nodded at the driver. "This is Parker. If I'm not with you, Parker will be."

"Hi." I smiled at the face in the rearview mirror.

"Nice to meet you, Duchess Rousseau." He nodded his head at me. He was close in age to Duvall, with gray streaks in the hair at his temples.

"Technically, I haven't gone through any ceremonies. I'm just Samantha."

"Ceremonies are only a formality. You were born a duchess."

I took a deep breath and looked out the window. I tried to not look behind us, not wanting pictures of me staring out a rear window to end up on the news. A car similar to the one we were in had taken the lead and I was pretty sure another had followed us.

"Do you think they'll follow us to the school?"

"It's likely, though the dean was notified and promised they would not be welcome on campus."

"The dean?" My heart stopped. Who had called the dean?

"It's a common courtesy to let the staff know when there may be an issue with media. Plus the duchess is visiting a couple of the programs while in town."

"Oh." It wasn't a long ride to my school. We had rented a house nearby. As if he could read my mind, Parker pulled into the parking lot for the Natural Sciences building.

Parker pulled the car up to the curb and Duvall hopped out immediately. He opened my door and I slid out. A man exited the car in front and a woman from the car behind us. They each took up a place behind me as I walked to the office. Duvall didn't take the time to introduce us as we hurried out of the cold. The people in the news vans and cars were all scurrying to try to follow us. We entered the building quickly and I flashed my student ID to the security guard. He waved us through and I took everyone up a flight of stairs to the floor with the offices.

We could hear the security guard telling the reporters they weren't allowed in the building as we climbed. When we got to the office I shared with several other graduate students, I sighed in relief. I turned and looked at the three people in suits.

"Samantha, this is Terrance Ross." Duvall nodded at the man. He was tall with a shaved head. I held my hand out to shake. His palm engulfed mine and his smile was very formal.

"A pleasure to meet you, Duchess."

"Sam or Samantha." I sighed when Duvall cleared his throat. "At least when we're alone, please."

"And this is Rebecca Meyers." The woman was younger than both of the men. Probably close to my age. She was wearing slacks and a button-up shirt under her winter jacket. Her blond hair was trimmed into a pixie cut that suited her face and friendly smile.

"Nice to meet you." She shook my hand firmly. "Please, call me Becca."

"Nice to meet you, Becca." I looked over my shoulder at the door and saw the shadows of my coworkers leaning toward the crack. "Well, might as well let you meet the idiots I work with."

"I heard that." Mary's voice hollered from the other side of the door as the shadows cleared out of the way.

I opened the door to find Mary and two other graduate students staring at us. I moved aside so the others could come in and waved in their direction. "Guys, meet the suits. Suits, meet my coworkers."

"Are you really a princess?" Mary leaned forward. "And please tell me we're going to meet the prince."

"What? No." I set my bag down on my desk and opened it to find my notes for the next class. "And no."

"But you're royalty, right? Your face was all over the news this morning." She reached over and turned the monitor of the guy next to her so we could see they were watching a live stream from one of the local stations.

"Turn that off!" I walked over and hit the monitor button.

"Geez, you can't blame us for being curious! We've known you for years and you never told us." Mary crossed her arms. I ground my teeth and counted to five before answering. Mary was not my favorite person in the program.

"I didn't tell anyone. Because I didn't know." I frowned at everyone. "C'mon, guys. Don't be weird. I'm the same ol' Sam. I just have a royal ancestor."

"Leave her alone, guys. We've all shoveled crap with her and spent hours studying manuals," David, one of the doctoral students, said from the back of the room. I let my breath out in relief. David was a good guy and the others listened to him. I smiled at him and he nodded in return. "We've all got enough to focus on."

I looked over at Duvall and lowered my voice. "Could you guys wait outside?"

"When is your class?" His accent drew the attention of some of the closer people.

"About thirty minutes."

"Very well. I'll wait outside with Ross. Meyers will stay with you. She tends to blend in and make people less uncomfortable."

"Why can't you all go?" I hissed the words between my teeth.

"Lady Rousseau, someone will be with you at all times in public. I must follow the duchess's instructions." His face was impassive and I knew our whispering was making everyone even more curious so I gave in.

"Fine. Becca stays. Everyone else goes." He started to say something so I cut him off. "Becca stays and everyone else hangs out in the background. No flying-V formations or people circling me like a mama bear protecting her cub when I go anywhere."

"Yes, my lady." Duvall bowed his head before exiting the room.

"I'm going to do a few things before I leave. Intro to Wildlife isn't for thirty minutes and it's in this building, so won't take but a minute to get to." I jerked my head toward my desk.

"Sounds good to me." One thing I had noticed right away was Becca had an American accent. A Southern accent, to be exact, and it made everything feel a little less foreign and crazy.

I dragged a chair next to my desk for her and pulled out some papers, thumbing through my notes for today's lecture, but my attention kept being pulled to the manila folders. I opened the one Rose had sent and studied the first few pages of notes. There were copies of birth certificates, a ship manifesto, and a few deeds for property in New York. Then I found the family tree. It was very generic-looking, no picture of a tree or fancy calligraphy. Just a chart, listing descendants. I traced down the lines until I found my mother's name. There had been other branches but they had all ended in one fashion or another. A blank space was next to my mother with a line that led down to my full name.

Tracing the line down to me, I looked at my name and frowned. Samantha Ellen Frances Rousseau. I'd always hated having four names. It seemed so silly growing up. Everyone else had managed with just three. I flipped through some more of the paperwork, looking for anything that caught my eye or seemed familiar. Copies of my mother's thesis and first write-up in a journal made me smile. She had been a brilliant scientist.

I looked up at the clock and decided I had enough time to look quickly through the other folder. The noise in the office soothed my nerves. The clicking of someone typing, the whispers of Mary as she flirted with David. David telling her to hush. It was nice to have a little normal for a few minutes.

Alex's folder had several paper-clipped articles from medicine journals about homeopathic solutions for cancer and dealing with chemo along with information about a new drug that seemed to be helping ease the pain of some cancer patients without affecting their quality of life. The articles were fascinating and I felt hope swelling in my heart. Maybe jumping the pond wouldn't be so bad. Especially if I was able to help Dad. Or at least make him more comfortable.

In the very back of the folder was a note in slanted text and a sticky note with a website address. Apparently this was a link to a doctor that worked strictly with patients suffering from prostate cancer. Alex wrote that the doctor lived in Paris and might be persuaded to give my father an in-depth examination.

Becca cleared her throat and I looked over to where she was sitting.

"Your class starts in five minutes."

"What?" I looked at the clock on my desk and frowned. The time had flown by. I grabbed my stuff and put it in my bag before jerking my head toward the door. "Let's go."

The lecture hall was on the other side of the building, so we took the back stairs. I hesitated just inside the door when I saw all the people in the room. Almost every seat was taken, which was unusual for such an early class. Duvall looked at me with a blank face from near the stage and I wondered what was running through his mind because I sure as hell didn't know what to think. My fingers tightened on the strap of my bag and I walked forward purposefully. Fake it till you make it would be my motto of the day. The room quieted except for a few whispers.

I set my bag down and turned toward the room. My eyes picked out familiar faces among a hundred or more that I had never seen before. "It makes my heart all types of bubbly to see so many people excited about the chapter on ornithology." A faint ripple of amusement spread through the room. "For those of you that didn't wake up this morning with a newfound love of birds, open your books to chapter twelve."

I pulled my notes out and grabbed a dry erase marker. While the true students rifled through their bags, I quickly outlined some key points on the whiteboard. I turned back to the class and swallowed. I'd never spoken to this many people before and it was intimidating.

Hopping onto the small desk on the stage, I decided to focus on what I was supposed to be talking about and forget that most of these people had only come to stare at me. "Who can define a bird?"

A young undergrad's hand shot into the air. I couldn't remember her name, but I tended to refer to her as Hermione in my head. I nodded at her.

"An animal whose body is covered in feathers and forelimbs that modified into wings." She smiled proudly.

"Yes, but that isn't all that defines a bird. Anyone else?" I looked around the room. Someone I didn't recognize raised their hand and I waited a beat before nodding for them to speak.

"Are you really a princess?"

"All little girls are princesses, didn't you know that?"

My heart sped up in my chest and I narrowed my eyes. Titters erupted around the classroom and I sat down on the top of the desk. "Now, who can tell me about birds?"

One of the male students raised his hand and I pointed in his direction. "They all have scaly legs, a beak with no teeth, and bear their young in a hard-shelled egg."

"Good." I jumped up and scribbled the definition on the board. "Does anyone have any idea how many types of birds there are in the world?"

There were more people with their hands raised when I turned back around. I tried to pick someone I recognized from the class, hoping they would stay on topic.

"Danni?" I looked at a small blonde.

"Five thousand?" I almost couldn't hear her tiny voice.

"Nope. Who else?" I pointed at a boy with a skullcap on.

"Four thousand, five hundred, and seventy-two." He smiled when people turned to look at him.

"Not even close." I glared around the room. "C'mon, guys. You're supposed to read the chapter ahead of time."

Someone in the back raised their hand, but I couldn't see their face. Reluctantly I pointed in that direction.

"Over ten thousand, four hundred." Alex's voice easily filled the room and I felt my face flush. My heart sped up and just his voice made me shiver. He was here, watching me? Some of the students turned around to look at him, the sound of his accent drawing their attention. A loud rustle filled the hall as people realized the Prince of Lilaria was among them.

"Correct. I believe the last count was at ten thousand, four hundred, and sixty-six." I wrote the number on the board, plowing forward, trying to calm my nerves. The class settled down and I did my best to keep things on track.

"How many orders of birds are classified by the International Ornithologists' Union?" I looked around the room. "Seriously, guys? You're going to let him come in here and show you up?" Laughter filled the room and I was relieved when Hermione raised her hand and had the correct answer.

By the time class was over I couldn't have been more ready. I had twenty minutes before the next lecture and I was considering putting a note on the door and hiding. As the students got up and left, a few of them came down to try to ask me questions. I did my best to shoo them away, but a few were much more dedicated to finding an answer. Becca had come to stand just to the side of me, her friendly smile replaced with a glower that made me rethink my original assessment of her personality.

"C'mon, Sam. It's the school paper. Just an interview. I'll let you decide which questions you want to answer." The editor for the student paper was leaning against my desk and I was resolutely trying to ignore him.

"I told you, Toby, I have too much going on right now. I'm sorry." Truth be told, I would always have too much going on when it came to having time for interviews. Especially with Toby. He was a pervert to the tenth degree. "If you don't mind, I have to finish grading some papers."

"Samantha—"

"This way, sir." Duvall appeared beside Toby, a friendly hand placed on his shoulder. "Lady Rousseau has asked for some space."

"But—"

"Another time, maybe." Duvall maneuvered Toby away from my desk and off the stage, to my relief.

Who would have thought I'd be grateful to see Duvall after all?

"You're an excellent teacher. You handled the class quite well." Alex's voice in my ear made me jump, bumping my head into his chin.

"Youch!" I rubbed the top of my head while he looked down at me with amusement. He rubbed his chin but smiled. "Good grief. Don't sneak up on me. And I would have handled the class much better if you hadn't shown up."

"I'd like to think I encouraged them to try a little harder." His blue eyes sparkled as he looked at me. "And I wanted to make sure they weren't giving you too hard of a time."

"Thanks, I think." I frowned up at him, trying to not get pulled into his eyes. "But I would have managed just fine. You don't have to take care of me."

"You've been thrown into a new world . . . I just wanted to help you get your feet." Instead of being annoyed with my reluctance to accept his help, he seemed entertained. "How many more classes do you have today?"

"Two more." I rubbed my forehead. "Then I go to the sanctuary."

"I see. Do you have time for lunch somewhere in there?" He leaned casually against my desk, his perfect rump perched on the edge. I tried to not think about it and just focused on the conversation.

"I usually eat in the office after the last class. Catch up on my paperwork before I head over." I bit my bottom lip, confused by his presence in my class, by his interest in me. His eyes focused on my mouth briefly before moving back to my eyes. Some flashes from the right side of the hall drew my attention and I realized some of the students were using their phones to take pictures of us talking. Becca jumped down from the edge of the stage where she was standing and headed in their direction.

"Would you mind if I join you? Or is that not allowed?" He cocked his head to the side and I found myself studying the way the bright lights of the stage played in his blond hair.

"Um, no, that's fine." My eyes traveled over his face, taking in the slight imperfections that only seemed to make him more handsome. "Uh, I usually just grab a sandwich or something. I guess we could order something in, if you'd like."

"A sandwich is perfect. Why don't I bring the food? I'll meet you there, that way you don't have to waste any of your time."

"Why?" The question exited my mouth before I could rethink it.

"Why save you time?" His eyebrows drew together.

"Why do you want to have lunch with me? Surely you have more important things to do."

"Well, I like your company for one thing." He leaned a little closer. "And you underestimate your importance. I'm starting to think you're very important."

I didn't know what to say. What could I say to that? There was no mistaking it this time. Alex was definitely flirting with me and I felt like a fish out of water. I was a terrible flirt, too blunt and not coy. And I blushed. Like I was doing right now.

"I make you nervous, don't I?" His gaze turned thoughtful. "And not because of my rank. That doesn't seem to faze you at all."

"A title is a title. It doesn't define the type of person you are." I closed the notebook with the quizzes and took a deep breath.

"Very true." Reaching out, he brushed a stray strand

of brown hair that had escaped my ponytail back from my face. I froze and our gazes locked before I remembered the cameras. I looked over to where the students had been standing, but no one was there.

"We're alone. Duvall and Becca saw everyone out and are watching the door."

We're alone. His words sent a shiver through my soul. Images of him and me on the desk filled my mind and my blush deepened. His fingers traced my jawline briefly before he stood up and gave me enough space to breathe again.

"Do you have a preference for lunch?"

"No mustard." I stayed in my seat, feeling safer there.

"No mustard. I can manage that." He turned and walked down the steps. I couldn't stop my eyes from following his backside as he went.

"My office, it's on the second floor." I cleared my throat. "I share it, so there will be other people there. They might pester you." In fact I was sure Mary would pester him.

"I'll find it." He smiled over his shoulder at me.

SEVEN

Chaos on Campus
—COLLEGE DAILY

"UNLESS YOU CAN tell me the number of toes a bird has, you have accidentally wandered into the wrong class." I put my hands on my hips and glared at the students. "And that means you need to drag your hungover self out of your seat and go find the correct room. Now."

I waited while half the room got up and left in an explosion of noise. Some people took pictures of me with their cell phones before they ducked out of the door, others laughed like it was all a big joke. When it finally quieted down, I looked up from my desk and tried to not groan. There were still too many people in the room, but at least a good portion of them had left. Taking a deep breath, I stood up and started the last lecture of the day.

By the time I was finished, I barely had any patience left. I had been asked if I was a princess, if I was really a teaching assistant, if I knew the Queen of England. People had taken my picture and recorded my lecture. Nothing had been accomplished in the lesson. I should have just canceled the class and hidden in a broom closet somewhere.

"Lady Rousseau, let's wait to move until the room has cleared and there isn't as much traffic in the hallways." Becca glanced at me over my desk with a look of pity.

"Can you just kill me? Carry me out in a box?" I looked up at her. "Do you even have a gun?"

"What kind of bodyguard would I be if I needed a gun to kill someone?" Becca smiled at my expression. "Besides, it could've been worse."

"That's not comforting." I leaned back in my chair and groaned. "Thank God I don't have any more classes today." I grabbed my notes and shoved them into my bag. My stomach was in knots and I wasn't sure if it was because of the classes or the fact that I was supposed to go eat with Alex.

"Ready?" Becca asked.

"Yeah." We left the room and headed for the back stairs. There were still people in the halls, but for the most part they moved out of our way. When I got to the office, Alex was leaning against the wall next to the door, a bag of food in one hand and a tray with drinks in the other. His head was against the wall, his eyes closed. I felt guilty that he looked so tired. He must've been up late to see to my truck and get me those notes. As we approached, one of the men in his detail said something quietly. He tilted his head to look at us and smiled. His gray suit made his blue eyes look almost silver and I felt my mouth go dry. Just being near him felt like something in my gut was tugging me to him. He was perfect, right down to the light stubble on his chin.

"No mustard." He held the bag up in victory and I laughed. He looked so proud of himself I couldn't help it. Some of my nerves melted away and I felt a bit more relaxed.

"C'mon." I opened the door so he could walk in and almost melted in relief when no one else was inside. I had been dreading the stares and awkward conversation. "That's my desk." I pointed at the one near the window and he stood next to the chair Becca had used earlier. I checked the message board, watching him from the corner of my eye before going to find some paper towels.

"Thank you." He sat down when I handed him the napkins. "I hope you like red meat. I have a weakness for hamburgers. The bigger the better."

"You're in luck. The hamburgers from the cafeteria are great." I spread the fries onto a napkin so we could both get to them. "So tell me. How did you manage to go in the cafeteria and come out alive?"

"Many years of practice." He took a bite of his burger and groaned. "Ah, now that is good."

"Why not just send someone else for them?" I took a bite of my food and mentally agreed with him.

"I was hoping it would draw away some of your fake students."

"You mean you prostituted yourself out to the masses? To draw them away? That was . . . sweet." He choked on his drink and coughed roughly. I set down my sandwich and slapped him on the back.

"I hadn't thought about it that way." He chuckled. "But it was worth it if it helped you."

"Well, thank you." I picked my sandwich back up and smiled at him. "For lunch and for pimping yourself out."

"I told you I wouldn't throw you to the wolves." He winked at me, and I didn't have the heart to tell him about all the people who had still crashed my classes.

"Did you have a chance to look through the notes I sent?"

"A little." I pushed some of the fries toward him. He seemed to like those just as much as he liked the hamburger. "I have to admit I'm interested in the specialist you listed."

"There is a great deal of information online, too much to print out."

"Thanks. I'll look it over before I talk to Dad." I pulled my phone out of my pocket and checked for new text messages. Still nothing from my father, so I texted the lady that came to check on him twice a day. Patricia was a neighbor who had been good friends with my mother. She wouldn't let me pay her, and honestly, I have no idea how I would have anyway. But knowing she went to check on Dad to make sure he didn't need anything was a huge relief.

Patricia: He's got one of his migraines today and is sleeping. I'll let him know you're coming over later.

I sighed in relief and told her thank you.

"Everything okay?"

"Yeah. Dad hasn't texted me since yesterday and I was getting worried. He gets terrible headaches sometimes."

"But he's fine?"

"Fine as can be." I chewed on some fries and thought about it. "A family friend checks on him a couple of times a day to help out. She said he was sleeping."

We didn't say anything else for a little while, just munched on our food and watched the light snowfall. It was going to be a cold afternoon. At least I wouldn't be in the truck. The heat took forever to warm up. Which reminded me . . .

"Thank you for seeing to my truck. Tell me how much the repairs were and I'll get the money to you."

"Don't worry about it. I was happy to see to it."

"Alex, I appreciate it, but I don't feel right letting you pay for it. It's not your fault the starter died." I set my sandwich down and looked at him. The thought of someone paying for me didn't sit well. Especially someone I had only met the night before.

"If we hadn't invited you out, you likely wouldn't have been stranded. It is my obligation." Alex leaned back in his chair as if amused by my obvious disapproval.

"In which case it wouldn't have started this morning and I would have been late for class. Arguing when it happened is silly. It's my car, my responsibility."

"Fine. You can pay me back after you're granted your lands and title."

I thought it over for a minute before I realized what he had done. He'd given me one more reason to go to Lilaria. I narrowed my eyes but couldn't help the smile that tugged at my mouth. "You're sneaky."

"That's one way of looking at it." I liked his laugh. There was something free and honest in it. I shook my head and picked up my food again. I'd let it slide for now until I figured out what I was going to do.

"So, what are you doing after this?" I looked at Alex, curious. I tried to squash the hope that was bubbling in my stomach. Being around him made me feel like I wanted more.

"Well, that depends. I have some phone calls to make and we were invited to dinner at the mayor's house, but I have a few hours free." He shook the ice in his cup before taking another sip. "I'd like to see your birds. I have to admit, I miss being around them when I travel."

"Well, you're welcome to come with me but it's going

to be pretty cold. And there will definitely be people there." I looked around the room. "I don't know how we got lucky for lunch. Normally everyone is here about this time."

"Lucky that you got me all to yourself?" Alex smiled and my face turned beet red.

"I just meant that Mary wouldn't have left you—I mean us—alone with all her questions." Good Lord, I was going to inflate his ego to unbearable proportions if I wasn't careful.

"A man named David sent everyone out of the office. I think he was worried about this Mary too."

"Mary isn't a bad person; she just takes some getting used to." I shook my head. "I've known her for two years now and she still shocks me."

"I'm glad it worked out this way. I've been trying to figure out a way to spend some time with you since you turned me down for drinks last night. Free time is often hard to come by." Little creases of amusement appeared at the corners of his eyes as he laughed at my expression. "From the shock on your face, I can tell I wasn't being obvious enough."

"I just thought you were being polite." I looked down at my food and tried to calm my racing heart. His warm fingers lifted my chin so that I was looking him in the eye. His face had turned very serious, his eyes intent.

"Wanting to spend a few hours getting to know a beautiful woman isn't about being polite." His thumb ran over my bottom lip and my breath stuttered. "I shouldn't chase you, Samantha, but I'm not sure I can help myself."

I didn't know what to say. Why shouldn't he chase me? Because I'm from diluted nobility? Or because I have enough going on to keep me busy? Did I want him to chase me? I did and I didn't. I wanted him, the man staring at me right now. But I didn't want what that included: the cameras, the politics, and who knows what else.

As I tried to sort out my thoughts, there was a knock on the door. I had been leaning forward, pulled in by his eyes, so sat back quickly. "Come in."

Becca stuck her head in the door and smiled. "Ma'am, someone named Jess is here."

"Oh, let her in." I shook my head as Jess walked through the door. Today was possibly the weirdest day of my life. Well, after yesterday, anyway.

"Heard your classes were crazy." She set her bag down and swiped a few fries from my desk. "Hello, Your Majesty." She looked embarrassed for roughly one quarter of a second and I had to assume it was because of her word vomit last night.

"Hello, Jess." Alex gave her a friendly smile. I wondered if she was breaking some kind of protocol by being so informal. He didn't look bothered, even if she was.

"Word is you had to shoo people out." She narrowed her eyes at me.

"You could say that." I frowned at her. I didn't want Alex to know I'd still been swarmed with strangers.

"Yeah?" She sat on the desk next to me but on the opposite side of Alex.

"Yeah. It was weird. Normally I have to worry about most of the class not showing up for the eight o'clock block." I snorted. Not the problem today.

"My prof gave a pop quiz. I think he was really offended that people might have skipped his class 'just to see some royals.'" She made air quotes with her fingers. "No offense, Alex. He's a stick-in-the-mud."

Jess was a teaching assistant for Dr. Woodrum, one of the most boring teachers you could get. Then again, the thought of pre-med classes made me squirm. Animals were one thing, but I didn't want to change any bedpans or give rectal exams.

"What class is it?" Alex asked.

"Beginner's Biology." Jess grabbed another fry. "Long story short, Woodrum hates all college students but knows the basics better than anyone."

"And he is your advisor?"

Jess nodded her head. "It'll look good on my résumé. He's written so many articles it's insane, and it lets me work on some really interesting projects. Even if I do have to put up with his comb-over and bean-dip breath." Jess sighed dramatically.

"You chose it." It was an old argument.

"I thought you might need someone to go with you to the raptor center, but it looks like you've got it covered." Jess's eyes darted between me and Alex. I knew she was trying to figure out if he was going with me. I could almost feel her mentally prodding me for answers. Or maybe that was the foot she was using to kick my leg.

"There are three bodyguards standing outside the door waiting on me." I batted her foot away from me.

"Not to mention the three that followed me." Alex laughed.

"Oh, are you going with Sam?" Jess turned bright eyes toward him. He seemed to pick up on her tone and leaned back in his chair, that little smile playing on his mouth.

"She was kind enough to offer to show me the birds."

"Uh-huh." She turned and smiled at me. I thought about shoving her off the desk.

"Alex has birds at home. I thought he might enjoy seeing the ones we have here." I stood up and started collecting the trash. Alex held open the bag so I could stuff the wrappers inside.

"Well, I guess I'll go on to my office then." Jess stood

up and picked up her bag. "Have you heard from Dr. Geller?"

"Shoot. I need to check my e-mail. Today has thrown me off." I sat back down at my computer and opened up my account, scanning the messages. I frowned when I saw the one from Dr. Geller. Apparently the dean had contacted him, so he knew a little bit about what was going on. He would be in early tomorrow to talk.

"Greeeaaat," I muttered.

"Geller unhappy?" Jess looked over my shoulder.

"The dean called him." I met Alex's eyes. His face was blank and I knew he was waiting for more information. "I think he was just surprised to not have heard the news from me."

"It's not like you exactly had time." Jess shrugged. "You'll be fine. Geller loves you."

"We'll see." Would he still love me if I went to Lilaria? He had invested a lot of time in my education. Was I really thinking about going?

"I'm going to run. I've got some papers to grade and I don't want to do it tonight." Jess looked over at Alex. "Enjoy the birds. Don't let the eagle bite you. He's a moody bastard."

"I shall endeavor to keep my fingers to myself."

"You do that." Jess moved out of his sight and winked at me.

I looked away from her and down at my computer to log off. "See you later." I didn't look up when I heard the door open. I was worried Alex would see the relief on my face. The longer Jess was around him, the bolder she would become in her jokes.

"She's a good friend." Alex said it like he knew for sure after spending less than an hour with her.

"I have good taste." I smiled at him as I picked up my bag. "Ready?"

"Lead the way." He opened the door for me and motioned into the hall. There were people in suits filling the area just outside the office.

"Uh, I need to head over to the center." I looked at Duvall, who motioned at the others. Someone handed Alex a winter coat and we headed down the stairs. There were more people in the lobby than normal and I had a sneaking suspicion it wasn't because of the snow. In fact, the ones that normally used the area to study looked irritated. I didn't blame them.

"Sir, should I send someone for your car as well?" A man who rivaled Alex in size leaned close.

"No, I'll be accompanying Samantha." Alex nodded at me.

"Yes, sir." The man moved ahead of us to clear the door.

A young woman with red hair broke away from a group near the elevator and stopped in our path. She was vaguely familiar, but I couldn't remember where I knew her from. Her shirt was unbuttoned much farther than it normally would've been considering the frigid air outside, and from the way her friends giggled, I was sure it was just for Alex's benefit.

"May I have your autograph?" She smiled around the bodyguards at Alex, her eyes practically shimmering like an anime cartoon. The guards continued to block her, allowing Alex to make the decision.

"I'm sorry, I can't sign anything." Alex flashed a panty-dropping smile and she made a little moue of disappointment before turning toward me.

"Would you sign?" She pushed the notebook toward me.

"Um." My eyebrows rose so high, I thought they might try to escape my face.

"You were the TA in one of my classes last semester.

I can't believe I know a royal." She shoved the notebook toward me and I had no choice but to grab it. I felt awkward and clumsy as I stared at this girl who acted as though she knew me.

"As much as we would love to sign it for you, we're not allowed to give autographs." Alex took the notebook from my hands and held it out to the girl.

"So you are a royal?" Something in her eyes shifted to a shrewd glint. With one simple sentence, Alex had confirmed all the news reports floating around and sent the rumor mill into overdrive.

"I'm a grad student." I tried to keep my face friendly, but I had a feeling she wasn't some silly coed.

"But you're also part of the royal family from Lilaria?"

"I'm sorry, we're going to be late." I tried to smile, but it probably looked deranged.

"My brother works for WKFS. He'd let you tell the story in your own words." She stepped closer and I saw the guards around us move into action. Duvall slid between us and Becca stepped close to my right side. Alex put a hand on my elbow and steered me away from the redhead.

"Let's go." A thread of anger slid through his quiet words as we tried to walk around everyone.

"Samantha, are you and the prince dating? Have you always known you were from a royal family?" The heat that would have normally flooded my cheeks was countered by the cold that seeped up my spine.

I didn't look back up until we'd gone through the security checkpoint. That was when I noticed the extra campus guards. Instead of the usual one, there were three. They each looked me over with interest but also made sure no one was following us.

The cold air slammed into me and I scrambled to

button up my coat. Alex had dropped his hand from my arm but stayed close by my side as we walked through the campus to the parking lot. Despite my earlier instructions to not walk around me like they were guarding the crown jewels, the team was carefully edging people away from us.

"It's a pretty campus. I imagine it's very nice in the summer."

"Are you trying to distract me?" I looked up at him, amused.

"Is it working?" He cut his eyes toward me. "You looked like you were leading a funeral procession."

"I did not!" I laughed, realizing he was right. "Okay. It's just weird. And strange. And disconcerting. All these people staring at me. I've been here for four years, but they're acting like I've suddenly sprouted a second head."

"You're a novelty." We got to the car and he opened the door. "It'll wear off. Probably."

"You Lilarians aren't a very comforting bunch." I pulled my bag off my shoulder so I could slide into the seat. He laughed as he closed the door and walked around the car.

EIGHT

Raptor Center Receives Large Grant
—MINNESOTA RAPTOR ASSOCIATION

THE RIDE TO the center was long, but it would have been shorter if people had stopped turning to look in our windows. When we pulled into the gravel parking lot where I had met Duvall yesterday, I hopped out of the car before Alex could get around to my side and shouldered my bag again.

"Well, this is it. Last chance to come up with something interesting to do. If you stay I might put you to work." I looked at him, not sure if I wanted him to stay or go. Logically, I knew I'd get more work done if he wasn't there, but I was also starting to enjoy his company.

"Use me as you see fit." Alex stepped close, his eyes lit with mischief. "I'm at your disposal."

"You may regret that." I tried to keep my voice calm but failed.

"I highly doubt it." Stepping around me, he opened the gate and we walked toward the main building. People stopped to stare at us, but for the most part no one really bothered me. For the first time that day I felt normal, like I could be myself.

I threw my bag down in a corner of the office and looked around for any notes. David had been here earlier in the day and checked on the birds. Thankfully everyone seemed to be handling the weather well.

"You might want to leave your suit jacket." I grabbed Dr. Geller's large snow coat from the rack and tossed it to Alex. He traded coats and hung his jacket on the rack.

This was the part of my day I looked forward to. Here, I didn't have to deal with students or idiotic questions. Most of the others were leaving or going to their offices to finish up paperwork. I could focus on my birds, get lost in research, and agonize over my thesis. It was my passion, and here nothing else got in the way. Nothing else came first.

Alex didn't talk much as I showed him the facility: the mews, the enclosures, and the area where we prepped the food. There was also a very small room where Dr. Geller performed examinations of the injured birds brought to us. It was a slow time of the year, considering most birds that could leave the cold did so. That was why Dr. Geller chose this time to take a team of students farther south. They had spent time in the Everglades and the swamps of Louisiana. I think it was also a convenient way for him to get away from the snow for a while.

"How many of you work here?" Alex was helping transfer some of the birds while I cleaned cages. He hadn't needed much direction. It was easy to tell he spent a great deal of time with raptors.

"Depends on the season." I hauled a bucket over to use for trash. "In the summer we have volunteers who help out. There are shows and education programs as well that help raise money for the birds."

"Education is the key, isn't it? The more people understand about these creatures, the more they will be able to see their vital importance." Gently, Alex coaxed the horned owl from her perch and onto his gloved arm. "That's one of the things I'm working on back home. I run a charity that goes to schools and town centers to help educate the public. The kids love it."

"What's it called?"

"The Future Bird Trust." He didn't look at me as we talked, his eyes solely on the bird, so didn't see my dumbstruck expression.

"You run the FBT? I thought they were based in France."

"Yes, we work very closely with the French government to uphold the laws protecting these beauties." He looked at me over the owl's head, his eyes full of determination. "It's my goal to spread the FBT to the surrounding countries to educate the public about the importance of raptors. I hope that with more knowledge people will understand why it is so important to preserve these birds."

"I've read about the FBT." I leaned the shovel I was carrying against the wall and went to wash my hands. "They've done some great things."

"Thank you." He looked back at the owl, examining the large gash on her beak. "What happened to this one?"

"Car." I turned back to the table to finish getting the food sorted. Rats and mice were the entrée for tonight. Not exactly my favorite part of the job, but I'd become immune to it at this point. Everything has to eat. I brought a small rat over to Dover, the owl Alex was holding. Alex took it in a gloved hand and proffered it to the bird.

"C'mon, sweetheart. Don't be shy." Alex clucked

when Dover turned her head away from the meal. "I saw you eyeing it while the lovely Samantha got it ready."

"She's a coy one." I smiled at him, not sure if I was more amused by the coaxing tone or by him calling me lovely.

He mumbled a few words in Lilarian, at least I thought they were Lilarian, and Dover turned to look at him. He chuckled and offered the rat again, which she deigned to accept. I didn't blame her for turning to look at him. While he spoke English easily with an almost British accent, those words were beautiful.

"Well, that may be the fastest she's ever accepted a meal from anyone."

"That so?" He smiled over at me.

"It's the accent. Women always swoon for an accent." I rolled my eyes.

"And does the accent work on you?"

"You wish." I fumbled with the gloves I was trying to put on. I looked at him over my shoulder to see if he was watching.

"Too true." He winked at me. My heart jumped and I turned to finish making the meals. Unfortunately I knocked over the shovel and was rewarded with a loud clanking that sent all the nearby birds into a flutter. I bent over to pick up the shovel and glanced at Alex. He was openly watching my backside.

When he realized he had been caught ogling, he smiled and raised an eyebrow. "Nice jeans."

"Thanks." I turned back to the task at hand.

"No—thank you." He chuckled and I blushed.

"Did you know what your aunt was going to tell me last night?" I asked, wanting to change the subject. I kept my back to him, not wanting him to see my red cheeks.

"No. She asked me to accompany her to dinner and

since I had no other plans, I agreed. She mentioned something about the university, but since we had been here earlier that day, I had no reason to think it was for anything else."

"Yeah, I saw you guys. You were busy flirting with a blond girl outside the library and I couldn't get through the front doors. I had to go all the way around to the back and they still wouldn't let me in with the fancy-schmancy prince visiting." He laughed at my barb and I remembered the way he had been laughing with the girl. Something in my chest tightened. I tried to stomp the emotion down because I had no reason to care.

"Jackie." He said her name with a fond tone and I felt my back stiffen. There was no reason I should care if he liked her. Just because he had been flirting with me didn't mean anything. And really, I had no use for a prince. "She was assigned to show us the campus. Part of a sorority, I believe."

I continued chopping up mice bits and ground my teeth. Of course she was. Cute, blond, designer clothes. Probably a business major so she'd have a degree when she went to work for the family company. Plus she'd looked adorable standing next to Alex for the cameras that had come to record the event. They had looked cute standing next to each other. And comfortable with each other.

I grunted. "Yes, she was the perfect little host, I'm sure."

"Yes, Jackie was an . . . excellent escort." Escort? *Escort?* Alex's next words cut through my thoughts with amusement. "How small are you planning on cutting those?"

"Shit." I frowned and looked at the mess I had made. I pushed it aside and started on another mouse. I'd freeze this for one of the birds we had to syringe feed.

"You know, if I didn't know better, I'd think you were jealous."

I spun around to glare at him. I opened my mouth and closed it. If I denied it, I'd look like an ass, but I couldn't just tell him the truth. Shit, shit, shit. I *was* jealous. *Snap out of it, Sam!*

"Your ego is something of a wonder, isn't it?" I glared at him as he put Dover on her perch to finish eating.

"I think I like this look on you." His eyes were a different shade of blue as he regarded me. "Jackie was nice, very friendly, and dumb as a rock. She is nothing compared to you." He pulled the gloves off as he walked toward me. I flattened myself against the counter with each step he took. Placing a hand on either side of me, he leaned forward. "Put down the knife, Samantha."

"Why?" I hadn't realized I was still holding it. My voice had been too high; excited. This close to him my brain was turning into mush. His blue eyes peered down into mine and I felt small and feminine.

"Because I'm going to kiss you and I don't want to be stabbed when I do it." His hand moved to mine and carefully plied my fingers away from the blade's handle. When he had disarmed me, he dipped his head down toward mine and I felt my heartbeat speed up. While his breath tickled my lips, he carefully pulled my work gloves off. One of his hands moved to cup my cheek, tilting my face upward. Our eyes stayed locked until his warm lips touched mine. It started out slow and tender, our breaths mingling while we touched with featherlight brushes. I was putty in his hands, my body no longer under my command.

I ran my hands over his chest, tracing the muscles I had caught hints of through his shirt. Eventually I tangled my fingers in his hair. He mumbled things I didn't understand and didn't need to, the tone making it obvious. He tasted like a dark, decadent dessert. I had a feeling I could live on that taste alone for months; that his kiss was something I could become addicted to.

The sound of wings flapping and loud squawking had us pulling apart. My breathing was heavy and I felt light-headed. Alex ran a thumb over my bottom lip, his eyes bright with a mixture of surprise and desire.

"I think someone is jealous." I bit my lip and looked over his shoulder to where Dover was glaring at us.

"Not much I can do about that." He leaned forward and nipped my bottom lip. I melted back into him, already craving his taste again. His hands moved up my sides, his thumbs barely grazing the sides of my breasts. I sucked in a breath at his touch and moaned softly.

One of the outer doors opened and we froze at the sound of voices. Alex smiled at the look on my face, but pulled away. I adjusted my shirt, hoping I didn't have that just-kissed look. Alex picked up my gloves and handed them to me. I pulled them back on and turned around to what I was doing.

"Hey, Sam?" David's voice heralded his entry into the room. Alex moved over to the sink to wash his hands and I heard David's footsteps pause.

"What's up?" I turned to look at him, the knife in my hand. His eyes moved from Alex to me, noting how close we were standing.

"I wanted to see how Dover was healing. Dr. Geller asked me to keep an eye on her while he was gone." Something in his tone changed and I realized he appeared pissed.

"She's doing good." I felt my eyebrows draw together. David was usually a bit distant, but friendly. Did he think I had ignored the owl because of everything going on? Everyone brought friends or family to the center, so he couldn't be upset at Alex's presence.

"Have you given her the medicine yet?" David glared at Alex, who had turned around to lean against the sink. There wasn't much space between us and I could see the calculating gleam in David's eyes.

"Yep." My response was curt, annoyed by the judging look in his eyes.

"Good." He grabbed a glove from one of the shelves and walked over to check out Dover. I turned back to my task and frowned.

"She's a beautiful bird." Alex had stayed leaning against the counter, so close that my elbow hit him when I went back to work.

"Yes. She is." David's voice sounded odd, so I tried to peek over my shoulder. Dover was sitting on his arm, but his eyes were trained on Alex. "She's been through a lot. I'd hate to see her hurt any more."

I turned back to the mouse I was holding and frowned. Why did he sound so angry?

"I'm sure everyone here takes very good care of her." Alex's voice sounded affable, but there was something odd about the way he phrased his words.

"Often people hurt things by accident." David's voice took on an edge. "No one plans on hurting anyone, but it happens."

Anyone? I froze and set down the knife I was holding. Slowly I turned around and glared at David. He was ignoring me, his gaze still glued on Alex.

"I have no intention of hurting Samantha." Alex's posture was relaxed, at odds with his words.

"She's been through enough. I've watched her fight her way through the death of her mom and now her dad. Don't pull her into something just for her to have to fight some more."

"David!" I felt my mouth fall open in shock. How had the conversation turned into this?

"She's like my sister and I'm tired of seeing her screwed over." His eyes turned to me apologetically.

"I can understand that." Alex stood up straight. "But I think she can take care of herself."

"Just remember there are people, here in the real world, that love her." My heart squeezed with David's words. I had grown really close to everyone in the office. David had been a big help when I was applying for a master's position. He wasn't one for too much emotion, so to hear him say that made me want to throw my arms around him in a hug.

Alex nodded his head, and David turned back to Dover. I stood there staring at them both, wondering what on Earth had happened to my life.

"Close your mouth, Sam." David didn't look at me, but his voice shook me out of my thoughts and I turned back to the task at hand.

Alex's phone rang and he walked away to answer it. I could hear him but couldn't make out what he was saying. When I had finished cutting up the food, I split it up and went to deliver it to the birds in the building. When I got back, David was finishing up his examination of Dover. He put her back in her pen and replaced his gloves on the shelf.

"See you later?" David looked at me from where he was standing and I nodded my head.

"Yeah. Geller will be back tomorrow."

"I know." He turned to leave. "See you then."

"David?" He stopped and looked at me. "I love you guys too."

He winked before turning and leaving the way he came. Alex was still on the phone, so I checked the time before going about cleaning. I was almost finished by the time he was done with his conversation.

"I didn't mean to leave you with all the cleanup." Alex took the broom out of my hand.

"There's not much to do." I shrugged and rinsed out one of the rags while he swept the trash I had collected into the dustpan.

"Still, I said I would help." He frowned.

"It's really okay." I headed for the office where our coats were hanging, with him following close behind.

As I reached for my coat, I was spun around and pressed against the wall. Alex leaned down to nuzzle my neck before dragging his lips across mine. There it was, my new drug of choice. His kiss was hot and hungry. His hands weren't patient this time as he slid them over my body. It was as if our first kiss had answered a question and now he was sure of what he wanted.

His phone beeped and he muttered something that had to be a curse. The kiss slowed. There was something serious and dangerous behind his kiss—something that made my heart stutter and my panties catch fire. When his phone beeped again, I pulled back so there was just enough space between our mouths that I could feel our breaths mingle.

"You should probably get that." My voice was husky and thick. It had taken a lot of willpower to pull away from him.

"They can wait." He started to lean forward again but I shook my head.

"I can't. I need to go see my dad."

He sighed but nodded his head. "I understand."

"Are you leaving soon?" I bit my lip, surprised I had asked him. Did it matter? I guess it did, considering how my heart was beating rapidly.

"I'm waiting to see what you decide." He brushed some of the hair out of my face.

"Is that why you're kissing me? To try to convince me to come to Lilaria?" The words seemed to freeze the air between us and I felt my stomach clench.

"You think I would kiss you to try to get you to come back?" He leaned farther away. "I'm not sure what you think having you in Lilaria would accomplish for me, but I assure you I don't go around kissing people to make political alliances."

"I'm sorry." I closed my eyes and thunked my head against the wall. "I just can't imagine why you . . . I'm just . . ."

He pulled away from me with a look of frustration. "Do you realize how insulting that is?"

"I'm sorry, I didn't mean—"

"You didn't mean to insinuate I would stoop to such a thing, or you didn't mean to insinuate you're not attractive enough to make me forget my senses?" He stood up and ran a hand through his hair. "I do want you to come to Lilaria. I think it would be good for you and for your father. I think if you would let yourself, there could be something good between us, as well."

"This is happening too fast. There's too much going on."

Alex pulled his coat off the rack. "Don't think your whole life is here. Your ancestors were courageous—don't let them down by hiding."

I watched as he walked out of the little office, my mind a complete mess.

NINE

**Lilarian Health Care Makes Headway
with Homeopathic Medicines**
—*DURREN PATHOLOGY CENTER*

*I*T HAD TAKEN a lot of arguing to get my security detail to stay in the car. Becca had insisted on standing at the door, but I finally convinced her she would get frostbite if she did. I used my key to let myself in and sighed in relief. It was nice to be back in my childhood home.

"I'm in here." Dad's voice drifted over the sound of the television in the living room. The smell of lasagna meant he was in the kitchen.

"Hey." I hung my coat on the back of the chair and smiled at Patricia. She gave me a hug and then held me out at arm's length.

"Girl, what on Earth have you been up to?" Apparently she had been watching the news.

"It's a really long story." I shook my head.

"A really crazy one, I'd guess." She narrowed her eyes at me and lifted my chin. She tsked under her breath and gave me a knowing smile and wink. "You're all flushed."

"It's minus ten outside. Of course I'm flushed." I tried to not grimace when she laughed.

"That's not the same kind of flushed." She lowered her voice. "I bet it has something to do with that gorgeous man I saw you on the cameras with."

"What?"

"There's video of you walking around on campus laughing with that prince. He's a good-looking guy. I'd let him get me all flushed too."

"I'll let him know you're interested." I laughed as I walked past her and into the kitchen. I threw my arms around Dad's neck and pressed my face against his shoulder.

"Don't make me spill this!" He was trying to transfer the lasagna from the dish onto plates. I had learned with my mom you never took time for granted, so hugged my dad as often as possible.

"I'm gone, you old fart!" Patricia hollered from the living room.

"Get out of here, woman!" Dad yelled back. I could hear her laughing even after the door closed behind her. I knew for a fact that even though they enjoyed pestering each other they were the best of friends.

"So, I thought you had a headache today." I carried our plates to the table and then went to get glasses out.

"I did, but feel a bit better tonight. I figured you might need your favorite dinner after I saw you on TV." He smiled at me as he brought the milk carton to the table. "Lasagna is always good for dinners where there's stuff to discuss."

"Did you know?" I sat down and looked at him. "Did Mom tell you?"

"I think you're going to have to start at the beginning." He passed me a piece of bread. "All I know is I woke up today to seeing you on the news and had voice mail from several news stations."

"Oh, Dad, I'm so sorry." I sighed and poked at my food. "I should've asked them to send someone over for you."

"Who to send who over?"

"Mom was from a royal family. I don't know if she knew or not, but I sure didn't. But they gave me a detail to keep the press away and I should have asked them to send someone over here for you too. I mean, the duchess that came to tell me about my family assigned a detail."

"Huh." We ate in silence for a few minutes, each of us working through things in our heads. "I don't guess they're going to bother me too much, since I'm just your stepfather."

"You're not *just* my stepfather. You're my dad." I knew he would understand the differentiation.

"I know, but that probably makes a difference to the people wanting to ask questions."

"Did she know?"

"Your mom was always a mystery, Sam. That's one of the things I loved about her. She was brilliant, funny, and the most loving woman. But I knew there were things about her I would never learn." He smiled at me, his love for her still as alive as ever. "She never told me she was from a royal line, but I know she placed a great deal of emphasis on family. I suppose that could mean something."

"I have this folder full of birth certificates and a family tree. Of ship itineraries and land deeds." I frowned. "And it all leads back to Duke Rousseau of Lilaria."

"Why did they hunt you down?" Dad had always been practical. It was probably why he had done so well in the military. "Seems like a lot of work just to tell you your great-great-great-grandfather used to own some land."

"They want to reinstate my title." I bit into my bread and chewed thoughtfully. "Supposedly the queen has made it her life task to bring back the families that left."

He looked at me, processing what that could mean. "They want you to move back, then?"

"Yes. I think so." I frowned. "They aren't pressuring me, but there's a lot to accepting the position. I'd be on the council to the queen." I laughed. It was such a ridiculous thought. "I'd be in charge of lands and a house."

"That's a very big honor." Dad looked at me seriously and I stopped my giggles.

"It is. But me? On the council to a queen?" I shook my head. "Can you imagine?" I snorted. "I don't know anything about their country and let's face it, I'm not the most diplomatic person."

"Maybe that's what they need. New insight and someone that isn't constrained by centuries of protocol."

The fact that he was echoing what Alex said scared me. I stared at him while he ate. Did he really think it would be a good idea?

"They also have a really great health care system." I watched him for any indications that this would excite him. "They have a really great specialist that would be willing to work with you."

"Don't base your decision on me, Sam. The truth is if it's my time there isn't anything to be done about it. You know that." My heart clenched and I fought the tears that gathered at the backs of my eyes.

"Anything has to be better than what you're going through." I reached out and grabbed his hand. He was only fifty-five and yet his hands looked like those of an eighty-year-old. There were bruises from all the IVs, shots, and blood work. This was only his second round of chemotherapy, and yet it had already taken so much out of him.

"I've had a wonderful life, Sam. You and your mom have given me everything I could need."

"Don't talk like that," I snapped at him, angry he seemed to have given up. He smiled and squeezed my hand, not bothered by my anger.

"Baby, I've always told you that you should travel. Here's a chance in a lifetime." Traveling had been Dad's favorite part of being in the service. He'd told me and Mom countless times about the places he had seen.

"This isn't the same thing. This wouldn't be a vacation."

"I know. If you decide to go, you need to do it for the right reasons. You need to do it because you're ready to accept the responsibility." He laughed. "Though I bet there are some amazing perks as well. It can't be all bad, can it?"

I smiled, even though I didn't feel like it. I remembered the media hounding me as I left the center and how the people I'd known for years had treated me differently.

Later that night, Dad fell asleep in his chair in front of the television. I went to the kitchen and sorted out his medicine for the night and got him a glass of milk. When I came back into the living room, I stopped and watched him for a minute. He looked so tired and worn out it made my heart ache. He'd barely started the chemo and I hated seeing him so vulnerable. He was my father; he was supposed to be invincible.

As I worked on setting up his medicine, I caught the glint of something out of the corner of my eye. I turned around to look out the kitchen window and froze. There was a man with a camera standing just on the other side of the glass. The light above the kitchen table must have reflected off the lens, because he wasn't using a flash. From the way his finger moved over the button on the top of the camera, I knew he was taking pictures.

Anger surged through my chest as I stalked to the window and turned the blinds down. Taking slow steps so I wouldn't wake Dad, I walked into the living room to close the blinds. Standing outside was a woman taking pictures of Dad asleep in the recliner.

"Get the hell out of here!" I ran to the window and twisted the blinds closed.

"What? What's going on?" Dad tried to sit up in his seat.

"It's nothing. Go back to sleep." I couldn't disguise the anger in my voice. They had been taking pictures of my father! He was sick. Did they have no morals?

"Doesn't sound like nothing." He wrestled with the handle on the side of his seat. "Is someone outside?"

"I've got it, Dad. I'll tell the security detail." Grabbing my coat, I yanked the door open and waved at the car idling in the driveway.

"Becca!" The sound of a camera drew my attention to the side of my house. The female photographer was snapping pictures. "Get the hell out of here! This is private property." I dug in my pocket for my cell phone, intent on calling the police.

"Stop where you are!" Becca was moving across the lawn in angry strides.

"I'm calling the cops, asshole!" The other photographer ran past the house and toward a van at the end of the street.

The cops said they would send a car out, but they wouldn't be able to stay at the house all night. I growled in frustration and asked Becca to stay and make sure no one bothered my dad. After she made some calls, another bodyguard showed up to stay. I grilled him, making sure he understood no one was to come on the property at all.

Dad spent a good amount of time trying to calm me down, but it only made me angrier. No one should be taking pictures of my father. Especially to sell to papers or tabloids. When I realized my anger was making him agitated I tried to relax—no reason to have him stressed over something I was handling.

I got him his medicine and helped him to bed even though he tried to wave me away. Patricia would be over bright and early so I didn't have to worry about him tomorrow. He hated having someone check on him every day, but I needed to know he was okay.

I didn't say anything in the car on the way to my house. When they told me someone would be staying overnight, I didn't argue. Duvall seemed to understand my quiet and spoke to Parker, who had taken a seat on the couch. Jess and Bert had already gone to bed, so the house was relatively quiet. I showed Parker where the bathroom was and told him to help himself in the kitchen before I went to my room.

Opening the computer, I searched for the specialist Alex had provided information about. Dr. Bielefeld was originally from Germany, but currently worked in France and Lilaria, enjoying a dual citizenship. He'd been written up in many medical journals for his work with holistic and natural methods for dealing with cancer. I read for hours, searching through the articles for patient health and longevity. While some of his patients responded well to his methods, others required a balance of the normal medicines with the herbal supplements.

From what I could tell, he seemed to believe each person required a program tailored for their individual needs. He apparently didn't have a problem mixing the more Western medicines with his holistic approach and obviously had a great understanding of them both. All the testimonials were glowing and happy; even the families of patients who died seemed to believe he had helped their loved one's quality of life.

At some point I switched topics. I read through all the paperwork about my family and their flight from Lilaria. Before they left, their name could be traced back for centuries. It was intimidating to see an outline of every ancestor and their achievements. There was so much history that I got sucked in and didn't realize how much time had slipped by. It was a bit like reading a historical novel, only I was somehow related to these people.

Eventually I leaned back on the bed and glanced at my clock. It was after three in the morning. I dragged myself down the hall to the bathroom. If I waited until the morning, I'd likely not get a shower. Jess and Bert were both bathroom hogs.

I leaned against the tiled wall and let the hot water run over my back. In less than two days my entire world had been turned upside down. Not just tilted or spun around and confused, but turned completely inside out. Nothing made sense. Every decision felt wrong. Every direction I looked led down a path I was unsure about. For years I had worked toward one goal, stayed focused on the one place I wanted to get. But now that goal felt like it wasn't quite right. I wanted to know more about where I came from. I wanted to take my father to a place where he could get the best possible care. I needed to know if I was meant to sit on the council of a queen or if this was all just a weird fluke in my life.

So I held on to the one thing I knew to be true. Family always came first.

TEN

How to Become a Bodyguard
—*GUNS AND BULLETS MAGAZINE*

THE CAR PULLED up to the school and I took a deep breath. Duvall looked back at me and I nodded my head. The press was waiting this time, ready for me to show up. Duvall opened my door and helped me push through the people gawking at me.

The security guards at the front door waved me past without even looking at my ID. Apparently my face had been plastered on enough TVs that they all knew me on sight. We took the stairs, but instead of heading for my office, I went to Dr. Geller's. I rapped on the door, hoping to catch him before anyone else showed up.

"Come in."

"Wait out here." I looked at Becca and Duvall. There was no compromise here. I would be going in this office by myself. Duvall grimaced but nodded. I'd take that small victory.

Dr. Geller was typing something on the computer, so I closed the door quietly and took a seat across from his desk. His salt-and-pepper hair made him look older than his forty-two years. I set my bag on the floor and tried to not shift in my seat. I was nervous, the want-to-puke kind of nervous. I was about to possibly make the biggest mistake of my life.

"Hey, Sam." He looked over at me and smiled, still typing. "Heard you had some crazy classes yesterday."

"Certainly wasn't my normal Tuesday routine." I pulled some of the tests I had graded out of my bag and set them on his desk. "They didn't do too poorly on Monday. A healthy average."

He looked through the tests quickly, glancing at a few of the questions and answers. "Good, good. They seem to have grasped that chapter rather well."

I didn't say anything, just gave him a tight-lipped smile. He set the papers down and looked at me expectantly.

"Did the dean tell you why the classes were so crazy yesterday? Or was he just upset I had caused an ordeal on campus?"

"On the contrary, he wanted to know why I hadn't told him one of my graduate students was from a royal family. I had to explain I didn't know myself."

"To be fair, I didn't know until Monday night."

Dr. Geller laughed. "Now that has to be a crazy story and is probably better than all the ones floating around."

"You know, it is pretty nuts." I shook my head. "I thought when they invited me to dinner they were planning on making a donation to the program. I knew David hated talking to the donors, so I thought maybe you had forgotten to tell me. Or I had missed the e-mail."

"So you went to dinner expecting to represent the school, only to be blindsided with this?" Dr. Geller chuckled. "I bet your face was hilarious."

"Hey! What would you have thought in my shoes?"

"Oh, I agree, it was a logical conclusion. So what does this mean? You're descended from royalty, but why did they look you up?" He leaned forward, his shrewd gaze pinned on me.

"They want to reinstate my title."

"Ah." He folded his hands on the desk in front of him. "And that would mean you would have to take up a seat on the queen's council and move to Lilaria."

"Yes." I couldn't help being surprised he knew so much about the country. "You seem to have a good grasp on it."

"I have a friend who works for the FBT and another that went on to teach falconry in Lilaria."

"I didn't know that." I fiddled with a hangnail and tried to decide how to broach the next part. "I have to decide if I'm going."

"And have you? Will I have another friend in Lilaria?" His words eased some of the guilt in my heart.

"I believe so." I paused, the words stuck in my throat. "I need to at least go and see if it's where I belong. If I'm a right fit."

"Well, we can unenroll you for the semester and I can give the classes you've been handling to one of the other grad students. If you decide to make it a permanent move, then we'll make it final." He smiled sadly. "I hate to see you go, Sam. You're one of the most dedicated students I've had in a long time, but I understand that at times life takes us in different directions than we planned."

"I still want to finish my master's, Dr. Geller. It just might take longer than I wanted."

"If nothing else, I will give you the name of my friend. Perhaps you will find a way to still work with birds." He stood up and moved around his desk.

"That would be great." I frowned. "I'm really sorry

it's turned out this way. I know . . . I know you've put a lot of time into my degree and I feel like I'm letting you down."

"Nonsense. If anything, you'll take a great deal of information with you. Lilaria's noble houses have been aligned with birds for centuries. Maybe you were meant to do this all along."

Something in my stomach loosened and for the first time I felt good about my decision. He seemed to understand what I was thinking because he laughed.

"Did you think I was going to yell and try to guilt you into staying?"

"Not really. I just hated to leave like this. It felt wrong."

"When will you be going?" He leaned against his desk.

"I'm not sure, but I probably shouldn't come back to the school. I'm causing too much trouble." I sighed. "In fact, I should probably clear out my desk today."

"If you need anything, let me know." He looked at me seriously. "I mean it. Anything. We're all going to be rooting for you."

"Thank you."

After I left his office, I went straight to the one I shared. Everyone was in there, and they all looked up when Becca and I came through the door. I walked over to my desk before stopping and turning to look at everyone.

"Well, looks like someone else is going to get the window desk."

"Oh my God, Geller kicked you out of the program?" Mary looked at me with wide eyes.

"Um, no. I'm withdrawing. I can't teach classes and uphold my course load if there are eight news vans following me everywhere." I started pulling stuff out of my drawers and shoving it into my bag.

"What are you going to do?" David spun around in his desk chair and looked at me seriously. "Are you going to finish your degree somewhere else?"

"I don't know yet." I started to tell them I was going to Lilaria but stopped. "I have several options to choose from."

"Like what?" Mary walked over to my desk with a box and helped me put some of my books and papers in it.

"Do you still have my field guide?" I brushed off her question.

"Oh yeah. Hold on." She ran to her desk and fished through her bag. "Here it is."

"So, you're just leaving?" David asked.

"I'll be in touch. It's not like I won't ever see you guys again."

"We should throw you a party!" Mary sat on the window ledge and looked at me. "It'll be fun. We can invite the whole department."

"Mary, I think that would be difficult right now." David narrowed his eyes at her. "She has security following her to the bathroom. You really think they're going to let her have a party?"

"Becca does not follow me into the bathroom." I glared at David. "And there isn't time. I'll probably be leaving in a couple of days."

"Are you going to Lilaria?" David leaned forward, his elbows resting on his knees.

"Possibly."

"We're going to miss you." Mary threw her arms around me, and I laughed when she knocked me off balance. Becca moved closer, but I waved her away.

"I'm going to miss you too. Don't drive David crazy, okay?"

"Bah. It's so much fun." Mary winked at me.

I walked over to David and hugged him before kissing his cheek. "Take care of yourself."

"You too."

I told everyone else good-bye, joking and laughing where I could. The truth was, I was crying inside. This had been my life for several years and it felt strange to leave it without having completed what I came for.

Parker took the box out of my hands when I left the office, and Duvall looked at me expectantly. "I need to speak with Rose."

"Very well. I'll see if she has time this afternoon. In the meantime, where would you like to go?"

"My father's."

I called Dad on the ride over, letting him know I was on my way. Seemed like the polite thing to do since there were two news vans tailing us.

"I mean, really. What do they expect to find out? That I'm really an alien sent from Pluto?" I glanced over my shoulder quickly.

"Good shots can make a reporter's career. Finding out the smallest bit of information can mean scooping another station. The fact is, right now you're news." Duvall looked back at me and if I didn't know any better I would think there was sympathy in his expression.

"They don't even know why they're following me right now."

"The little bit of information they have—"

"Misinformation!"

"Yes, the little bit they think they know means you're a story their viewers would find interesting."

I just shook my head. Dad was waiting for us when we pulled up. I could see him peeking out the side window. Since there were people following us, Duvall and Becca escorted me into the house. I hugged Dad and then introduced him to my shadows.

"Nice to meet you. Would you like something to drink?" Dad smiled at Duvall and Becca, who both declined.

I threw my box of books on the floor and sat down on the couch. Dad nodded his head and sat across from me. "You're going?"

"Yeah." I sighed, knowing he would probably put up a fight, but I was ready. "You're coming with me."

"Sam, I'm in the middle of chemo. I can't just leave."

"We'll talk to your doctor and figure out what to do." I sat up and looked him in the eye. "Have you been to Lilaria?"

"No." Dad shook his head.

"There's no time like the present." I knew he loved to travel and damn it, if he was going to be okay with whatever happened, then he might as well live a little in the meantime.

"I may have to wait until after the last round of chemo." He leaned forward and patted my knee. "But if you want me to come, I'll come after that."

I didn't like it. I wanted him to meet with the specialist right away, but I understood he would be better off finishing what he started. "I might have to go before that. The duchess made it sound like I only had a few days."

"Then go! I'll be fine. Patricia will take me to my appointments."

"Just call me cabby, why don't you?" Patricia hollered from the kitchen. She leaned against the door frame, a dish towel in her hand. "You're going to Lilaria?"

I nodded my head. It still didn't feel real. The entire last few days felt dreamlike. Especially the part where I had been plastered against Alex before sticking my foot in my mouth. Well, the foot in my mouth part felt pretty real. I'd been doing that my whole life.

"Good! Don't you worry about your dad. I'll keep him in line."

"Samantha, the duchess said she would be free in an hour." Duvall stepped forward. "Should I tell her you are coming?"

"Yes." I pulled my phone out of my pocket and checked the time. "Where is she?"

"She's at the Parallel."

I glanced down at my clothes and sighed. I had worn jeans and a sweater, but it would have to do. There wasn't enough time to go back to my house, change, and make it to the hotel.

"Okay. I'll have to go like this." I turned back to my dad and wrapped my arms around him. "You call the doctor today and tell him you're going to be moving to Lilaria. Tell him you need all your charts for Dr. Bielefeld, okay?"

"Samantha, I'm sick, not stupid." Dad kissed my forehead.

"Yeah, yeah. Don't forget." I laughed as I pulled my coat back on. How long had I been here? Five minutes? Six? Is this how life would be once I accepted the family title?

"Be careful."

"Love you." I smiled at him over my shoulder as I followed Duvall back to the car. The news crews were still setting up, obviously expecting me to be there longer than the amount of time it took to say hello.

"Love you too."

Becca pulled the door closed behind us and we left for the Parallel.

ELEVEN

Reluctant Royal
—LILARIAN GAZETTE

THE HOTEL WAS busy, guests checking in and out, people meeting for lunch or relaxing in the lobby. When we pulled up, the doorman opened the car door and Becca exited first. He smiled at her before looking at me. When he realized I was in the car as well, his whole demeanor changed. He bowed his head a little and made a sweeping gesture with his hand.

I looked at Becca to see if this guy was serious but she just smirked. As I walked past him, I realized he was the same guy who had been on duty the night I'd met the duchess and Alex for dinner. I squashed my urge to demand if he had been the one to sell photos to the press and walked past him with just a mumbled thank-you.

Inside, Duvall and Becca took us in an elevator to the penthouse. I found myself wondering if Alex would be there and tried to calm my racing heart. I wanted to see him, to tell him I was sorry again, but wasn't sure if that would be a welcome thing or not. There was a short hallway outside the elevator that led to a large double door. Duvall knocked and we waited until another suit-clad person opened the door.

"Samantha!" Rose stood up from a small desk next to the windows and walked over to me. She kissed my cheek and squeezed my shoulders. "So good to see you."

"Thank you for seeing me on such short notice."

"Not a problem at all." She led me over to a small sofa and offered me some tea. "Have you come to a decision?"

"I have." I took a polite sip from the teacup before setting it back on the table. "I would like to go back with you if the invitation is still open."

"Of course! That's wonderful news." She leaned back in her chair and smiled. "And will your father be joining us?"

"He has to finish his current chemotherapy treatments, but he'll come shortly after." I frowned, realizing there was a great deal for me to take care of, like plane tickets for him and setting up appointments. "Alex gave me some information on Dr. Bielefeld, but I'm not sure how to go about contacting him for my father. I imagine he must have a large client list."

"Oh, no worries there. I'll have someone set that up for you. In fact, there will be several things to take care of." She turned and motioned over her shoulder to a lady in a blue dress. "You're going to need access to your accounts, someone to help get you organized and to help you in the country since you've never been."

"Um." I looked from Rose to the lady in blue and back. "I have no idea where to start."

"That's okay, dear. I knew there would be a lot to take care of."

The front door opened and Alex walked into the room. The lady in blue and the waitress were setting up dishes on the dining table and bobbed a quick curtsy.

Alex nodded his head in acknowledgment before his eyes fixed on me. He smiled politely at me and I felt queasy. There was a distance in his eyes that hurt.

"Samantha." He sat down on the other end of the short sofa and my body automatically tilted toward him. It was like being caught in a gravitational pull. "Are you joining us for lunch?"

"Oh, no." I turned back to his aunt, wanting to focus on anything other than the man next to me. "I didn't mean to interrupt your meal. I can come back later."

Rose was watching me with that calculating look again. It wasn't unfriendly, just thoughtful. You could see her trying to figure out what was going on between me and Alex.

"Have you eaten? I called for four people in case you would be hungry." Rose nodded toward the table and the three place settings.

"Thank you, but I really don't want to intrude."

"Nonsense. We have a lot to discuss." She turned her attention back to the lady in blue. "Sarah, can you please bring me the green folder on my desk? And call the office and see if Chadwick is available."

"Yes, ma'am." Sarah hurried back with the green folder and then quietly left the room to make her phone call.

Rose flipped through the folder before handing it to me. "This holds your account numbers and access codes, including several cards that are linked to them. There is also a brief summary of the lands you hold, your official title, and an itinerary for the next two days and when we land in Lilaria."

"Accounts? Itinerary?"

"Yes, your family's holdings have been guarded by the crown. When they left to protect themselves, they only took what they could carry. This meant leaving a great deal of money and valuables in banks and trusts." Rose sipped her tea while I digested that bit. "The itinerary is to help keep us all on schedule. Since you've decided to accept your title, we will need to do a press release. This will help clear up the rumor mill some."

"You've decided to accept your title?" Alex looked at me with interest.

"Yes." I met his eyes and tried to calm my racing heart. My decision had nothing to do with Alex. At least that's what I kept telling myself over and over.

"Good. Will your father be joining us?"

"He has to finish his current course of treatment."

"Excellent. I'll make a call to Dr. Bielefeld and see that he is aware of your father's case." Alex leaned back in his seat.

"Thank you." I was trying to not be bothered by his behavior, but I found myself wishing the friendly, flirty man I had spent the day with yesterday was sitting next to me. He'd pulled back and I knew it was my fault.

I looked at Rose, who was watching us with a small smile. When Sarah came back into the room, she brought a small notebook to Rose. "It took some arranging, but Chadwick is delighted to help Lady Rousseau."

"Chadwick?" I asked.

"Chadwick is a member of the royal household staff. He has agreed to become your personal assistant, at least until you find one that suits you better. But I think you'll get along with him quite well." Rose smiled. "His mother is Lilarian, but his father is American, so he will be able to help you adjust to the customs better than some might."

"Oh. How does one pay a personal assistant? Is it an hourly thing or a salary?" I ran my fingers over the folder in my hand. Not sure what to expect when I opened it.

"He's currently employed by the crown, which means he's being given to you as a courtesy since we invited you to the country. However, if you decide to take him on as part of your staff, you'll be able to make whatever arrangements suit you." Rose stood up and I set my teacup back on the table. "I need to make a phone call, but I'll be back in a few minutes."

"Go ahead and open it." Alex nodded at the folder in my hands. "You need to know what you have."

I looked from him to the folder and frowned. There was a crest pressed into the paper and I ran my fingers over it. Was this the Rousseau crest? I went ahead and opened the folder and peered at the papers. There were credit cards attached with paper clips inside, and several papers were bank statements I had to look at several times. My eyes rose to meet Alex's, only to find him with a small smile.

"This is . . . mine?" I literally couldn't wrap my mind around the numbers. There were millions in each account. There were so many zeros I thought my eyes would cross. I needed a calculator.

"Yes."

There was a map with a highlighted area and several spots marked in another color. I traced them with my finger, not sure what they meant. While the other papers had been in English, the map was in Lilarian.

"What are these?"

Alex scooted closer on the couch so he could look at the paper. "That is a map of your estate. It is roughly four miles by two." He traced a finger along the green line before tapping one of the red dots. "And this is one of your oil wells."

There were four red dots on the map and I stared in disbelief. "They're all active?"

"The two with orange around them are active. The

others are closed right now. The blue dot is the village or township that belongs to the Rousseau family."

I looked up at Alex, my eyes wide with fear. Suddenly those bank accounts didn't feel as big. "I'm responsible for an entire village?"

He laughed, some of the amusement from yesterday creeping back into his eyes. "They pay a tax to your family, and you in turn take care of them."

"Take care of them from what?"

"Think of it as a town where you're the mayor. If there is a natural catastrophe, you help find a way to take care of it. If it's too big for you to handle, you would plead the crown, who would take it to the parliament. If they needed a new road or a new school, you would take care of that through your taxes."

"Oh sweet baby Jesus." I looked at him in horror. "I have no idea how to do any of that!"

"I promised I wouldn't throw you to the wolves." He leaned his head closer to me and I took a deep breath, enjoying his scent. "As the crown prince, it's my job to help you understand your duties. Eventually, I'll be the one you're reporting things to, so it only makes sense."

"I see." I lowered my voice so no one could hear me. "Alex, I'm a wildlife biologist. I'm in way over my head."

"You're a smart woman who will rise to the occasion." His eyes dipped down to my lips and I fought the urge to lick them.

"I'm sorry about yesterday."

"You were right." He frowned. "I should know better. I'll be good if you are." His eyes glinted with the dare. "Just know if you feel like changing your mind, I'm right here."

"I'll remember that." I couldn't help but smile at the

challenge in his eyes. "Does this mean we can be friends for now? I have a feeling I could use some people on my side."

"I'll try for you." His eyes ran over my body and I shook my head. "For now."

"Friends don't ogle friends."

"I said I'd try. I didn't promise anything." Sitting back in his seat, he chuckled. "I have a feeling our friendship will have a shelf life."

"A shelf life?"

"You'll either end up hating me or in my bed." His eyes grew dark. "And I know which one I'd prefer."

Heat raced over my body and I had to take a deep breath. Unfortunately, that meant inhaling more of his delicious scent. His eyes narrowed and he leaned a little closer to me.

"If you keep looking at me like that, we're not going to even be able to pretend to be friends." His voice was husky and the room seemed to narrow around us. Like tunnel vision. I forgot there were members of the detail and the maid in the room. It wasn't until Rose cleared her throat that I came back to my senses.

"This is going to be an interesting challenge." Alex smiled as he leaned back in his chair.

"Well, I think they're ready for us to order." Rose looked at me with a suspiciously bland face. "I hope you're hungry, Samantha."

I stood up and brushed my hands on my jeans, embarrassed to be caught in the staring contest with Alex. I took the menu Sarah handed me and took a seat at the table.

Alex sat next to me, his knee brushing mine. I should have moved my leg but I didn't. Apparently I felt like torturing myself today. When Rose sat down across from me, I had to bite my lip to keep from laughing at the ridiculousness of my life. Sarah joined us for lunch, discussing the itinerary for the next two days.

"So we leave on Friday?" I picked at my salad, pushing the cucumbers out of the way.

"I know that is soon, but I have several engagements coming up." Rose tore a piece of bread in half and put a little butter on the slice.

"No, I understand. I just have a lot to take care of by then."

"I'd be happy to help make any arrangements." Sarah smiled at me over her food. "It would really be no problem. Just let me know what you need."

"I'll have to make a list. I'm not sure I'll think of everything."

"That's part of my job. I'll sit down with you before you leave. Do you have a passport?"

"I do. I need to pack and talk to my roommate. Thankfully, I'm paid up on rent for the next few months." The waitress whisked away my half-eaten salad and replaced it with a plate of small sandwiches. It had seemed like the safest choice, but now I was regretting not ordering something heftier.

"Is there anything we need to address in particular with the press release?" Sarah opened a notebook next to her plate.

"No matter what we say, they are going to latch on to the story." Alex sipped from his water glass and watched me over the rim. "Another reason to make a hasty exit."

"Why are they so interested?" I looked around the table. "So what if my ancestor was a royal? It's another country. It has nothing to do with anyone over here."

"You don't get it. You're like an American Cinderella." Alex laughed at my expression.

"Last time I checked, I didn't own any glass slippers." I scoffed at the idea. It wasn't like I was being rescued by the prince. Or whisked away to be married. Not that I would say that part out loud. "No wicked stepmother forcing me to sleep at a hearth."

"It's the idea of it all. A young woman who's been working hard finds out she's the long-lost descendant of a royal family. It's exciting. Even in Lilaria, you're going to be an object of interest." Rose sighed thoughtfully. "There isn't much to be done about that."

"There have been other families, right? You said other families left Lilaria and the queen was looking for all of them."

"You're only the second to come back. Two of the other lines have ended." Rose frowned. "And while you're the second to reclaim your title, Duke Thysmer is quite a bit older than you."

"You mean he is almost seventy years old." Alex laughed. "No, you're going to be far more interesting because you're a young American. People will be curious about your background, how you adjust to your new life, and if you make any waves."

"I wasn't planning on it." I frowned at him, wondering why he seemed to think I would.

"Sometimes waves are a good thing. Rock the boat a little." Alex's smile was entirely too sexy to be in the friend zone, so I looked back at my food and tried to ignore him. I wouldn't mind rocking a boat with him.

"You're going to do fine, dear." Rose smiled at me. "And we will make sure you have someone to help you every step of the way."

After lunch, Alex had to leave for some diplomatic engagement I was entirely too overwhelmed to even think about. He lifted my hand to his lips and I felt my breath catch at the feel of his mouth on my skin again.

"I hope to see you soon." I didn't respond, just nodded my head. Words had failed me.

Once he was gone, Sarah had me cornered on the couch and was giving instructions on what to pack while Rose changed clothes.

"You won't have to worry about any immunizations, just your passport. Do you speak any Lilarian?" When I shook my head she sighed slightly but didn't look too put out. "That's fine. I will get you one of the audio programs to listen to. For the most part, we are a bilingual country, but all the formal ceremonies will be held in Lilarian."

"Of course." I swallowed and questioned my decision for the umpteenth time.

Rose came out of her room dressed in formal wear. "Samantha, I have to meet with the governor tonight. If you need anything, let Sarah know. We'll send you a copy of the press release in the morning. The sooner we get that done, the sooner we can try to keep things in check."

"You look spectacular." She was wearing a small diadem in her hair and a long, plum-colored dress that made her silver hair shine.

"Thank you, sweetheart." Rose smiled, pleased with my compliment. She patted her hair gently. "I hate wearing these, but since it's a formal event it's part of the uniform."

"Is it heavy?" I eyed the diamonds.

"This one isn't too bad, but even after an hour it starts to weigh on you." Sarah stood up and helped Rose into a dressy winter coat. "You'll have to practice at home so you learn how to hold your neck and get used to the weight for your ceremony."

"Excuse me?" I looked at her like she'd grown a second head.

"You will have a choice of jewels for the ceremony, but the Rousseau family jewels would be the most appropriate." Rose picked up a small purse from a table and laughed at my expression. "You look like I told you you'd have to wear a bear head, not a crown."

"You guys don't wear bear heads, do you?"

"Only for the secret ceremonies." Rose winked at me as she left in a whirlwind of purple and black.

"She was kidding, right?" I looked at Sarah but she only smirked.

TWELVE

The Weight of a Crown
—NEW YORK CONSTANT

"You're going to Lilaria?" Jess sat on the couch next to me.

"Yeah. I think I need to do this." I looked over my shoulder to where Becca sat in the kitchen. "Jess, there are millions in the bank accounts. And there's a specialist to work with Dad."

"What did Geller say?" Jess crossed her legs and leaned toward me.

"He gave me the name of someone he knows in Lilaria and seemed to understand. It's not like I can teach any of the classes right now. It was a fiasco."

"It could calm down." Jess frowned. "Okay, not any time soon, but it just seems like a huge decision."

"It is." I picked at the blanket over my legs.

"Look, if you think this is a good idea, then you should do it." She sighed and flopped back on the cushion.

"I thought you would be excited. You told me I needed to know more about my family." I leaned my head against the armrest and closed my eyes.

"I'm playing devil's advocate. I just want to make sure you're happy."

"You really need to stop hanging out with Bert so much." I opened my eyes and glared at her.

She just laughed at me. "I just can't believe you're leaving me. Who am I going to torture?"

"I'm sure you'll find ways of bugging me and you'll have to come and visit." I chewed on my thumbnail for a minute. "Are you going to have someone else move in?" I couldn't imagine someone else living in my room.

"Bert and I talked about it. I think we're just going to make it official and stop paying rent for two places." Jess smiled, her face bright with excitement.

"About time. I guess I've been holding you up, huh? No wonder you don't look upset I'm leaving. You get to officially shack up with your boy toy." I laughed when she threw a pillow at me.

"You guys realize I'm sitting right here, right?" Bert was sitting in the ugly old recliner by the curtain, a book opened on his lap.

"Shut up. I'm upset you're leaving and you know it." She frowned at me. "Will you be back here at all? If your dad is going there you won't have a reason to visit."

"Of course I'll have a reason to visit." I shoved her shoulder. "You and even you," I said, pointing to Bert. Besides, I had a feeling it wouldn't be long before they were mailing out wedding invitations.

"Speaking of boy toys, how's Prince Yummy?"

I heard Becca sputter in the kitchen and I kicked Jess.

"What? Don't act like you haven't thought it." Jess raised her voice and craned her neck to look at Becca. She smiled and got up from the table to go to the sink. "Fine. Pretend if you want to."

"Alex is fine." I tried to keep my tone normal.

"Mm-hm. He sure is." Jess wiggled her eyebrows and I groaned.

"Please tell sixth-grade Jess that I'd like to talk to adult Jess."

"Fine. Has he kissed you yet?" She narrowed her eyes at me. "Oh ho! Your silence speaks volumes!"

"Bert, stop letting her read your textbooks. I'm begging you." He didn't respond other than to shrug.

"C'mon. You have to tell me!" Jess looked at me with pleading eyes.

"It's not going to happen again." I sighed, knowing I had to spill if I wanted any peace.

"Oh my God. Alex really did kiss you! How was it? Why on Earth is it not going to happen again? Was it bad?" Jess sat up straight. "That's the saddest thought in the world."

"It was good." I shook my head. "Really, really, good. The best. But it shouldn't have happened. I have too much going on to deal with that too! I mean, I'm not interested in a fling."

"What makes you think it would be a fling?" Jess narrowed her eyes at me. "Did he say that?"

"No." I bit my lip and then blurted it out. "I'm an American! He's a freaking prince! What use would I be? He probably needs to end up with someone from a royal family that can help him rule a country."

"Um, aren't you from a royal family?" Jess raised one eyebrow and looked at me like I was stupid.

"It's not the same thing, Jess. He'd need someone from a respected family." I wrapped my arms around my chest. "I'm not really royal. I'm an American related to someone who was a royal."

"That doesn't seem to matter to Rose and Alex."

"Jess."

"Don't Jess me. I saw the way you looked at him.

The way he looked at you. Don't be stupid, Sam. You overthink things."

"I do not! I make educated decisions." I shook my head. "I have way too much going on to be mixed up in anything complicated."

"Complicated is the best kind." Jess smirked.

"I'm going to bed." I threw the blanket off and stood up. "I have to pack tomorrow and get ready for the trip." I could barely wrap my mind around the fact that this was my next to last night at home—the next to last night living with Jess. She had become my family over the years.

"I see my argument skills have forced you to retreat. I claim victory."

"Shuddup!" I looked over at Becca, who was leaning against the kitchen door frame. "Do you need anything?"

"I have everything I need." She smiled at me.

"Okay. Spill. Why do you have a Southern accent but work for Lilaria?" I frowned at her.

"I went through training with the FBI. When Rose came over a few years ago, I was part of the team assigned to her." She smiled. "I stopped an attempt to kidnap her and she asked me to work for her."

"Someone tried to kidnap her?"

"Holy shit." Jess stood up and walked over. "You stopped a kidnapper?"

"Yes. Did you think I was just here for looks?" Becca asked.

"Well, no. I just thought you were to keep people from bothering Sam." Jess looked at Becca with weighing eyes. "I bet people underestimate you a lot."

"It works to my advantage." Becca shrugged.

"Do I need to worry about something like that?"

"I'm just a precaution," Becca assured me.

"I'm so done for tonight. I'll see you guys in the morning." I started to turn away.

"You want help tomorrow?" Jess asked. She normally didn't have any classes on Thursday and often worked from home.

"That would be great."

As soon as my head hit the pillow, I was out. It had been one of the longest weeks of my life and it was nowhere near being over.

The next morning I was woken up by the sounds of voices in the living room. It was barely seven o'clock and I already had twelve e-mails according to my phone. I sat up and stared at the sun streaming through my window.

I grabbed some jeans, a long-sleeve T-shirt, and tennis shoes. Once I was ready, I threw open my door and went in search of coffee. Sarah was sitting at the kitchen table with Jess and Bert. I nodded my head at them but went straight for the coffeepot. I didn't have the brainpower yet to deal with why Sarah was in my house.

I poured in a healthy amount of creamer and sugar and stirred until my coffee was creamy brown. I took a sip and sighed. Just right. I rummaged around in the refrigerator and found some yogurt. Grabbing a spoon, I took the last chair at the table.

"Good morning, Duchess." Sarah smiled at me.

I grunted.

Jess snickered. "Wait until after the first cup."

I frowned into my coffee. Who would be in Lilaria to warn people that I needed caffeine in the mornings?

"Ah. I understand." Sarah smiled brightly. "It usually takes me two before I'm fully awake."

I grunted again. I bet Sarah woke up ready for anything. She probably slept in her clothes with that notebook clutched in her hand. She had it open next to her with a bunch of notes scribbled in the shorthand I had noticed the day before. I took my time with my coffee and yogurt, listening while Jess asked questions and Sarah answered.

Finally I got up and threw away the yogurt cup and poured some more coffee. I turned to look at them and sipped from my cup. "Okay."

"That's her way of saying tell her what's going on," Jess explained.

"Well, I brought you some more information about your arrival in Lilaria. There will be a ceremony to welcome you home. After that there will be a delegation to bring you to the palace to meet Queen Felecia. You'll be spending the night there before being given a small reception the next day where you will be introduced to some of the other nobility and members of parliament." She took a breath and I waved my free hand in the air.

"Whoa, whoa, whoa. I'm going to be presented to the queen after flying across the Atlantic for hours and hours? What type of plane are we taking? Will I be able to take a shower? I mean, I'm supposed to go meet the Queen of Lilaria just like *that*?" I turned around and fished through the cabinets. "Shit. I need a bigger cup." I grabbed the giant mug with the saying "I said good day, sir!"

"It's customary that the queen welcome visiting dignitaries or nobles. The fact that you are 'coming home' is an even bigger reason for her to invite you to the castle. Prince Alex also asked that you stay at the palace before being taken to your lands. I believe he wants to escort you to your home." Sarah smiled politely, but I caught the twinkle in her eyes. Apparently my moment with Alex hadn't gone unnoticed yesterday. Or maybe it was because he had spent the day before with me.

"That's not necessary. I'm sure he has more important things to take care of."

Jess glared at me, her nose wrinkled and her mouth pressed into a firm line.

"He was quite adamant." Sarah smiled again before turning back to her notebook. "Chadwick is going to the Rousseau estate today to make sure everything is ready for your arrival. There has been a steward appointed to the lands while your family was away, so I'm expecting everything has been kept in good shape."

"What is the steward's name?" I grabbed the grocery notepad off of the counter and looked in a drawer for a pen.

"Stanley Wessex." Sarah looked over her notes. "He is in his late fifties and has been in charge of the estate for the last twenty years. I'm sure he will be an extraordinary help when you take over."

"Or he'll hate me for taking his job," I muttered under my breath while scribbling down his name.

"I've also set up a secure e-mail for you and arranged for a new cell phone." She reached into the bag next to her and pulled out a white phone. She rattled off the new number while I quickly copied it down in my notes. "I've set it up so the monthly payments will be deducted from your primary account."

"Will I be able to use this worldwide?" I looked at the iPhone and frowned. I'd been an Android user for years.

"Yes, ma'am. It's a Lilarian number, so you will have to use the country code when calling a number in the States." Sarah pulled out some more paperwork. "I e-mailed you the press release we sent out this morning—have you seen it yet?"

"Yeah . . . That would be a no." I frowned at her. Apparently I was going to have to start getting up at the butt crack of dawn to keep up with these people.

"Well, here is a copy for you to look over. I also went

ahead and sent a contingent to your father's house. It's likely there will be some reporters sniffing around for a story." Sarah looked at me carefully. "Once they realize your father has cancer, I fear it will be a bigger story."

"I see." And I did. The Cinderella comment from yesterday would be blown out of proportion when they found out my stepfather was sick. "How do I go about hiring people to stay with him?"

"I'll take care of that. How many do you think would be appropriate?" Sarah held her pen ready over her pad of paper and looked at me expectantly.

"Um, two?" I swallowed. "So they can take turns and stuff, I guess?"

"That sounds like a good plan. While he will likely have to deal with some of the media, it won't be as much as you. Not to mention it should calm down once you leave the country."

"Heh." I didn't know what else to say, so looked over the press release. The queen had announced that after a long, thorough search, they had located one of the missing royal families in America. There was a quick bit about me, my schooling, and that I was returning to Lilaria to accept my title. It was brief and to the point. I approved.

"Samantha, I think you're going to have to leave the packing to me and Bert." Jess crossed her legs in her chair and propped her chin on her hand.

"What? I have to get this stuff over to Dad's today. I leave tomorrow."

"Exactly. And you need to go shopping."

"What on Earth for? Toiletries? Travel soaps?"

"Clothes, Sam. Clothes. You can't meet the Queen of Lilaria in blue jeans." She turned to look at Sarah. "Am I right? There has to be a dress code of some sort for that type of stuff."

"Yes. The reception at the palace will be black-tie formal. Your reinstatement will be white tie. And I'm sure that there will be other things that would require dresses or skirts." Sarah didn't look up from her notebook.

I stared at both of them. "Black tie? White tie?"

Jess sighed. "Black tie—you can get away with a fancy cocktail dress. White tie requires a long gown, gloves, jewels."

"Yes, for white-tie affairs you would need to wear one of your family diadems." Sarah was still scribbling in her notebook.

"Diadems. You mean tiaras? Crowns?" I shook my head. "My family has diadems."

"Diadems, never crowns." Sarah looked up at me. "And yes. I believe you have several. I recall a painting of one with gorgeous emeralds."

"Emeralds." I shook my head. I needed to stop repeating everything that was said to me. "Okay. So, shopping. And packing." I started to think about how much money I could spend on a dress and then realized I had three other accounts to consider. "What time are we leaving in the morning?"

"I'll send a car for you at four." Sarah closed her notebook. "There are several shops downtown that would have appropriate attire. When would you like to go?"

"I guess now." I looked around the kitchen, feeling lost.

"Wear some comfortable shoes—we're going to be busy." Jess hopped out of her chair and scurried down the hall. I guess that meant she was going with me. Thank God for stylish roommates.

THIRTEEN

How to Pick a Dress for the Ball
—THE JOLENE WATERS SHOW

Ａ FTER THE THIRD store I was ready to kill Jess and hide her body under a mountain of snow. Sarah seemed amused by Jess's way of talking to me. Then again, it probably looked funny to everyone that saw me standing in front of a mirror in a giant monstrosity of a pink dress.

"I will not wear this." I glared at her. "I wouldn't bury an enemy in this dress."

Someone sniffed beside me and I realized the store owner was watching us. Apparently she didn't think much of my style choices either. The fact was that I was incredibly nervous about meeting a queen, parliament, and a bunch of royals. The thought of trying to walk in this dress while meeting a queen, parliament, and a bunch of royals made me hyperventilate.

"It's gorgeous! You look like you could be in a magazine." Jess fluffed the skirt a little more. I stared at her until she finally sighed. "Fine. Let's try something a little more boring."

"Good idea." I stepped off the little platform and

gathered up the skirt in my arms. Jess followed close behind so she could help me undo the four thousand little buttons along the back.

"You know, this is a huge moment. Your chance to make a big statement." Jess looked at me seriously. "You need to go in there, large and proud. Don't let them treat you like the dirty cousin from America. Show 'em you're someone to contend with."

"You make this sound like high school." I wiggled out of the dress and helped her put it back on the hanger, which promptly bowed in the middle, struggling to support the weight of the dress.

"I'm serious. You need to go in there and let them know you're Samantha Effing Rousseau. You're gorgeous, you're brilliant, and you won't take any shit." Jess stood up and looked at me. "They need to know that right away."

I thought about what she was saying. First impressions were important. If I would dress up to give a speech at a bird convention, there was no reason I shouldn't dress up for a meeting with the queen. I turned and looked at the next dress on the rack and contemplated it.

"Okay."

"Okay?"

"Okay, but we need to make the right statement. No froufrou stuff." I pushed the hangers aside and met Jess's eyes in the mirror.

"I know just the dress." She ran out of the little room and I stood there contemplating what I was doing. I hated that I was making these decisions. I felt like I was doing this blind. And the worst part was there were people standing outside the store with cameras, trying to see what I was buying.

When Jess came back and held up a dress, I knew she had nailed it on the head. It was simple but elegant. Sexy but discreet: simple cap sleeves with an A-line skirt, the black material shining softly in the dressing room lights. There was a simple black belt that added a little something extra and gave it even more personality. I ran my hands over the gown and almost squealed in delight. There were pockets.

"You've been saving this one." I turned my eyes to Jess and glared at her. "You made me try on those god-awful dresses, knowing full well I would hate them. And this was in the store the whole time!"

"So you like it?" Jess smiled from ear to ear.

"You sneaky bitch! That last dress was torture!" I held my hand out for the hanger and she laughed.

"It worked, didn't it? I could have brought a trash bag in here and you would have been excited." Jess helped me pull the dress up and work the hidden zipper.

When I turned around to look in the mirror, I froze. The dress fit perfectly, which was lucky considering there wasn't time for alterations. Jess did something to my hair, twisting it up off my neck in a messy bun that countered the streamlined look of the dress.

"Understated elegance." Jess nodded her head like she had designed the dress herself.

"It's perfect." I turned so I could see the back of the dress.

"Let's go show the others." Jess swung the door open and motioned for me to go out first. I had to pick the skirt up to walk, but with heels it would be perfect. Outside, the curtains had been pulled over the large front windows and Sarah was waiting in a chair, her notebook in her lap. She looked up and a smile pulled at the corners of her mouth.

"Oh, you look lovely."

I stepped onto the little block in front of the mirror and looked at myself. It was silly, but I suddenly felt royal. I guess that was the magic of a beautiful dress. The shop owner brought over a pair of black high heels in my size. I slipped them on and looked again at the mirror. They were the perfect height. The skirt no longer hung too low, but they weren't so high I couldn't walk.

A phone beeped and I looked around to see who it belonged to, but no one moved to answer it. The phone beeped again and I looked at the shop owner, but she shook her head. I stepped down from the pedestal and walked over to my bag. I picked up the new phone and looked at the screen.

"Who has this number?" There were two text messages.

"The duchess and the prince, Jess, and your father." Sarah looked back through her notebook. "And your security detail."

651–555–1212: How is the dress shopping going?

I grabbed my other phone and checked to make sure it really was Alex's number before replying.

ME: I hate it, but I found one.

I quickly added his name to the contact list so I would have it in the new phone.

Alex: Send me a picture.
ME: Nope.
Alex: Then send me a picture without the dress.
ME: Pervert.
Alex: You have no idea.

I laughed and turned the phone off. When I looked up, I realized everyone was staring at me. "What?"

"Who was that?" Jess asked, her eyes amused.

"Alex." I cleared my throat and turned back to the shop owner. "I'd like to get this one. Do you have anything else made by this designer?"

"As a matter of fact, I do." The shop owner's eyes lit up and I realized I hadn't thought to ask the price. I tried to see the tag under my arm, but there were no numbers—never a good sign. I looked back at the mirror and decided that at this point, it didn't matter. I was getting the dress.

I tried on several more: a ball gown, a pearly silver sheath with a boat neck, covered in sequins and jewels; a red tea-length dress; and another black dress Jess had insisted on. It was form-fitting with short sleeves and a slit in the collar that went well into my cleavage. It was daring and beautiful. I couldn't imagine ever wearing it.

After the dress store, we stopped at a few more boutiques, grabbing a few business suits, jackets, and the normal necessities. It was dark by the time we headed home, but I had one last stop to make.

The car pulled up to the curb at the largest bookstore in town. I ran inside, knowing exactly what I was looking for. An *Idiot's Guide to Lilaria* and a language program to listen to on the plane. I sent Jess to the cash register with my card and waited in the music section with Becca. A few people seemed to recognize me, but thankfully no one said anything. We were back in the car and on the way to my dad's in no time.

Sarah had left to go over things with Rose, so it was just me and Jess with Dad. And the contingent of bodyguards waiting outside or in the living room. Dad made dinner and we talked about things to do when he came to Lilaria. Patricia was there, refusing to let me help clean up.

I sorted Dad's medicine for the next week and went

over things with Patricia. Dad had been happy and cracking jokes, but I caught him closing his eyes a few times. My heart clenched and tears sprang to my eyes. There was a picture of him and Mom in Hawaii above his chair and I wanted to cry at seeing them so happy. No matter how much he pretended, I could see the toll that cancer was taking on him. When it was time to leave, I could barely bring myself to get out of my chair.

"Hey, is there anything you want to take from here with you? A picture, maybe?" Jess asked. We'd known each other long enough that she understood how hard this was for me.

"There's a picture in my room, on the nightstand. Would you grab it for me?"

"Sure." Jess left the room, leaving me and Dad alone.

"Stop it." Dad's voice drew my attention back to him.

"Stop what?"

"Worrying. You've got those little lines between your eyebrows." He used his thumb to try to smooth them away. "I'm going to be fine. And I'm going to come see you soon."

"I know. I just feel like I shouldn't be leaving you right now." I frowned and looked down at the table.

"You're giving me something to look forward to." Dad grabbed my hands. "Do you understand that, Sam? I'm looking forward to going to Lilaria and seeing the land you and your mother came from. I got a travel book today and highlighted some of the stuff I want to do."

He stood up slowly and shuffled over to the kitchen counter before coming back with a dog-eared book. He handed it to me and I flipped through some of the pages.

"Wow. There's a waterfall?"

"Yes! And it's huge. I want to have my picture taken in front of it." Dad laughed. "And there is a huge lake in the Rousseau holdings. The book says there's good fishing."

"I saw that one on the map." I frowned. I really needed to spend some time on the Internet tonight.

"Yes! And there's a very popular local dish I want to try. Some kind of fish and potatoes. It looks delicious."

"Hm." I closed the book and looked at him. "Promise you'll be okay."

He squeezed my hand and smiled. "Promise."

"Have you talked to Patricia about coming with you?" I needed a subject change.

"Patricia? You think she should come with me?" Dad looked surprised. "I hadn't thought about it."

"Why not? She's not working anymore and I'd pay for everything." The money was certainly a perk and while I was terrified to spend it, having my family—even my adopted family—with me would be worth it.

"I'll think about it." Dad's eyes turned thoughtful. He and Patricia got along well, and while I knew there was nothing romantic between them, they seemed to complement each other.

"Think about it. She's retired and her son never calls her. Why not bring her with you? It's the least I can do for her after all she's helped us."

Jess came back into the kitchen carrying the photo frame that held the picture of my family. "Got it! Was there anything else?"

"That's it for now. I don't know how much I'm allowed to bring. I'll just come back for the rest when I can."

"Ready to go then?"

"Yeah. I still need to pack and do a little research." I leaned over and wrapped my arms around my dad. "I'll see you soon."

"Yes, you will! Make sure there are fish for me to

catch." He kissed my cheek and I caught the shimmer in his eyes. My throat tightened as I had a wild thought that I might never see him again. I had to remind myself that he was doing really well considering everything that he had been through.

"I'll order more if there aren't." I kissed his bald head and grabbed my coat. If I stayed much longer I was going to turn into a blubbery mess.

Later that night I sat on my bed with my laptop and stared at my empty room. There were four suitcases crammed with all my stuff, several giant garment bags, and a box with some books I refused to leave behind. I'd had to borrow a suitcase from Bert because I hadn't been able to fit everything in mine. The furniture would stay since I wouldn't need it, and Jess promised to take the rest of my stuff to my dad's next week.

I looked back at the search bar on my computer. I typed in "Lilarian Royalty" and waited for the results. It didn't take long before sites popped up. There were articles about the line of succession, scandals, history. I clicked on the one that detailed the line of succession, then clicked on the tab for the queen and smiled at the picture that came up. Alex favored her a great deal. I read the facts quickly. She was a little older than my dad, was an avid outdoorsman, and had three children. That made me pause. In all this time, I hadn't asked Alex much about himself.

His Royal Highness Alexander Patrick Fitzwilliam, the Duke of D'Lynsal and heir to the crown of Lilaria, was the oldest child at twenty-seven, with a younger brother, Maxwell Jameson Trevor, and a sister named Catherine Marie Rose. I clicked on the tab for Alex and read about his schooling, charities, and hobbies. I chuckled at the thought of him fishing and building things. Then again, I remembered his strong hands and decided it made perfect sense. There were several pictures of him alone, professional shots, and some candid pictures of him with his family or working with children.

I went back to the main menu and scrolled through some of the other royals. I stopped on Rousseau in surprise. Surely they wouldn't have me listed yet.

But they did. Thank goodness there was no picture, but my full name, date of birth, schooling, and honors were listed. There was a short explanation about my upcoming reinstatement, but not a date. I was the twenty-fourth person in line for the crown. I almost shit my pants when I saw that little detail. I sat up straight and barked a laugh. I was in line for the crown. May every soul ahead of me live a long and prosperous life because that was not something I would ever want.

Below my information was a beautiful black-and-white picture of my mother with her birth and death dates. I ran my fingers over the screen and wondered where they had found the image. She was smiling at the camera, her head angled as if amused by something. Her biography and a list of her publications were listed below the picture. It was a small thing, but I was glad they had included her on the list.

I left that page and looked back through the other names. I looked through a list of charities the family was involved in and at pictures of state events. Jess deserved something nice for saving me from looking like an idiot in my jeans and boots. Thankfully, from what I could tell, my new clothes would fit in perfectly. The site didn't really offer too much else for me, so I closed that page and went back through the other search results.

After a while I gave in to my impulses and typed Alex's name into the search bar. I instantly regretted it. Headlines about a sex scandal popped up, links to stories about women he could be tied to, and speculation about what royal he would eventually marry. There were stories with the words *player, model, stud, betrayal,* and *heartbreak* in the titles. Like watching a train wreck, my eyes were drawn to the images icon. Maybe it was a sick impulse to torture myself or the need to make him feel even more unattainable, but I clicked on the link.

There are some things you can never un-see, and images of Alex in bed with another woman were on the top of that list. His bare back with sheets barely covering his hips and the look on the woman's face would forever be etched into my psyche. There were pictures of the woman taking off her clothes while he watched from the bed. Pictures of her sitting on top of him that had to be from another day because she was wearing a different bra. It made me insanely jealous—angry enough to push my computer away and get up and pace around the room. I counted to ten. And then to twenty. I closed my eyes and scrubbed at my lids with the palms of my hands. I needed to calm down and think about this rationally. I knew he was a flirt and of course he had been with other women. It wasn't like I hadn't slept with guys before. Alex and I hadn't shared anything but a couple of kisses. And yet . . . and yet, it still bothered me. After a few minutes I grabbed the computer off the bed and started to close all the windows, but a headline grabbed my attention.

"BETRAYED BY LOVER" was in huge letters over one of the pictures that thankfully had the more indecent parts fuzzed out. I needed to know, needed to see if this was something important. Maybe I just hoped it was important.

Prince Alex D'Lynsal of Lilaria is currently in a legal battle over pictures that were sold by an on-again, off-again ex-lover. In an official press release, the prince claimed the photographs had been taken without his permission and then used as blackmail. The royal family of Lilaria has taken a firm stance on the matter and refuses to answer any questions by the press.

It's been speculated that the woman in the photos, Melissa Piaf, was trying to force the prince into marriage, but we've found no information to confirm those rumors. One thing is clear—the former model has made a name for herself. She announced on a national television show that several publishing and production companies had offered her money for her story. It remains to be seen if any of those deals come to fruition.

I sat back away from the computer and chewed on my thumbnail. If the press release from Alex was true, this Melissa woman was a real bitch. I couldn't imagine waking up to find pictures of me with Max or Thomas in the paper one morning. It must've been a terrible day—to have your personal bits flashed all over for the world to see. I checked the date on the article and sighed. Six months ago. I went back through the listings to see if there was any recent information. There wasn't much else I could find. In fact, there were no recent images or stories about Alex until he came to the States. A few stories with pictures of us on campus or at the restaurant. It made my stomach turn. They talked about him like he wasn't a real person, as if he shouldn't care what they said about him. Now instead of feeling jealous, I just felt sick for Alex.

The thought of searching for my own name crossed my mind, but I quickly dismissed it. Just the idea made me shudder. I closed the laptop and stuck it in my carry-on bag. Staring at the ceiling, I tried to turn my brain off, to stop thinking about the pictures and how terrible it was to imagine someone selling images of your intimate moments. Rolling onto my side, I punched my pillow, trying to get more comfortable.

He had told me he shouldn't chase me. Was this what he had been talking about, not my questionable heritage? Did it matter?

I was asking myself that question a lot when it came to Alex. I still wasn't sure of the answers.

FOURTEEN

No Pumpkins Here
Cinderella Leaves for the Palace in a Shiny Gulfstream
—*MINNESOTA DAILY*

$\mathcal{T}$HE THREE HOURS of sleep I had managed to get did not go well with my hatred for mornings. All my stuff was piled into the cars waiting outside and I was looking around my room for any last-minute items. My outfit was dressy yet casual—jeans, riding boots, and a comfortable shirt with a big chunky scarf—since I knew the press would be taking pictures. Jess was standing by the door holding my new black peacoat and looking a little misty-eyed. Tears this early in the morning were scary.

"I've got your coat." Jess sniffed and I looked up at her with wide eyes.

"Oh no."

"You're going to need it. I checked the weather and it's snowing there." She sniffed again. "Don't want to get sick right when you get there."

"Jess, don't do this." I shook my head, frozen in place.

"I know that good-byes aren't your thing, so I'm just going to give you this and then go to my room." Sniff. Hiccup.

"C'mon, you're killing me." I felt the skin around my eyes tighten and I blinked quickly.

"I'm going to miss you." She thrust the coat out in front of her.

"You're going to come see me this summer, right?" I didn't take the jacket. "This isn't good-bye forever."

"But I'm going to miss your grumpy morning face and the way you double-check all the dishes I've cleaned." She pouted.

"Bert's grumpy in the morning, you'll be fine."

"Am not." He grunted.

"Right. Not grumpy at all." I shook my head. Jess gave up waiting on me to take the jacket and threw her arms around me anyway. I hugged her back, knowing it would be a while before I got to see her again. No one else would understand me the way Jess did. I squeezed her a little tighter and then let go.

"I'll send you a souvenir. Maybe one of those little figures that's pooping on a lawn." I hugged Bert too and turned quickly toward the door but stopped with my hand on the handle. I looked over my shoulder one last time and threw them a smile.

"I'll see you soon." Biting my lip, I pushed through the door, scared that I'd start crying if I stayed any longer.

The news vans that hadn't left in the last few days were still there, the reporters standing on the curb with cameras and microphones.

"Sam! Sam! Are you excited about going to Lilaria for the first time?"

"Are you going to stay in Lilaria?"

"Are you and Prince Alex an item?"

"Samantha! How do you feel about being America's Duchess?"

I couldn't help but laugh at the last comment and looked over at the reporter. "America's Duchess?"

"Our very own royalty! What do you think?" He seemed elated I had found his comment funny.

"I'm a grad student." I shook my head and ducked through the open door of the car. It was weird that I had gotten used to having a driver already. Even though my truck was a pain in the butt, I did miss the old thing. Bert and Jess were going to use the truck to move the rest of my stuff to my dad's house and then leave it there.

The trip to the airport was surreal. We passed some of the landmarks that had been part of my life for the last ten years, buildings I had known forever, it seemed. Vans full of reporters and cameras followed us at a respectable distance—thank goodness. I'd hate for them to photograph the tears that were running down my cheeks.

Duvall had come to escort me and I was starting to wonder why I was being protected by the head of the detail. Thankfully, he hadn't said anything about my crying, just handed me a tissue and turned back to the front of the car. As we neared the airport, I checked my bags again to make sure I had everything I would need. It was pointless because I had already checked twenty times while at the house. The anal retentive in me was satisfied, so I sat back and wiped at my face to make sure there was no moisture left to betray my emotions.

When we pulled up to the drop-off point, there was a huge area blocked off by a police escort. Alex was standing at the curb, smiling and chatting with a few people wearing press badges. I wondered how he could look so chipper talking to the people who would just as happily post embarrassing pictures of him. When Duvall exited the front seat, Alex excused himself with a wave and came over to my car. I put on a small smile and let him help me out.

"Ready?" His eyes studied my face and I wondered what he saw there. I was a giant ball of emotions and wasn't even sure myself what the most prominent was at this moment. Sadness, definitely, but there was also a thread of excitement, and to be honest, I was happy to see Alex.

"Think so." I took a deep breath and shouldered my bag.

He smiled at me, but I could see a little guilt in his eyes. "Nothing is ever as good or as bad as you think it will be. Lilaria is just a place. It's what you make of it that counts."

His voice was quiet, so I knew no one else could hear us except for Duvall, who hadn't left my side. Becca was standing close as well, but she had given Alex a little space when he obviously wanted to say something privately. I nodded to let him know I had heard him. He was right—I could make this as good or as bad as I wanted.

"My lady, may I take your bag? I'll see to it that it's on the plane before you leave," Becca said quietly.

I handed it over, feeling naked without anything to do with my hands. Alex was wearing a suit and I suddenly felt underdressed in my skinny jeans and boots. At least I would be comfortable on the flight. I frowned and hoped I wasn't breaking some kind of protocol by not wearing a dress. Okay, so I wasn't going to wear a dress just to please them, but I could have at least worn nice slacks.

"Smile at least a little, okay?" Alex smiled widely to illustrate just how little I was supposed to smile and I laughed. I could see all his teeth.

"Got it."

"That's my girl." My breath hitched at his words and he seemed to catch my response because his smile widened even more.

"Samantha! Samantha!"

"Sam! Over here!"

"Are you excited?"

The last question made me stop and I turned to smile at the cameras. It was early and I'd only had one cup of coffee before leaving, but it was time I at least said something to the press. Especially if I was leaving. I might not like being a news story, but I loved my home and saying good-bye seemed appropriate.

"I hate leaving Minnesota, but I'm looking forward to seeing my homeland." I smiled widely and let them take a few pictures. Not exactly a good-bye, but I hoped it would work. "Hopefully it won't be as cold there."

My last statement produced a few chuckles and I gave a quick wave before going through the sliding doors to the airport. Alex walked next to me, not touching, but close enough that I didn't feel alone.

"Well done." He winked down at me. "You're already slipping into the part."

Rose was speaking to some officials near a door and I let myself be guided toward her.

"Yes, thank you. That will be perfect." Rose smiled graciously and I studied the way she handled the people, mentally taking note of how she spoke to them. Friendly, but with a small sense of detachment—most likely to keep them from overstepping any bounds. "We appreciate all you've done for us."

"It's been a pleasure, ma'am." The airport official smiled at her before turning to me and Alex. "Good morning, Highness. Duchess."

"Good morning." Alex reached out and shook hands with him.

"Morning." I was still on the fence over how good it was. I let him shake my hand and tried to hide my nerves.

"Samantha, have you ever been on a private jet?" Rose leaned forward and kissed my cheeks in greeting. She linked her arm through mine and led me toward a side terminal.

"I flew on a Cessna once while on a trip to South America." Did that count? Not exactly a jet, but it was privately owned.

"Oh, you're in for a treat. We have a Gulfstream. The seats are comfortable and much better than flying long distances in those of a large airline." She patted my arm, her fingers squeezing gently, and I knew she was trying to put me at ease. Rose did make me comfortable and I didn't want her to think I was unhappy, so I smiled enthusiastically. Probably a little too enthusiastically because I heard Alex snort.

The security guards didn't even stop us. There was no going through the metal detector, they just unclipped a rope and led us straight past. I smiled at the men and women gaping at us. Airport workers were peeking out of shops, the cleaning crews had parked their carts in the hallway. At the end of the terminal, we were led out onto the tarmac.

The plane glowed a beautiful pearl white in the early morning light. A long pinstripe of blue and green ran along the plane, matching the flag that hung in the cockpit window. A blue rug led straight from the exit all the way to the jet. A row of marines stood along the rug, saluting us. There were also a few members of the press, but I was more shocked by the military. I looked up at Alex, the confusion in my eyes obvious.

"It's customary when a member of royalty comes to a country that the military serves as an honor guard."

Alex ducked his head so I could hear him over the wind. "I believe they are also showing their support for you. The governor was very taken with your story and excited you are from his state."

"Um, wow." I smiled at the men and women who lined the carpet. They had gotten up at a god-awful hour just to stand in the cold for us. I murmured thank-yous as I passed them even though I knew they wouldn't be able to respond since they were at attention.

At the plane, Rose entered first, taking the steps smoothly. Alex motioned for me to go ahead of him. I had to duck in the door and there wasn't much space between my head and the ceiling of the plane in the center. Even with the height restrictions, there was a spacious feel and sense of opulence. Leather seats, all the electronic conveniences, and special lighting. Soft classical music played over the speakers and there were throw blankets on some of the chairs.

"Good morning, Duchess." A woman smiled at me and motioned for me to move to the center of the plane. She was wearing a flight attendant uniform with a little Lilarian flag attached above her heart.

"Morning." I looked at the seats, not sure where to sit. Finally I decided on one of the large seats next to a window, opposite Rose. I'd always enjoyed flying. One of my favorite parts was watching the takeoff and landing.

Alex nodded to the woman at the door before taking the seat across from mine, a small table separating us. The attendant brought him a satchel and a stack of newspapers, which he flipped through quickly. Rose had a similar stack of things on her table. She was watching me and Alex, though, her shrewd eyes moving back and forth as if searching for invisible strings.

"What do you think?" Rose asked.

"It's beautiful. Certainly puts flying coach to shame." I ran my fingers over the buttons on a panel next to my chair. "None of these will accidentally open a door or flush the toilet, will they?"

"Don't worry about the doors, but I'm not sure about the toilet." Rose laughed.

"You can use your new phone to control the lights and call the attendant." Alex looked at me over the paper he was holding. "Even turn on the television, if you want. There is a large selection of movies. The little icon at the bottom."

"Oh." I reached into my pocket and pulled out the new phone. There was a text message, so I opened it quickly. There was a picture of Bert in my bed eating cookies, with crumbs everywhere. I laughed and pointed out I wasn't the one who was going to have to clean it up. I showed the picture to Alex, who smiled.

"Will they come to visit you sometime?"

"I think they're going to try to come this summer. I'm betting I'll be back for a wedding soon too." I smiled thinking about it. "I'm kinda relieved I won't have to go dress shopping with Jess." I shuddered.

"Isn't that supposed to be one of the enjoyable parts?"

"Not for me." I shook my head. "Jess would drag me to every store in the country to go dress shopping if she could. Of course, I'll probably end up wearing a puke green bridesmaid dress now."

"How long have they been together?"

"Almost four years." I sighed, remembering how Jess had hated Bert at first. "She thought he was a pompous putz; he thought she was a spoiled shopaholic. Love at first sight. Couldn't keep their hands off each other."

He laughed, amused by the obvious contradiction. "Sounds like a movie."

"A book. Classic love story." I laughed. "Very Jane Austen."

"Do you read often?"

"Not as much as I'd like. Lately it's been all journals and textbooks." I looked around for Becca. "Actually, I brought my e-reader for the flight. Thought I might actually read something fun for a change."

"And what kind of book will it be? Romance? Science fiction? Mystery?"

"Paranormal romance." I sighed. "The Elemental Mysteries series by Elizabeth Hunter. The last book came out a while ago and I haven't had the time to read it yet."

"So, vampires? Ghosts?" Alex smiled like this amused him.

"Hot, sexy vampires with a good helping of historical mystery. Perfection." I leaned back in the chair when the engine started. Sarah came up the steps, followed by Becca and Duvall. Sarah took the seat across from Rose, and Becca handed me my bag before moving to a couch in the back. A pair of guards came up the steps carrying one of my garment bags and carry-on. I sighed in relief. When the engine had started I'd worried I would have to meet the queen in my blue jeans. As it was I wasn't sure how I was going to change into my dress in the plane.

"I wish I had been able to meet your father before we left," Rose mentioned while going over her papers, and I realized she was talking to me.

"You were very busy. Maybe you'll get to in Lilaria."

"That would be wonderful. Perhaps if he is feeling up to it, you could come out to my estate for dinner."

"He would love that." And he would. Getting to go to another country had seemed to excite him.

"Then we'll set it up!" Rose smiled before turning back to her paperwork.

I fished through my bag for my e-reader and earbuds.

I'd loaded the language CD so I could listen to it while I was reading or staring out the window. I really hoped some of it would stick.

Alex settled into his paperwork and I watched out the window as the workers cleared the plane for takeoff. It wasn't long before we were in the air and I was watching my home disappear.

After a while I pulled my headset off and set down my book. Alex was sketching in a notepad and I'd been curious to see what he was working on. "So, you draw?"

"Some. Not much." He looked at me over the pad of paper, his eyes thoughtful. "When something strikes me."

"Can I see?" I leaned over the table and tried to peek at the paper.

"Hm. I don't know." He tilted the book away from me. "I'll play you for it."

"Play me for it?" I sat back in my seat. "Play what?"

"Don't do it, Samantha. He never loses." Rose didn't look up from her paperwork.

"We'll see." I narrowed my eyes at him. He was smiling like he had already won. "What is it?"

"Well, wait a minute. If you win, you get to see my sketch. What do I get if I win?" He leaned forward, his eyes sparkling.

"I warned you." Rose shook her head and stood up from her seat, stretching. "I think I'm going to try to nap for a while." She moved back to one of the open benches and pressed a button. It slid out from the wall to make a small bed. I shook my head at the idea of a bed on a plane.

"Well? My prize?" Alex brought my attention back to him.

"What could you possibly want?" I had been thinking he had everything, but as soon as the words left my mouth I realized my mistake. His eyes flashed with triumph and his smile made my blood race.

"Oh, there are a lot of things I want." His eyes ran over my face. "What are you willing to give?"

"Friends, Alex," I hissed at him under my breath, worried the others had heard him.

He chuckled and leaned closer. "If you win, you see the sketch. If I win, you have to volunteer at the FBT."

"Seems a bit uneven."

"Take it or leave it." He leaned back in his chair, his eyes watching me carefully.

"What would I have to do at the FBT?" I narrowed my eyes at him.

"Whatever I think appropriate."

I studied him for a minute, considering what he could possibly force me to do. Clean out birdcages? Been there, done that. Cut up mice? Didn't bother me anymore.

"Fine. But I get to keep the sketch if I win."

"Deal." He held out his hand and I shook it even though he still hadn't told me what we were going to play. Hopefully not cards. I hated poker.

He stood up and moved toward the back of the plane. When he came back with a box in his hand, I laughed.

"Monopoly?"

"What? You're too good for Monopoly?" He set the box down on the table and proceeded to set up the game. "What do you want to be?"

"The shoe."

"The shoe?" He looked at me doubtfully. "Are you sure?"

"My mom was always the shoe." The words popped out of my mouth without thought. I hadn't thought about that in a long time.

"Very well. The shoe it is." He set out the shoe and the top hat before distributing the money.

It didn't take long to see why Rose had told me to not take the deal. Alex was incredibly lucky when it came to the game. Always passing Go, always collecting money, never landing on any of the spots normal people feared.

"You're cheating! Give me the dice!" My sad stack of paper money was shameful.

"How dare you!" He mock-glared at me.

"No one is that lucky. How are you doing it?" I reached over the table, trying to swipe the dice from his hand. He laughed while I tried to pry his fingers loose.

"I don't cheat! I'm just incredibly smart. And it's my turn again."

"Being smart doesn't get you to land on the Go spot every time!" I sat down and Alex opened his hand to show me the dice.

"Normal dice. Nothing to see here." He rolled double sixes and I groaned loudly. Another good move.

"You're so cheating. Magnets or something." I grumbled as I collected the dice for my roll. Eight spaces put me on one of his hotels. Cursing under my breath, I took half my remaining money and threw it at him.

He laughed. "Thank you. I appreciate your patronage."

"Shut up and roll, cheater."

FIFTEEN

The Royal Price Tag
—*FINANCIAL TALLY*

In only a few more rolls I was completely out of money and Alex was gloating. "Ah, what shall I do with you?"

"Again?" I raised my eyebrow. He was competitive, but so was I.

"But I've already won." He smiled. "And I like to win."

"Bet you can't do it again." I narrowed my eyes. We still had two hours before we landed to refuel.

"Oh, I can do it again." He leaned forward and lowered his voice. "But I'll only play again if we up the stakes."

"What are you betting?" The last couple of hours had gone by in a flash as I laughed and joked with Alex. I hadn't realized we'd started flirting until I was almost out of money.

"If I win I stop pretending we're just friends." His voice dropped an octave and he glanced at my lips. "And I get to kiss you. Whenever I want."

My body temperature rose as I considered what he was asking. "One kiss?"

"Maybe." He leaned even closer. "But we both know we'll want more than that."

"And what do I get if I win?" I licked my lips, his smell invading my senses. A kiss didn't sound too bad. In fact it sounded like a pretty good idea right now.

"What do you want?" He smiled cockily, knowing exactly what I was wanting right this minute.

"You teach me Lilarian." I frowned. "I don't want to sound like an idiot at the ceremony."

"You realize this means I win either way." He ran a hand over the scruff on his jaw and I was mildly fascinated by the sound it made under his fingers.

"No. If I win, you have to teach me Lilarian while keeping your hands to yourself." I picked up the dice and rolled. "Like a good friend."

"Where's the fun in that?" He kept his voice low. "I can think of some really fun ways to teach you my native tongue."

"I bet you can." I let out a nervous chuckle, thinking about the things I'd like him to do with his tongue.

"I can think of some things I'd like to hear you say in Lilarian too." His eyes stared holes into me as he moved his top hat five spaces. "Loudly."

"Then you better bring your A game."

"I always bring my A game."

"Is that so?"

We set up the board for another game. Alex's eyebrows had drawn together as we worked our way around the board and I realized he meant business. It excited me to know how serious he was about winning a kiss, but it also scared me. Possibly because I was excited by the idea.

Eventually I bought a hotel and put it on Park Place.

I needed to reel in my hormones and focus. Even if he won, I wasn't going to just give in to him. It was too complicated.

Alex landed on my carefully laid trap. "Pay up, Prince Yummy." The nickname burst out of my mouth as I mentally screamed in slow motion, trying to stop my lips from uttering the words.

"Prince Yummy?" He threw his head back and laughed loudly. When he looked back at me, there was heat in his eyes. "Care to explain that one?"

"Jess." I shook my head, trying to not look embarrassed. I was going to kill her the next time I saw her. "That's her nickname for you."

"I'm liking her more and more." He leaned forward again. "Looks like you agree with her."

"There goes your ego again." I narrowed my eyes. "If you hear something enough it gets stuck in your brain."

"Hm." He pushed the dice toward me. "That's one explanation."

"I'm going to kill her." I frowned at the game board.

"Just make sure you hide the body well." He chuckled, his hand reaching out to brush over my fingers. "I don't think I've enjoyed a game of Monopoly this much in a long time."

"I'm developing a deep hatred for it."

"That's because you're losing." He narrowed his eyes. "In fact, you're losing so badly I'm starting to think you want to lose."

"Har, har." He was right. I was losing. Badly. "Maybe we should try another game."

"Nope. You agreed to Monopoly."

"That was before I realized you had some kind of Monopoly Jedi skills."

"This is not the hotel you are looking for."

"Shut it, Obi-Wan Cheater."

Something shifted, and I began to take the lead. Alex looked miffed, and eventually frustrated. When he landed in jail I stood up and did a little dance in the aisle. He watched me with hooded eyes and it dawned on me I was shaking my butt in his face. I sat back in my seat but couldn't stop smiling. He leaned his elbows on the table and stared at the board with confusion.

"I can't remember the last time I lost." He looked at me with a small smile. "I might lose more often if I get treated to your victory dances."

"Oh, c'mon. I'm sure you've lost before." I started putting the pieces back in the box. The captain had started the descent for Ireland. I wanted to watch out the window and try to catch a glimpse of rolling green hills. I'd always wanted to visit Ireland but hadn't had a chance.

"I was distracted." He smirked.

"That's not my fault."

"On the contrary, it's completely your fault." He gave me a slow smile that made me want to knock the rest of the pieces off the table and pull him on top of it. "You may have won this time, but I still think we won't last as friends for very long."

"Why? I have plenty of guy friends."

He narrowed his eyes briefly. "There's something here, Samantha. Deny it if you can, but I don't think you'll be able to for long."

"Seriously. Your ego is at dangerous levels." I bit my lip and focused on cleaning up. He took the stack of money out of my hand and sorted it into the right places.

"You can deflect all you want. It doesn't make it any less true."

"You said there were two options." I didn't meet his eyes.

"I have a clear preference."

We lapsed into silence as we waited to land. Sarah woke Rose as we started the descent and I stared out my window. I pulled my feet up into my seat and leaned on the wall to try to see better. It was late in the day and the sun made the clouds glow a soft golden hue. It was beautiful, but I wanted to see all the green. As if listening to my thoughts, the sky split and I had my first hint. The greens were blurring into blues in the dusk and then we were over Dublin.

Fueling the plane didn't take near as long as I thought it would and after a fast meal, we were back in the air. There was a renewed sense of energy in the plane. Sarah was making phone calls and Alex had opened up his laptop. At some point Duvall and Rebecca changed into suits that would blend into the background but still had a formal look. Rose went to the little area in front of the kitchen and pulled a curtain shut. She called for Sarah to help before coming out in a silver dress with a matching jacket. It was simple but elegant.

"We don't have much longer if you want to go ahead and change." Alex nodded toward the little curtained area.

I stood up and made my way to the alcove. I pulled the curtain shut and opened the tiny closet that held my garment bag. I quickly undressed and fought the dress out of the bag before remembering that I needed to put on panty hose. Cursing under my breath, I dug into the bottom of the bag. The plane hit a bit of turbulence and I bounced into the wall before almost falling through the curtain in nothing but my underwear.

"Holy crap!" I stood up and prayed I hadn't knocked the curtain open.

"Samantha?" Alex's voice was nearby and my eyes grew large. "Are you okay?"

"I'm fine! What are you paying these pilots?"

A few people chuckled while I wrestled the panty hose up. Worried about more turbulence, I slid the dress on as fast as possible. Reaching behind me, I tried to grab the zipper but ended up spinning in circles like a puppy.

"Sarah?" I called for Rose's assistant, giving up.

"I've got it." Alex's voice made me freeze. I heard the curtain whisper as he stepped into the area. "Zipper?"

"Um, yeah." I turned my back to him. The zipper started low and I was highly aware of the fact that he could see the lace panties and bra I was wearing. His warm fingers grazed my skin as he unhurriedly pulled the zipper over the top of my butt and up my back.

"Lift your hair." He leaned down and whispered in my ear.

Slowly I reached up and gathered my hair in my hands. He slid the zipper into place before reaching down and sliding his hands around my waist. He pressed his chest against my back while he looked over my shoulder. Deftly, he pulled the belt through the loops and fastened it in the front. It was painfully erotic to know that he was taking his time dressing me, and my breathing was matching the excitement of my thoughts. When he pulled back, I let my hair fall and turned to face him without stepping out of his hold.

He was already wearing a tux, the bow tie hanging open, and no shoes. It was a look that worked for him. He looked down at me with hungry eyes. "You look gorgeous."

"Thank you." His hands were still on my waist and I was having flashbacks to our kiss.

"This is going to be difficult." He leaned back a little so he could run his eyes over my body. "Very difficult."

"All good things are worth the work." I didn't have

to ask him what he was talking about because I was thinking the same thing. Being friends with Alex would be one of the hardest things I'd ever done.

"It would be difficult either way." Alex's voice was serious. "I'm not sure I can keep my hands off you, but I swore off women in the public eye. You make me want to take that back."

"Anyone in a relationship with you would be in the spotlight." I chewed on my bottom lip. "I don't want to be in the spotlight; I just don't think I could handle it."

He leaned forward and whispered something in Lilarian.

"What does that mean?"

"Consider it your first lesson to find out." With a small smile, he turned away and left the curtained area. I stood there, trying to catch my breath before going back out. After a minute I grabbed my shoes and carry-on. I went to the bathroom to put on makeup before twisting my hair into a messy knot at the base of my head, then put on diamond stud earrings that had been my mother's before going back to my seat.

"Perfect, dear. You look absolutely perfect." Rose touched the dress gently.

"Thank you."

"Are you ready?" Rose sat down. "When we land, the authorities will board the plane to check passports and then we will be taken to cars that will deliver us to the palace."

"I would suspect there will be a bit of fanfare for our arrival. Bringing back one of the royal families is an important occasion." Alex was sitting across from me and his voice took on a hard edge. "There will be a great deal of media no matter what. Don't do or say anything you think you might regret."

"I understand. People will try to hurt me just to make

a few dollars." He caught the undertone in my voice and regarded me with sad eyes.

"Yes." He looked out the window at the lights of the city below. "There are those people."

"Do not forget there are also people worth trusting. Those who will love you for you and nothing else." Rose looked at Alex sadly. "Who will love you in spite of your title and money. They are out there."

Her eyes darted to me before looking at the paperwork on the desk. Was she warning me? Or was she worried I would hurt Alex? I turned back to my window and watched as we circled the airport.

When we touched down, my anxiety rocketed. I was here, I was doing it. And I was so nervous I wanted to puke.

"How do I greet Queen Felecia?" I scrubbed my hands together.

"When you're introduced, you'll curtsy once just inside the door and then again a few steps into the room. Go straight to her and introduce yourself. She will shake your hand and welcome you to the country. After that, you'll be introduced to several other people." Rose waved her hand in the air as if she was explaining how to get to a class in a new building. "A few of the nobles that are in town will be there, as will a few key members of parliament. They always love a good reason to come to the palace. After the initial introduction, it will be less formal. This isn't the official ceremony for your reinstatement."

"Okay. Curtsy, walk, and curtsy again. Shake her hand." I took a deep breath. "Monopoly. Why did we play a board game when there is so much I need to know?"

"You needed to relax." Alex grinned devilishly. "It was one of the only ways I could come up with to help."

One of the ways. I could imagine the other ways he could have done to help me relax. Shaking my head, I pushed aside the thought and frowned. "And what do I call her? Your Majesty?"

"That's appropriate the first time you meet her. Then you can switch to something simpler. Ma'am is the most common." Rose smiled at me. "You're going to be fine. No one is going to expect you to know everything tonight."

"The staff is used to walking people through first meetings. Don't worry," Alex said.

The plane was taxied to an open area and I was shocked at the amount of people. A blue rug was rolled out to the plane and a line of cars pulled up. There was a military honor guard in place and a sea of flashing cameras. The door to the plane was opened and an official in a suit stepped up to the entrance.

"May I enter?" His voice held the interesting accent that Alex spoke with.

"Please," Alex said. Even though Alex had been laid-back in the States, I realized that as the highest-ranking royal, everyone would defer to him.

"Welcome home, Your Highness."

"Thank you, Matthew" Alex stood up and shook his hand. They must interact with this official often.

"Welcome home, Duchess." Matthew shook Rose's hand and then turned toward me. "A heartfelt welcome to you, Duchess Rousseau." Matthew smiled warmly at me.

"Thank you."

"I'm afraid I need to see your paperwork." He looked embarrassed.

"Of course." I handed him my passport.

"Excellent." He looked over the passport, and I found it oddly comforting that he hadn't just waved me on. He pulled a stamp out of his pocket and quickly used it. "I hope you find Lilaria to your liking."

"I'm sure I will." I smiled at him and tucked my passport back into my bag.

Alex stood up and held my coat out for me. I slid into the sleeves and buttoned up the front. I was about to set foot on Lilarian soil, the homeland of my ancestors and my new life. Rose walked to the exit and waited for Duvall and Becca and Sarah. Duvall jogged down the stairs to the cars, a finger to his ear as he listened to something on his earpiece. Rose turned to me and smiled.

"Welcome home, Samantha. I'll be waiting in the car for you." Rose winked at me and then quickly made her way down the stairs. There was a cry from the photographers, calling her name, but she simply waved and went straight to the vehicle. The air blowing in through the open door was cold but that wasn't why I shivered.

"I'll be right behind you." Alex put a hand on my back.

"You promised you wouldn't throw me to the wolves." I tried to smile, but it came out weak.

"Trust me."

"I do." I took a deep breath and stepped out into the cold night air.

SIXTEEN

The Reluctant Royal
—*AMERICAN TODAY*

THE SOUND WAS almost deafening. The flashes of the camera were blinding. I froze at the top of the steps and looked out at the people chanting my last name. Alex's warm presence jarred me back to reality and I started down the steps, careful to not trip on my dress. There was a roar from the crowd at the sight of Alex, and it grew when he stepped down from the bottom step next to me and placed his hand on my back.

"Smile and wave." Alex ducked his head down so he could speak in my ear.

I did as I was told, completely overwhelmed. I smiled and waved because I had no idea how to handle all this attention. For the most part, I ignored the people shouting my name and made eye contact with no one. When we got to the car, Duvall opened the door and Alex helped me in. My skirt made it difficult, but I finally managed to take a seat. Rose was sitting on a bench across from me, a smile stretching from ear to ear.

"Brilliant. I knew people were excited, but I hadn't expected it to be quite this large of a reception." Rose patted my knee. "You did great. It's very overpowering at first, but you'll get used to it."

I didn't say anything. I had no words to explain what I was feeling. Terror with an edge of excitement and adrenaline pumped through my system. I just looked out the windows at all the people and tried to not jump when Alex slid into the seat next to me. He kept his gaze focused out his window, smiling at the people, but where no one could see, his fingers slid over mine and clasped my hand tightly.

Some of the panic fled at his touch and I didn't feel so alone. The pressure of his fingers helped ground me. If Rose noticed, she didn't say a word, but I saw her smile at us before turning her attention back to the crowd. The trip through the city was winding and I had a chance to see some of the buildings and statues. It looked a lot like the pictures I had seen of France. People lined the route with signs and cameras, hollering our names.

"Are they always this excited when you come home?" I looked at Alex.

"That's not my name they're shouting." Alex met my gaze with an easy smile. His fingers tightened on mine. "This is an important day for our country. For your family."

I bit my lip and looked back at the crowds. I raised my hand and gave a small wave when we passed a group of children holding a sign with my name on it. They jumped up and down, the little girls giggling. Soon the gates for the palace came into view. I leaned forward in my seat and craned my neck so I could see out Alex's window. He scooted over a bit so I could see better, his hand never letting go of mine.

It looked like something out of a fairy tale. The walls were made from stone and old brick. When I finally got a good look at the castle, I smiled my first real smile since landing. The palace was made from the same stone as the walls. Guards in ceremonial dress flanked a huge door in the center of the old building. It was breathtaking. Duvall opened our car door and Alex helped Rose and me out. A man in a tux took pictures as we climbed out and I tried to not look frustrated. I had hoped we would be through with the photographers at this point.

"That is the palace photographer. You can trust Cecil." Alex seemed to sense my hesitation.

"Duchess Rousseau, may I have you stand here in front of the car? Look up at the castle for me. That's perfect!" Cecil snapped pictures quickly before standing up. "Duchess Sverelle, Your Highness, will you stand with Duchess Rousseau for a moment?"

They moved next to me and gave practiced smiles for the camera. Alex didn't put a hand on my back like I was growing accustomed to, but kept a friendly but respectful distance. I blinked at the flashing and hoped my smile didn't show all my teeth.

Once Cecil was satisfied, the guards saluted Alex and opened the front door for us. I digested everything around us, staggered by the amount of history contained in the walls. Rose and Alex looked like they were just coming home. Their relaxed expressions made me wonder if they were going to kick their shoes off and go dig through the fridge. Instead, we were greeted by a group of people just inside who bowed and curtsied to Alex before taking our coats.

"It's good to have you home, Your Majesty." An older man smiled at Alex. "And lovely to see you, as always, ma'am. Welcome home, Duchess Rousseau." He dipped his head at Rose and me.

"How are things tonight, Ryan?" Alex asked.

"Good. Dinner should be ready shortly and your

mother is waiting in the front sitting room." The man checked a clipboard he was carrying. "The prime minister and his wife are here along with your sister, Duke Constal, and Duke and Duchess Marion."

"Excellent." Alex smiled at the others. "Chadwick, let me introduce you to Duchess Rousseau. Samantha, this is Chadwick. He's offered to be your assistant until you decide on something permanent."

"A pleasure to meet you, Duchess." Chadwick was a tall, thin man. He bowed his head in a formal greeting.

"You too, Chadwick." I held out my hand to shake his. His hands were gentle, but firm. "I think you've got your work cut out for you."

"I do love a challenge." He smiled.

"Well, then. Let's go meet Mother, shall we?" Alex turned away from the aides he was speaking with and looked at me.

"Let's." I took a deep breath.

Alex held his arm out to me, and I slipped my hand in and let him lead me down a long, formal hallway. Portraits of monarchs lined the walls, interspersed with images of gardens and forests. There was a man in a tailcoat waiting next to golden double doors. He stood to attention when we neared and opened the door.

"You'll enter last, but we'll be waiting inside." Rose patted my shoulder as she nodded at the man. He knocked on the door and waited for an answer. When he heard what he needed, he opened the doors and stepped inside.

"The Duchess of Sverelle, Your Majesty." Rose followed closely behind him, curtsying once just inside of the door. She walked out of sight and I fought the desire to peek around the corner.

"His Royal Highness, the Duke of D'Lynsal." Alex stood up straight and winked at me before turning the corner. I could hear voices inside, but not what they were saying. Or maybe they were speaking in Lilarian.

"The Duchess of Rousseau." The man announced my name and I took a jerky step forward. There were ten or eleven people standing in the center of the room. The queen was right in the center, complete with tiara and flowing dress. She was an attractive woman and I could see a great deal of Alex in her features.

I remembered to curtsy once inside the door and took a few more steps before pausing and doing it again. I didn't curtsy too deep, scared I would fall in my heels. When I looked up, the queen was smiling. When I reached her, she held out her hand and I shook it.

"Your Majesty, it's a pleasure to meet you." I looked down at her, surprised that such a small woman had given birth to such a tall man like Alex.

"Welcome home, Duchess Rousseau. We're very glad that you've come." The woman smiled. "We were very excited when we found you."

"Thank you, ma'am."

"Let me introduce you to everyone." The queen placed her hand on my elbow, gently guiding me away from Rose and Alex. I tried to keep a hold on the beating of my heart. It was beating faster than that of a kitten facing down a dog. "This is my daughter, Catherine."

A tall girl with blond hair and Alex's bright eyes smiled at me. She held out her hand and I shook it. There was a lot of handshaking in my future, it seemed.

"Nice to meet you, Samantha. I've heard a lot about you." Catherine smiled widely. She was breathtaking—model perfect. Her eyes were bright and she seemed genuinely happy to see me.

"Nice to meet you."

"I'd be happy to show you around the city if you'd like. It can be a bit confusing the first time you visit."

"I've already set up some time to take Samantha around." Alex's voice rumbled behind me. I looked over my shoulder and into his eyes. "I promised I wouldn't throw her to the wolves."

"I'm not a wolf!" Catherine shook her head and laughed.

"You would want to take her shopping, and I have it on good authority that Samantha is not a fan."

"That's because she hasn't been with me." Catherine smiled and I wondered if men threw themselves at her feet. "Well, we can just go sightseeing if you'd like."

"You could come with us," Alex replied. I hadn't known he was planning on taking me around town.

"Not letting her out of your sight, hm?" Catherine gave me a thoughtful look. "Okay. It's a date."

"Sounds like fun." The queen was already leading me away from Catherine, but Alex stayed with his sister.

"This is Prime Minister Tomas Derry." Catherine smiled at the man. He had lively eyes and curly gray hair. "Prime Minster, this is Samantha, Duchess of Rousseau."

"My pleasure." He took my hand and pressed a kiss to my knuckles.

The queen didn't waste any time moving me to the next few people. The members of parliament seemed very interested in the fact that I was American, and then I met a couple with two small children.

"This is the Duke and Duchess of Marion."

"Call me Heather." The woman held out one hand while keeping a tight grip on the small boy. "This is Leo." She pushed him forward and I leaned down to shake the young boy's chubby hand. He smiled at me before rubbing the back of his hand across his nose.

"Nice to meet you, Leo."

"Barry." The duke shook my hand with a friendly

smile before motioning toward the little girl in his arms. "And this is Violet."

"Nice to meet you both." The little girl was leaning against her father's shoulder with her eyes half closed. "I'm sorry we got in so late."

"Don't be sorry! We're glad to meet you. I know you must be tired after all that travel."

"I'm happy to be here." The queen pulled me away from the young family and toward a grouping of young men. Two of them were smiling in a bored sort of manner, but one of them leered in a way that made me wish I hadn't taken my coat off.

"The Dukes of Minsington, Bowdell, and Sheferd. Otherwise known as Daniel, Barney, and Kyle." The queen leveled her eyes at the men and they shifted where they stood. "This is Samantha, Duchess of Rousseau."

They all shook my hand, Kyle lingering a little longer than was necessary. "A pleasure to meet you, Samantha."

I smiled at him, not really thinking the meeting was so pleasant. He reminded me of the school reporter. The one you wouldn't leave your drink with while you ran to the bathroom.

"Kyle and Daniel both went to the university here in town. Perhaps you can find a program to finish your studies with." The queen smiled at me as if this was a brilliant idea.

"I'll have to look into it when I have some time." I really hoped I would be able to escape this conversation soon.

"Maybe I could take you to the campus and show you around. There are a lot of great places to study." He emphasized the last word so I knew he meant something else entirely.

"Right. I'll let you know if I need the help." I had no

poker face and I was certain Kyle could see my irritation.

"I look forward to it."

"Your Majesty, dinner is ready," a man in palace livery said. I hadn't even noticed him approaching.

"Excellent. Samantha, I will leave you with these gentlemen while I check on things." The queen squeezed my elbow gently before walking away. I watched her leave and my eyes landed on Alex. He was laughing with the Marion family and was holding the little girl against his chest, patting her back while she drooled on his shoulder, sound asleep. I wanted to go to them and put as much distance as possible between myself and Kyle.

"What did you study, Samantha?" Daniel looked at me, interested.

"Good God, Danny. Don't you read the papers?" Barney took a long sip from the tumbler in his hand. "She's a biologist of some sort."

"Wildlife biologist," I explained.

"You know I don't read that trash. It's a waste of time." Daniel frowned at his friend. "Good for you, Samantha. You'll have a lot in common with Alex."

"Is that so?" A woman came over with a tray of drinks. I picked a glass of white wine and sipped.

"Yes, our illustrious future monarch has a degree in wildlife biology. He specialized in birds, I believe." Daniel smiled. "What's your specialty?"

"Raptors."

Daniel laughed and pointed at Kyle. "You might as well give up right now."

I looked at them confused. "Excuse me?"

"Let's just say that there aren't many eligible female nobles right now." Daniel laughed at Kyle's expression. "It's a lost cause."

"We don't know that." Kyle winked at me. "I've got a lot to offer."

"Are you guys serious? I'm not looking to get married."

"You're fresh meat, sweetie." Barney leaned forward and I could smell the bourbon on his breath. "Daniel here couldn't care less since he's not into skirts. But for every other eligible man in the country, you're a potential wife. With a lot to bring to the bank . . . and bed." He stared down at my breasts. I squeezed my hands into fists so tight I could feel my nails digging into my palm. All of the responses that popped into my head were wildly inappropriate for a queen's sitting room.

"Barney." Daniel glared at him. "That's enough. We're not all terrible, Samantha."

"What are you talking about?" Catherine moved next to me. "You can't monopolize the guest of honor."

"I was hoping you'd come over here to check on her so I could enjoy that pretty dress up close." Kyle tilted his head and looked up and down Catherine's slim figure. She blushed, but didn't look all that upset with his perusal.

"Dinner is served." A door off to the side of the room opened and I couldn't have been more relieved.

"Your Highness, may I escort you to your seat?" Kyle bowed to Catherine, who accepted with a roll of her eyes.

"Samantha?" Daniel held out his arm to me and I let him guide me into the dining room. There was a long rectangular table, with place settings for each guest. Little cards with handwritten names told everyone where to sit. Daniel leaned close when we got to my seat.

"I may not be worried about finding a wife, but I am always happy to make a new friend." He smiled at me, and I felt a little better.

"That would be nice." I let him pull my chair out and help me sit, before he went to find his own seat.

"Welcome to Lilaria." Daniel winked at me as he walked away.

"Kyle is not someone you should befriend." Alex sat next to me and leaned close. "He's only interested in what kind of dowry you have." He glared over to where his sister was joking with the young duke. "Among other things."

"Thanks, Captain Obvious," I whispered. "Tell me you've told your sister this."

"Sisters don't like to hear that kind of stuff from brothers, but yes, I've tried." Alex opened his napkin and laid it over one leg. "You, on the other hand, have no one else to tell you this."

"Not true. Barney has already informed me that I'm fresh meat."

"He told you that? Those exact words?" The skin along his jaw tightened and he glared at where Barney was asking for a refill.

"Calm down. I'm not an idiot." I shook my head.

"He can be very convincing when he wants to be. I don't want to see you be taken advantage of." He looked at me with frustrated eyes. "Consider it a *friendly* warning."

"Are you upset that you can't stomp around like a caveman and pee on my leg?" I poked his shoulder. "I'm not a tree, Your Highness."

He laughed, and several of the people at our end of the table turned their attention toward us. "What happened to my nickname?"

"That was an accident. Not going to happen again." I looked around the table, noticing how everyone was watching us. The queen was smiling behind her wine-glass and Rose was decidedly ignoring us as she spoke with the prime minister and his wife. Catherine, however, was grinning widely from her seat next to Kyle, a complete contrast to the glower he was shooting my way.

The food was delivered quickly and no one wasted time before eating. I could understand why; the food was delicious. I answered questions about my schooling, my family, and what I thought of Lilaria. I answered everything with the simplest answers I could manage. I didn't want to tell these people my life story. By the time dessert was placed in front of me, I was exhausted.

When the queen stood to signal the end of the dinner, everyone raised a glass. "We're honored to have back among us one of our family. Samantha, may you find happiness in Lilaria."

She left shortly afterward with Rose and the prime minister, signaling that we could leave if we were ready. Catherine and Kyle made their way to where I was standing up. Alex had his back to me, talking to one of the parliament members.

"We're heading out, want to come along?" Kyle had his hand on Catherine's back but smiled at me in a way that made me want to punch him. He was definitely a worm and the fact that Catherine seemed oblivious worried me. He was an attractive guy, but he oozed creep.

"Maybe another time. I'm ready to call it a night."

"Would you like me to show you to your room?" Kyle dropped his hand from Catherine and stepped forward. Her eyebrows pulled together as she watched him.

"I've already offered to show her to her rooms." Alex placed a hand on my back.

"Is that so?" Kyle glared at Alex. "Is it the same room Melissa used? Or the one Lora or Maggie stayed in? Maybe the room Adriane used the last time she stayed at the palace? How about the one Tabitha used? Maybe that was the same room Melissa stayed in."

"Kyle!" Catherine gasped. Alex's fingers stiffened against my back and I knew he was worried how I would react to a list of his conquests.

"I see pedigree has no bearing on whether or not you're an asshole." While it bothered me to think of Alex with all those women, I was more disgusted by Kyle's behavior. "Now, if you'll excuse me, I need to get some rest."

Kyle sputtered, apparently surprised I had spoken up. Catherine looked at me with something close to jealousy and awe. Alex nudged me gently toward the exit. I left Kyle staring after us while Catherine watched thoughtfully.

SEVENTEEN

Will America's Duchess Fit In with the Other Royals?
—*CELEBRITY TALK MAGAZINE*

"*I* APOLOGIZE FOR THAT." Alex ground his teeth when we were in the hallway.

"Don't. It's not your fault." I was barely paying attention to the direction we went. I was so tired I had to focus on putting one foot in front of the other. I was also mentally chanting the list of women who had been with Alex, the image of him and Melissa flashing in my head. He stopped at a door and turned the ornate handle.

I stepped inside and looked at the giant bed and lavish furnishings. My bags had been unpacked and nightclothes were laid out on the mattress. I turned to look at Alex.

"Thank you. I guess I'll see you sometime this week." I bit my lip. I had no idea what the rest of the week held for me. Much less the rest of my life.

"Are you forgetting something?" Alex raised an eyebrow.

"What are you talking about?"

"Your dress." He nodded toward me. "Or do you think you can manage on your own?"

I frowned. As much as I had complained about having to wear it, I was sort of fond of the dress and didn't want to rip it. I looked up at him and nodded once before turning around so he could see the zipper. He closed the door behind him and moved toward me. I reached down to undo the belt at my waist but his hands slid around and closed over mine before moving them out of the way so he could do it. Slowly he pulled the belt from the loops and tossed it onto the bed. His fingers tugged the zipper at an almost torturous pace. His knuckles dragged along my spine the whole way and I shivered in response. When he slid the zipper over my bra I took a deep breath, but he never hesitated.

I knew I should stop him once he reached my waist, but I didn't. I closed my eyes, enjoying the smell of him and the feel of his hands on me. I heard him take a deep breath of his own and he stopped the zipper just above my panties. I could feel his hands shake just before he let go and stepped away.

"I think you can take it from there." Need mixed with frustration in his voice.

"Thank you for helping." I took a step forward, clutching my dress to my chest as I turned around.

"How long are we going to play this game?" He was irritated and I didn't blame him. He wasn't the only one feeling frustrated.

"I'm not going to be another conquest, Alex. I don't do one-night stands. I'm not that person."

"And I'm not looking for a notch in my bedpost." He took a step toward me.

His words scared me more than if he was just looking for a quick tumble in the sheets. Falling in love with Alex would leave me open to too much hurt. Anything I had with him would be short-lived. He'd eventually have to move on and marry someone who could help him rule a country. I looked around the room, at a loss for words. Refusing to say the words that would reveal my cowardice.

"Samantha, none of those women stayed at the palace." Alex looked at me with serious eyes. He had taken my silence for something else. "At least they didn't stay at the palace with me. Tabitha and Adriane have stayed here because they are from noble families. Kyle was just trying to upset you."

"Alex, I don't need to know." I shook my head and grabbed at the excuse he had provided. "Besides. We're friends. You don't need to give me the list. I don't care." The last sentence sounded forced and desperate.

He narrowed his eyes at me. "You're a terrible liar."

"I know." But I wasn't ready for anything else. Would never be ready for anything with Alex. I knew with just the little that had happened between us it would hurt too much when it fell apart. I had lost so much already and was on the verge of losing my father. Losing my heart would be unbearable. "I feel like my entire world was just shaken by a massive earthquake. I don't know how anything works or what I'm supposed to do with myself. I can't fall—" I stopped and swallowed. "I wouldn't be a good girlfriend right now and I'm not up for sex with no strings. Once my dad gets here I won't have any time."

"All good things are worth the work. And what we could have would definitely be good." He threw my words back at me and I had no response. I just stood there silently as he turned and left.

I let the dress fall to the ground and sat on the bed, staring at the door. My heart was still racing and I felt like kicking something. Mainly myself. And Alex. And Kyle.

Eventually I pulled myself up and got undressed. I

checked out the attached bathroom and whistled. There was a huge jetted tub, separate shower, and everything was shiny. Apparently the inside of the palace was much newer than the outside. After sending a text message to Dad and Jess, I went to bed. I had no idea what tomorrow held for me.

SUNLIGHT WAS STREAMING into the room and I woke to a knock on my door. I sat straight up and looked around the room in confusion. The knock came again and I slipped out of the blankets and padded to the door. I pulled it open and glared at Chadwick on the other side.

"Good morning, Duchess. I brought you some coffee." He held a cup out to me that I took without hesitation. It could have been poison, but as long as there was some coffee mixed in I'd die happy. As I drank, he made his way into my room and set up a laptop and notebook on the desk in the corner. "I've already ordered another cup for you and can call for food if you're hungry. I wasn't sure if you'd want breakfast or lunch."

"Slower, please." I looked at him in confusion. "Breakfast or lunch?"

"Yes, it's almost noon."

The cup stopped halfway to my mouth. "Oh my God. Why didn't you wake me up?"

"There was nothing pressing this morning." He sat down and went through the drawers until he found a pencil. "I thought you might need the rest. You've had a busy week."

"You could say that." I sat down in the chair across from the desk.

"I've gone through your schedule and set up some of the meetings you'll need to have in the next few days, including time for you to see some of the country. Alex insisted you get to spend a few days here in the capital before leaving for your estate." Chadwick sat primly at the desk. "I believe Catherine is hoping to join you as well."

"Okay." I pulled my feet up in my seat and finished off my cup. "First, food. Then we start doing what we need to do."

"Excellent. We've already received requests for appearances and you've been invited to several dinners here in town. I've told them everything was pending approval at this point."

"Appear where?" I latched on to the thing I thought most important.

"The American embassy has requested you meet with the ambassador. I believe they want to check on you." He smiled fondly like it was cute. "There was also a request for you to make an appearance at a local American school and the local zoological gardens sometime this week."

"An ambassador, a school, and a zoo." I thought it over in my head. "I haven't technically been granted my title back."

"That's a formality. Speaking of which, the queen would like to perform the ceremony in two months, unless you have other plans?" His voice rose at the end, letting me know it was a question.

"I do believe my calendar is clear."

"Not exactly, but I understand what you mean. I'll let the lord chamberlain know." He smiled at me. "I've also spoken to Dr. Bielefeld's staff and gotten them in contact with your father's doctors. He should be looking over his paperwork at any minute."

"Great! Is he here in town?" I sat up and leaned forward.

"Not yet. He was in Paris for a convention and to see

a few patients. He keeps in regular touch with his office though, so we can expect steady updates." Chadwick smiled a bit mischievously. "Apparently the doctor was excited to help out America's Duchess."

"Oh no. Tell me that hasn't stuck."

"It certainly has. Catchy, if you think about it. There's a definite fascination with royals in America. Probably because they don't have any of their own." Chadwick flipped open his notebook to a different page. "I hope you don't mind, but I had your luggage inventoried and I believe shopping may be in order. You have several lovely dresses and outfits, but the fact is you're going to need much more."

I glared at him and set down my cup. He picked it up and put a coaster underneath. "You inventoried my clothes?"

"Well, yes. That's part of my job. Helping make sure you have everything you need." He looked at me with patient eyes. "I know it feels like an intrusion, but try to not look at it like that. Besides, I couldn't care less about your bras and panties—they wouldn't fit me. Though I would recommend getting more nightclothes. You only brought tank tops and giant shirts." He said it like it was a crime.

"Hey!"

"No offense. They're very nice tank tops and giant shirts if you like that sort of stuff, but if you're going to let Prince Alex help you undress each night you might want something a little sexier to slip into." He wiggled his eyebrows. "Not that I'll say a word about it of course. Not a word."

"It's not like that!" I sputtered. "He's a friend and I couldn't reach the zipper . . . I just . . . It wasn't like that!"

"Of course not, honey. Not that I'd blame you if it

was. That man has sent many a heart fluttering." Chadwick smiled up at me through his red hair and winked. "And if you need any help next time, let me know, I'd be happy to assist. I was coming to see to you, which was when I caught Alex leaving your room."

"Oh, um." I wasn't exactly any more comfortable with the idea of Chadwick helping me undress.

He laughed at my hesitation. "I'm not going to be ogling you, if that's what you're worried about. Not the right bits, okay?"

"Oh. Okay." That explained the joke about my bras and panties. "Listen, you really can't tell anyone what you saw last night. It was nothing and Alex has had enough trouble with the press."

"You can trust me, ma'am. I wouldn't have been given this job if there was a chance I'd leak stuff to the press or start any rumors." He smiled at me and patted my hand. "Now, I'm going to order some food while you get dressed. Any preference?"

"Fruit? Maybe some yogurt or oatmeal?"

"Done. I'd wear the blue suit-dress. It'll look lovely on you. And it would be appropriately patriotic." Chadwick disappeared out the door and I wondered what had just happened. I did as he said though, grabbing my clothes and taking a shower. I hurried because I wasn't sure how long I had before the food would be back. There was a blow-dryer in the bathroom, so I quickly dried my hair and pulled half of it back out of my face. The sheath dress fit perfectly, but I hated I had to wear hose with it. It wasn't really a suit, but rather a simple dress with a fitted jacket over it. I put my mother's earrings back on and slipped into the nude pumps Jess had insisted on.

Breakfast was sitting on the table near the fireplace. Someone had stoked the fire, so I was very toasty as I watched the light snow flutter outside the window while I ate. Chadwick had a bowl of soup as we went over the schedule for the rest of the day. Once I was ready to leave, Becca and another "suit" came to escort us. We went straight to the embassy to meet with the ambassador for the United States. There were photographers outside the palace gates and more when we reached the embassy. I stopped and smiled for a few pictures before ducking inside out of the cold. If Chadwick hadn't given me puppy eyes, I wouldn't have stopped for a picture at all.

Chadwick turned out to be invaluable. He knew everyone by name and could tell me all about the things they were currently working on. The ambassador was a nice lady with blond hair, serious eyes, and quick smile. She introduced me to her aides and offered help getting my things moved over and arranging transportation for my father. I was there for an hour total. It was like a whirlwind history class. There were dates, stories, and pictures. I could only pray I wouldn't be tested on any of it. Then again, Chadwick would make an excellent cheat sheet. We made an appearance at an elementary school that American workers and expats sent their children to. I enjoyed that visit much more than I did the one to the embassy. The children had all kinds of crazy questions. I took a picture with one of the classes, and a tiny girl with dark brown hair in braids crawled into my lap. The palace photographer had met us at the school and while thorough, he seemed to understand too many pictures would drive everyone crazy.

After the school, we went shopping. Becca seemed to enjoy watching me suffer through it all. And suffer I did.

Chadwick was a slave driver, constantly handing things over the door. It was as much fun as I thought it would be, but I left with several dresses from a Lilarian designer, dressy slacks, and new sweaters. I was fairly certain I had offended Chadwick with my sense of style. He would shake his head and put something on the counter I had originally declined.

"Trust me. If I wasn't the assistant extraordinaire, I would have gone into fashion." He mock-glared at me and I pretended to roll my eyes. "This will look great on you, ma'am."

"Why did I even have to come if you were going to pick everything out?" I looked at him in disgust.

"You did find that gorgeous sweater, so you're not completely hopeless. Think of me as a fashion guru and you're my reluctant protégée."

I laughed at him, glad we were getting along so well. It was a bit like having Jess with me. She had texted me to let me know I had been on the news. Apparently my landing had been streamed on live TV in the States. I had been horrified, but she seemed to have loved it. Said it felt like she had been there. My father had another chemo treatment today and I was feeling incredibly guilty for shopping while he went through that torture. Patricia had texted me to let me know he was fine and that they had watched me on the news.

I needed to call Dad soon and made a mental note to try later tonight. I wanted to hear his voice. I had been busy from the moment I set foot here, but I was still more than a little homesick.

EIGHTEEN

Romantic Dinner or Friendly Get-Together?
—LISA TALKS

ONCE THE SKY began to darken, Chadwick started to hurry me along.

I rolled my eyes at him. "Do you want me to get new nightgowns or what? There's a billion to choose from."

"Yes. I got down on my knees this morning and prayed you would get rid of those hideous nightshirts, but we're running out of time, ma'am." He tapped his watch. "Prince Alex and Princess Catherine will be waiting for you, so just pick something."

"All right, all right." I grabbed several different colors of the one I was looking at and headed toward the clerk. "And stop calling me ma'am. You're older than I am. Just call me Sam."

"Sam?" He wrinkled his nose at me. "I don't know."

"Why not?"

"It's just that Sam doesn't really seem like the name of a duchess." He looked at my face and backpedaled. "Not that there is anything wrong with Sam. What about Samantha?"

"Fine." I shrugged. "Anything is better than ma'am."

"Well, only in private of course. It would be highly inappropriate if I called you that in public."

I ground my teeth. "Okay."

"It's not so bad." He patted my arm.

The staff hadn't batted an eye when I'd come through the door, but it made me feel awkward to buy anything like a nightie. What if it ended up on the news? The cameras and news vans had lowered in numbers the longer we shopped, but as soon as I left the store I ran into a crowd of people hollering my name. Chadwick put an arm around me while Becca made a path for us to the car.

I thought we were in the clear as we pulled away from the curb, but cars surrounded us almost immediately.

"What are they doing?" I leaned forward to look out the window. "This is dangerous!" I squeaked when a car swerved close to us around a corner. Our driver slammed the brakes and we skidded, just missing the curb.

"Sit back, Samantha." Chadwick moved to make sure I was buckled in.

"This is cr—"

A light blue van slammed into the back of our car, making my teeth snap shut. Blood pooled in my mouth from where I nipped my tongue. I covered my lips with my hand and looked around wildly. Camera flashes blinded me as I tried to see just what had happened. A motorcycle stopped in front of our car and the person on the back snapped pictures through the front windshield.

"Are you okay?" Becca turned around in her seat.

"Yeah." I nodded my head and tried to quell the nausea that was bubbling in my stomach. Adrenaline and anger ran through my body. Balling my hands into fists, I glared out the window at the people still busy taking photographs.

"Can you get us out of here?" Chadwick asked.

"As soon as I have an opening." The driver never took his hands off the steering wheel.

"Should we call the police?" I looked from Becca to Chadwick.

"Best to get out of here fast." Becca shook her head.

My door handle made a loud noise as someone tried to open the door. I turned to check that it was locked and almost sighed in relief when I realized it was closed for sure. The driver took his foot off the brake and edged forward. I watched as he pushed the bike with the front fender and almost cheered when the motorcycle driver pulled away from us.

Our car shot forward and I felt like celebrating, but I still felt sick. I couldn't wrap my mind around the fact that someone had hit our car just to get a picture of me.

"It'll calm down, Samantha. They just don't know what to make of you." Chadwick patted my arm.

"Are you kidding? They could have hurt us! They did hurt us! I bit the shit out of my tongue." I waved my hand in the air. "All that for a picture of me? Me? Why?"

"You're interesting and they make the most money by selling photos of interesting people." Chadwick pursed his lips.

"I'm not interesting. I'm the same as every other person. I have to brush my teeth, use the bathroom, and take a bath, same as everyone else."

"You also just found out that you're the duchess to a huge estate in a foreign country." He frowned. "I understand what you're saying, and they shouldn't behave the way they are, but it's because you *are* interesting. Things will calm down."

"Please don't say eventually." I shook my head. "Everyone keeps telling me that it will calm down eventually, but it just seems to be getting worse."

"I know." He frowned and looked out the window as we reached the palace gates.

The car deposited me and my bags at the main door while Chadwick basically pulled me into the palace. That was fine by me. I didn't want to stay in that car another second.

Catherine and Alex were chatting near the entrance to a room. They were both wearing jeans and I felt incredibly overdressed. This was the first time I had seen Alex in jeans and I had to admit it might be my favorite view of him. His worried gaze found mine immediately.

"Are you okay?" He took a step toward me and stopped.

"Yeah. I'm okay." I ran a hand through my hair but dropped it when I realized it was shaking. "It was pretty crazy."

"We heard the bodyguards talking about it. That must've been scary." Catherine shook her head. "I'm so sorry they're hounding you like this."

"Maybe when they figure out how boring I am, they'll leave me alone." I tried to make a joke, but it sounded a bit too hopeful.

"I'm sure it's going to calm down." Alex's fingers opened and closed by his legs. He looked antsy. In fact he looked as shaken up as I felt.

"You went shopping without me!" Catherine glared at the bags someone carried in. I was grateful for the subject change. I didn't want to think about what had just happened.

"It was Chad's fault. He made me do it." I pointed at my assistant, who rolled his eyes at me.

"Trust me, there is still *much* more to do." He lifted the bags. "I will take care of these, Samantha. Enjoy your night out with these two." He gestured with a full hand toward Alex and Catherine. My heart froze. I'd almost forgotten I would have to go back out in that mess. "Don't let them get you into any trouble, and call me if you need me when you get back." He winked at me as he turned around so the others couldn't see.

"Thanks, Chadwick."

"We don't have to go out." Alex watched me carefully, a small tic running along his jaw.

I thought about it for a minute. I didn't want to go out. I wanted to curl up somewhere quiet and hide. But I also didn't want to stop living just because some nutso person wanted my picture.

"I'll call for extra security," Cathy offered. "If you want. Or we can try again another day."

"No. Let's go." I was glad my voice sounded so sure, because the rest of me wasn't. "Mind if I run and change? These shoes are killing me." My feet were screaming in agony. I'd throw them away if I could forget how much they had cost.

"Of course." Alex leaned against the wall and tucked his hands into his coat.

"I'll be quick." I hurried down the hallway in the direction of my room, only to stop and look around, confused. I looked back behind me and Catherine was smiling. Alex pointed to the right, so I nodded my head and took that hall.

Chadwick was standing at my door and held up one of my new sweaters.

"Be careful tonight."

"I will." I blew him a kiss as I took it out of his hand and ducked into the room. I changed quickly, pulling my hair down from the clip I had been wearing and grabbing my scarf. I threw my necessities into my pockets and headed back to the others. The entire walk back

I chanted in my head: *I can do this. I will have fun. I can do this. I will have fun.* I didn't want the media to stop me from seeing my new country.

By the time I got there, my stomach was growling and Catherine laughed. "I think someone needs dinner."

"I haven't eaten since noon." I winced.

"We can fix that. Do you have a preference?" Alex opened the door for us and I shook my head. I noticed there was a second car behind us, containing several bodyguards.

"I'd settle for a peanut butter sandwich at this point."

"We can do better than that," Catherine said as we climbed into the car.

"What do you have in mind, Cathy?" Alex sat next to me, his leg brushing mine.

"How about that little place you like in the South District?" Cathy poked at his stomach. "The one with all the greasy burgers."

"I don't know. I just got back from the States, I'm not sure these will measure up. Why not get some local food?" Alex turned to look at me.

"Sounds good."

Cathy gave the name of the restaurant to the driver and we headed into town. Reporters followed us as soon as we left the palace gates. Cathy shook her head, but I could see how tense Alex was next to me.

"What's the big deal? We're just going to dinner." I frowned. Maybe we should have just stayed at the palace. Ordered pizza or something.

"They're hoping to catch an embarrassing shot." Alex sighed. "It's their livelihood."

"Like ketchup on our chin?" I was trying to lift some of the dreariness that had settled over the car.

"Like us stumbling drunk out of a bar." Catherine shook her head. "Like we would ever do that."

"It happens." Alex frowned at her. "Kyle is often photographed acting like a baboon at nightclubs."

"Kyle just likes to have a good time." Cathy looked out the windows. "Look, Samantha! There's the Rousseau monument!"

I looked out the window, surprised. "Really?"

"Yes. Your family fought off a northern invasion and gave the capital enough time to rally troops." Alex looked out the window with me as we drove past the large statue. A man rode a rearing horse, sword held high.

"How about that." I felt a little bubble of pride in my chest. My family had faced down invaders.

"Just down the road here is the Lilarian library. There are paintings of some of the earliest families inside. You should go visit them when you have time." Cathy was proving to be an excellent guide. "Oh! And that's the Sverelle Bridge. Our mother's family is responsible for it being here. It's one of the few that survived the Nazis' occupation."

"Wow." And I meant it. There was intense pride in her voice for the work of their family and that of their country, and I understood. This was their home and they could literally trace their ancestors back to massive historical moments or places. It gave the history a life, a face.

We pulled up to a small family-style restaurant situated between two buildings. There was faint music spilling out of the door, and I could smell food as soon as Duvall opened the car door. The press were on us immediately and I felt my hackles rise. I was trying to get used to the idea, but they certainly weren't giving me any adjustment time. Alex opened the door for us and a tall, thin man greeted us inside.

"Your Highnesses, Duchess. A pleasure to see you." He bowed to us.

"We've been coming here since we were kids, Luca. Why are you suddenly bowing?" Cathy pulled her coat off and hung it on a rack near the door. A few of the patrons inside turned to look at us, but for the most part seemed more interested in their food.

"Ah, but this is Duchess Rousseau's first visit!" Luca smiled widely. He motioned us to follow him, and he sat us at a booth in the back. It was far from the little window at the front and I knew he was used to dealing with public figures.

"You're going to love this place." Cathy smiled at me over the table. She pushed a menu at me. "I already know what I want."

Alex eyed the booth for a minute before taking a seat next to his sister. I was relieved. Sitting next to him in the car had been difficult enough. It's amazing the little things you notice about someone when you have the hots for them. Like the way he smells or how long his legs are compared to mine. Then there are the other things, like wondering how his hands would feel running over my skin. Things I wouldn't think about sitting next to just anyone, but here I was thinking about them and trying to pretend that I wasn't.

I opened the menu and looked over the selections. I frowned when I realized it was in Lilarian. There weren't even any pictures to help me pick. I looked up at my companions and Alex was watching me with shrewd eyes.

"Need help?"

"A translator would be nice." I winced and laid down the open menu on the table. "I have no idea where to begin. I want to try something new."

"I hadn't thought about that. You don't speak Lilarian, do you?" Cathy shook her head. "You need a teacher."

"I have a teacher." I raised my eyebrow at Alex. "I won one in a bet."

"Really?" Cathy looked at her brother. "You lost at something?"

"Don't." He shook his head. "It'll never happen again."

"What was it? The bet?" Cathy looked at me, her large eyes wide with curiosity.

"I beat him at Monopoly." Alex groaned and leaned back in his seat.

"No way!" Cathy leaned forward. "Did you figure it out? He has to be cheating. There's no way he's won that many times otherwise!"

"Maybe the karma gods thought it was time he lost." I shrugged.

"Karma gods, huh? Well, it's about time." Cathy sat back in her seat.

"So, foreign-language teacher. Tell me what this is!" I pointed at the first thing on the menu.

"Well, that is the word for stuffed." Alex grinned while Cathy laughed.

"Oh." I looked at the menu and wondered if there were any words that wouldn't trigger naughty thoughts.

"And I said I'd be your teacher, not your translator." Alex shook his head.

"Well, you're not doing such a good job. I've been here a day and know nothing. I think I should get the drawing as forfeit." I narrowed my eyes at him. Luca brought over three glasses of water, wineglasses, and a bottle before quickly departing.

"Drawing? Is that the one I saw on your desk?" Cathy turned toward Alex with a small smile.

"Miss Nosy wanted to know what I was working on, so I made a bet. I won."

"So she hasn't seen the picture?" Cathy narrowed her eyes at Alex.

"No. But she does owe me a week of volunteer work for the FBT."

"Then how did he end up being your Lilarian teacher?" Cathy looked at me, confused.

"It was a long flight. He lost the second game."

"Ha! Alex, you better start teaching her, or that lovely sketch isn't going to belong to you anymore."

"Fine." He leaned forward and pointed at the menu. "This is the word for stuffed. What do you think would be good stuffed?" His eyes twinkled at me in the candlelight. I could think of something I'd like to stuff, all right. And who I'd like to do the stuffing.

"Chicken? Lamb? Some kind of pasta?" I ignored the innuendo, though it was hard to do.

"Chicken. So, this is the word for chicken, this is stuffed, and see how these words are in the front? They tell you what the chicken is stuffed with. Here." He turned the menu so that it was facing me. "See if you can figure out any of the other dishes with these words."

"What is this? Advanced classes? What happened to starting with the alphabet?" I let my eyes run over the menu and tried to pick out words that seemed familiar. There were a few words I remembered from my high school French class.

"Go over there and help her! She's starving and Luca will be back any minute." Cathy shoved his shoulder.

He looked at me and I could see the hesitation in his eyes, but he slid out of the booth and in beside me. Leaning close, he pointed out some of the words that would help me most. After a minute I'd found a dish that sounded great and we were ready to order. Luca came over, blocking Alex's exit from my side of the booth, and started pouring wine.

"This is one of my favorites. A celebration of the duchess coming home!" Luca smiled at me and I lifted my glass before taking a sip. I wasn't much of a drinker, so had no idea if it was a good vintage or not. It also struck me as odd every time someone welcomed me home. I understood why they said it, but home would always be in the States where I had grown up.

"To the Rousseau family." Cathy lifted her glass.

"To Samantha." Alex looked at me over his glass of wine.

The food was delicious and I was completely satisfied by the time Luca brought several bowls of chocolate mousse.

"I don't have room!" I groaned.

"Make room! You don't turn down Luca's mousse. It's amazing." Cathy dove into her bowl with relish and I looked at Alex. He had finally relaxed next to me and stayed there through the dinner. His arm lay on the back of the booth and his long legs stretched out under the table.

"Where does she put it all?"

"No idea, but if you want to try it, you better do it before she finishes hers."

"You only live once, Sam! Try it!" Cathy nudged my bowl with her finger and I realized that was the first time she had called me by my nickname. A little piece of me relaxed and I picked up my spoon.

The dessert melted in my mouth and it was like I had swallowed a tiny piece of heaven. I closed my eyes and just enjoyed the flavors. There was a hint of raspberry from the sauce that made me consider pouring the rest of the bowl in my mouth. Forget the spoon. When I opened my eyes, Cathy was nodding her head in agreement, but Alex was watching my mouth with a stony expression.

"Told you! It's like crack. Or, I think it's like crack. What drug is it that only takes one time?" Cathy tilted her head thoughtfully. I was struck in that moment by her youthful eyes and guarded upbringing. No wonder she didn't see Kyle for what he truly was.

"That would be it." I took another bite but tried to keep my reaction sedate. "And this is definitely addicting."

"Don't tell the head chef at the palace, but his chocolate mousse doesn't even compare." Cathy sighed.

"My lips are sealed."

As we were finishing up, there was a commotion at the door. I looked over the booth to see Luca talking angrily to a man at another table. The man tried to calm him down but eventually stood up and pointed a camera at our table. A large chef and waiter joined Luca as they tried to push the man out the front door. Luca was hollering in Lilarian, but from his tone I could tell it wasn't very pleasant. Becca and Duvall showed up at the table, blocking our view of the scene. Or, more importantly, blocking the camera's view of us.

I tried to calm my racing heart. There were a lot of people in the little restaurant who wouldn't let anything bad happen to me. I just couldn't believe the trouble the photographers were going through for a picture.

"Oh, poor Luca." Cathy sighed and set down her spoon.

"Duvall, make sure we take care of that man's dinner. I don't want Luca losing money just because someone was trying to take our picture." Alex leaned toward the people standing outside our booth.

"Of course, sir."

"Why are they so focused on us? Is it like this all the

time?" I frowned at them. What had I gotten into that I couldn't go enjoy dinner with friends?

"I haven't seen them this rabid since . . ." Cathy trailed off at a quick look from Alex. "I'm sure it'll calm down, Sam. They just want pictures of the new duchess."

"Did they do this with the other guy? The duke that was reinstated?" I had a feeling what she had been about to reference.

"No." Alex shook his head. "But you're younger, so they feel like you're more interesting."

"Not to mention beautiful." Cathy smiled at me. "All that dark hair and your dark eyes."

"That too, of course." Alex gave me a small smile.

"There's also a lot of press about you and Alex. They love to drum up romance stories." Cathy leaned forward, resting her elbow on the table. "They'd just love it if you two were an item."

"We're friends," Alex and I said in unison. I chuckled weakly.

"Of course you are." Cathy sat back in the booth with innocent eyes.

I felt queasy and I wasn't sure if it was from all the food or the reminder of what life would be like if I did give in to Alex. We ended up leaving through the back door. There were too many people out front for us to be able to reach the cars. Luca had boxed up some of his chocolate mousse for us to take and apologized that our dessert had been interrupted.

"That wasn't your fault!" I shook my head.

"I should have realized he was paparazzi." Luca said the word like it was an insult.

"Thank you for watching out for us." Alex followed his words with a few in Lilarian, which seemed to make Luca happy. We left, getting in the cars and zipping out into the streets.

We drove around for a little while, Alex and Cathy giving instructions to the driver so that I could see a bit more of the city. We never stopped and got out, but I didn't complain. It was cold and I was tired. Not to mention, I didn't want to deal with the press again. When we got back to the palace, I took my little box of chocolate mousse and dragged my sorry tail inside.

"Do you remember how to get to your room?" Cathy asked, a hint of mischief in her eyes. "Alex can show you. His room is down that way too."

"I'm heading to bed anyway. I have to be up early tomorrow for a meeting." Alex kissed Cathy's cheek.

"Thanks for showing me around," I said to Cathy.

"No problem. When things calm down we'll do some more." Cathy reached out and hugged me. "It's nice to have another girl here."

"Looks like there are lots of girls." I frowned, thinking of her mother, aunt, and the women I'd seen working earlier that day.

"It's not the same thing." Cathy looked at me with shimmery eyes. I handed her my mousse and she instantly brightened up. "You don't want it?"

"Nah. Your puppy-dog eyes just broke my heart a little. Take it."

"Thanks!" Cathy took off in a flash and I stood there with my mouth open.

"C'mon." Alex chuckled beside me. He placed his hand on my back and I almost sighed with relief. Just a few days ago I had thought it was silly when he did it, now I had come to look forward to it. "You better build up a tolerance to Cathy's anime eyes or you'll never get another dessert."

"Ha! They did look like a pathetic anime waif. She's got it down pat."

"You have no idea. She has four dogs and two cats.

Dad couldn't tell her no. They're all incredibly old now and the staff is always having to clean up behind them." Alex chuckled.

"She must've been very young when you lost him." I watched him out of the corner of my eye. We hadn't talked about it, but I knew that Alex's father had died from an aneurysm almost ten years ago.

"She was, but Mother has made sure she never felt neglected."

We turned onto the hallway my room was on and I stopped at my door. I pulled the key out of my pocket and played with it for a minute. "Thanks for taking me out to see a bit of the city."

"You're welcome. It was nice to get to relax." Alex smiled at me. "I don't get to spend as much time with Cathy as I used to."

"She's great." I bit my lip. I was making small talk because I didn't want to say good night yet. And I sucked at it.

"We can do it again sometime." He was watching me closely.

"That would be fun." I sighed. "I really suck at this."

"At what, exactly?" He smiled his devil smile.

"This whole small-talk thing. I'm not good at it." I motioned between us. "But I want to be. I don't want stuff to be weird between us."

"I think you're doing just fine. I don't seem to recall you having a hard time in Minnesota."

"I'm out of my element here. And I tend to blab whatever I'm thinking when I'm nervous."

"I've noticed." Alex lowered his voice. "It's quickly becoming one of my favorite things about you."

"Why is that?"

"Because when you blab whatever you're thinking, I find out you're thinking about me."

"You get all that from me being worried about small talk?" I shot him a skeptical look.

"You don't worry about it with anyone but me." He leaned down and kissed my cheek. "Good night, Samantha."

"Good night, Alex."

In my room one of the new nightgowns was laid out with a robe. I looked at it for a minute before picking it up. I stuck it in the top drawer next to my big T-shirts and grabbed a tank top and pair of shorts instead. On my desk was a stack of papers, including a schedule for the next day. I had to okay shots that the royal photographer had taken, sign a form detailing how much it would cost to fly my father over, and there was paperwork from my college to terminate my classes.

I glanced at the pictures and initialed the paper, agreed to whatever it cost to get my father over safely, and stared at the paperwork from school. It was all so bland and boring; nothing in the wording pointed out how I was giving up a lifelong ambition or how much I already missed my birds. I squeezed the pen in my hand and flipped through the pages again. There were no personal notes, nothing telling me they cared that I'd left the program. Just a blank line waiting for my signature.

I signed my dreams away with angry strokes. Throwing the pen down, I got up and went to sleep with tears in my eyes.

NINETEEN

Getting Frisky at the Zoo
—THE DAILY GOSSIP

THE NEXT MORNING I put on slacks and a nice shirt. Breakfast was brought up early and Chadwick wasn't far behind. He came in carrying a newspaper and clipboard. He sat down with me while I ate and looked through notes for the day.

"I've barely set foot in this country and people are asking me for interviews and to come to openings." I set the newspaper down and took another sip of my coffee. "I'm used to cutting up mice and tracking birds. Shaking hands and taking pictures with strangers is not something I'm accustomed to."

"That can't be true." Chadwick looked at me over his paper. "I'm sure you shook people's hands in America. You're not completely uncivilized over there."

I threw one of the raisins from my muffin at him and laughed when he blocked it with the paper. "You know what I mean. I'm just ready to go see my house and learn more about the area I'm going to be spending my time in. I feel like I'm winging everything. I don't like that."

"I get it, Samantha. I do. And we're heading out to your family estate at the end of the week." Chadwick frowned. "But the reality is that this is your life."

I set my muffin down and looked away out the window. He was right, but that didn't make all this craziness any better.

"I'm scheduling only the important things. I've turned down a hundred meetings." He looked sad, so I tried to smile. I felt a little guilty for being so difficult. "That's just pathetic."

"I'm trying here." I gave up and glared at him instead.

"That's better. I like it when you're all saucy." He winked at me before going back to his paper.

By the time I finished my muffin and coffee, we were moving out of my room and toward the car. Chadwick went over the schedule for the day and he gave me a quick run-down of the people I'd be meeting.

"So, the zookeeper that requested me to come out is American?" I smiled at the man who opened the door. Becca was standing next to the car, talking to one of the other suits.

"Yes. He is relatively new to the position." Chadwick held my purse while I climbed into the car. "I think he's excited you're a wildlife biologist and I thought you might prefer this to the luncheon planning the garden fund-raiser."

"Nailed it."

"Of course." He flipped through the paperwork while I tried to ignore the cars that followed us as soon as we pulled out of the gate.

The zoo was a little ways out of the city center and I really enjoyed getting to see some of the scenery. It was a heavily forested area with a lot of hills. As we exited the highway, I could see the sign for the zoological gardens, thankfully written in English as well as Lilarian. I really needed to spend more time learning the language, but I would probably try to find a real teacher. I still hadn't figured out what it was that Alex had whispered in my ear. I had tried online translators, but I must not be spelling it right, because all I ever got was gibberish. Something about a hamster—and I was pretty sure he hadn't been talking about a hamster.

We pulled right up to the gate and were ushered through after a few pictures were taken in front of the signs. It was a pretty zoo: lots of plants, trees, and decent-sized enclosures. An attractive man a few years older than me met us just inside. He walked straight up to me and held out his hand.

"Duchess, it's a pleasure to meet you. I'm Jeremy."

"Nice to meet you, Jeremy. Thank you for inviting me out here." I shook his hand and noted the calluses. He wasn't someone to sit back and let everyone else do all the work.

"Thank you for coming! We're honored that you accepted our invitation. I know you haven't been in the country very long." He motioned for us to walk, so I fell in step beside him. My detail kept a close proximity, but I did my best to ignore them.

"Not very long." I nodded my head. "But I have a weakness for animals."

"I was hoping so." He smiled at me and I realized he would likely be someone that would have made my heart flutter before Alex. My stomach clenched. Before Alex.

"So, why did you invite me out here?" I bit my lip. I wasn't very good at doing the political dance around things.

"Straightforward. I like that." He touched my shoulder, leading me toward an aviary. "A few reasons, actually. One, I figured you would enjoy seeing the zoo since you're a wildlife biologist. Two, I was hoping to meet America's Duchess." He winked at me and I felt my face heat. I really hated being called that.

We walked through the large aviary while he pointed out some of the species they had managed to obtain. It was an impressive enclosure with a large array of birds that I hadn't seen in person before. I stopped to admire one of the waterfalls in the habitat and he stopped with me. There was a tile mosaic at the bottom that glistened under the water.

"I designed the enclosure when I first arrived about three years ago."

I didn't blame him for being proud—it was a beautiful and efficient building. "I like the way you have the feed dishes dispersed. Very natural-looking."

"Thank you." He held his hand out to help me from my kneeling position by the water. "I spent a lot of time studying some of the ones in the larger zoos. I really wanted people to feel like they were observing the birds out in the wild. This design is what got me my position."

"Mission accomplished." I smiled at him. I was wondering how he had managed to be in charge of so much at such a young age.

"Lilaria has a long relationship with birds, and I was very excited to receive a spot at this zoo. I feel that I can do a lot of good for our avian friends here." He led us through the exit door and into a small schoolhouse setting. There were models of birds, a poster listing extinct species, and a wall with windows into a nursery type of room where tiny birds hopped around and chirped loudly. There were TVs along the top of the room, showing footage of birds in flight, raptors chasing ever-changing clouds made up of thousands of sparrows. It was an impressive educational tool and obviously directed at getting people interested in birds—especially children.

"The Future Bird Trust helped pay for this building." Jeremy put his hands on his hips and looked around the room. "There is a heavy emphasis on education."

"That's excellent. We need to teach children why it's so important to preserve what we have." I watched some of the hatchlings with a smile. I missed the birds.

"It is important, but I feel like we should also reach out to the adults in charge of things now. Otherwise, there won't be as many birds when the children grow up." Jeremy stood next to me and stared into the nursery. "I'd like to start a promotion that targets adults."

"What do you have in mind?"

"I have several ideas, including setting up falconry classes and holding events for parties, wedding receptions, and conventions here at the zoo. A set fee would go to the care of the animals, but it would also give us a chance to introduce large and sometimes influential groups to the birds." He leaned against the glass and looked at me. "I'd also like to run advertisements in the papers and with the news stations. There is a community-sponsored channel that is willing to do a series on birds with the zoo."

"Those are all ideas that could work." I tilted my head in thought. "I'd also say to not underestimate the amount of power a well-educated child has on their parent. I've seen a lot of families take up recycling because their children insisted."

"Oh, we'll keep the programs we have in place, but I'd like to target the immediate threat directly." He moved a little closer toward me and I found myself stepping backward to put space between us.

I nodded my head and moved farther away, walking

around the little room, taking in the posters and little odds and ends that had been strewn about the room. Becca was watching me closely and had taken a closer spot to where I was standing. I knew she could tell that I had become uncomfortable. Chadwick was checking his watch and raised an eyebrow in my direction.

"May I call you Samantha?" Jeremy followed close behind me and I had to keep from rubbing at my skin. He seemed nice and he was bright, but I had a feeling that he didn't see me as a human or even as a biologist— he saw me as a means to an end.

"Sure." I didn't look at him, instead I motioned toward Chadwick. "Look at this, Chadwick. This is an article my advisor was credited in."

"Oh? That's interesting." Chadwick flipped through the periodical. "He must be very good at his job."

"Yes. He's one of the best."

"I heard you studied with Dr. Geller." Jeremy looked over Chadwick's shoulder. Suddenly I had a feeling the periodical had been placed there just for my benefit.

"Yes, I was very lucky."

"You must have hated giving up that spot." Jeremy shook his head. "I know how much work goes into that stuff."

"Yes, it hurt, but I hope to resume my studies in the future."

"Well, if you'd like to work with the birds here, we'd be happy to have you." Jeremy sat on the bookshelf next to me and crossed his arms. "We're always in need of knowledgeable volunteers. And it might be nice for you to get your hands dirty again."

I laughed. It was true that I would probably enjoy working here, but the fact was I'd also be under constant scrutiny. "I'll keep that in mind. I'm sure I'll have a chance to be hands-on once on my property."

"Will they let a duchess do any work?" Jeremy laughed. "Lilarians take their royals very seriously."

Chadwick glared over at Jeremy. Even though I was American I could see why that statement would bother those born here. It was in his tone that he didn't think that much of the royals in general.

"I know that Prince Alex does a lot of hands-on work with the FBT, so I'm sure if I want to help out here, no one would say otherwise."

"And that's why you're America's Duchess." He gave a throaty laugh and I felt myself cringe again. So he thought I would do what I wanted just because I was American? I guess he had a point, but it still seemed rude to bring that up while I was invited here as a Lilarian duchess.

"So, what other animals does the zoo house?" I walked toward the door, not acknowledging his comment.

"A lot of the basics: lions, apes, antelopes." He jumped ahead of me and held the door open. "We had a baby elephant two days ago. Would you like to see her?"

"I'd love to." And I meant it.

"Right this way," he said.

The baby was still ungainly and stayed close to the mother, but I was in love with all the adorable wrinkles and clumsy feet. "Chadwick, look at its legs! They're all wobbly."

He laughed. "Looks a bit like you when you got off the plane!"

"Hey!" I slapped his shoulder, even though he was probably right.

"Samantha would be a great name for her!" Jeremy nodded his head. "You both arrived in Lilaria the same day."

I looked over at Chadwick, who had covered his

mouth with one hand. I wasn't sure if I should be flattered or insulted that he wanted to name an elephant after me. He seemed to understand my inner dialogue because he smiled.

"I believe there is a rhino named after the queen."

"Oh." I smiled at Jeremy. "That would be sweet."

"I'll have to put it up for discussion, but I have a feeling that it will stick." He leaned against the railing. "She is a cute little thing, though."

He cut his eyes toward me and I looked away quickly. Jeremy was cute enough, but obviously not really interested in me.

He showed us around the other exhibits. A few of the people visiting the zoo would stop and ask for pictures, and there were members of the press, but the security detail kept them at bay for the most part. By the time we had completed a full loop, I was ready to hit the road.

"Would you like to grab some lunch? Maybe chat a little about raptors?" Jeremy leaned close.

"I'm sorry, I believe that I have another engagement soon." I shot a glance at Chadwick who cleared his throat.

"Yes, we need to leave shortly to stay on time."

"Maybe another time?" Jeremy touched my elbow and I could hear cameras clicking away.

"Thank you for the invitation, but right now I'm so busy I barely have time to tie my shoes." I smiled at him and moved out of his reach.

"Okay." He stepped back and let his hands fall to his side. "I wanted to ask if you would consider throwing in your support for the television show. If we have someone with your background we could get a lot of financial help. I think you'd make an amazing host."

I stared at him for a minute, flabbergasted. I had been expecting him to ask for a donation, to write a check for something, but to be on camera? He was trying to capitalize on my newfound public interest.

"I'm really not good at public events. Being in front of cameras makes me nervous." As if they knew they were being discussed, the cameras following us clicked away intensely. "You're very sweet, but I think I'd be a terrible host."

"You'd be great. The media would eat it up and so would the public. They'll love your American accent."

"You mean they'll love seeing a duchess." I frowned at him. "I'm not the one for the job, but I wish you the best of luck."

"I'm sorry to hear that." He ran a hand over his jaw. "Would you be interested in donating to the program? We're always looking for people who have a genuine interest in wildlife."

"I'll think about it. For now I need to focus on my lands and the people there. Once I know more, I'll look into donating to worthy causes." I held my hand out to him. "Thank you for inviting me, Jeremy. It was nice to see the zoo. I enjoyed the aviary and especially the baby elephant."

"It was nice to meet you as well, Samantha." He looked disappointed, but I wasn't about to offer any money. I could barely understand the amount I had, and I still didn't know what my responsibilities would be when I got to see my actual home.

Once we were in the car, I melted into the seat and frowned at Chadwick. "Please tell me we don't really have anything else to do today?"

"Well . . . there are two more stops." He cringed when I sat up straighter.

"God, Chadwick, you're killing me. I'm already exhausted."

"From avoiding Mr. Flirty?"

"Yes! And from everything else." I closed my eyes. "I'm not cut out for this life. Eventually I'm going to snap and say what I'm really thinking."

"Ah, don't focus on all the bad. Think about it! You're going to have a baby elephant named after you!"

I laughed. "Yeah. She was adorable."

"A cute little thing is what he said."

"Shut it, Chad."

"I hate it when you call me that." He frowned at me.

"Good."

TWENTY

**Already Stepping into the
Shoes of Her Royal Family**
—*LILARIAN GAZETTE*

$\mathcal{T}$HE NEXT TWO days were full of similar events. People eager to meet me and then turn around and ask for money. I even spoke with Dr. Beilefeld, which had been the most important thing to happen since my arrival. He seemed genuinely interested in my father's case.

Even with the little breaks Chadwick had planned into my schedule, it was exhausting and I was on the verge of a temper tantrum when my phone rang. When I checked my screen I sighed in relief. It was my dad and I quickly answered.

"Hey! How are you?"

"Good. You're on the news every day. Looks like they're keeping you busy." His voice went a long way toward calming my frayed nerves.

Chadwick stood up from his seat at my desk and pointed to his watch before exiting the room.

"Something like that."

"Well, the doctor said I could leave after my next

scan as long as everything comes back okay. I only have one more week of chemo."

"That's great! I can't wait to see you." I smiled. "Has Patricia given you an answer about coming?"

"Yep. She said I couldn't shake her just by moving to another country." He laughed. "She's boxing up stuff right now. Won't let me help. Stubborn woman."

"I heard that!" Patricia's voice squeaked through the tiny speaker on my phone.

"Tell her I'm hiring movers! She doesn't need to do that."

"She knows. It's like she's got a compulsion."

"Well, keep her from doing any lifting."

"Right. Like that woman has ever listened to me." I could hear Patricia laugh in the background. He was right.

"Okay. Well, how are you feeling? What did the doctor say?"

"I have another scan after the chemo is finished." He never hesitated talking about it all. He was very no-nonsense. "But we're hopeful that it will have helped."

"Let me know as soon as you have the results. I wish I could be there with you."

"Nah. It's fine!" Dad laughed. "I'm a big boy, Sam. You don't need to hold my hand."

"I know." My voice cracked. "I need you to hold mine."

"You okay?" Dad's voice softened. "You sound tired."

"I am. It's just really different here. I feel like everyone wants something from me." Even my new friends. Chadwick wanted me to find my groove, Cathy wanted me to be her best friend, and Alex . . . I hadn't seen Alex in days.

"You take care of yourself. You can't help anyone else if you don't start with you."

"You're right." I sighed. "I miss home."

"It'll get better."

"I know." Chadwick knocked on my door and I sighed. "I have to go, the warden says my time's up."

He laughed. "Love you, baby. Call me when you have some time."

"I will. Love you too." I hung up the phone and took a deep breath. Time to go play tea party.

I grabbed the jacket for my dress and went out into the hall. "I'm ready."

"Good. The queen has a very strict schedule."

"I know."

"How's your dad?" Chadwick led me through the hallways. I still got turned around in the palace.

"One more week of chemo and then he has another CAT scan. If everything checks out, he'll be here next month."

"Excellent! I checked out the fishing at your house and it's supposed to be good. Stanley even has a chair picked out for him. Said it's the most comfortable."

"Stanley . . . How does he seem about the whole new-royal-coming-to-the-house thing?" I watched Chadwick out the corner of my eye.

"He seems excited, to be honest. I'm sure you guys will have to get used to each other, but he seems happy about having someone live in the manor house." Chadwick glanced at his paperwork. "He is having everything freshened up for your arrival."

"He doesn't need to do that. I can clean up or fix anything when I get home."

"Samantha, your homecoming is a very big deal. He will make sure everything is just right."

"Okay." I took a deep breath. It didn't take long until we were at the doors for the queen's parlor. The man standing there nodded to me to make sure I was ready before knocking softly and waiting for a response. I followed him into the room before stopping to curtsy.

"Your Majesty." The footman bowed. "The Duchess of Rousseau."

"Samantha, so glad you could have lunch with us."

"Thank you for inviting me, Your Highness." I smiled at the queen and at the people behind her. Cathy, Alex, and Rose were all standing, waiting on me to join them. I hoped my eyes hadn't lingered on Alex for too long, but his were locked on me the same way.

"Not at all. You've been busy and we thought it might be nice to have a quiet lunch." She motioned for me to take the open chair next to Alex. He held the seat out for me and I managed to slide under the table with no problems. I was getting better at this manners stuff.

"How are you?" Rose asked.

"Good. Trying to find my footing."

"Samantha, how have you found Lilaria?" The queen smiled at me over the flowers in the center of the table. I'm not sure why, but Felecia made me nervous in a way that Alex and Cathy didn't.

"It's lovely, but I hope I get to see more of it soon." I put the napkin in my lap and tried to calm my nerves.

"Eager to get to your estate?" Felecia took a sip from her water glass.

"Yes, ma'am."

"It's beautiful out there. The D'Lynsal property runs adjacent to the stream on the backside. I used to fish there with my father." Felecia looked over at Alex. "Do you still go out that way? I know you used to fly birds back there."

"Yes, it's a good area to hunt." He looked over at me. "Don't forget you said you'd join me sometime." Was he flirting with me in front of everyone?

"I didn't realize your property ran alongside mine."

I looked at Alex while the staff placed salads on the table.

"You should have studied your map a little better." He laughed.

"I would if my teacher would ever get around to helping me decipher Lilarian." I gave him a pointed look before taking a bite of my salad.

"I'll send you some homework."

"Alex, you still haven't taught her anything else?" Cathy was watching us carefully. "So, the only words she knows in Lilarian are *chicken* and *stuffed*?"

I heard Rose snort but she quickly turned it into a sneeze. Felecia looked like she was trying not to laugh.

"I need to know more than that?" I winked at Cathy.

"It will certainly make your reinstatement ceremony more interesting if that's all you know." She giggled.

"Would certainly be entertaining," the queen offered. "Alex, if you've promised to help her with her Lilarian, you need to do it. What is on your schedule for the next few weeks?"

"FBT work, a trip to the mines, the normal stuff." Alex wiped his mouth with his napkin. "Actually, Samantha is going to be doing some work with the FBT. I could help with her Lilarian then."

"That's perfect." Felecia nodded her head like she was confirming an order.

"I really need to get to my property." I tried to not sound annoyed. When was I ever going to get to see my new home?

"We're going this weekend," Alex said. "I won't need any help with the FBT for at least another week."

"Oh, are you going with her to Rousseau?" Felecia looked up, interested.

"Yes." He didn't offer an explanation, and the queen's thoughtful gaze turned to me.

"Let me know if you need to rearrange your schedule, Alex." Felecia smiled before looking down at her plate. That was the first time I felt like she was working something and I couldn't help but wonder what.

"That's great, Alex. I'm sure Samantha will appreciate having a friend along for the ride," Cathy interjected.

"A friend will be appreciated amongst all this change," Rose said primly.

"You have had to adjust to a lot this week," Felecia said. "I think you've done wonderfully."

"Thank you. I have to admit that I'm flying by the seat of my pants." A woman cleared the plates. I was starting to understand why Alex loved hamburgers so much—the fancy food lost its appeal after your eighth straight meal of it.

The rest of the lunch was filled with chitchat. The longer I talked to Felecia, the more comfortable I felt. She was a quick thinker, directing the conversation easily but not leaving me feeling like she wasn't listening.

By the time lunch was finished, we were all laughing and I'd even joked with the queen. Alex had one arm thrown over the back of his chair while he teased Cathy about her collection of frog figurines.

"Frogs? Why frogs?" I leaned forward and propped my chin on my hand.

"It started when I was little. They're cute and green." She shrugged while Alex and Rose laughed. "And then it just exploded. Everyone would bring me frog figurines when they came back from a trip."

"She still has all of them." Alex shook his head.

"They're special! You guys got them for me. What am I going to do? Throw them away?" Cathy glared at him.

"Your closet looks like a frog shrine."

"I don't know where else to put them." Cathy shrugged.

"So, you have hundreds of frog figurines stuffed into your closet?" I laughed. "This gives the whole frog-prince thing a new meaning."

"Oh hush." Cathy laughed.

"Well, as much as I've enjoyed lunch, I have to go." Felecia set her napkin on the table and stood up. "I've really enjoyed getting to know you better, Samantha."

"Yes, ma'am. Same here." I stood up.

"We'll have to do it again when you come back."

"I'd like that."

Once Felecia left, Alex stood up and smiled down at me. "I hear you have portraits tomorrow afternoon."

"Don't remind me."

"Aren't those normally done in the morning?" Cathy asked.

"I asked them to move it to a later time." Chadwick chuckled under his breath and I shook my head. "Okay. I begged them to move it to later. I'm not a morning person and didn't think it would be appropriate for me to be glaring at the camera in each picture."

"Not a morning person?" Alex asked.

"I can get up and do what I need to do, I just don't want to talk to anyone while I do it." I shrugged. "Just takes me a little while to warm up."

"And a lot of coffee," Cathy added. "Or so I've heard."

"It's not a very well-kept secret." I sighed.

"Speaking of the portraits, you still need to decide if we're doing them inside or out." Chadwick raised an eyebrow. "I believe it's supposed to rain tomorrow."

"Lilaria has the strangest weather." I frowned. "I guess we'll do them inside."

"What are you wearing?" Cathy asked.

"I'm going with the black dress from the other night." I caught Alex's eye. I didn't want to admit that I had chosen that one because he had said he liked it.

"That dress looks great on you. Have you had any jewelry delivered? It's customary to wear family jewels." Cathy watched me thoughtfully.

"The Rousseau family had three tiaras in the royal vault, and Samantha prefers to wear her mother's ear-rings," Chadwick supplied. We hadn't talked about the tiaras, but I had said I wanted to wear Mom's earrings.

"Would you like to borrow a necklace? I have a few that would look great with that dress." Cathy pulled a phone out of her pocket and tapped on the screen. "I can have Selene bring them to your room."

"No, it's fine. Thank you." I hadn't thought about wearing a necklace, but Cathy's taste and mine differed greatly. I'd rather have something simple and she was all about jewels.

"The offer stands if you change your mind." Cathy leaned forward and kissed my cheek. "I've got to run. I'm signing up for my first semester today." She practi-cally vibrated eagerness. Sometimes it was easy to forget how young she was. After a quick kiss for her brother, she left in a swirl of excitement.

"How are you doing?" Alex asked. He stepped closer, ignoring Chadwick. "You've been really busy for just getting here."

"I'm fine." I sighed. "Okay. I'm a little overwhelmed, but Chadwick's keeping me sane."

My assistant hummed to himself before looking up. "I'm going to run a quick errand—I'll be right back and then we've got to move on to our appointment."

"Sure." I frowned as I watched him disappear out the door. He was leaving me alone when we had something to do?

"Samantha?" Alex's voice drew me back to him. "He's giving us a few minutes to talk."

"Oh." I looked up into his eyes and words left me. Again.

"You say the most profound things." Alex laughed softly.

"Shut it, Your Highness." I narrowed my eyes.

"And then when you do find something to say, it's always so sweet." Alex reached out and tucked some of my hair behind my ear.

"Why do you do that?" I wanted to hear that he needed to touch me as much as I wanted to touch him. He did something to me that I had never felt before.

He rubbed some of my hair between his fingers. "You know why."

I stood there, enjoying his nearness. I felt like I was trying to soak him up to get me through the craziness of the rest of the week. "You're the least normal person I know and yet you're the only person that makes me feel grounded."

He took a deep breath. "I don't understand why you're so intent on fighting this."

I'm scared. I wanted to tell him, but I couldn't make my mouth utter the words. How silly would that sound? He'd think I was a child.

He slid his hand over my cheek and I looked up at him with wide eyes. He leaned close so that his breath tickled my mouth. "Ask me to kiss you."

"I can't." I wanted him to. I wanted him to kiss me badly. I wanted to not worry and to get lost in the moment. To get lost in him.

"You want me to. I can see it in your eyes." The rumble of his voice dropped even lower.

His lips were so close to mine I could barely think. I wanted to say something, anything. My heart was screaming for me to beg him to kiss me. And yet my throat was frozen. After a moment he pulled back enough to look at me.

"Tell me when you're ready, Samantha."

Disappointment flooded my body. My heart was more than ready, it was my brain that was holding me back.

There was a knock on the door and Chadwick stuck his head in the room. "Ma'am, it's time."

"I have to go." I turned away and walked to the door.

"Samantha?" I stopped and looked over my shoulder. "The ball's in your court."

I nodded my head and hoped my face didn't show my regret.

TWENTY-ONE

**The New Duchess of Rousseau
to Host Nature Show**
—*LILARIAN PROPHET*

"I'M NOT WEARING that much makeup." I grabbed a washcloth and rubbed at my cheeks. I looked at Chadwick in the mirror and hissed under my breath. "I look like a prostitute."

He barked a laugh. "You do not."

I glared at him in the mirror as I rubbed off an inch of foundation.

"Okay. A very classy one."

"Damn it. I smeared the eyeliner!" I rubbed at my face harder. "Now I look like a crying prostitute."

"Stop that! You're taking off skin." Chadwick grabbed the towel out of my hand. "Look at me."

I turned toward him and sat very still while he carefully wiped around my eyes. He picked up something that I couldn't see. "Close your eyes."

I sat there patiently while he reapplied the eyeliner. He tsked under his breath while he worked. "The makeup artist I hired had a family emergency."

"Where did you find her replacement? A brothel?"

"It's not *that* bad."

I peeked one eye open. "Yes it is."

"Okay. It was pretty bad." He spun me toward the mirror. "But I fixed it."

"Why didn't you just do it in the first place?" I checked my reflection out, feeling much better about the way I looked.

"Bah." He helped me out of the chair. "Now hurry. We need to pick a diadem for the photos." He led me into the room where we were doing the shoot. There was a bland-looking background set up in one corner with lights focused directly on it. Off to the side was a table with a large wooden box. Chadwick went straight to the chest, produced a large key, and unlocked the lid. He opened it and stepped back so I could see what was inside.

"These belong to my family?" I ran my fingers gently over the jewel-encrusted tiaras.

"These belong to you."

There were three in the box, each as beautiful as the next. One had large, clear emeralds set between diamonds. The next one was large and flashy—it would make Cathy proud. The last one was small and had been worked to look like vines. It was simple but breathtaking. It was intricate, but not over-the-top, and I knew it was the one I wanted immediately.

"Do you know anything about them?" I lifted the tiara out of the box and watched as the light played along the jewels.

"I had a feeling that would be the one you chose." Chadwick took it from my hands and nodded toward the chair. I sat down and let him place it on my head before securing it with a hundred pins. "This one was designed in the seventeen hundreds for the marriage of Duke Rousseau to the Duchess of Minsington."

Cecil, the photographer, entered the room with a large smile. "Duchess Rousseau, you look lovely."

"Thank you." I stood up, trying to ignore the priceless heirloom tucked into my hair. "What would you like me to do?"

"Have a seat right here on the stool. That's it." He grabbed a camera from a small worktable. "Now, there are a few basic shots we have to get and then we can try a few different things."

I let him tell me how to sit, which direction to look, and when to hold my breath. I smiled big, small, with teeth, without teeth. I made serious faces, thoughtful faces. He put a table in front of me and told me to prop my face in my hands. I did as he said and tried to not laugh as images of glamour shots flashed through my mind.

I heard the door open quietly, but I couldn't tell who it was that had snuck in. The lights focused on me were so bright I couldn't see much past the table. The shadowy figure moved toward the corner and Chadwick joined whoever it was. I squinted but still couldn't make out the newcomer.

"What kind of face is that?" Alex's voice rang through the room. I scrunched up my nose, but couldn't help the smile that pulled at my mouth. I heard the camera clicking, but didn't care. My heart felt a little lighter.

"This was wonderful, Samantha. I think we have some great images." Cecil set his camera down and walked toward me.

"Thank you." I hopped off the stool and shook Cecil's hand. "I hope some of them are usable."

"I think I have some you'll enjoy." Cecil gave a short bow and grabbed his camera off the table before leaving the room excitedly.

I made my way over to Chadwick and Alex. "Well, how'd I do?"

"I think you deserve the night off." Chadwick smiled at me.

"Excellent!" I rubbed my hands together. "I saw a little bookstore on the ride to the zoo. I think I'll make a run over there and poke around. I promised I'd send Jess some souvenirs. Oh! I can wear jeans for something like that, right? Please tell me I don't have to wear another pantsuit. They're giving me hives."

"Not so fast." Alex narrowed his eyes. "You need to have a lesson in Lilarian."

"You're going to deny me the chance to wear jeans? I miss them." I gave him my best puppy-dog eyes.

"You're getting better at the anime eyes. Have you been practicing with Cathy?" Alex smirked when I frowned. "I rearranged my schedule so I could help you with Lilarian. Besides, I thought you hated to shop."

"I hate shopping for clothes. Books are something else." I widened my eyes, empowered by my close freedom. "Come with me. You can teach me Lilarian in the car."

Alex shook his head. "You're definitely getting better at that look. Okay. We can practice in the car. I need to buy a gift for someone anyway."

"Thank you!" I threw my arms around him without thinking. His hands slid around my back with no hesitation and pulled me closer for just a moment.

"Well, I'm going to go unless you need anything else, Samantha?" Chadwick cleared his throat. "Let me help you with the tiara first, though."

"Of course! You need a night off too." I pulled myself away from Alex and smiled at Chadwick. "Sorry, you've been just as busy as I've been."

"It's my pleasure." He made quick work of the pins

holding the tiara in place before locking it back into the wooden box. Chadwick picked up the chest and ducked a small bow. "Good night, Alex. Samantha."

"Good night, Chadwick." Alex slapped him on the back as Chadwick made his retreat.

"I'm free!" I smiled up at Alex and did a little dance. "Free!"

"Has this week been that bad?" Alex looked down at me with sad eyes.

"It hasn't been torture." I frowned, remembering him telling me that I was a bad liar. "Okay. It wasn't peeling-your-eyelids-off bad, but I need a break. I need to be Sam, not America's Duchess or the weird, long-lost cousin."

"Peel your eyelids off, American duchess, and creepy cousin." Alex shook his head. "I think I followed that."

"Why are you here, anyway?" I ran a hand through my hair and found another pin.

"I came to bring you this." Alex held his hand out, revealing a small black box.

"What is that?" I looked up at him. Jewelry? Why would he give me jewelry?

"I saw this the other day and thought of you." He held the box out a little farther and I picked it up off his hand gently. "When Cathy offered to lend you a necklace, I decided to get it for you. I know Cathy's style wouldn't really fit your personality. Unfortunately, it took a little longer than I had planned and wasn't in time for the shoot."

I opened the lid slowly, not sure what to expect. I shouldn't have worried. Inside was a simple gold chain with a bird charm trapped among the links. I pulled it free, careful to not tangle the chain. I looked at it and realized that the charm wasn't meant to hang at the bottom, but sit along the side of your neck so that it looked like it was in flight.

"It's beautiful."

"Would you like to wear it?"

"Yes, please." I handed him the necklace and turned so that he could put it on me. He took his time, his warm fingers sending goose bumps racing over my skin. When he was done, I peeked in the mirror on the wall. It was dainty and wouldn't draw a lot of attention, and I absolutely loved it.

"It looks good on you."

"Thank you." I met his eyes in the mirror.

"You're welcome." He tilted his head to the side, watching my reflection. "Now, go change into the jeans that had you salivating."

"Yes!" I hurried for the door and hesitated. "Should I meet you out front?"

"Perfect."

I smiled at him as I made my way through the door. Once inside, I quickly snagged one of the passing maids to help with the zipper and then threw on my favorite pair of jeans. Closing my eyes, I sighed in happiness. It was like slipping into my favorite pj's after a long day. I dug through my clothes and found my favorite sweater. My warm peacoat, scarf, and boots completed the outfit—I was ready to be me.

I stopped at the mirror briefly and checked my hair before running my fingers over the necklace. Smiling, I wrapped the scarf around my neck, turned the lights off, and headed for the front of the palace.

Alex was talking with a blond woman wearing a cocktail dress, her hand lying on his arm. She laughed at something he said and stepped a little closer to him. I looked down for a minute and tried to rein in my jealousy. I had told him I wanted to be friends and I had no right to envy the way she was touching him.

She said something in Lilarian and he chuckled while shaking his head. I couldn't understand anything they were saying, but thankfully I didn't hear the word *stuffed*.

I cleared my throat when I got closer, not wanting it to seem like I was creeping up on them. The woman turned to look at me, her expression open and friendly. I tried to not focus on the fact that her hand was still on his arm.

"You must be Samantha!"

I held out my hand to shake hers and smiled. "That's me."

"Samantha, this is Adriane, the Lady Minsington—Daniel's sister." I hoped my face didn't falter as I realized this was one of Alex's past flames. No wonder she was so comfortable with him.

"Nice to meet you."

"You too. Alex was just telling me that you were going out to do a little shopping." She looked over at him. "I offered to let you take my car. I figured it might keep some of the reporters off your tail."

"Thank you, that's very generous."

"You've been hounded this week and need a break." She shook her head. "It's hard enough for us who are used to it. I can't imagine what it would feel like being thrown into all this."

"It's definitely been an experience." I buttoned up my coat. "But I'd hate to take your car and leave you stranded."

"I'm in town for a charity event, so will be staying at the palace. It won't be a problem at all." Adriane checked her dainty watch. "In fact, I'm supposed to be meeting with the president of the organization shortly."

"Would you like to try to duck out?" Alex looked at me, assessing my response to her offer.

"Will you hum the *Mission: Impossible* theme song?" I smirked.

"You two have fun. I'll chat with you again, Samantha." Adriane's eyes slid between me and Alex. She gave me a sly smile before heading down the main hallway.

"So, the palace is like a cross between a Motel 6 and a dorm." I followed Alex as he led me away from the front door.

"That's a rather apt description." He put his hand on my back as we walked through the kitchen.

"So this is where they hide the food." I looked at the industrial-grade appliances and open pantries. "Now I can get my own midnight snack."

"They keep ice cream in the third freezer on the right." Alex winked at me.

"Nice." We exited a large door, and I whistled when I saw the car.

"Adriane has always had a fondness for fast cars." Alex clicked the key remote and opened the passenger door.

I slid into the low seat and ran my hands over the leather. "Not exactly low profile."

"The press will assume it's just Adriane, and she's not the one they're after." Alex revved the engine and I could understand why Adriane loved this car. It was sexy and powerful without feeling too masculine. He moved the car around the palace and toward a rear exit. A guard waved us through the gate and we were off.

"Why don't we leave through the back gate all the time?"

"If we give them a little of what they want, we can keep a little for ourselves." He glanced over at me. "When you leave through the main gate for official royal tasks, it keeps them from looking everywhere else."

"Seems a bit lazy that they didn't have someone watching the back exit." I reached up and grabbed the handle above the door as he turned onto an expressway.

"They have people watching, but they can't see the door we left from."

"In other words, we really did look like Adriane leaving."

"Exactly." He shifted gears and the car rumbled.

"Do you use this trick often?" I was trying to not be bothered by the fact that we were in one of his ex-girlfriend's cars. I was trying really hard.

"Only when I need to, and I think you really needed a break."

"Thank you."

"Anytime." He smiled at me. "Are you ready for your first real lesson?"

"Just don't teach me to say something horrible and embarrassing, okay?"

"Never!" He smirked. "Well, not for this event."

"Great." I shook my head. He rattled off a song that sounded much like the alphabet song Americans learned in grade school. I tried to follow his lead but tripped up on some of the sounds.

"Do you know any French? That would help. Our languages are closely related."

"I took a couple of classes in high school." I frowned. I tried again, this time keeping in mind the French I had learned years ago. It went a little smoother.

"Much better." He sang it again and then waited for me to follow suit. After the third time I was fighting the giggles. The Prince of Lilaria was teaching me the alphabet. "What's so funny?"

"Just this. You. Teaching me the alphabet."

"You have to start somewhere."

"True. Okay. How about some numbers and then key phrases? Like 'Where is the bathroom?'" Just in case I needed to puke before the ceremony.

"I'm the teacher here," he protested. "And I think we should try some numbers and then key phrases."

"By all means, teach on."

We made the drive, him correcting my pronunciation and me laughing at his frustration. The drive came to an end all too soon.

TWENTY-TWO

An American-style Night on the Town?
—*PARIS OBSERVATEUR*

$\mathcal{I}$T DIDN'T TAKE long to get to the little bookshop. Apparently Alex had found out from Chadwick which one I was talking about. He got out of the car and opened the door for me, which I was starting to get used to. A bell chimed when we entered the store and I took a deep breath, enjoying the smell of all the books. I might love my e-reader, but I'd never pass up the chance to browse real books.

The woman behind the counter greeted us in Lilarian before doing a double take. She dipped a quick curtsy and I tried to not be disappointed that even after our sneaky exit, I was still Duchess Rousseau.

"Your Highness. Duchess Rousseau." She gave us a small smile. "Can I help you with something?"

"Samantha wanted to find some gifts for friends back home."

"I saw your store while I was out earlier today and wanted to come back." I looked around the open area we were standing in. There were rooms and hallways that appeared to go farther back into the building. "I've always had a difficult time turning away from a book-store."

"We're happy to have you." She motioned toward the bookshelves. "We have a large selection of books, new and used. Many are in English. There are rooms toward the back with older books. We also have an assortment of the more standard souvenirs, including some pottery my sister makes."

"Thank you." I smiled at her and headed for the books. I ran my hands over the spines. She had a lot of the most recent best sellers. I stopped on a copy that had a "Signed" sticker and pulled it off the shelf. It was the UK version of *Fall Guy* by Liz Reinhardt. I tucked it under my arm and kept looking. Jess would love this one. We'd read the American version months ago. I browsed the shelves a little more and found an interest-ing book titled *Inhale, Exhale* by Sarah Ross. I grabbed that one for myself. It was set in the States and looked like it would be pretty steamy.

I left that room and wandered down the little hall and peeked into some of the doorways. A room with old, leather-bound books drew me in like a moth to flame. I took a deep breath, enjoying the musty smell of the old pages. Alex followed me into the room and drifted down one of the aisles to the side. I stopped to stare at some of the names on the spines. I didn't rec-ognize all the authors, but I hesitated when I hit the A section. I scanned the books carefully, looking for one name in particular.

When my eyes landed on Austen I gulped and care-fully pulled the volume off the shelf. Gently I opened the book and checked the publication date. Eighteen thirty-three. It wasn't a first edition, but that was okay. There wasn't a price tag, which was intimidating, but I couldn't walk away from the book.

"What is it?" Alex looked over my shoulder.

"*Pride and Prejudice*."

"What year?" He looked over my shoulder at the title page. "First edition?"

"No." I closed the cover carefully. "But my mother always wanted an old copy of *Pride and Prejudice*. It was her favorite book."

"We could keep looking. Maybe the owner has one, or knows of someone that does."

"I need to ask how much this is—there isn't a price tag." I turned the book over and then checked over the binding. "I only checked out of habit. I've never seen one this old. Mom would have gone gaga."

"Then get it." Alex moved so he was leaning against the bookshelf.

"It's probably very expensive." I bit my lip.

"Get it anyway." Alex shook his head. "You should do something nice for yourself."

"Buying an ice cream cone or new shoes would be doing something nice for myself. This book probably costs more than some people spend on groceries for a year."

"If you don't buy that book, I will." He stood up straight and held out his hand.

"What? I don't need you to buy it for me." I pulled the book against my chest.

"Who said I was going to give it to you?" He smiled and took a step toward me. "Maybe I have secret love for Fitzwilliam Darcy. We do share a name. I also need to get a gift for someone who would love it."

"If I can't have it, no one can." I narrowed my eyes in mock threat.

"Is that so?"

"You'll have to pry it from my cold, dead fingers." I backed into the bookshelf behind me.

"Maybe I just need to distract you long enough to steal it." He put a hand on the shelf by my head.

"And how do you plan on doing that?" I licked my lips.

"I have a few ideas." He moved his other hand, caging me in, and leaned down.

I clutched the books to my chest and my heart beat against them like a drum. Alex brought his mouth close to mine but stopped a centimeter away. I inhaled his scent and fought my urge to close the distance. Slowly he moved his mouth to my cheek, close enough that I could feel his breath wash across my skin. His journey continued down my jaw and to my neck. My head tilted of its own accord, letting him have better access. One of his hands moved from near my head to just beside my waist, the sleeve of his jacket brushing against my arm.

As he moved from my right side to the left, I tilted my head again, my body alive with anticipation. I wanted him to kiss me. Needed his kiss, and I was near my breaking point—no more waiting. His other hand slid down from the shelf and closed on my waist while he took a step closer, pressing his body against mine. He brought his head back up and looked into my eyes.

"I want to kiss you, Samantha." He took a deep breath and moved a little closer. "But I'm not going to kiss you again until you ask me to."

"What?" I jerked my head back at the same time he pulled the book from my arms. "Hey!"

I made a grab for the book but he held it above his head. Embarrassment and anger flared through my system. He had gotten me all worked up just to steal my book? The book I wanted so badly?

"You jerk!" I grabbed at his arm and tried to pull it down, but he was too strong.

"You can tempt me all you want, crawl all over me,

but I meant what I said. I won't kiss you again until you ask me to." His eyes sparkled with his own frustration. "I've made it clear what I want. You need to decide."

I stopped and looked at him. "You were right. This is difficult."

"And I plan on doing my very best to get what I want."

"C'mon. Let me get the book." I changed the subject. The truth was, what I wanted was quickly outweighing my concerns.

"Nah-uh. I got it fair and square. I was looking for a gift for a friend."

"Fair and square? You stole it out of my hands."

"I did, didn't I?" He smiled with pride.

"Fine." I still had my other two books, so I hadn't lost everything. I marched out of the back room and to the counter to pay for my selections.

The shop owner asked how I was enjoying Lilaria and if I'd read any of Reinhardt's or Ross's books before. We chatted about the authors and then I moved so Alex could buy his book. When she announced the total, my eyes almost popped out of my head.

"Thank you. I have a friend who will really enjoy this." Alex calmly handed over a credit card and smiled when she handed him his bag.

"My pleasure, Your Highness. I hope you both enjoy the rest of your night." She dipped a quick curtsy as we left.

"Where to now?" Alex opened my door.

"I don't know. I didn't even think we'd be able to come here without being followed." I set my package in my lap while he took his seat. "What is there to do for fun around here?"

"There's the movies."

"Too many people." I shook my head.

"Then I guess the clubs are out." He raised an eyebrow.

"Definitely." I frowned. "What about a museum?"

"Too late. Most of them are closed by now." He narrowed his eyes. "We could go to the zoo."

"No, thank you." The thought of running into Jeremy made me cringe.

"That's right, you've already been. There was a very nice picture of you and Jeremy in the paper saying you're going to work together."

"What? I didn't see that and—wait a minute. Are you jealous?" I twisted in my seat to look at Alex. It was sad but the thought brought a little bubble of excitement in my chest. "Nice segue there with the whole zoo option."

"Should I be jealous?" He turned away from me and started the car. "You have made it very clear that you want someone normal, to be out of the spotlight. And Jeremy would love nothing more than to have a royal girlfriend."

"Hey! First of all, I don't want anything to do with Jeremy." I didn't mention that he'd made passes at me. "Second of all, we're in your ex's car, which is a really weird place to be having this conversation. And thirdly, I don't want someone normal, I want to be normal. To be just me. Not America's Duchess. Just Sam."

"You're not just anything." His voice rose a little and he snapped his mouth shut for a minute. He pulled out of the parking lot and headed toward the city. "You're not just anything. Even 'just Sam' is something special."

I looked at him as my heart slammed in my chest. I wanted to say something, anything, but my mouth was frozen. Fear ran through my body and my mind wrestled with my heart. I wanted Alex. I was scared of what that would mean, where it would lead.

I opened my mouth and shut it. I opened my mouth

again and shut it again Neither of us said anything else, just rode in silence. I had no idea where we were going, but I didn't ask. Alex eventually pulled into a small restaurant that wasn't too busy.

"Let's grab some dinner." He got out of the car and walked around to my side. I climbed out and followed him inside. Everything was in Lilarian: the sign, the menu, the words on what I thought were ketchup packets.

The man behind the counter said something friendly to Alex and then to me. We had covered basic greetings in the car, so I tried to say, "Nice to meet you." The man chuckled and his smile grew.

"Nice to meet you too," he responded in English.

Alex looked at me and shook his head. "We might need to hire a professional. You just said, 'Nice to leave you.'"

"I'm sorry." I grimaced.

"They're very close words." The man motioned toward the back of the place. "Have a seat. I'll bring you some drinks."

"Thank you."

Alex picked a booth in the back and pulled his jacket off. I set mine next to me in the booth and tried to not fidget in my seat. Alex passed one of the menus to me.

"Thank goodness there are pictures." I stared at the images in relief.

"I wouldn't let you order something nasty."

"Sure, sure."

"Well, not too nasty." He laughed and it eased some of the tension gripping my shoulders.

"So, this is the burger joint Cathy was talking about?" I let my gaze drift over the pictures and tried to pick apart some of the descriptions. "*Laitu?*"

"Lettuce." He set his menu down. "And yes, this is

the best burger in Lilaria. I thought maybe after this week you could do with some familiar food."

I smiled because he was right. We ordered our food and went back to working on my Lilarian. I was seriously lacking in the language department.

"I feel like I'm trying to cram before a final."

"Cram?" He raised an eyebrow.

"You know, pull an all-nighter studying. Cram in as much information as possible before the big test." The waiter deposited our food and whisked off to another table.

"Ah." He picked up some fries.

"I'm really unprepared."

"I think we need backup." He frowned. "If we had more time, you'd pick it up just fine, but it wouldn't hurt to have someone with more practice helping you."

"What about the bargain? I won!"

"I'll still help."

"Oh no. You're not getting out that easy. I want the picture."

"You don't even know what I was working on." He laughed.

"Doesn't matter. A bet's a bet."

"Okay." He took a sip from his water.

"Okay?" I frowned. "Just like that?"

"You're right. I can't hold up my end of the bargain, so I have to do something else." He polished off the rest of his burger while I watched him.

"All right." I took another bite of my food and thought about it. "What is it of?"

"You'll see."

"You're frustrating."

"I warned you."

I rolled my eyes. He had said I'd end up hating him if I didn't end up in his bed.

People at the restaurant had started to recognize who we were and had turned to look at us. Alex threw some money on the table and stood up. He pulled his jacket on and held his hand out to help me stand up.

"Time to get out of here."

We took a scenic route around the city and Alex pointed out some of the places we hadn't seen the other night. After a while we ended up back at the palace. The guard nodded us through the gate and Alex parked back by the kitchen while I tried to guess what he had been sketching.

"It's a bird."

"No." He shook his head.

"A plane?"

"Not a plane and not Superman either." He held the kitchen door open for me.

"Kyle with devil horns?"

He laughed. "Now that would have been a good idea."

We made our way through the kitchen and to my room and I looked down the hallway. "Maybe we should go get the drawing now so you don't try to back out."

"Are you trying to find a way into my room?" Alex asked.

"If that's what I was looking for, I'd just drag you into *my* room." I bit my lip. His eyes focused on my mouth and I thought about asking him. Asking him to kiss me. Asking him to come into my room. Asking him to let me get lost in him.

"You'll have to wait. I sent it out to have it framed."

"Oh. I didn't realize it was something you wanted to keep." I looked away from him. "You don't have to give it to me if it means something to you."

"I want you to have it."

I touched the necklace and looked up at him. "Thank

you for tonight. It's the first time I've felt like myself since I got here."

"Be you, Samantha. No one can ask for more than that."

I stood on my tiptoes and pressed a soft kiss to his cheek. I lingered for a moment, breathing in his smell before turning and going into my room.

When I closed my door, I leaned against it and took a deep breath. I was in trouble.

TWENTY-THREE

Is Your Man a Prince?
—*THE JOLENE WATERS SHOW*

*T*HE NEXT COUPLE of days were a blur, except for the angry meeting with Duvall where I was told not to duck my security detail again. Becca had not been a happy camper either. I'd had to explain that going out to the bookstore hadn't seemed like a thing I would need security for, but they seemed only slightly mollified. The only bright spots were the lunches I had with Cathy at a small table tucked away in the kitchen. She gave me the gossip about some of the royals and local celebrities. She was also full of information on the upcoming events and charities.

"What about politics? I know royals don't vote or run for office, but is there anything I need to be on the lookout for?"

"Mainly you want to do the political dance if you're ever on the spot. Vague answers, smiles, and hoping-for-the-best stuff. Anything else can come back to bite you in the arse." Cathy took a bite of her sandwich.

"So what is our job exactly?" I sipped at the soda I had found in a pantry.

"We host dignitaries, advise parliament, lead charities, and see to our own lands. When something tragic happens in our districts, it's our job to try to help. Sometimes that's with money, other times it can be with connections or a simple friendly hand." She stopped and thought for a minute. "Actually, we're really busy. It probably feels like you're doing a bunch of things that don't matter right now, but you can't think of it that way. Think of it as networking. You're building a base of people who might be able to assist you in the future."

"And in turn I need to help them in some way." I thought about it. "Oh man, Cathy. This is such a bad job for me. I'm terrible at keeping my opinions to myself. I'm likely to piss someone off and not by accident. It's a miracle that I've gotten through this week without doing it."

"Are you kidding me? You're American and they expect you to be curt and adorable."

"Uh, that's offensive." I shook my head. "There are a lot of Americans that would go out of their way to not insult anyone. I'm just not one of them."

"Exactly. And people like it. They think it's refreshing."

I snorted and almost dribbled soda out of my mouth. "Refreshing. Right."

"Seriously. I heard you shot down Jeremy and he still wanted you to do his show." She waved her chip in the air. "He thought it was great that you were so transparent and upfront. No tiptoeing around stuff."

"Jeremy is a weird guy and I'd rather stab myself in the eye with a spork than be the host of a television show."

"A spork?" Her mouth twitched.

"Weird little spoon that thinks it's a fork."

"You're kind of crazy." She smiled. "I can see why Alex is so smitten."

"Excuse me?" I looked around to see if anyone was listening, but the closest person was washing dishes on the other side of the room.

"C'mon. I'm not blind, Sam."

"We're just friends." I looked down at my food.

"Why?" She pushed my plate with her finger so that I'd look up.

"What?"

"Why are you just friends? You're wearing the necklace he gave you, he hovers around you like a mommy bear, and the chemistry is disgustingly obvious." She narrowed her eyes. "Is it because of Melissa? You have to know how much that hurt Alex."

"No, it's not that." I frowned. "There's just so much going on and I don't think I can handle a relationship on top of it all."

"So, it's because of your father?"

"No. Yes. Partly. It's everything. I'm trying to learn how to do all this." I motioned around the kitchen. "Plus, I'm leaving soon and Dad will be here. He's going to need me."

"Is that all of it?" She leveled her gaze on mine and I squirmed.

"Did you take classes as a child on how to get what you want?"

"Don't change the subject, Samantha. What is this really about?" She leaned forward.

"I just told you!"

"You think your father would want you to miss out on something—someone—that would love you because of him? All this change, it's scary. I get that. But it can be good too. You don't see it because you're living it, but to those of us watching, it's obvious that you were meant for this job, for this life."

I chewed on my lip while I pondered what she was saying. "That's pretty deep for an eighteen-year-old."

"I might have come from a life of privilege, but that doesn't mean I don't have any perspective." Something in her eyes shifted and I saw a much older girl looking back at me.

"I'm scared." I said the words in a rush. Maybe if I said it out loud it would make it less real.

"Of what, exactly?"

"Alex—it wouldn't be a fling. It wouldn't be simple or easy. If I let myself, I'd just end up hurt and then it would be in every newspaper and on every gossip site."

"Why do you think Alex would hurt you?" She sat back in her seat. "No one knows Alex the way I do. When Daddy died, Alex stepped up and became the man of the house. He watched out for me and Max. Max has classic middle-child syndrome and left for school as quickly as he could, but every decision Alex has made was based on how it would affect us. And I can see how much he already cares about you. He would never do anything to hurt you."

"Not on purpose." I played with my napkin. "I don't think I could handle the scrutiny, the media attention."

"That'll die down after a while. Or you'll get used to it. It's overwhelming right now, but we do have real lives. We go on vacations and sometimes have lazy Sundays like everyone else in the world."

She didn't understand. She'd been born into something that was so foreign to me I felt as if I'd been dropped on another planet. And Alex would break my heart—he'd have to when it came time for him to take the throne. I'd read enough in my *Idiot's Guide to*

Lilaria that I knew he had to marry someone of royal blood who would be able to help him rule the country.

"The wheels are turning in your head; I can practically hear the gears squeak." She leaned forward and lowered her voice. "You know what I think? I think you're worried about what it would mean if it all worked out. Alex comes with some heavy baggage. Crown prince isn't nearly as fun as they make it out to be in the storybooks. Whoever he chooses will be queen."

I groaned. "Exactly. I'm an American, for crying out loud. Remember? The adorable little foreigner that says whatever she's thinking? No one would accept me as their queen and God knows I wouldn't blame them. When I think about being with Alex, I can't just think about how he makes me feel, I have to think about how it would affect an entire country. If they reject me, he would have to leave me. And if they don't reject me, how badly could I screw it all up?"

Cathy smiled and leaned back in her chair. "He could always abdicate."

"Geez, Cathy, that wouldn't make me feel like an ass or anything." I glared at her. "Our entire relationship, I would be the reason he wasn't king."

"The very things that have you worried are the exact things that mean you would make an excellent queen."

"You don't understand. You've been brought up your whole life with that as a possible future. I was brought up in a land with no kings or queens. The very idea makes me nervous."

"You do realize you're from a line of royalty that once held the crown of Lilaria?" She snorted and picked up her plate. "Sam, get it together. Sometimes all our plans for life go to shit. You end up doing something you never dreamed of and you know what you do?"

I stood up and followed her to the sink with my plate. "What's that, oh wise one?"

"You make the best out of it you can. Nothing is ever as good or as bad as you think it will be. It's what you make of it." Alex had said that exact same thing to me. She tossed her leftovers and handed the plate to the dishwasher. "But I can tell you this: You will never find another man that would love you the way Alex would."

"Riddle me this. If you're so smart, why are you hanging out with Kyle? He's a scumbag." I looked over at her as we walked.

"Oh, I know." She shrugged. "I know exactly what he's after, but when it's just us, we have fun. I might understand how the world works, but that doesn't mean I don't want to just be a little wild."

"Be careful there. The lines become blurry when we're living it."

"I will." Her blithe answer did nothing to make me feel like I had gotten through to her. Kyle was dangerous and I'd hate to see some of her sweetness smothered by the scars he would leave on her heart. "You leave tomorrow?"

"Yep. Bright and early. I think we're driving." I shrugged. "Chadwick already packed up my clothes and sent them to the house."

"You'll love it out there. Lots of trees and quiet."

"I've seen some pictures online, but I'm really looking forward to being there in person." I stopped near my bedroom door.

"Alex is going too?"

"Yes." I took a deep breath. I hadn't seen him since our trip to the bookstore. It felt like ages and I was eager but also nervous to see him again.

"Lighten up, Sam." She pushed my shoulder. "I expect an invitation to dinner soon."

"Pizza party at my place."

"Sounds perfect." She hugged me quickly. "I've got to run."

"See you soon."

I spent the rest of the afternoon going through my e-mails. I was almost through with the list of unread messages when a new one popped in. When I saw the return address I grinned. It was from Bert, probably telling me about something silly Jess had done. I clicked on the icon and almost screamed when I saw the attached pictures.

From: BERT
To: "Sam Rousseau" PRIVATE
Subject: Important Question!!

Sam,

    I was going to ask you to come with me to look, but since you're all the way in Lilaria I'm sending you pictures. She'll kick my ass if I pick the wrong one. What do you think?

                                  Bert

I looked over the pictures of rings and chewed on my lip. I was so happy for Jess, but also sad that I wouldn't be there to listen to her squealing. I looked over the choices carefully, trying to pick out what Jess would and wouldn't like. I debated for a minute over a couple of settings before responding.

From: Sam Rousseau
To: "BERT"
Subject: RE: Important Question!!

Bert,

   It has to be the round-cut; they have the most facets so sparkle the most. And we know how much Jess loves to sparkle!

   Congrats! Really happy for you guys.

                                        Sam

I hit the send button and sat there staring at my computer monitor. I wasn't there, but I had still been able to help Bert. I sent a quick e-mail to Dad with pictures I had snapped with my phone. Looking through the snapshots made me realize how much of the city I had seen. Cathy was right. I needed to stop focusing on the parts that made me miserable and enjoy the good things that came with this new life.

I decided to relax the rest of the night. Chadwick was so busy he hadn't scheduled me anything after lunch. It was like coming home and having no homework. I made use of the big tub and finished the book I had started on the plane. In fact, I was so engrossed in the book that the water chilled and I had to get out. It was the most peaceful night I had spent in Lilaria and I was grateful for it. I had needed to recharge my batteries. I felt like I had been handing out little pieces of myself to everyone I met and took pictures with. After a while I had begun to feel like a shell of the person I was, and having the night off was working wonders.

I fell asleep with the e-reader on my chest and didn't move the entire night.

TWENTY-FOUR

America's Duchess Finally Goes Home
—*CALIFORNIA TRAVEL AGENTS' ASSOCIATION*

THE NEXT MORNING was a blur of activity. For the first time since I met Chadwick, he looked flustered. I dutifully wore the dress he had left in my closet and checked the guest room for anything I might have accidentally left behind. I packed up my laptop and stuck my e-reader in my bag to carry in the car. It would be a two-hour drive—nothing too long, but not a trip around the corner.

I finished up my breakfast while looking through the local papers. Thankfully some of them were in English. Unfortunately, my picture was on the front page of most of them.

"How can they do this? They just publish whatever they want without checking facts." I held up the one I was reading. "I'm not pining away for some lover back home." I set that paper down and picked up the next one. "I'm also not suffering from an eating disorder. Look at this! This one says I refuse to eat and the queen is worried. This other paper has a picture of me stuffing a burger in my mouth and calls me an American slob. Which is it? Am I anorexic or a fatty?"

"Best advice you will ever receive is to not read the papers." Chadwick opened my closet.

"This is crazy! They just post whatever will sell." I growled and threw the papers in the trash can next to the desk. "What are you doing?"

"Making sure we haven't left anything." He opened the drawers of the nightstand.

"I already checked." I shook my head. "Are you okay? You seem flustered."

"I'm fine." His snappy tone made my eyebrows rise. "No. I'm not. I had a fight last night with my . . . friend. I apologize. I shouldn't take it out on you."

"Want to talk about it?"

"We don't have time." He sighed. "Are you ready? I believe I saw Alex leaving his mother's sitting room."

"Sure." I pulled my coat on and grabbed my bag. "Chadwick, would you be interested in making this a permanent job? Work for me? I know you've been living here, so if you have a life out here and aren't interested in moving, I get that." I wrapped my scarf around my neck. "I really would understand, but I've gotten used to your brand of nagging."

"You're so darling. How could I resist?" Chadwick said.

"So, that's a yes?"

"I've already packed." He opened the door for me and we made our way to the main entrance.

"What if I hadn't asked you?"

"It's my job to be prepared for everything." He looked down at his clipboard and a terrible thought came to me.

"That's not why you fought with your friend, is it?"

He didn't look up from his notes. "Chadwick, don't move out there for me. I mean, I want you to move out there for me, but I don't want you to leave something good behind."

"I'm happy with my decision, but thank you." He smiled at me. "Besides, I think we make a good team."

"I think so too." I frowned as we walked a ways. "Maybe . . . maybe your friend could come with you. I wouldn't mind, if that's what you're worried about."

"That's incredibly kind of you, but that's not an option."

"Oh." I hated to see my peppy assistant so despondent. "Well, if that changes, the option is open."

"I appreciate that." He smiled at me but still looked sad.

"So long as I don't find you in your underwear drinking milk out of the carton in the middle of the night."

"What if I pour it in a cup first?" Chadwick was starting to loosen up and I was relieved.

"That's mildly better. How about we agree on at least pajama pants or a robe with the glass of milk?"

"You do realize that there is an entire suite for me?" He looked over at me with a smile. "I believe in the States they are referred to as a mother-in-law suite."

"Still. You might run out of milk and try to swipe mine."

"Then I believe that's an acceptable deal as long as it applies to you as well."

"Hey, it's my house." I laughed. "No promises."

We waited at the entrance for Alex and his assistant. I'd seen him a few times with Alex, an older gentleman who was very proper. While we killed time, I studied the paintings hanging in the entranceway. There was some beautiful work and some of them even looked vaguely familiar.

"Yes, yes. Tell them that I'll be out there next week." Alex's voice reached my ears and my heart thumped. I was starting to feel like a schoolgirl. "I have some things to take care of at D'Lynsal and then I will go to Paris." I turned to look at him and he smiled. His eyes ran over me like a man in the desert looking at a glass of water. My heart rate sped up and I watched as he made his way to me. He quickly hung up and stuck the phone in his suit pocket. "Are you ready to see your home?"

"Very." I didn't even have a joke. I was more than ready to see my place, to find my groove. Not to mention, as usual, the sight of Alex had erased the majority of my vocabulary.

"Then let's go. Ned, I'll be riding with the duchess."

"Of course, sir." The older man nodded his head.

Alex and I took the second car in the line; the first car was the escort that seemed to go with us everywhere. Chadwick winked at me as he took a spot in the backseat of the front vehicle.

We left with little fanfare except for the ever-present reporters and their cameras. "There are more of them today."

"You're going home." Alex looked over at me. "They're documenting history."

"And here I was excited to get somewhere I could drink milk out of the carton while wearing my underwear."

"You drink milk out of the carton while in your underwear?" Alex laughed.

"You've never done that? Gotten up in the middle of the night and wanted a snack?"

"Yes, but I wouldn't bother to put on my underwear." He watched my face as his words sank in.

"What do you . . . oh." I frowned. "Wouldn't that be cold?"

"It's not so bad when you have someone warm to get back to." His eyes ran over me, lingering on my hose-clad legs.

"Good point." I looked back out the window as he chuckled.

All in all, the car ride wasn't that terrible. We spent the majority of the ride discussing my property with the occasional phone call or message interrupting us. I spoke to my dad and was thrilled to hear him sounding more like himself. Patricia was in the background, telling him to ask me for more pictures. I laughed and joked with them while Alex took care of paperwork. It was a pleasant, easy car ride that only seemed odd because neither of us was driving.

As we left the city behind, I enjoyed watching the rolling hills and wooded areas flash by outside the window. Despite the time of year, there was green everywhere. It peeked out from underneath the snow-covered ground and from beneath the frosted branches of trees. We passed small villages and houses that seemed to spring up out of nowhere. There was a lot of farmland and horses. Cathy had been right—while I had enjoyed the city, I loved it out here.

Eventually the driver turned off the main street and took us down a meandering road. Nestled among the trees was a clearing filled with houses and shops. People lined the roadway with signs and flowers. My heart swelled with excitement. I was finally here.

People waved as we drove by and I rolled down my window to wave back. The driver seemed to understand that he should take his time because he slowed to a snail's pace. Alex rolled down his window too and would point out buildings or people from his side. I hadn't known what to expect—part of me had been waiting for them to all hate me for coming back, or to at least be indifferent, but I never would have expected them to be excited. As we neared what must be the village center, I was surprised to see a small stage and a band playing music. It looked like a holiday celebration.

"Do the children not have school today?" I asked as I waved at a young group.

"The local school closed for your homecoming." Alex looked over at me in curiosity. "Didn't Chadwick tell you this morning?"

"He may have mentioned it." Chadwick must've been even more frazzled than I had realized if he had forgotten to tell me about all this. "Am I supposed to speak?"

"That would be a nice gesture."

"Shit." I drew the word out and he laughed quietly.

"Unprepared?"

"Guess I'll have to wing it." I looked at him with worried eyes. "How do you say thank you again?"

He said the words a couple of times while we waved and I practiced it under my breath. When we pulled around the center, Becca was out of the car ahead of us in a flash and by my door. Chadwick was right behind her, but at a more respectful pace. The cars behind us unloaded Alex's security detail. We were led to the stage where there was a small podium and several important-looking people. I shook the hand of the woman that was the equivalent of the mayor, but I couldn't pronounce her official title. Thankfully, she told me to call her Simone. There were a clergyman and several other men who made up the local council, all smiling and bowing.

Alex received bows and thank-yous from everyone. They all seemed to be floating on a high, as if my coming home and Alex's presence was something to celebrate. It weirded me out. Chadwick handed me some paper while the woman in charge spoke to someone offstage.

"This is a speech I wrote on the way here. I forgot to tell you about all this and I feel terrible." He shook his head. "But we don't have time for that right now. Look it over while Simone speaks. It's short and sweet. I tried to channel you."

"Sounds good." I smiled at him, hoping he would understand that I wasn't angry. Everyone makes mistakes.

I glanced at the speech and tried to memorize the highlights. There was no way I would be able to say it all verbatim. If I tried I'd get tongue-tied.

The reporters who had followed us from the palace set up beside the locals, all waiting to hear what I had to say. Or rather, what Chadwick had written for me to say. Alex's voice brought my attention up from the notes and I realized he had left the chair next to me and was speaking to the crowd.

"I'm very pleased to be able to bring Samantha Rousseau home and I'm proud to say that she lives up to her family's reputation. She is sensible, loyal, and intelligent. I have no doubt that Duchess Rousseau will fit in here with all of us. I'm very glad to be able to call her neighbor—and my friend. So, without further ado, I present Samantha, the Duchess of Rousseau, and the real reason we're all here today." Alex turned toward me and smiled.

Chadwick cleared his throat and I realized it was my turn to talk. I stood up slowly and brushed at my skirt. The three steps to the podium were the longest three steps of my life. Never before had I worried about tripping and falling so much. Alex held his hand out to me and I shook it in turn. When he pulled me in to kiss my cheeks, I felt my face flush, and the sound of whispering and cameras clicking filled my ears.

"Relax," Alex whispered in my ear. "Just keep it simple and be yourself."

"Thanks." He let go of my hand and took his seat while I was left to face the crowd. I had no way of judging how many people were actually standing in the village center watching me, but it felt like I was giving a State of the Union address. I squeezed the paper in my hand, the one I couldn't remember anything from, and gave the crowd a smile.

"People use the word *honored* in award speeches, they talk about how grateful they are and humbled. Well, I'm not sure how to catalog today, but it feels as though I've won an award and I am all of those things: honored by your reception, humbled to be a part of such a wonderful legacy, and grateful that Her Majesty sent His Highness to find me." I paused, trying to remember what else I was supposed to say, and was surprised by the applause. I looked over the crowd, stunned. "I'm going to keep this short because I hate to keep you all out in the cold—you might turn into Popsicles." There were chuckles from the crowd. "Thank you so much for coming out here to meet me. I look forward to learning more about each and every one of you." Very carefully, I said the words for *thank you* in Lilarian and silently prayed that I got it correct.

People stood up and clapped. I should have felt proud, but I just felt silly—like they were humoring me. I stepped away from the microphone and let Simone shake my hand. She turned toward the crowd, still holding my hand, and motioned to me again while the crowd cheered. Not sure what to do, I waved with my free hand and smiled. When she let go, I moved to where the others had stood. They shook my hand like they hadn't already been introduced to me and told me how happy they were that I was back. It was very surreal and I didn't really understand why they were so excited. I was starting to think I never would understand.

People stopped me just off the stage. There was a lot of handshaking and smiling. So many names and faces I would never be able to keep up with. Through it all, Alex stayed by my side. He was a living, breathing wall of support. Every person that he spoke to felt at ease; the women swooned and the men felt important. By the time we got back in the car, I felt like I had seen a whole new side to Alex.

"Why are you looking at me like that?" He settled into his seat and raised an eyebrow at me.

"Thinking."

"About how incredibly sexy I am?" He turned to look at me with a smirk.

"How do you have room in your head for anything other than your ego?" I laughed. "And no, I was thinking that you make a really great prince."

"Why is that?"

"You put people at ease and they still respect you." I smiled. "You're a natural."

"I've had years of practice. You didn't do so bad yourself." He pulled at my coat pocket and retrieved the speech Chadwick had written. "Was that really what Chadwick told you to say?"

"I couldn't remember it." I winced.

"So you winged that?" Alex whistled in appreciation as he unfolded the paper. "Wow, this wasn't bad either, but I think you nailed it." He read over the paper quickly.

"It may have been the shortest speech in history." I looked out the window as the car finally began to move.

"It was exactly what you needed to say." He folded the paper and stuck it back in my pocket. "It's exactly what the crowd wanted."

"Thanks." I met his eyes and bit my lip. Would it be wrong to take what I wanted? Would it be worth it if I let myself give in? The more time I spent with him, the harder it was to fight my attraction to him.

"You're welcome."

Surprisingly there were no cars following us except for our own detail as we drove through the winding roads. When we came to a thin driveway with a gated entrance, the first car pulled in and the driver punched a code into the small keypad. I craned my neck to try to see the house through the trees, but they were too dense.

I sat up in my seat and leaned forward as we pulled through the gate. Seeing this house in person would clinch the whole deal for me—it was where I thought I'd finally be able to understand my place in this weird direction my life had taken. The trees cleared and I was rewarded with a breathtaking sight. The house wasn't really a house. With the stone walls it looked more like a castle.

A short burst of laughter exited my mouth. I had seen pictures, but they hadn't done it justice. There was a large staircase that led up to a massive door with elegant statues and stonework on either side. There was a small garden in the center of the circular driveway, a light frosting of snow sitting on top of the sculpted bushes.

"It's something out of a fairy tale."

"Welcome home, Samantha." Alex's warm voice drew my attention from the house. His eyes were soft and there was a gentle smile pulling at his lips.

"Thank you." I whispered the words. I meant for everything—for coming with me, for not running away every time I pushed, and for being my friend when I needed one.

He reached out and wrapped his fingers around mine before lifting my hand to his mouth and pressing a soft kiss on my knuckles. There were no words, no explanations, but they weren't needed. He had said he wouldn't kiss me until I asked, but this didn't count. It was less than the kiss I had wanted in the bookstore, but more than I could ask for right now.

He got out of the car and walked around to open my door. I stepped onto my family land for the first time while Alex stood next to me. It felt right for him to be here. A shiver ran over my body as my eyes drank in the surroundings. A long time ago, my ancestors had lived here. Not many people could trace their family as far as the queen had done for me.

The front door opened and a man stood at the top of the stairs. He was tall with a friendly face and silver hair. I took the stairs carefully, Alex a step behind me. The man at the door bowed and I held my hand out.

"Duchess Rousseau, it's a pleasure." The man shook my hand briskly. "I'm Stanley Wessex." He motioned to the open front door. "Welcome home."

TWENTY-FIVE

Our Very Own Royal Upgrades Homes
—*COLLEGE DAILY*

THE INSIDE WAS much more spacious than I would have thought. Two women stood just inside and curtsied when I entered the house. Stanley introduced them as his wife, who was the cook, and a slight woman named Jeanette, who was the housekeeper.

I took the time to talk with them each, but I was itching to run through the rooms. The furnishings were elegant, but nothing too grand. It felt like an ideal French chateau. After depositing our coats, Stanley led Alex and me through the rooms. He took the time to point out important furniture pieces and rooms that were used for something special.

"Two years ago we decided to upgrade the kitchens and bathrooms. The queen felt like it was a worthwhile expense and now I know why. She must have been close to finding you." Stanley showed me the lovely kitchen, large enough to make food for a big party, but nothing like the industrial kitchen of the palace. "Margie has really enjoyed the changes."

"It's beautiful." I liked the counters and soft colors of

the walls. "I don't think I would have picked anything different."

"I'll have to tell Margie. She worried that you wouldn't like the things she chose and wouldn't feel at home."

"No, I love it."

"I'm glad." Stanley ushered us through the formal dining room, the sitting parlor, and the more relaxed living room. As he led us up the stairs, he looked over his shoulder at me. "I'm afraid that we kept most of the renovations and upgrades to the main levels. We felt that if any of the family came home they would want to have a say in their bedrooms. There are eight bedrooms total, six bathrooms on the top level, and two bathrooms on the bottom level."

At the top of the stairs was a landing with a desk and two hallways that ran in opposite directions.

"The right wing is typically used for the family, while the left wing is used for guests." He started down the right hall. "There are four bedrooms on either side, and four bathrooms on the family wing. The one on the end will be yours."

He led me straight to the last room down the right-hand hallway and opened the double doors. The room was beautiful. While the furniture was on the older side, it had a more antique feel rather than being outdated. The ornate furnishings and decorations were balanced by a simple white bedspread and gauzy curtains. This room spanned the entire wing, which meant there were plenty of windows and natural light. The detailing along the walls and ceiling was beautiful. I looked around, trying to believe that it belonged to me.

"What do you think?" Alex asked from his vantage point in the doorway. He was leaning against the wall, his hands tucked in his pockets as he watched me.

"It's beautiful." I shook my head. "I can't believe it's mine."

"We did update the master bath, of course, and the mattresses." Stanley opened a door so that I could look at the bathroom. "Simple and clean. If you want to change anything to have a more American feel, it should be simple enough."

"Thank you, but everything really does look great." I smiled at him. "You've done a wonderful job of maintaining the home."

"My pleasure." Stanley smiled. "I'll leave you to look through everything. I'm sure you'd like to have a peek without someone breathing down your neck. I'll be downstairs helping Margie with the food if you need me."

"Thank you." I chuckled, relieved. I did want to poke around, but it felt odd with someone watching my every move. It was my home, but not my home. Like when you're house hunting and you want to check the closets to see how much room there is, but someone's stuff is inside.

"Well?" Alex was still leaning against the wall.

"Wow." I laughed. "Completely surreal."

"There's a library." He stood and motioned for me to come with him.

I followed him out of the room and into the other wing. He stopped at one of the doors and motioned for me to go in. I turned the handle and was rewarded with a beautiful sight. Floor-to-ceiling bookshelves that made my knees weak.

"Oh, that's gorgeous." I walked inside and sighed. It even smelled like a bookstore. I couldn't wait to explore the titles and see what was in there.

"I thought you might like it." He peeked around at the books. "Looks like you'll have a lot of exploring to do."

"It's like a treasure hunt." I ran my fingers over the large desk in the corner. "I don't know what I'm going to find next."

"What are you waiting for?" He gestured to the door.

I bit my lip, thinking, before pulling my shoes off and running out. I opened every door, peeking into each room and closet. Alex followed me at a more sedate pace, but chuckled each time I found something that made me "ooh" or "ahh."

"This is really mine?" I looked at Alex over the giant antique bed in one of the guest rooms.

"It's really yours." He placed a hand on the ornate poster at the end of the bed. My heart sped up when I realized we were staring at each other over a very inviting mattress.

"I keep thinking there's a mistake." I looked away from him. "I know it's real, but it doesn't feel real."

"But the house helps?"

"Yes. I think so." I shrugged. "Last week, I kept thinking if I could just get here it would fall into place. That I'd find my groove."

"I shouldn't have asked you to wait for me. I didn't realize how uncomfortable you really were." Alex frowned.

"No, I'm glad you came with me. It feels right that you were here." I met his eyes, hoping he could see what I meant. "And I met some great people in the city and learned a lot."

"Things will calm down eventually."

I forced myself to nod. Out here, away from the crush of the city, I could almost believe it. "I hope so."

"Are you ready for some lunch?" He stepped away from the bed. "I have to leave soon. I have a meeting at home I can't miss."

"Oh. Of course." I didn't move. My heart stuttered

because I realized that I might not see him for a long time. "Will you be going back to the city soon?"

"I haven't decided yet." He watched me carefully.

"Can I see you again before you go?" My hands were sweating, so I set my shoes down on the floor and stepped into them. I hadn't asked him to kiss me, but maybe if I took small steps I'd get there eventually.

"I'll make sure of it." One side of his mouth curled up.

"Good." I felt my own mouth turn up.

We joined everyone else downstairs, where Margie served us a large meal. It was much more laid-back than it had been at the palace and I found myself relaxing. Stanley joined us at my insistence, though Margie politely declined, intent on serving all the food herself. We talked about the property, about the village, and about the local people. We discussed the fishing and hunting in the area. Stanley was looking forward to my father's arrival. He was an avid fisher and was excited to share his favorite spots.

Chadwick was as lively as ever. With some of the pomp removed from our surroundings, even he relaxed with the protocols. When Margie finally delivered the plates of tiny desserts and a cake, she sat down with us and Chadwick grilled her for recipes. After a short while Alex checked his watch and looked over his shoulder to where he could see his assistant, Ned, sitting in the hall. Despite the fact that Chadwick had sat with us, Alex's assistant claimed that he wasn't hungry.

"You need to go?" I sat up straighter in my seat. I had been slouching forward, laughing at Chadwick.

"I'm afraid so." Alex bowed his head. "Duty calls."

"Thank you for coming with us today." I stood up and everyone else did as well. I moved to the door and Alex followed closely behind. Once we were in the hallway, Ned moved ahead of us and out the front door.

"I enjoyed it." He turned to look at me just inside the door. "I'm sorry I have to leave."

"Me too." I bit my lip and stepped forward to press a kiss to his cheek. I leaned back just enough to look up into his eyes.

He looked down at me, searching for something. His fingers touched mine briefly before he pulled away and left. I watched out the window for a moment before turning back and looking at my new house. I could hear the laughter from the dining room and something about it struck me as familiar. I was standing there enjoying the sound when it hit me. It sounded like home.

I made my way back to the dining room and threw myself into the conversation. Stanley and Margie were easy to talk to, offering up information about the house and the staff. The two of them lived in a small house just off the side of the main driveway. Jeanette had a small flat above their apartments.

"Where will poor Chadwick live?" I winked at my assistant. "And Becca. Will she be staying here as well?"

"Just clear out the barn." Chadwick laughed.

"No, no. There is a small house behind the manor home. A very short walk and it has plenty of room," Stanley said. "We already put your bags in there. And Becca has a room attached to this house in the back. It is completely self-sufficient but closer for security reasons."

"Though if you'd prefer the barn, I could clear out a stall." Margie winked at Chadwick.

"I think I'll be glad of the house." Chadwick shook his head. "Looks like your milk will be safe, Samantha."

"As will my eyes." I laughed when Margie and Stanley exchanged a confused look. "It's a long story."

"How have you found Lilaria so far?" Margie cut a

piece of the cake and put it on a plate for me. "You've been in the papers every day. I imagine you haven't had a chance to see much."

"It's a beautiful country, but I'm looking forward to things settling down." I took a bite of the cake. "I'm also looking forward to having my father here. I think he'll enjoy the area."

"When you have had time to settle in, we can talk about what type of changes you'd like to make in the home." Margie smiled. "There are a lot of excellent local artisans."

"I can't imagine what I would want to change right now. The house is beautiful." I finished up the cake and stretched. "I do want to see more of the town and the area."

"I'd be happy to take you around," Stanley offered. "I imagine that you'll only have a few days before the locals start making requests of your time."

"You're probably right, and thank you—that would be nice." I picked up my plate to take it to the kitchen, but Margie tsked at me and took it out of my hands. "Margie, I'm happy to clean up behind myself."

"No, ma'am. I'm happy to do it. Especially today!" She smiled. "Imagine, we finally have a Rousseau back in the house. This is a wonderful day."

"It must feel weird. You've been here your whole lives and I just show up and it's mine." Chadwick choked on his drink, but I wanted to get that out in the open. "I hope there won't be any hard feelings. I'm going to need your help."

"You have it." Stanley stood up and grabbed some of the dishes. "I assure you there is no resentment. Taking care of the Rousseau Manor and its holdings is a job passed down through the generations of my family. It's something that we take very seriously."

"Thank you." I picked up some of the other dishes since Margie's hands were too full for her to take them.

"Have you thought of what you'd like to do tonight?" Margie asked. "For dinner, I mean. We weren't sure if you'd want to eat here or go out."

"I'd like to unpack and relax a little." I looked over at Chadwick to make sure he didn't have any other ideas. He nodded his head and I felt relief wash over me. "In fact, I'd like nothing more than a big sandwich for dinner and to spend some time getting to know the house."

"Are you sure, ma'am? I'd be happy to make anything you would like." Margie stepped in front of the sink so she could keep me from doing any of the cleaning.

"Margie has even scoured the Internet for American dishes." Stanley smiled at his wife proudly.

"Honestly, one of my favorite things to eat is a giant turkey sandwich with lots of cheese and mayo." I sighed. "It's comfort food."

"Then a turkey sandwich it will be. Do you have a preference for when you like to eat?"

"Margie, I can make my own sandwich. You don't need to do that." I frowned. "Really! I'll call you for the big dinners or anything fancy because I'm pretty helpless in the kitchen. But I can make a turkey sandwich."

"Are you sure, ma'am? I truly don't mind."

"I'm sure, and please call me Samantha." Margie's eyes widened and I heard Chadwick sigh.

"She's having a hard time adjusting to being royalty," Chadwick explained.

"He's right. Everywhere I've gone in the last week or so people refer to me as Duchess, ma'am, or some other title. I've shaken hands with a million people and had my photo taken two million times." I paused, trying to find the right words. "But here? Here I want to be Samantha. I'd prefer Sam even, but I'm willing to compromise. I just want to feel at home."

Margie smiled sadly at me. "All right then, Samantha. I'll let you make your own dinner tonight."

"Thank you." I felt relieved that we'd gotten that out of the way. I talked to them for a while, standing in the kitchen, laughing as they told me stories about the locals and their families. Stanley offered me a glass of wine and I forced Chadwick to take one as well.

After a while, Chadwick and I meandered around the house, looking at the rooms. The mixture of Chadwick's sly jokes and the wine had given me the giggles. When we opened a closet only to have an avalanche of blankets fall out, I died laughing as Chadwick tried to push them all back in. I held his glass while he cursed under his breath and used his shoulder to force the door shut. Eventually we ended up in the library upstairs.

We were looking at a painting when I saw the package on the desk. There was a note tucked into the twine that held the brown paper in place.

I wanted you to have something here that would make you feel as if your mother was with you.
Happy Housewarming.
—A

I shook my head as I unwrapped the copy of *Pride and Prejudice* we had argued over. I opened the book and gently flipped through the pages as Chadwick looked over my shoulder.

"Oh, is that *Pride and Prejudice*?"

"Second edition." I closed the book and ran my fingers over the spine.

"I'm guessing this was from Alex?" Chadwick stood back and narrowed his eyes.

"What makes you assume that?" I looked around the room, trying to pick a place to put the book.

"One, you haven't had a ton of guests today. Two, that silly smile." Chadwick wiggled his eyebrows over his glass.

"Shut it, Chad. Yes, it was Alex." I sighed. "I guess this is why Ned didn't join us for lunch. He must have snuck up here while we were eating."

"You like him."

"Ned?" I laughed.

"You like Alex." It wasn't a question. I looked at Chadwick, wondering what I should tell him. Maybe it was the wine, but I felt like I could trust him with just about anything.

"Yes." I groaned. "A lot. So much more than I should. I'm starting to not even care that he's a prince."

"His title is why you're playing hard to get?"

"I'm not playing hard to get. What the hell would I do with a boyfriend who's in line for the throne?"

"What the hell would he do with an American duchess?"

"Harsh, but true." I fell down into the old leather chair behind the desk. "And you summed up the whole problem in one sentence."

"I don't get it. You like him. He likes you. Why fight it?" Chad leaned against the desk. "You're making this more difficult than it should be."

"Maybe. I don't know." I leaned my head back and stared at the ceiling. "Hey, there's a pattern up there."

"You're drunk." He looked up at the ceiling. "Ew, someone put wallpaper under the molding. That needs to go."

"Heh. Tipsy, not drunk." But I was on my way to being drunk. This is why I didn't drink in public. He was also right about the wallpaper.

"Samantha?"

"Yeah?" I leaned my head to the side so I could see him.

"What would your best friend tell you to do about Alex?" He lifted his glass to his mouth.

"Jess would tell me to hit that." He sputtered into his cup and I laughed. "Actually, she has told me to hit that. Several times now."

"She sounds like a smart woman."

"You'd love Jess." I turned my attention back to the ceiling. "Her boyfriend e-mailed me pictures of engagement rings. He's going to pop the question soon. I was sad at first that I wouldn't be there to celebrate with her, but then I realized it had worked out for the best. They're going to need their own space."

"I'm sure she'll still want you to celebrate with them. Maybe you guys can go dress shopping this summer when she comes to visit."

"Oh God. You take her dress shopping. I'll send my card—just don't make me go with you."

He laughed at me. "I'll set her up right."

"Good." I bit my lip before turning to look at him. "Why did you argue with your boyfriend?"

"It's complicated."

"Oh, come on! I spilled, you spill. That's how this works." I sat up straight and tried to give him the puppy-dog look. He laughed at me so hard he tipped his wineglass and had to use his jacket to wipe the liquid off the desk.

"Okay, okay." He sighed. "Daniel technically isn't supposed to be gay."

"Daniel?" I leaned forward. "Adorable Daniel, the Duke of Minsington?"

"That's the one." He sighed into his cup. "Want another glass of wine?"

"Why not? I sense a good story coming." I stood up and we made our way back to the kitchen. Stanley and Margie had left, but the bottle of wine was still sitting on the island. I poured us both another glass and headed for the family room. Stanley had stoked a fire, so we sat down and watched the flames.

"Okay. Daniel and I have been seeing each other for years now. It works, because I was living at the palace and he usually makes a trip to the city at least twice a month." He sighed. "The thing is, it can't last the way it's going. He won't officially come out. He's worried that his family will cut him off."

"Can they do that? I thought Lilaria legalized gay marriage." I set my glass down on the table.

"Yes, gay marriage was legalized, but that doesn't mean his family is a fan." Chadwick stared into the fire. "Danny could stand up to his family. They can't take away his title or disown him, but they could make his life hell."

"And that's enough to keep him away?"

"No. He keeps trying to figure out a risk-free way. He's all about playing it safe and covering all his bases." He took another swallow of his wine. "I'm just tired of waiting."

"Chadwick, you didn't have to come here." I frowned. "You could have stayed and figured something out."

"We didn't fight because I moved out here with you. I wanted to come. His estate is only an hour from here. We fought because I'm tired of being careful. I don't want to have to keep my distance or only stay in. I want to live life with him and we can't do that in a bedroom. Well, there's only so much we can do in a bedroom."

"Oh." I looked at the wine in my glass. "Even without the wine, I wouldn't have any sage advice."

"Ah. Well, maybe I do." He pursed his lips when he

turned to look at me. "You have someone who wants to be with you. Do you know how much he had to rearrange to be able to come out here with you?"

I shook my head no.

"A lot. A ton. He called in favors to get people to cover some of his appearances. That man is willing to go out of his way for you. Stop being dense."

I blinked at him in surprise. "Sorry."

"Don't tell me. Tell him. Everyone has baggage, Samantha. His just happens to be very public. He needs someone who will be with him that he can trust. He needs someone who isn't going to use him or let him forget that he's human." Chadwick reached over and poked my shoulder. "He needs you."

"You just poked me." I looked at his finger.

"I did. I poked a duchess." He snorted. "That's a first."

"You really think he needs me?"

"I think you need each other."

"Oh geez." I sighed. "What if he breaks my heart? It'll be all over the tabloids. The American duchess that was dumped by the prince."

"Maybe you'd be the one doing the dumping," Chadwick pointed out.

"And what if there is no dumping?" I said the words quietly.

"You mean, what if you guys decide to tie the knot and make adorable little babies?"

"I hadn't thought about babies, but what if we fall in love? Where does that leave him and his title? I just can't imagine starting something with him, knowing there's an expiration date."

"Oh, honey. I think it's too late to be worried about falling in love." He chuckled. "And why would it affect his title? You're a royal. There's no reason he couldn't marry you. Heck, Prince William in England married a commoner. The world is changing."

"But me? I'm not from Lilaria. Not really." I frowned. Chadwick thought it was too late for me to worry about falling in love? It wasn't love. It was fascination. I liked him, yes. I respected him. I certainly lusted after him. But it wasn't love. Yet.

"Royals have married royals from other countries throughout history. The key is to make the person feel loved. Let them know you would put them first." He said something in Lilarian that made me sit up straight.

"What does that mean?" It was the exact phrase Alex had used on the plane after helping me with my dress.

"All things are possible with love." He smiled at me. "It's a very common expression here."

"All things . . ." I let the words sink in and tried to apply them to me and Alex.

"Think about it." He stood up and stretched. "I'm going to bed."

"Thanks, Chadwick." I smiled at him.

"For what?"

"For letting me be me." I stood up and hugged him. "For poking me, for talking this out with me."

"Ah, you're a sap when you drink." He laughed. "Go get some sleep."

"All right, but I'm not drunk."

"Good night."

I took our glasses to the kitchen and rinsed them out before heading upstairs. Chadwick must have had someone unpack my bags because my clothes were in the closet and dressers. On a whim I grabbed one of the satin nightgowns and slid it on. The wine had made me hot, and the cool material felt good against my skin. I brushed my teeth and climbed into bed but couldn't get comfortable. My mind kept going over the phrase Alex had used. Could it be true? Could love get someone through anything? I ran my fingers over the necklace around my neck.

After a while I decided to get a glass of water. In less than thirty seconds out of my bedroom door, I stubbed my toe and ran into a small table. I held onto the stair rail and took the steps slowly. How ironic would it be if they brought me back here and I fell down the stairs my first night? A small lamp in the corner of the kitchen gave me enough light to find the glasses. I poured myself some water and leaned against the counter.

I was contemplating making a snack since I had never gotten around to making my sandwich when someone knocked on the front door. My body froze in place except for my heart—it sped up. I set my glass down and made my way through the living room. Maybe Chadwick had gotten lost on his way to his house. I wasn't crazy though and grabbed a large bust from a nearby table. Edging to the door, I tried to peek out of the small window at the top, but I couldn't see anything.

"Who is it?" I called.

"Alex."

TWENTY-SIX

A Royal Sleepover?
—*LILARIAN TALE*

*I*F I HAD thought my heart was beating fast earlier, it didn't compare to what happened when I heard his voice. I twisted the lock and peeked out the door.

"What are you doing here?" I brushed some of my hair out of my eyes. He was standing there in jeans, a dark T-shirt, and a simple jacket.

"I have to leave tomorrow afternoon." He tucked his hands into his pockets. "May I come in? It's cold."

"Oh, yeah." I pulled the door open wider and stepped back. His eyes raked over me and I realized I was standing there in my nightie.

"What were you going to do with that?"

I looked at the statue I was clutching and set it back on the table. "I don't know. Bash you on the head I guess."

"I see." He definitely saw something. His eyes were locked on me like laser beams. "I thought you slept in your underwear."

"That was a joke." I frowned.

"This isn't so bad either." He took a step forward, his

fingers grazing the material along my waist. "Were you sneaking down here for a glass of milk?"

"Water." My voice caught and I had to swallow to wet my throat. "Why are you here?"

"I told you I'd see you before I left." He didn't move his hand from my waist and his fingers were causing waves of need to wash through my body. "And I found out I have to go to Paris tomorrow afternoon."

"Oh." I chewed on my bottom lip. "Thank you."

"I was hoping to catch you before you went to bed, but I never expected to find you dressed like this." His fingers slid up a little farther to trace the thin strap.

"I wasn't expecting company." My fingers itched to run over his chest.

"What would you have worn had you been expecting company?"

"Shorts and a T-shirt, if I have any left after Chadwick packed my stuff. He hates them and made me go shopping." I took a deep breath when he shifted closer to me. "Lucky you."

"Lucky me." His breath rushed over my skin and I shivered. "Why did you want to see me, Samantha?"

His fingers had moved to brush the hair off my shoulder and grazed along the skin of my collarbone. I don't know if it was the wine or the fact that I didn't want to fight it anymore, but I threw caution to the wind.

"Kiss me."

"Not exactly a request." His eyes darted down to my lips.

"It's a demand."

"About damn time." His mouth crashed down onto mine as his arms wrapped around my body. I ran my hands over his chest while I greedily returned his kiss. When he pulled me against his body, I groaned in pleasure. Spinning around, he pinned me against the front door and I could feel the bulge in his pants pressed against my hip.

He pulled away from my mouth to trail kisses over my neck, his tongue flicking over the pulse point below my ear before he bit down gently. I let my head fall back against the door and moaned. His hands ran over my waist, down to my hips, and back.

"Jesus, I can't get enough of you." He whispered the words right before he captured my mouth in another scorching kiss.

He wasn't the only one that couldn't get enough. I'd opened Pandora's box and there was no turning back. I pushed his jacket off his shoulders and he let go of me just long enough to let it fall to the floor. His hands slid up over my body, his thumbs tracing my nipples through the material of the nightie. Fire ran over my skin, every cell in my body alive with need.

I ran my hands under his shirt to trace the ridges of his muscles before tugging the material up. He shrugged the shirt off quickly and threw it to the side. The moonlight poured in through the windows, making his eyes glow as he moved back to me. He slid his hands down to cup my rear and lifted me from the floor. I wrapped my legs around his waist and sighed in relief when he pressed his hard body against my hot center. His mouth teased my lips open and he kissed me as if he was drowning. I shifted my hips in a slow move, enjoying the feel of him between my legs. Then again, harder.

"Oh fuck." He pulled away from the kiss and groaned against my neck.

"I want you." I whispered the words into his ear as I moved against him again. Forget caution. Forget willpower. I wanted Alex and I wasn't going to fight it anymore.

He stepped away from the door, still holding me

against him. I kissed along his jaw as he stumbled through the house and up the stairs. When we reached the landing he moved much more steadily and we were in my new room in no time. He set me down next to the bed and cupped my face in his hands.

"You're sure you want this?" He was breathing heavily and pressed his forehead against mine. "There's no going back."

"I told you." I traced the top of his jeans with my fingers before tugging at the button. "I want you, Alex. All of you. Right now. No more games, no more waiting." Slowly I slid his zipper down before pushing his jeans off his hips.

"Are you on birth control?" He kicked his shoes off, stepped out of his jeans, and let his boxers go with them.

"Yes." My breath caught in my throat. He was gorgeous. "Should I worry about you being tested?"

"Done. I'm clean." He looked at me seriously. "You?"

"After my last boyfriend. No problems."

Taking a step closer, he grabbed the bottom of my nightgown and pulled it over my head. His eyes ran over my breasts and down to the tiny black panties I was wearing.

"I've wanted to undress you since I helped you with your zipper on the plane." He wrapped a hand around the back of my neck, tilting my head up. "If we'd been alone, I would have torn that dress off right then." His lips touched mine in a slow, teasing kiss while his free hand ran over the outside of my breast and down to my hip. "It was torture to leave you that night in your room."

He moved us back until my legs touched the bed, and he lowered us down carefully. The warmth from his erection against my skin was intoxicating. He slid a hand up to cup my breast while he kissed me, his fingers pinching my nipple gently. I moaned and my hips bucked against him.

"So eager." His deep chuckle rumbled out of his chest. He shifted so that he could slide his hand between us, rubbing the growing moist spot between my legs. "So wet."

Carefully he peeled my panties down my body and I helped kick them off my feet. He slid back up my body, his face skimming along my skin. I sucked in a deep breath when he nuzzled the curls between my legs, but he didn't stop until he reached my breast. I fisted my hands in his hair when he closed his lips over the peak of my left breast. Pleasure washed through my brain and I could only form one thought. More. I wanted more.

His hand slid between my legs and I opened willingly. With sure fingers he explored between my folds and slid deep inside. I dug my fingernails into his shoulder and groaned loudly.

"You're beautiful."

I opened my eyes to meet his gaze as he worked my body slowly. I slid a hand between us and he shifted so I could touch him too. I ran my fingers along him, enjoying the way he sucked in a deep breath. After a moment he pulled away and slid his mouth down to my other breast to tease it gently with his teeth. When he shifted to his knees between my legs, I reached down to stroke him again, taking the time to touch every bit of him.

He growled loudly and sat back, his eyes running over my body. I was breathing heavily, more than ready for him. I leaned up enough that I could pull his head down to mine, needing his kiss, while he teased my opening. With painful restraint, he slowly entered me. Much slower than I wanted.

"Damn it, you're tight, Samantha."

I couldn't respond. My breath was caught in my throat as he finally rocked his hips home. He stayed there for a minute, letting me get used to him, until I moved under him to let him know I was ready. When he finally started moving, I couldn't think. I couldn't do anything other than experience this moment.

"Oh God." I moaned.

He brought his mouth to my ear. "Alex. My name is Alex, not God. I want to hear you say my name."

"Oh God. Alex. Alex." I said his name over and over again with each thrust of his hips.

"Samantha." He whispered my name in my ear and I understood what he needed. I dug my heels into the bed and lifted my hips for a better angle. He groaned loudly and picked up his pace.

"Samantha, I can't wait much longer." He gripped my hip with a hand, slamming into me. It was too much and I couldn't hold on any longer.

"Alex!" I screamed his name as I fell over the edge into oblivion. He came right behind me, burying his face against my shoulder, his hot breath tickling the hairs at the nape of my neck.

We lay there limply, our hearts thudding in our chests. After a moment, he shifted so that he was supporting his weight on one arm while he slowly kissed my neck where the charm of my necklace rested. When his mouth touched mine in a soft, gentle kiss, I sighed in contentment. He finally left my mouth, but only to nuzzle my hair. Rolling, he slid out of me and pulled me onto his chest. I traced the planes of his face with my eyes, appreciating the way his features cut sharp shadows in the moonlight. I liked the sated look he was giving me, pride and possession mingled together.

"You look smug."

"I feel a bit smug." He chuckled.

"I can't think of a better way to have christened my new bedroom."

He kissed my cheek. "Well worth the wait."

"Maybe we shouldn't wait so long next time." I propped my chin on my hand and used my finger to stroke the stubble along his jaw.

"Couldn't agree more." He ran a hand over my hair and I closed my eyes. "But right now, I don't think I can move."

"This could be addicting." I let my head slide onto his chest, enjoying the sound of his heartbeat.

"Get some sleep." I felt him shift a bit before pulling a blanket over us.

"Are you staying?" I asked. I was in that sweet spot between wakefulness and sleep.

"As long as I can."

TWENTY-SEVEN

Does the Return of the Duchess Herald New Jobs?
—*LILARIAN DAILY*

THE CHIRPING OF birds woke me up. I opened my eyes slowly, enjoying the laziness that permeated my muscles. I shifted and tried to untangle myself from the sheets when I realized I was pressed against Alex.

"Good morning." His voice rumbled out of his chest. He was propped on his elbow looking down at me.

"Uh." I made a face and closed my eyes against the bright light streaming in through the windows. "That's weird."

"What?" He chuckled.

"Watching me sleep. Is this going to be like those movies where we have sex and then the really hot guy turns out to be a creeper?"

"You make little mewing sounds."

"I do not."

"Like a baby kitten."

I narrowed my eyes at him. "I am not a baby kitten. I'm sleepy and annoyed."

"It's cute and sexy."

"Oh no." I groaned. "You're a morning person."

"Mm-hm." He moved so that I was lying on my back and nuzzled my neck.

"We're going to have a hard time." I sighed as his hand ran over my stomach.

"I think you're right." He moved so that I could feel him pressed against my leg.

"Oh boy."

"You can say that again." He chuckled as he slid under the sheet, his mouth trailing over my skin.

"Oh boy." His mouth covered one of my breasts, his tongue running over it teasingly. "Oh boy."

When he spread my legs and pressed kisses to the tender skin there, I whimpered. I was starting to think I had been waking up to the wrong alarm clock all these years. As he took his time tasting and licking, I closed my eyes and floated along the bliss. When he slid his fingers inside, my hips moved in response. I was tender in a good way, like after you exercise for the first time in a while. One thing was sure, he had given me a good workout.

He focused all his attention on the sensitive place at the top of my mound while he worked the perfect rhythm. His fingers flicked just the right spot and I groaned loudly. I reached down, tangling my fingers in his blond hair. My movements increased and he understood the cue. Crawling up my body, he licked and sucked as he made his way out of the sheet. Reaching between us, he rubbed the head of his manhood against me.

I whimpered, needing him, and he smiled smugly. "Ask me."

"For what?" My voice came out breathy.

"What you didn't ask for last night."

I licked my lips. "Please kiss me, Alex."

His mouth covered mine and I could taste us mixed together on his lips. His tongue slid into my mouth while he continued to tease me under the covers. He eased in just enough to make me moan, then pulled right back out. I growled into his mouth in frustration. When he did it again I slid my hands over his ass and pulled at him. I made some headway before he chuckled and pulled away.

He sat up and the sheet fell behind him, letting me enjoy the sight of him in the morning light. Gripping my hips, he pulled me to him, tilting me upward so that he could slide in. My breath left on an exhale of pleasure as he filled me. I wiggled against him, wanting more, but couldn't get enough traction. I reached above my head and placed my hands against the headboard and pushed, making us both groan.

He ran a hand over my stomach and between my breasts before cupping the back of my neck. He pulled me against him and moaned, his hips setting a slow rhythm that was just enough.

"I could watch you all day." He groaned louder when I pushed harder against the headboard, slamming him deeper. "God, that feels good."

"Samantha. I'm Samantha, not God."

"Samantha." He leaned forward, bracing himself on the hand that had been holding my neck. "Samantha, you feel so damn good." His words slipped into Lilarian and I only paid attention to the sound of his voice.

As we moved together it wasn't fast or rushed, but a steady pace to find the finish line. When his breathing hitched, I was right there with him, my orgasm slamming into me as I felt him jerk inside of me.

He lay on me and rolled so that we were on our sides but still connected. It was a comfortable feeling and I liked knowing he was still inside me. My body was still twitching with aftershocks of pleasure. His hand lazily ran up and down my arm.

"That's a great way to wake up." I sighed against his chest.

"Glad I could help." I looked up into his blue eyes and enjoyed his smug grin.

"But now I want a nap." I rubbed the tip of my nose against him.

"That sounds like a great idea." He pulled me tighter against him. "Unfortunately I have to leave soon."

Disappointment crashed into me, even though I had known he would need to go. I didn't say anything for a minute, just listened to his breathing and wondered what he was thinking. His hand continued its steady movement against my skin and I sighed. I fought against the nerves that were starting to bubble up underneath my skin. The realization that I was already in deep was sinking in slowly.

"Do you have time for breakfast?" I looked up at him. We couldn't lie here all morning if he needed to go. And I needed to do something other than obsess about my fears.

"I have time to eat." His eyes twinkled down at me. "And to take a shower."

I rolled away from him and stood up, looking over my shoulder as I walked to the bathroom. "What are you waiting for?"

I turned the knobs for the water until I found a comfortable temperature. I was checking to make sure we had enough towels when he slid his hands around my waist. I sucked in a breath and fidgeted in his grasp.

"Your hands are so cold!"

"That's why I'm trying to warm them up."

"Dirty." I stepped away from him and pulled open

the shower door. I smiled at him as I moved under the water. He followed close behind and turned a knob so the extra shower head came to life.

"You already know I don't play fair."

My soaps had been put in the bathroom, which was kind of creepy, but I didn't linger on it for too long. I poured body wash onto the bath sponge and began to lather my arms when Alex plucked it from my hands.

He didn't say anything, just ran it over my body in slow circles. I had thought I was more than sated, but when he knelt down to wash my legs, my hormones came alive. He looked up at me, his wet hair trailing water down his shoulders as he lifted one of my feet and then the other. There was something gentle in his expression as he took his time cleaning me and it made my heart thump in a different way.

When he had finished I took the sponge and gave him the same treatment. I took my time cleaning every inch of his body. When I moved my hands down his thighs, he twitched and started to grow hard. Alex grabbed my wrists and wrapped my arms around his neck. He kissed me slowly before pressing his forehead to mine.

"I'd like nothing more than to stay locked away with you, but I have to go to Paris." He twined his fingers with mine. "And if you kept doing that we aren't going to make it out of your room."

"Now you have something to look forward to."

His eyes bored into mine. "I won't be able to think of anything else."

Eventually we finished getting clean and dried off. Thankfully, there were extra toothbrushes in the cabinets. I pulled out some new clothes and got dressed while he slipped his jeans from the night before back on. He stood there for a minute, looking around the room.

"What?" I tugged on a sock and looked at him as he frowned.

"I think my shirt is downstairs." Alex looked at me and raised an eyebrow.

"Oh." I realized we had left evidence. "Oh! I'll go down and grab it." I opened the door, but someone had folded and stacked his shirt and jacket neatly just on the other side. "So much for no one knowing what happened here."

He took his shirt and pulled it on. "They won't say anything, Samantha."

"I know." I frowned. "It's not them I'm worried about."

"The press?"

"I just got here and this would be even more fodder for the tabloids." I bit my lip. "But it's not just me, Alex. The papers would eat this up because it's you. I mean, can you get in trouble for this?" I motioned between us.

"I'm a grown man, or hadn't you noticed?"

"I noticed all right." I smiled and sat down on the edge of the bed next to him while he put on his shoes. "I just don't want to cause trouble for you."

"People are going to be interested in us no matter what. That's not going to change whether we're together or not." He looked at me seriously. "And there is no reason I would get in trouble over us."

"Is there an us?" It sure felt like there was an us after last night. And this morning. And the shower.

"You told me you don't do one-night stands." He brushed some of the wet hair away from my face. "And while the sex is awesome, that's not all I'm looking for either."

"So, us." I shook my head. "Alex, I—"

"Don't make this complicated." He frowned. "We can keep it quiet, see how it works."

"Someone already knows."

"There's no getting around that. People are going to know; some people have to know." He didn't look happy about this plan and I felt guilty.

"Alex, it's not that I don't want people to know—it's that I don't want people to put pressure on us. I've been famous for a week and I already know that we would never get a break." I grabbed his hand.

"I understand." He stood up and pulled me with him. "Let's go get some breakfast, I'm starved."

We went downstairs and were met with the sound of voices in the kitchen. Alex laced his fingers through mine before lifting our hands to his mouth and kissing my knuckles. Whoever had picked up the clothes by the door had to know what had happened. Or at least had a good idea. There was no reason to try to hide it.

Chadwick was sitting at the island, a plate full of food in front of him, while Margie moved about the kitchen. Margie was the first to spot us and smiled.

"Good morning, Samantha. Sir." She dipped a quick curtsy. "I wasn't sure what you like for breakfast so made a little of everything."

Chadwick looked over his shoulder at us and smiled. "Good morning."

I grabbed a plate off the island and picked out some food. "Thank you, Margie. You didn't have to make breakfast."

"I like to cook and I love that I have new people to cook for." She smiled as she cut up some fruit. "Chadwick did tell me you enjoy fresh fruit for breakfast."

"Thank you." I sat next to Chadwick and he pushed a cup of coffee in my direction.

"Where's the normally grumpy Samantha this morning? Is there a coffeepot in your room?" He took a bite of his toast and looked at me with innocent eyes.

"It's a pretty morning." I shrugged and sipped my coffee.

"A very pretty morning." Alex sat across from me and smirked. I glared at him over my cup, but that just seemed to amuse him.

"Spring is definitely on its way," Margie said. Her back was turned to us, so she didn't notice the looks that were being passed around.

"I believe I heard some birds this morning," Alex said as he ate his pancakes.

"I wonder when the bees will make an appearance," Chadwick said thoughtfully. "Pollinate a few flowers and such."

"Really?" I shot them both looks.

"Ignore them, Samantha." Margie looked over her shoulder at us. "Do you think you're the first people to fall into bed together? Or the first people that had a lot on the line?"

I closed my mouth and set down my cup. Alex cleared his throat and turned to look at the older woman. "I'm sorry if we've put you in an uncomfortable position, but this is something we would like to keep to ourselves if possible. The less people who know about us, the better."

"Oh, I understand. That's why I folded up your clothes and set them next to your room."

"You had clothes all over the house?" Chadwick chuckled. "Jess would be very proud."

"How did you know Alex was here?" I asked. He hadn't seemed surprised in the least.

"His Land Rover is out front." He shook his head and looked at Alex. "And Ned called me. I told him that I thought you had come over early to make sure Samantha was settled."

"Thank you." Alex nodded his head.

"Of course, I didn't tell him that you were the one doing all the settling."

"I've created a monster." I groaned. Chadwick winked at me.

"I should have turned my phone on this morning, but didn't want to deal with it yet." Alex polished off his food.

"Why do you have to go to Paris?" I hadn't asked him earlier. There had been more pressing things at hand.

"One of the head chairs was hospitalized last night and he was scheduled for a large appearance. They need me to cover for him this week." He leaned back in his chair. "It's mostly promotion."

"Parties and fund-raisers?" I pushed the food around on my plate.

"There's a gala and a few plaque unveilings." He sighed. "Get used to the idea of unveiling plaques. You will lose count of how many you've done before this year is over."

"Plaques?"

"To commemorate one thing or another." He scratched at his chin. "For some people the monarchy is an outdated institution. We hold a little more sway than some of the other remaining royal households because we have retained ownership of the lands that made our country what it is. However, we do so much more than some people notice. We're the ones sent to rally people for events, to congratulate someone on a job well done. In a time where real, honest successes often go unnoticed, we are the ones who make sure they don't. If someone has spent fifty years of their life dedicating work to a charity or an important cause, we honor them. If the people feel they are being neglected by the government, they can petition us to bring their troubles to parliament."

"Did you know that Lilaria is considered one of the happiest countries?" Chadwick asked me.

"I didn't." I finished my coffee. I hadn't really thought of the monarchy as offering support and guidance. Then again, as an American I hadn't really spent a lot of time thinking about what a monarchy did. "It's almost like you guys are the parents and the country is your child."

"You're part of that too." Alex leaned forward.

"And you know how you can tell if there are good parents?" Chadwick asked.

"Happy children," Margie said.

"Exactly." Chadwick smiled.

Alex stood up and put his plate in the sink. I could tell from his face that it was time for him to leave but he didn't want to. He leaned against the counter and crossed his arms over his chest, watching me as I finished my food.

"Have to go?"

"Unfortunately." He pushed away from the counter and walked around the island. I stood up, intending to walk him out, but he pulled me into his arms and kissed me right there. It was a tender kiss that left me feeling breathless. So much for keeping things quiet. "I'll see you soon."

"Okay." I looked up at him and couldn't help the smile pulling at the corners of my mouth. So far I was kicking myself for having not given in sooner.

He pressed a kiss to the charm on my necklace before letting me go, then turned to smile at the cook. "Thank you for breakfast, Margie."

"My pleasure, sir."

"Chadwick, always good to see you." Alex shook his hand.

"Have a safe trip."

He pulled on his jacket as he left and my knees felt weak as I watched him go. I slid into my seat and sighed.

"You're welcome." Chadwick bit off a piece of toast and smiled at me.

"For what?"

"My pep talk. Maybe I should become a life coach."

"Oh, good idea since you're about to lose your current job."

"Apparently your pleasant morning attitude left with Alex." He shook his head.

"What are we doing today?" I sipped my coffee, ignoring him. "I'd like to see more of the property."

"I've kept the next few days clear so you can take your time learning the area."

"Great. I want to see the lake."

After breakfast I headed out with Stanley to see the property. The lake was a short walk from the house, but long enough that I worried my dad might not make it.

"Do we have anything that would be able to carry my father here?" I stared out over the water. It was beautiful.

"Yes, we have a golf cart that can make the drive as long as there hasn't been any bad weather." Stanley put his hands on his hips. "We also have furniture that we can put up and leave once spring sets in."

"That sounds good." I walked along the edge of the water. The call of a hawk drew my attention up to the sky. The weather had cleared up a great deal, and standing there in the sun with the birds flying overhead, I felt like I could finally breathe.

"The lake also runs along the prince's estate." Stanley pointed off in the distance. "I'm sure the land was divided in such a way that the original landowners could both have access to the water."

I nodded my head. That made perfect sense. "What else is out here? Tell me about the land."

"There are a few hiking trails and a running trail that circle the lake." Stanley pointed out the entrance. "Jeanette runs in the early mornings and I walk the trails from time to time to make sure there haven't been any problems."

"That's nice. I like to run when it's not freezing out." I picked up a small rock and ran my fingers over it.

"We also have horses. Most of the hiking trails are perfect for riding."

"We have horses?" I looked over at him with a smile. "I haven't ridden since I was a little girl."

"Three. Let's go check out the stables."

The stables were tidy, and several grooms were tending to the horses. They all stopped what they were doing to bow while Stanley introduced them and I spent some time asking about their jobs. The horses themselves were gorgeous and one of the mares was with foal.

"How many other people work on the estate?" I asked as we walked through one of the gardens.

"We have ten full-time staff and five who work part-time. Many of them only work on certain days or on rotation."

"Wow. That many?" That was intimidating. Fifteen people coming in and out of my property all the time?

"Actually, we run on a very tight ship and those numbers include me and Margie. I was planning on hiring more people now that we have you in residence." Stanley picked up a rake that had fallen over.

"Why do we need more people?"

"I'm sure you'll be hosting dinners or fund-raisers." Stanley stuck his hands in his pockets. "We'll need more staff to keep up with the influx of people."

"Dinners? Fund-raisers?" I laughed and rubbed my face.

"Eventually all this will feel normal." Stanley laughed. "I have to admit, I'm looking forward to what you will do. I think this place is going to be much livelier from now on."

"I guess we'll see."

We spent a lot of time going over the things that were done on a regular basis. It probably felt silly to him, but Stanley answered every question with as much explanation as possible. The more we walked around the property, the more I fell in love with it. There was so much history, and one of my favorite parts of the whole place was a little area near a stone wall. The trees overlapped and I could see much of the property. There was a worn stone bench and I imagine it had been used by many over the years.

I checked out the cottage that would be Chadwick's home and the garage. I took pictures as we walked. I couldn't wait to send them to my dad and Jess. They were going to love it here. Cathy called to see how I was settling in and said she wanted to come visit next weekend. Once we had it figured out, I spent the rest of the day unpacking the boxes I'd brought with me and trying to make the place feel like home.

I was sitting on the floor in my room and sorting my books when my phone rang. I pulled it out of my pocket and smiled like an idiot when I realized it was Alex.

"Hello?"

"Miss me yet?"

"Nope." I smiled.

"Liar." He laughed.

"You should be studied for that giant ego of yours. It's unhealthy." I set a couple of books on a shelf I had cleared.

"I think it's well deserved."

"You would." I laughed. "Aren't you breaking some kind of dating rule? Like wait a full day before calling?"

"What can I say? I'm thinking about that shower and wishing I had stayed."

My breath caught as an image of him covered in water flashed in my mind. "Well, I did warn you."

"True."

"Have you made it to Paris?"

"I'm here, have unveiled a plaque, finished a conference call, and am now back at my apartment."

"You have an apartment there?" I was wishing I hadn't wanted to keep our relationship quiet. I'd always wanted to visit Paris.

"I do. It's in the seventh arrondissement." I could hear him walking around. "I can see the Eiffel Tower from my bedroom."

"Wow. I thought you'd have to stay at the Lilarian embassy." I leaned back against my bed.

"I like having my own place. Then I don't have to explain to anyone when I get up in the middle of the night for a glass of milk."

"I have no idea how to respond to that." My imagination went into overdrive at the thought of him walking around naked.

"I do. Come here and keep me warm." His voice took on a serious tone.

"I just got here, Alex. And your sister is coming in a few days." I chewed on my thumbnail.

"It's for the best, I suppose. The press here can be vicious." He sighed. "Not to mention you're a blanket hog."

"I am not!"

"And you make weird noises."

"You said that was cute!" I laughed.

"And sexy." He chuckled.

We talked for a while and he explained some of the internal workings of the FBT and I talked to him about the estate. We didn't run out of things to talk about and it wasn't until he got another call that we hung up. I couldn't wait to talk to him again.

TWENTY-EIGHT

Royal Shopping Spree?
—*PARIS POST*

THE NEXT DAY I convinced Chadwick and Margie to run to town with me. Becca came along just in case we needed her, but I felt like it was overkill. The good news was I didn't have to dress up for something like this and no one was expecting me to show up.

We parked the car in one of the public lots and hit some of the local shops. I wanted to show my support of the family-run businesses, so I avoided the chain stores. When we entered a florist shop the woman inside seemed shocked. Chadwick was laughing to himself while the woman tried to hand me every bouquet I looked at. I ended up buying flowers for my room and a set for Chadwick, but only because I insisted on paying.

"Sheesh. I can't remember the last time someone didn't want me to pay for something." I tucked the flowers under my arm and fiddled with my purse. "When I was eating macaroni and cheese in college, everyone wanted me to pay for things. But now that I have money, I have to force them to take it. I thought I was going to have to pull rank!"

"Don't worry, there will be lots of people happy to take your cash." Margie shook her head.

"Too right." Chadwick shot me a look, obviously thinking about Jeremy from the zoo.

It was actually sort of fun to walk around the town. Some of the people didn't know what to say and just stared at me while others talked nonstop. I wasn't sure if that was because they were nervous or because they thought it might be their only chance to talk to me. Margie and Chadwick often stepped in to help me escape when that happened, but for the most part people seemed to understand I had other things to do.

At one point a young mother with a baby in a stroller stopped to welcome me to the town. Just when I was getting ready to go pay for the homemade bubble bath I was holding, she asked me to take a picture with the infant.

"Sure." I smiled at the little girl and turned to face the mother's phone for the picture when I felt something warm cover my arm. I didn't say anything until she had gotten her pictures, but there was no hiding the wet spot on my jacket.

"Oh my Lord! Duchess, I'm so sorry. So sorry. Here, let me buy you a new coat." The young woman handed me a towel from her diaper bag.

"It's fine! Really, don't worry about it." I couldn't help that a laugh bubbled up out of my throat. "My first picture with a baby and I get peed on. It's pretty funny."

"I've never been this embarrassed before in my life." The young woman looked close to tears.

"Here, hand me the baby and take another one. When she grows up, you can use it as blackmail."

She chuckled weakly. "Oh no. I couldn't do that to you."

"Just send me an e-mail with the picture. My father will think it's hilarious." I held my arms out for the baby and made a silly face while Chadwick laughed. He gave her his e-mail address and she promised to e-mail it that night.

"What if that ends up in the papers?" Margie asked me.

"I don't care. What're they going to title that article? 'Duchess Gets Peed On'?" I laughed. "Maybe it'll make everyone realize I'm just human."

"It was really sweet of you to make sure that mother didn't feel so bad."

"Meh. It was funny. I mean, who else would get peed on? It would only happen to me." I shrugged out of my jacket and shirt in the dressing room of a nearby shop. "Or I'd be the mother whose baby peed on someone famous."

"Still very nice of you." She passed me a shirt over the door.

"Not really. I could have been upset or laughed it off." I opened the door and walked out. "There was nothing to do for it at that point."

The rest of the day went smoothly. We ate in a local pub, which I loved. For the first time since arriving in the country I felt like I was experiencing the real culture. People spoke a mix of English and Lilarian, often in the same sentence. I liked how birds were a common thread. They were painted on signs and featured on wind chimes.

The pub owner came over to introduce himself but didn't stay. Most people smiled in our direction, and apparently the story of the peepee picture was already starting to circulate. One of the waitresses was related to the baby and brought us a basket of chips.

"Sally was so embarrassed, but she couldn't get over how sweet you were."

"I didn't do anything special." I shook my head.

Most of the people who came in would shoot me a look and then act like I wasn't there. It was perfect. By the time we headed back to the house, I was tired but happy.

I worked with Stanley through the week to understand more about the running of a manor and found that it was as intimidating as I had thought it would be. Simone made a visit, but since my title hadn't been officially reinstated, I couldn't take on any of the local cases to present to parliament. I enjoyed her visit and found myself looking forward to working with her. She was a bright woman who loved her home.

Alex called every night and I found myself looking forward to his voice more each time. Despite the demands on his time, he never seemed frustrated or angry, even though I could hear how tired he was. He asked questions about the manor and how I was adjusting. When I told him about the baby incident he laughed so hard I thought he was going to snort.

"It's not that funny!"

"Oh, that is priceless." He chuckled. "And you thought the best thing to do would be to take another picture?"

"Yeah. I mean what else was there? Wave her off and leave her feeling horrible?" I shrugged my shoulders even though he couldn't see me. "It was the first thing that popped into my mind. I was hoping it would make her laugh."

"And has it shown up in the papers?"

"The local post contacted Chadwick and requested a copy. Apparently Sally, the mother, told them they needed my permission." I laughed. "They were good sports about it."

"That was right of her." I could hear his voice growing thick.

"I think so." I sighed. "Go to bed. You sound exhausted."

"Sorry, today was incredibly long."

"I'll talk to you soon."

"Good night."

Later, after my shower, I plugged my phone in to charge and realized there was a text message from Alex.

Alex: Miss you.

I bit my lip for a second before responding.

ME: Miss you too.

By the time the weekend rolled around, I was itching to see him again. I had almost forgotten that Cathy was coming until she texted me Friday morning. Stanley and I were in the front yard discussing some of the fencing damaged by the last snowfall when she arrived. She was wearing jeans and boots, which was the first time I had seen her looking so relaxed.

She hopped out of the car with a package in her hands. Running straight to me, she threw her arms around my neck.

"Hey!" I hugged her back.

"You look good." She pulled back to look at me. "I knew you'd feel better once you got out here."

"I'm really starting to love it." I took her inside and she handed me the package.

"Happy housewarming."

"You didn't need to get me anything." I held it in my hands and examined the wrapping paper.

"Hush. You don't go to a person's new home without a gift!" She smiled at me. "Open it."

I pulled the bow off and tore into the wrapping.

Inside was a beautiful bird statue. I pulled it out and examined the detail. It was a merlin, small but fierce.

"It's gorgeous."

"It's considered good luck. Most homes have a bird tucked somewhere. When I saw this was a merlin I had to get it."

"Thank you. I love it." I reached out and hugged her with my free arm. "Where should I put it?"

"A lot of people keep them in their kitchens or offices." She shrugged. "But it doesn't really matter."

"I know just the place." I led her upstairs and put it on the desk in the library. "Perfect."

I showed her the house and told her about the few things I had decided to change. While I loved all the history, I wanted to make it feel a little more personal. Most of the things would be very small but would help me settle in.

I had invited Cathy for a pizza party, but I hadn't known there wasn't a pizza parlor anywhere nearby. Instead of ordering in I had bought all the ingredients and we were trying to figure out how to make pizza dough.

"You've never done this before?" She looked at me over a glass of wine.

"How hard can it be? A little flour, a little water, knead. We can do this." I shrugged nonchalantly. "Grab the measuring cup."

I had told Margie to take the night off, so it was just me and Cathy. She looked behind her at the cups on the counter and frowned. "How big?"

"What?"

"Which one do you want? There are four measuring cups here."

"I don't know." I picked up the instructions and read over them. "Three-quarters of a cup."

"These are in metric." She laughed but handed me the right one. "Here."

"I forgot about that." I frowned. "I hope I don't mess this up."

Forty minutes later we were both covered in flour and giggling. The dough had been runny, so I had added more flour, but that hadn't helped. Cathy was trying to scrape the sticky mess off the counter when the doorbell rang.

"I'll get it." I grabbed a towel on my way and tried to scrub the mess from my hands. I pulled open the door and my heart thumped in my chest. Alex was standing there with a small duffel bag and a huge smile.

"Hi."

"I thought you weren't coming back until tomorrow night!" I smiled and stepped back so he could come in.

"I managed to get stuff done early, so hurried home." He dropped his bag and walked toward me.

"Is that why you were so tired last night?" He had snored at one point, but when I told him about it, he denied it.

"Maybe." He pulled the cloth out of my hands and threw it onto the entryway table. "It was worth it."

His hands wrapped around my waist and I melted into him. When his lips slid over mine hungrily, I returned his kiss with fervor, devouring his taste. He growled against me and lifted me in his arms so that my feet didn't touch the ground. There was no hesitation when he turned and started walking for the stairs.

"Now I know why you look so happy." Cathy's voice had me pulling my head away from Alex's. "No, no. Don't stop for me. I'll just eat this nasty pizza all by myself." The fake hurt in her voice made me roll my eyes. I looked over at her and laughed. There was flour all over her face and sticky dough clumped in her hair.

"Funny, huh? You don't look much better," Cathy pointed out.

I looked at Alex, who was still holding me off the ground, and realized I had rubbed flour on his face. "Oh no. I must look a mess!"

I wiggled and he set my feet back on the ground before kissing my nose. "I don't care."

"When did this happen?" Cathy leaned against the kitchen door frame. "And I can't believe you didn't tell me."

"Last weekend." Alex watched as I retrieved my towel and wiped at my face.

"So your big plan worked."

"Big plan?" I narrowed my eyes at him.

"Yes, it did." He smiled, completely unbothered.

"Oh, it was a doozy." She snorted. "Incredibly intricate and well thought out."

"Is that so?" I looked from her to him.

"Stick around as much as possible until you gave in." He shrugged.

"And it worked!" Cathy laughed.

I shook my head with a smile. It certainly had.

"Are you going to tell me why you're covered in goop?" Alex reached out and scooped a chunk from my hair.

"Pizza party." I led him to the kitchen.

"The pizza party from hell." He whistled. "Margie is going to have a heart attack."

I looked around and cringed. He was right—we had made a mess. "Yesh."

"You're lucky I'm a good cook." He moved past me and went to work. I looked over at Cathy, who was nodding her head.

"Sit! Talk." She patted one of the chairs at the island. "What happened?"

"Um." This wasn't really a talk I wanted to have with Alex's sister, especially not when he was listening in. "I just realized I was being dense."

"And what was your big clue?"

"Chadwick poked me."

Cathy threw her head back and laughed. "I'll have to remember that in case you decide to overthink things in the future."

"I need to tell him thank you." Alex winked at me over his shoulder. His hands were busy turning our sloppy mess into something familiar.

"I thought you left last weekend for Paris." Cathy grabbed some of the cheese from a bowl on the island and popped it in her mouth.

"I did. I left the next morning." Alex laughed while I blushed.

"Then you definitely owe Chadwick a thank-you." She shook her head. "And I'm leaving after dinner."

"But I invited you to stay the weekend!" I frowned.

"I have to go back in the morning anyway. And there's no way I'm staying here while you two act like horny teenagers." She winked at me. "I'll stay at D'Lynsal tonight."

"I can behave myself." I frowned.

"I can't." Alex didn't look up from what he was working on.

"Yech." Cathy grimaced. "Really, it's fine. You can make it up to me and come out with me in the city. I'm tired of it being a boys' club."

"Cathy, I hate clubs and bars." I shook my head. "I'll do anything else."

"Please?" She looked up at me with her big eyes and I almost caved.

"Hey! Stop that! No anime eyes."

Alex chuckled. "I thought Tabitha was still in town."

My stomach clenched at the name of his ex and I had to stomp on the jealousy. Who cared if she was at the palace? Alex was here in my kitchen.

"It's not the same. She's all over her new boyfriend."

"What about Kyle?" I narrowed my eyes. He was the person she normally went with to the clubs.

"That's who I'm talking about." Cathy frowned.

I reached over and grabbed her hand. No wonder she wanted someone to come out with her. It was obvious that even though she had thought she was being careful, she'd still ended up hurt.

"I just don't want to stop doing things because it's uncomfortable." She sighed. "Besides, you'll have Alex to keep the guys away."

"Samantha and I are keeping this quiet for now." I could see Alex's shoulders tense.

"Why?" Cathy narrowed her eyes at me.

"I just don't want the attention." I shrugged. "Or the pressure."

"We're just taking our time." Alex slipped the pizza into the oven before turning around.

"Oh." Cathy's mouth pulled to the side and I could see she thought it was a bad idea. "It won't stay quiet forever."

"We know." Alex shot me a look.

After dinner I called Becca and asked her to drive Cathy to Alex's home. Even though she'd only had one glass of wine, I didn't like the idea of her making the trip. I took my time cleaning the kitchen because I didn't want to leave a mess for Margie, but it took a lot of willpower. I wanted nothing more than to drag Alex up to my bedroom. I figured if I took care of cleaning up now I wouldn't have to worry about getting to it in the morning.

I was wiping off the island when Alex moved behind

me. He placed a hand on either side of me on the counter and nuzzled my neck, sending shivers over my body. When he pushed against me so I could feel how hard he was, my breathing picked up. He tugged my rubber band loose, letting my hair fall around my shoulders.

I leaned on the counter for traction so I could rub against him and was rewarded with a growl of pleasure. He pressed against me so I was almost bent over completely, his body bracketing mine. Pulling my hair to the side, he ran his lips over my neck and up to my ear.

"Are you expecting anyone else tonight?" His teeth tugged at my lobe.

"No." The word came out on a groan as he ground against me.

"Good." He slid his hand between me and the counter to undo my jeans. "Because I don't think we're going to make it upstairs."

His hand slipped into my pants and I moaned with desire. Pressed between him and the counter, I had nothing to do but enjoy the attention. My breaths were coming in pants and my knees were starting to feel weak. I moved my hips so that I was rubbing against him, and he groaned deep in his throat.

"I really like those jeans." He leaned forward to press a kiss to my neck. His free hand gripped my hip as he moved in a slow rhythm.

When he pulled away from me, I made a sound of disappointment. Thankfully he was just giving himself a little room and yanked my jeans down to my ankles. I gasped and started to turn, but he kept a hand on my back so I couldn't see what he was doing. When I heard the zipper of his pants, my breathing picked up and I wasn't sure if it was in nervousness or anticipation.

He moved his hands over my ass in appreciation, squeezing gently. I'd never been taken like this and I didn't know what to expect. When he reached around to massage me again, I groaned loudly. I was putty in his hands, weak with wanting.

"Is this okay?" He pressed against me so that I could feel the heat of his erection.

I nodded my head, unable to find my voice. His fingers continued to rub me until I was slick with need. He pushed at my opening and my breath caught. I froze and had to take a deep breath.

"Samantha?" I could hear the strain in his words.

"I'm okay." My voice sounded raspy so I swallowed and tried again. "I want you."

He pressed against me again, but this time didn't stop. Slowly he slid inch by inch inside me until I could feel his balls pressed against my swollen mound. He groaned something in Lilarian and I took a deep breath. It was different, but good. From this angle he filled me completely.

When he pulled back out, I gasped and then whimpered with his reentry. Soon my hips were rocking with him and I was moaning against the counter, my hot breath leaving little clouds of condensation on the cold stone.

"Alex." I groaned his name loudly as his thrusts sped up.

"I missed you." He slammed into me and I could feel the orgasm building to its peak. His thrusts came faster and faster until words were impossible. With one final push, he jerked inside of me and pleasure exploded over my body. My legs shook weakly and my breath came out in heavy pants.

"Missed you too."

TWENTY-NINE

A Prince on the Streets, a Freak in the Sheets?
—*THE GOSSIP CROWN*

"*I* THOUGHT WE WERE going to ride horses."
I twisted the reins in my hands. "This is not a horse.
This is a prehistoric beast." We had saddled some of
the horses from my stable, but they sure didn't feel like
"mine." I ran my hand over the mane of the horse I was
riding. Serenade was a gorgeous dappled stallion.

"You said you had ridden before." Alex laughed
from his perch. He was riding a black stallion named
Alto.

"Yes. Horses, not elephants." If I wasn't so nervous
I would have been extremely turned on by how sexy
and manly he looked sitting on a horse. It was completely unfair that he really did look like a prince while
on horseback.

"Elephant, horse. It's the same thing." He urged his
horse toward the trail.

"Not even if you squint," I muttered.

"Come on, scaredy cat. We only have so much day-
light left."

"Nag, nag, nag. What kind of king are you going to

be if all you do is nag?" He laughed loudly. "Besides, it was your idea to have breakfast in bed." I smiled just thinking about it. I had enjoyed my breakfast very much. Even if it had been cold by the time we got around to eating it.

"I didn't hear you complain." He looked back at me and smirked. "Do I need to come get you?"

"Pfft. No. I'm just letting you get a head start." I sneered. "I didn't want to make you look bad."

The truth was, I loved horses, but it had been years since I'd ridden one, and even then it had been with a guide. This was a little different. It was riding for real. Just me and a horse.

And Alex and his horse. Which were both waiting on us.

Taking a deep breath, I moved forward. Alex navigated the trail easily and I soon found my body moving in rhythm with the horse. In fact, once I eased up the horse seemed to relax and I barely had to give him any direction.

We moved around the lake at a leisurely pace and I could feel myself unwind with each step. I had missed being out in nature. Even during the Minnesota winters I would have carved out a little quiet time outside. No buildings, no walls, no people arguing on cell phones. Just me and nature. I took a deep breath and exhaled quietly. I had missed it.

I had needed it.

The trail opened up to a clearing along the lake's edge and Alex came to a stop. Hopping down, he tied his horse to a tree and walked to the water's edge. I managed to dismount without embarrassing myself and joined him. Leaning down, he picked a smooth stone out of the dirt before skipping it across the water.

"Not a skill of mine." I shook my head. "Dad spent

hours trying to teach me one day, but the rock always sinks."

"You just need a different teacher." Alex picked up a stone and ran his fingers over it before passing it to me. "Try this one. It's nice and smooth."

I took the stone but laughed. "It's no use. I'm terrible at it."

"Everyone can skip stones." He raised one eyebrow.

Shaking my head, I turned the rock over in my fingers before launching it out over the water. It seemed to hang in the air for just a moment before sinking into the water with a soft plunk.

"You're holding it wrong." Ducking down, he grabbed another rock and walked toward me. "Here, hold it between your fingers like this." He positioned the stone between my fingers.

"This is pointless, Alex." I smiled when he moved to stand behind me.

"Shh." He pulled my arm behind me, keeping my hand at waist height. "It's in the wrist."

Sighing, I focused on the water and what he was saying. This was never going to work, but I'd humor him. He stepped away from me and I took a deep breath before loosing the stone from my fingers. For half a second I thought it might work, but my hope was dashed with a loud splash. Turning to look at Alex, I shrugged.

"Again. Try flicking your wrist." He handed me another stone.

"Alex—"

"We're taking the day off, remember?" His eyes twinkled in the afternoon sun. "We've got time to skip some stones."

Looking back at the lake, I moved the rock into position and contemplated the water. Flick my wrist. I needed to flick my wrist. Biting my lip, I pulled my arm back before whipping it forward. At the last moment, I flicked my wrist just a little.

The stone seemed to glide over the water before barely touching the surface once and then twice. When it entered the water, I stood there with wide eyes. I had done it!

"I did it!" Turning, I smiled at Alex. "Holy shit, I did it!"

"Told you anyone could do it." Wrapping one arm around my shoulder, he kissed the top of my head.

"Let me go! I want to do it again!" I knelt down to find another rock while he laughed.

"Are you hungry? Margie packed us some food." He moved to the horses, but I stayed by the water.

"Sure." I turned the rock over in my fingers until it felt right. This time the stone went much further but didn't glide along the surface. Instead, it made a large splash that startled a nearby bird.

"Damn." I picked up another stone and tried again. That one never touched the water, but landed in a nearby bush. "I did it once. I can do it again."

"Eat; then skip stones." Alex handed me part of a turkey sandwich.

"Not yet." Frustrated, I glared at the water and took a bite of my sandwich. "I can do it again."

"I've created a monster. To think I was going to bring you out here and seduce you under the trees, but all you want to do is skip stones."

"Under the trees, huh?" That got my attention. "Haven't you had enough of me today?"

"Not possible." He pulled me against his chest, his tender kiss coaxing a sigh from my lips. His fingers undid the zipper of my jacket before sliding in along my waist.

When he tried to slide my jacket from my shoulders, I leaned back. "What about my sandwich?"

"We'll get you another one." Plucking it from my fingers, he tossed it into the woods before pushing my jacket off and pressing his mouth to my neck.

"Okay." I moaned when his hands slid up to cup my breasts. "But after this we eat and skip stones."

THE NEXT MORNING I woke up to the sound of Alex's gentle snoring. I opened my eyes to see him still sound asleep. I didn't want to wake him because I knew he was exhausted after his week in Paris. I couldn't believe he had worked so hard just so he could come back early.

I studied the planes of his face as he slept, committing them to memory. I didn't think I'd ever get tired of looking at him. What had surprised me over the last month had been how much I loved just being with him. I hadn't thought it would be possible to feel so comfortable with Alex, but I was quickly finding that I didn't know how I had lived so long without him. My phone beeped on the nightstand and I carefully dislodged his arm so I could turn to see who was calling.

When I realized it was my dad I rolled off the bed and tiptoed out of the room.

"Hello?"

"Hi, Sam." He sounded tired and I tried to figure out what time it was back home, but my mind was too foggy to do the math. I knew it was way too early for a phone call.

"What's wrong, Dad?" I went to the library and grabbed one of the blankets off the small sofa.

"The doctor wants me to push back my trip."

"Why?" I chewed on my nail, waiting for the bad news. There was no way it could be anything else.

"There was no change in the scan and they've put me

on a different medicine." He sounded so tired it made my heart clench.

"Then we need to get you over here even sooner."

"I want to wait. The medicine makes me feel pretty bad." He sighed. "They said it would take a little while for me to get used to it."

"Dad, why can't they try something else?" I shook my head angrily. "That's crazy! They need to change it." He didn't say anything for a while and I listened to his labored breathing. "Dad?"

"This is the best thing for me right now. Even Dr. Bielefeld thinks so."

"You've spoken to Dr. Bielefeld?" That made me feel better. "Is he working with your doctors in the States?"

"Yes. They contacted him when they got the scans back. I've spoken to him several times now." His voice was so strained.

"What are you doing up so early? You sound terrible."

"Gee, thanks, honey." He chuckled and for just a moment sounded like his normal self.

"I'm serious. Why are you calling me so early?"

"I wanted to catch you before your day started. I know how busy you are and didn't want to interrupt anything later."

"What does the medicine do? I mean, what's making you feel so bad?"

"Just makes me sick to my stomach." He sighed. "And I have a hard time sleeping."

"I'll come home." I rubbed at my cheek. "Chadwick can get me a flight tonight or tomorrow."

"Absolutely not," he snapped. I froze, surprised, because he wasn't one to raise his voice. "I'm coming there, remember?" His voice softened. "I just need to let the medicine get into my system good."

"I want to be there. I wouldn't have left if I'd known."

"I know." His tone made my eyebrows pull together. "It's okay. I didn't mean to upset you, but I knew you'd want to know."

"Why didn't Patricia tell me? I talked to her yesterday."

"I wanted to tell you." He heaved a sigh. "I knew you would be upset."

"Damn right, I'm upset."

"Don't be. It's just part of the deal. Hey, do you have any pictures of Patricia's room? She was asking me about it yesterday."

"I can take some. I think she'll like it." I stood up and paced the length of the library. "Nice change of subject there. I'm still worried."

"Don't be." I heard him moving and realized that he must be in his bed. "I'm going to try to sleep. I'll call you soon."

"I miss you." I took a deep breath.

"Miss you too, baby."

I hung up the phone and stared out the library window for a minute. Having Dad so far away broke my heart. Especially with everything else going on. Taking a deep breath, I decided I'd call Dr. Bielefeld tomorrow morning to see if we had any options for getting here sooner. And if there weren't, I'd blow everything else off to get home.

Using the blanket as a wrap, I tiptoed back down the hall to my room. Alex hadn't moved, so I climbed back into bed and curled around him. His mouth pulled up into a smile and he wrapped an arm around my waist.

"Good morning."

"Morning." I closed my eyes and breathed in his scent.

"Everything okay?" He shifted so he could see my face.

"Dad called. His scan wasn't good and they've changed his medicine." I took a deep breath. "He wants to wait to come over, see if his body can get used to the medicine first. It makes him sick."

"We could get a flight and go to him."

I looked up at him, my heart bouncing a little. The fact that he had included himself in the plans made me warm all over. Brushing my fingers over his face, I kissed him softly.

"What's that for?" He looked down into my eyes.

"For being you." I cuddled closer to him. "He doesn't want me to go over there. I think he's worried that if I do, he won't ever get to come here."

"Is it that bad?" He rubbed a hand over my hair.

"He didn't say so, but I'm worried. I'm going to call the doctor tomorrow and see what he thinks." I sighed. "Dad sounded really rough."

"Why don't we do something fun today? Take your mind off it until tomorrow." He propped himself up on his elbow.

"What do you have in mind?"

"Come to D'Lynsal and I'll introduce you to my birds." He raised an eyebrow. "Spend a little time outside. It's supposed to be nice today."

"That sounds great." I sat up and turned to look at him. "Can we go now?"

"Sure."

D'Lynsal Manor was less than an hour from Rousseau. I fiddled with the radio as we drove, amused by the wide range of music. Alex played tour guide and pointed out some of the local landmarks we passed. Becca and Duvall were in a car behind us, which helped make it feel like it was just us.

When we pulled up to D'Lynsal, Alex waved at the gate guard and we were let in. If I had thought Rousseau was breathtaking, it was nothing compared to Alex's home. Instead of a house that looked a bit like a castle, this *was* an actual castle.

"Wow." I leaned forward in my seat as we pulled up. A turret along one of the corners had arched windows and a flag flying on top. Much like Rousseau, there was a circle driveway with a garden in the center. Unlike the home that was now mine, there were a lot of extra buildings nearby.

"What's that building?" I pointed at the one closest to the house.

"The people who work here have rooms." He parked at the front door. "Then there are a few storage buildings and work sheds. The stables are behind the house."

A butler opened the front door for us with a bow. I realized that here would be a lot more people who might possibly sell us out to the press. I stepped away from the hand Alex had on my back and smiled at the people who greeted us. I tried to ignore the look Alex shot me and focused on seeing everything around me.

The house was amazing. The stone walls from outside were also inside and I was reminded of a fancy hunting lodge. Where my home was large, I could still find all the rooms with a quick search. Here, I had no idea where a kitchen would be, much less a bathroom. I stood in the grand room and turned in a circle, taking it all in. Alex watched me as I surveyed the splendor that was his life.

"You grew up here?"

"We have a few other places, but most of my childhood was spent here and the palace." He motioned for me to follow him up a large staircase. "There is a smaller family area upstairs. These areas are more like a pass-through for us, unless we're having a special event."

I thought about the tiny house I had lived in with my mother before she married my dad. The house we had moved into together was larger and newer, but still nothing fancy. There had been signs all over the place that it was a home; dings on the walls, a little dust in the corners. Despite all the family portraits hanging along the wall of Alex's home, it felt impersonal and I couldn't imagine being a child here.

"I bet you never got to watch TV with dinner."

"Not true. My grandmother used to let us eat with those little tables in front of the sofa." He smiled at me over his shoulder. "She was addicted to *The Price Is Right*."

"You guys get *The Price Is Right* here?" I laughed.

"I think they were reruns, but she didn't care."

He showed me the family room upstairs and the small kitchen. There was a separate TV room, which amused me. In the States the family room was typically where everyone gathered to watch shows or movies. When he showed me his room, I was ready to be wowed. He opened the door and stepped inside. There was a large four-poster bed along one wall, but the rest of the room felt very modern.

"I'm jealous." I looked around.

"Why?"

"There's not a stitch of wallpaper in here."

He laughed and pulled me toward the bathroom. "Wait until you see the tub."

"That's a pool." He was right. I coveted the tub.

He laughed as we left his room and headed outside. I was so excited to see his birds I practically jogged down the stairs. He led me around the stables, which housed ten horses, and around to the mews. The cages were much more elegant than what I'd worked with at school, but it was familiar all the same.

The hawks were gorgeous. Alex retrieved gloves for us and brought me a bird.

"What's her name?" I looked over her feathers and feet.

"Tweety."

I looked over at him and smiled. "Tweety?"

"Remember the little boy you met the first night? Leo?"

"Ah. He named Tweety?"

"I named her Talon, he disagreed. You can see who won."

I snickered. Remembering how Alex had looked with the kids that night convinced me Leo hadn't had to put up much of a fight.

"Want to take them out?" He closed the mew and stepped out with his own hawk. "Tweety and Sylvester work together really well."

"By all means." I looked at Tweety. "Let's see what you've got."

We spent hours out with the birds and I could have stayed longer. There was something spectacular about watching the birds fly, their wings spread as they rode the currents and searched for game.

"My father loved birds." Alex watched as the birds swept the area. "I can't remember a time when we didn't own any."

"There's a freedom that comes with flying." I looked over at him.

"Exactly. Nothing ties them down unless they want it to." He looked over at me. "I think that's part of the reason he was so fond of them. They could go wherever they wanted, whenever they wanted."

"Did he feel trapped?"

"No more than anyone feels trapped." He shrugged.

"Everyone is tied down in some way. Work, family, medical problems. It's what you make of it. That's why it's so important to surround yourself with the things that make you happy. If you have a bad day at work but get to come home to a woman you love or your favorite hobby, the rest doesn't matter as much."

I thought about what he was saying as I watched the birds. Was that why he had kept after me even though I tried to keep him at arm's length?

Someone with food actually drove a small golf-cart-type vehicle out to where we were when lunchtime came around, so after seeing to the birds we spent some time enjoying the warmer weather while we ate. He told me about his family and described holidays with nobles running around. It was obvious that his family was much closer with some of the nobles than others, but there was still a very tight-knit feel.

"Do any of the nobles have regular jobs? Or do you all focus on royal tasks?" I tucked my legs under me on the blanket that had been spread out and picked up a carrot.

"A lot of us have jobs on the side. Daniel has a degree in marketing, but he uses it more for the family than anything else. I believe he does take on contract work from time to time. When not drunk, Kyle is working on a business degree, but I have no idea if he'll ever use it. Mother doesn't send him on assignments for the crown, so it would be best if he figures out something to do with his life."

"What about Cathy? She's starting school soon."

"Cathy is going for a history degree. She's wanted to work in a museum since she was little." He leaned back on the blanket and looked up at the sky. "The problem is that she'll never be able to have a full-time job."

"Why not?" I lay down next to him but kept my distance. His hand snaked out and wrapped around my fingers.

"She's too close to the throne. Until I have children, Max and Cathy are the next heirs and are required to speak for the crown."

"That's such a foreign thought to me. It's like you guys aren't real people, just objects." I frowned. "What about after you have kids? Will she be able to take a job then? And Max is away at school now. Will he be able to do anything with his degree?"

"She might, but will most likely find a charity to focus on. The crown can't keep up with every single thing required of them and the other nobles are counted on to help. Max and Cathy will always be a part of the day-to-day operations of the monarchy. Going to school is just a chance for us to live a little before we are immersed in the running of things." He turned his head and looked at me. "There are lots of perks, though. It's not all work. We don't have to worry about as much as the English royal family, which means we're not as spread thin."

"Will I have to do things for the queen?" I knew I had responsibilities to the Rousseau village, but hadn't thought about much more than that.

"It depends. She tends to pick and choose carefully." He smiled. "I think it's reasonable to assume she'll have some things you'd be perfect for."

"Hm." I looked back up at the clouds and wondered if that would change if our relationship did go public. When I thought about all the people who would follow my every move it made me nauseous. Alex was worth it. More than worth it, but it was still something I was going to need to ease into. And there was a big part of me that worried what we had might not last. Then I'd be left to pick up the pieces of my very publicly broken heart.

"You've got a while before you have to worry about it. She can't ask you to take on any official duties until you've gone through the reinstatement ceremony." He squeezed my fingers.

"Good to know." I started to pull my hand away, but he tightened his grip.

"Samantha, you don't have to worry about people here. They won't say anything." He rolled over to his side and propped his head up. "Most of the employees here are generational. Their families have worked for my family for years. In a lot of ways they're like extended family."

I bit my lip and looked up at him. "I'm making this difficult. I know it. But . . ."

"You're scared." He cupped my cheek. "I do understand. I'm willing to wait until you're ready, but that doesn't mean I have to like it."

"Doesn't it bother you?" I frowned. "That people will speculate about us?"

"People always speculate about couples." He laughed.

"But not on the front page of the papers!"

"That'll calm down. Eventually they'll find something else to focus on." He shrugged.

"I'm just not used to it." I sighed. "I'll get there. I promise."

Slowly, so that I had time to move, he leaned forward and brushed his lips across mine. My body's response to him was immediate and I forgot about who might be watching. He continued to tease me with feather-soft kisses until I nipped at his bottom lip. That did the trick and he deepened our kiss. I ran my hands through his hair, enjoying how warm it felt on my fingers.

When he finally pulled away, I snuggled close to

him and he chuckled. "I should kiss you more often. It makes you much more agreeable."

"Shut it and cuddle me."

The rest of the weekend was spent with the birds or learning more about the area. Alex was good at keeping me distracted, but the closer it came to Monday, the more anxious I became.

THIRTY

A Royal Rendezvous?
—*L.A. DAILY*

"H E STILL HASN'T returned my call."

I shoved my cell phone in my pocket and glared out the car window.

"Samantha, it's been two hours and Dr. Bielefeld was in surgery." Chadwick lowered his paper and looked over at me. There was a picture of Cathy on the page he was reading. "I know you're worried, but give the man a break. He can't run out of the operating room to talk."

"I know." I sighed. "Dad was really snappy this morning. I'm starting to think it's the medicine."

"Yes, I've heard that can happen with certain prescriptions." Chadwick folded up the paper. "He will call you. You can't do anything right now, so focus on why we're in town."

"Meetings with politicians." I leaned back in my seat. "This is going to be awesome."

"Deep breath. It's only for an hour and then you get to go home and wear jeans again."

"And sit through Lilarian lessons." I picked at my jacket.

"You'll do great."

I met with the local council of leaders, listening to what all they did and how they thought I might be able to help. It was an interesting morning and the breakfast was delicious. Simone, the local mayoral figure, kept everyone on track and we actually got a great deal accomplished. When I was leaving, she pulled me to the side to thank me for coming.

"No, I enjoyed seeing how everything works. I know I can't petition the parliament on behalf of the people yet, but if there are any cases you can think of, let me know. I have time to look into them, even if I can't do much yet."

"I like that. You'll be able to dive right in when the time comes."

"I like to be prepared." I shook her hand.

"Wonderful. I hope you don't mind my bringing this up, but I realize you might not have thought of this." She took a step closer, still holding my hand. "I know you've been worried about how the locals would feel about your coming home and I thought of something that might make you feel better. The royal families that represent the different provinces typically hold open houses or parties for the locals at least once a year. It encourages conversation and makes the villagers feel appreciated. Once you're reinstated, it might be nice to consider holding one."

"I'll look into it. Thank you."

That afternoon was spent with a nice woman named Mrs. Rewell who refused to speak anything but Lilarian to me. I thought about hiding in the blanket closet but Chadwick kept careful watch. By the time she left I could sing the alphabet easily and count to twenty. I felt like I had run a marathon.

Alex had gone back to the city to work on a few projects that required his attention. He hadn't wanted to leave until I'd spoken with Dr. Bielefeld, but I insisted. I didn't want him to put off things that were important just because I was worried.

By the time dark fell, I was in a very bad mood. Not only had the doctor not returned my call, but I couldn't find my e-reader. When my phone rang, I didn't even check to see who it was.

"Yeah?" I pulled stuff out of my carry-on bag, hoping I'd stuck the e-reader in there for some reason.

"Hi to you too." Alex laughed. "Bad day?"

"Yes. The doctor never called me back and a very nice lady spent three hours refusing to speak any English." I shook out my jacket, but still no e-reader.

"I'm sorry Dr. Bielefeld didn't call you back." The rumble of his voice went a long way to soothing me. "Something important must've come up."

"Probably. I just want to know more about my dad's scan and medicine." I sat on my bed and sighed. "Just a frustrating day."

"I can tell." He was quiet for a minute. "Did you learn any Lilarian?"

"A little. I guess she's doing her job."

"Well, that's good." He sounded distracted.

"What's going on?"

"Eh, it can wait."

"Oh no. Just get it out of the way." I leaned back on the bed. Today was not going well.

"I don't want to upset you."

"What is it?" My stomach clenched.

"Someone published a picture of me at your house."

"That's not so bad."

"Well, they also titled it 'Royal Rendezvous.'" I could hear the worry in his voice so I tried to curb my immediate response. "Samantha?"

"It's okay, Alex." I chewed on my lip.

"I can hear in your voice that it's not okay."

"It's fine."

"Oh, now I know it's bad. No matter what language a woman says those two words in, it means bad things."

I chuckled weakly. "Seriously, it's okay. I mean, they don't know anything for sure. Maybe it'll just blow over."

"It might."

"I think I'm going to call it an early night." I closed my eyes.

"Okay. I'll talk to you soon."

"Good night."

The next morning my phone rang during breakfast and I almost dropped it in my rush to answer.

"Hello?"

"May I speak with Duchess Rousseau?" an accented voice asked politely.

"This is Samantha."

"Ah, this is Dr. Bielefeld. I apologize for not returning your call yesterday. I had an emergency pop up."

"That's understandable. I just had a few questions about my father. He said that his scan hadn't shown any changes and he was taking new medicines." I got up and walked outside. "He seems pretty miserable."

"Yes, I have his file here. Mr. Thompson's scan didn't show much change, so after speaking with his physician in the States we decided to try a medicine that is a lot more powerful. He's likely experiencing some side effects."

"What kind of side effects?"

"Nausea and insomnia are the most common, but he may also experience a change in mood and temperament."

"I believe he's dealing with all of those." I sat down

on the steps leading from the kitchen door to the yard. "Is this medicine necessary?"

"Duchess, I wouldn't have suggested it if I didn't believe so."

"Doctor, how bad is this? I thought he was doing better."

"Cancer often leaves us scratching our heads, but we're doing everything we can. Once Mr. Thompson is up to traveling, I'll be making a trip to Rousseau to examine him personally."

"I'm really worried." I said the words quietly. "I thought he was doing better and this is a bit of a blow."

"Samantha, I can only tell you so much. Your father's cancer was never an easy case because it went so long without detection. At this point, we just need to try to keep it from spreading."

"I understand." I gripped the phone tightly. "Will we be able to get him over here soon?"

"I'm supposed to have a phone conference with his doctors tomorrow. I'll let you know if there is anything I can tell you."

"Thank you."

I sat there on the steps and looked out over the yard. The main reason I had decided to come out here and accept my title was so I could get health care for my father. Now I was over here and he was too sick to travel. I leaned forward, rested my elbows on my knees, and took a deep breath. I was here now and there were some things that had turned out pretty good. I'd made some friends. Cathy was the little sister I never had, and it felt as if Chadwick had always been a fixture in my life. And then there was Alex.

Alex was by far the best part of all this mess. Even with all the media and scary pressure of what it meant to be in a relationship with a prince, he was worth it. In the middle of all this mess, he made me feel normal. We spoke every day and I missed him while he was gone. I missed him a lot. Taking a deep breath, I stood up and tucked my phone in my pants. There was no going back at this point. The scariest part was that I wasn't sure I wanted to.

Mrs. Rewell spent the majority of the rest of the week working on my lessons. By Friday I could manage most of the phrases I would need for the ceremony. There had been speculation about me and Alex, but no one brought it up. In fact, the last time I'd seen a picture of Alex in the paper, the reporter had been speculating that Alex was secretly dating Adriane again. It had hurt, but I knew better than to give it any credit. Alex had attended a charity event that Adriane had set up, but had asked me to come with him. In fact, he asked me to go to every event he attended. I was the one who kept saying no. I just wasn't ready to deal with the media explosion that would happen when it was official. I refused to look at the papers after that, and even Chadwick had stopped reading them when I was around.

When Alex came that weekend, he didn't bring up that I had turned down his invitations. Instead we spent time in his giant tub and relaxed. Well, relaxed some. I really liked his tub and not just because of the jets, though those were nice.

"You know, when you picture having sex in a bathtub, it always seems romantic and erotic, but then when you actually attempt it, there's nowhere to put your legs. And you slosh water over the top." I crawled onto his lap and wrapped my arms around his neck.

"Is that so?" He ran his wet hands up over my back.

"Mm-hm." I tilted my head back while he trailed kisses over my collarbone and down to my breasts. "Not this one though."

"Why is that?" His words were muffled because he was paying so much attention to my nipple.

"Because it's so—" He gripped my thighs and lifted me so I could slide down over his thick shaft.

"So what?" His teeth caught my earlobe and tugged gently.

"Big." I moaned as he shifted under me.

The rest of our conversation consisted of nothing more than the sound of our lovemaking. His growls of desire answered my moans of pleasure. When we finally fell over the edge, it was a blinding sensation that left me gasping.

Later that night we collapsed in his bed, the sheets tangled around our legs.

"I've never had this." Alex trailed his fingers over my arm.

"Never had what?" I lifted my head so I could see his face.

"Being able to relax." He sighed. "With anyone else I would have taken us away somewhere more private— to a chalet or apartment. I never let someone stay at D'Lynsal."

Jealousy flashed over me and my muscles tensed. Then the rest of his words sank in. I was here at D'Lynsal, he felt safe letting me into his home.

"What happened with Melissa?" I forced my hand on his chest to unclench and waited for his response. We hadn't talked about his ex or the photos. For me, it was in the past, but maybe he needed to tell me, to clear the air.

He shifted under my hand and grunted. "She wanted more than I did."

I didn't say anything, just waited for him to clarify. The thought of her brought the images I had seen on the Internet to mind and made me want to break things. It was an irrational feeling—she was the past. I had my past too, and thankfully it hadn't ended up in the tabloids.

"I met her at a fashion show. She was modeling for a line Cathy loves and we hit it off. I wasn't looking for anything serious, just someone to spend time with." His hand wrapped around my arm. "It wasn't like with you. It was just—"

"It's okay. I get it." And I did. I'd had my moments of lust as well.

"When she started insisting on more, I pulled away. I told her I wasn't looking for that and said we should stop seeing each other." His hand tightened a little and I could feel the tension coursing through his body. "She didn't take it well. I wouldn't answer her messages or go anywhere I thought she might turn up. She started harassing Cathy, which upset my sister greatly. Melissa threatened to commit suicide." He paused for a minute and I could feel the anger vibrate under his skin. "Cathy was a mess and felt like it was her fault if she didn't do something. I hadn't even known Melissa was hounding her until she told me about that message."

"Oh my God." I closed my eyes, imagining poor Cathy and Alex. Sweet Cathy would have been distraught and Alex . . . he would have felt obligated to make sure she was okay.

"I contacted her to see if she was really unstable, but she wasn't. Not suicide unstable, that is. She was just trying to find a way to get back in touch with me and played on Cathy's conscience. That's when I found out about the photos." His chest rose under me and he let out a heavy breath. "It was not a good day."

"I can't imagine how I would have reacted."

"She seemed to think that if she sold the photos I would have to marry her." He let out an unamused snort. "What she did was force me to get a restraining order. My family was very supportive, thankfully. Even Max, who hates all things to do with the media, took the stage and picked up appearances for a while."

"What an idiot." Fury bubbled under my skin. "Who would want to marry someone like that? No one marries the skank that puts out sex photos."

He chuckled and pulled me tight. "She thought I would have to marry her to calm the gossip. After she released the photos she sent my lawyer an e-mail, telling him that we could work together to make it seem like we, as a couple, had been violated—not just me. That everyone would feel sorry for us and it would be good publicity."

"What a crazy bitch." My jaw clenched and I sat up, looking down at Alex. "You deserve so much more than that." Anger made my voice tight. I wanted to beat Melissa's face in for abusing Cathy's sweet nature and betraying Alex's trust.

Looking up at me, he touched my cheek. "I hope so."

I covered his fingers with mine and warmth filled his gaze. I didn't say it, didn't need to, but I would never do anything to hurt Alex or his family. I would go to war for them and fight anyone who would try to harm them. In such a short period of time, they had become mine. And I would do anything for those people I considered mine.

And Alex would do the same for me. I had no doubts. Was that love?

"I hated knowing that you would see those pictures." His eyes grew stone hard. "That they would always be floating out there on the Internet."

"We all have a past, Alex." I sighed and laced my fingers with his. "Don't let it haunt your future."

He pulled me back down on his chest and I curled

against him. The feel of my skin against his had quickly become my safe haven—my home.

"Are you staying?" His fingers ran over the skin of my back and I sighed in contentment.

"Do you want me to?"

"Yes." There was no hesitation to the reply.

"Then I'll stay as long as you want." I pressed a kiss to his jaw and snuggled closer. The nights I spent with Alex were always the best and sleep came easily. Being with him quieted my anxiety and the constant worry. I almost didn't hear what he said next.

"Forever." He mumbled the word against my hair. "Stay forever."

My heart did a little dance and I smiled as I cuddled even closer to him. Alex had wiggled his way into my heart despite my best efforts, and I couldn't be happier about it. Who would have guessed that the day he blocked my way into the library, he'd also changed the entire course of my life?

The following week was much the same. No news about Dad, but he did seem to be adjusting to the medicine. He wasn't as grumpy and Patricia said he was finally keeping food down. Dr. Bielefeld hadn't called me with any more information, but his assistant had sent me a package of potential treatments to look over. I also spent a lot of time with Simone. We went over cases from local families who had issues with land or tax problems, and I wrote my first check for charity after seeing a home destroyed by fire. I had folders full of notes and names. Chadwick and I spent several evenings researching computer programs that were easy and efficient to use. I needed a filing system and while I preferred to take notes by hand, I wasn't fond of the idea of having eight hundred file cabinets.

I found that I actually enjoyed the problem-solving

aspect of my new job. It was work, but it gave me something constructive to do. The brightest spot of the week was Jess's call to tell me Bert had proposed. My heart had felt much lighter after listening to her squealing. When I told her she should wait to go dress shopping until she came to visit, I thought my eardrums would explode. Not only was she excited about shopping in Europe, she immediately assumed it meant I was going too. I didn't have the heart to tell her no, so I decided I'd just suck it up and look for a dress with her.

It wasn't until Friday arrived that I started to feel blue. I'd stayed so busy I'd managed to not worry too much. Unfortunately, Chadwick was pretty strict about keeping my weekends free. He felt I deserved time off just like everyone else. Normally that would be a great thing, but Alex had called to let me know he couldn't come back this time. He was attending a formal dinner at the palace and wouldn't have time to make it here and back.

"Why don't you go do something? Call Cathy." Chadwick looked at me over lunch. "You need to think about something else."

"Are you sick of me?" Not that I'd fault him for it. I was being grumpy. I stood up and put my plate in the sink. Margie was getting used to the idea of us eating in the kitchen and I was getting used to her cooking everything.

"I'm sick of you looking so frustrated." He threw his napkin on the counter. "Your dad wants you to stay here, but you feel like you should go to him. You miss Alex, but don't want anyone to know you're together. It's like you're trying to torture yourself."

"I am not!" Margie tsked under her breath while she wrapped up the leftovers, and I frowned. "You think I'm being stupid too?"

"Of course I don't think you're being stupid. I think

you're afraid to see the good." She set the plate she was holding in the refrigerator.

"What do you mean?"

"The man you love loves you just as much." Her back was to me, so she didn't see the look on my face.

"Close your mouth, Samantha." Chadwick rolled his eyes. "You're the only person who doesn't realize you're in love with him."

"How would you know I was in love before I did?" I crossed my arms and glared at him.

"Because we're not the ones living it. It's easier to see when you're not wrapped up in it yourself."

"Speaking of being wrapped up in things. How are you and Daniel?"

"Nice subject change. And we're okay. His sister, Adriane, is helping with his parents." He leaned back in his chair. "I don't think he understood how much it upset me until I set an ultimatum."

"So you're working things out?"

"We're trying. Instead of talking about it, he's actually taken steps." He smiled. "Alex told him that the crown stood behind him and they wouldn't put up with any prejudice."

I smiled. Alex and I had talked about the predicament Daniel was in with his family. It made me happy to know that he had made an official move to back his friend.

"So, are you pushing me out of the house so you can go see your boyfriend?" I raised an eyebrow and smirked.

"I certainly wouldn't complain . . ."

"Okay. I'll call Cathy. She's been bugging me nonstop to go out with her." I didn't want to go to the clubs, but I had told her I would and this gave me an excuse to see Alex as well.

THIRTY-ONE

President Gregory Visits Lilaria
—*LILARIAN DAILY*

$\mathcal{C}$ATHY WAS WAITING for me at the palace. When I got there, she grabbed my garment bag out of my hands and made a beeline for the guest room that I'd used last time. I'd shooed Chadwick away, promising I would be fine.

I wanted to surprise Alex, so hadn't told him I was coming. He should still be in a meeting, but I was hoping that I'd be able to drag him with us later. Even if there wasn't going to be any PDA, I'd at least like to spend the time with him. The door to his room was open as I walked down the hallway and I hurried my steps. His meeting must've finished early.

He was sitting at his desk with his laptop open and a stack of papers. I watched him for a minute, enjoying his look of concentration before I knocked on the door frame.

"Samantha?" He stood up and crossed the room in quick strides.

"Hey." I stepped into his room and pushed the door shut.

He wrapped his arms around me immediately and I sighed into his kiss. It had been a long week without him.

"What are you doing here?"

"I promised Cathy I'd go out with her and figured that I'd get to surprise you and make her happy at the same time." I ran a hand over his cheek and the five-o'clock shadow there.

"You came to the palace to see me?" He tilted my chin up. "I know you don't want to go to the club."

"I missed you." It was the truth. The club had been an excuse to come be with him.

"I missed you too." He leaned down and kissed me once more. "But it's a lot harder to keep secrets here."

"We'll just have to be careful." I stepped away from him. "Besides, I'm not going to be sitting around waiting on you. I have to go to the club tonight." I tried to look excited. "In fact, your sister is probably in my room right now going through the stuff I packed."

"You're going tonight?" He glanced down at his watch. "I have to finish up some paperwork, but maybe I can catch up."

"I think it's supposed to be a girls' night out." I laughed.

"Well, I'll come over and tell you bye before you leave." He grimaced. "I really do have a lot of paperwork to catch up on."

"Sounds good. Now I need to go before she decides my clothes aren't good enough."

"Go." He swatted my ass as I turned around and I looked at him, shocked. He chuckled and winked at me. "Don't be surprised if I sneak in your room later tonight."

"I'm counting on it."

I'd been right. Cathy was going through my clothes, but she hadn't tried to find something else for me to wear. In fact, she was so in love with the dress I'd brought, she was looking up the designer on my laptop.

"Well, help yourself," I teased. The dress was risqué, but the high heels I brought to wear with it made me the most nervous.

"Who picked that out?"

"Why do you assume someone else picked it out?" She just stared at me. "Jess."

"That's your friend who just got engaged?" She tapped her chin. "She has a good eye. Is she going to do her dress shopping when she visits?"

"Yep. I'm sure she wouldn't mind if you come with us." In fact, Jess would think it was a hoot to have a princess helping her decide.

"That sounds like fun!" Cathy was already dressed for the night. Her long hair was pulled up and she was wearing a sexy, but appropriate, short blue dress. "Get ready! We don't want the VIP section to fill up before we get there."

"I thought it was better to make an entrance." I grabbed the dress from the hanger and slid it on. Once I had wiggled it into place, I touched up my makeup and went out to get my shoes.

"Oh, we'll be making an entrance." She whistled.

I pulled on the heels and looked at myself in the full-length mirror. You could see the necklace Alex had given me through the slit in the front. I ran my fingers through my hair so it had that tousled look and turned toward her for inspection.

"Do I pass?"

"I'd say so." She nodded in approval. "But we need to test it out first."

Grabbing my hand, she pulled me down the hall to Alex's room. He was back at his desk working when she barged in with me in tow.

Alex looked up and froze. His eyes ran over me hungrily. "When are you leaving?"

"Now," Cathy responded. "I just wanted you to know what you would be missing out on."

"Oh, I'm not going to be missing out on anything." He leaned back in his chair, his eyes locked on me. "I'll meet you there."

"I thought you had paperwork." I smirked.

"There's no way you're going without me in that dress."

"Then you better hurry up." Cathy grabbed my hand again and pulled me toward the door. "We'll see you there."

I rolled my eyes at her. She was a handful and I'd agreed to go out with her. There was a limo out front instead of one of the normal cars. Becca was present as usual and I knew better than to complain. There was no way we would be able to go to such a public place without a guard.

"You'll love this place. The lounge is above the main floor, but there is plenty of dancing room. And the owner is more than happy to help us if we need to sneak out."

"Why would we need help sneaking out?"

"If the press gets too rowdy. Not that I think we'll have any issues." Cathy smiled. "This is going to be fun! I never liked Tabitha and now that she and Kyle are together, it's miserable."

"What happened? Kyle seemed to have his sights set on you."

"I told him no." She sighed. "The serious no. Not the flirty one."

I wasn't sure if I was following her, but I let her keep talking.

"So he moved on?"

"In about two point one seconds. He told me to make a decision, I did, and he left with Tabitha." She looked down at her nails. "I wish it didn't bother me so much."

"He was your friend." I shrugged. "It may have been based on the wrong stuff, but he was the person you spent time with and now he's gone. That makes sense."

"You're right. I've been trying to figure out why I've been upset. I mean, I never wanted more than friendship. I'm not sure I even wanted that much with him."

"You just wanted a friend." I sighed. "I get that."

We pulled up in front of the club and my heart raced at the sight of all the people. A bouncer opened the door and helped us out. There was no waiting in line, no showing ID or paying a cover charge. We were allowed right in and a hostess took us up to the VIP lounge.

The club was nice, but underneath all the shiny surfaces was the same thing you find in every club. Loud music, alcohol, and people needing to let off steam. It wasn't that I was against any of those things, but when you put them together, it often had ugly results. Like waking-up-next-to-Jabba-the-Hutt kind of results. Or being groped by a man wearing a bow tie and lavender slacks. Not that either had happened to me. Okay, bow-tie-loving groper had happened, but I'd never drunk enough to mistake Jabba the Hutt for Brad Pitt.

The VIP box was full. Kyle was busy making out with a redhead I assumed was Tabitha and several other people were dancing in the middle of the room. Becca had followed us up the stairs but stopped just inside the door.

"What do you want to drink?" Cathy pulled me to the bar.

"Cosmo." I didn't plan on doing anything but sipping the drink.

Cathy ordered our drinks and then pulled two chairs together. She introduced me to the people closest to us, always careful to use my full title. I was called the American duchess more times than I could count. At first the music had been annoying, but I was getting used to it.

Cathy had been pulled out on the floor by one of the guys she'd introduced, and his friend asked me if I wanted to dance.

"I think I'm going to sit this one out." I smiled and then looked away, hoping he would go. Instead he pulled up the seat next to me.

"How are you enjoying Lilaria?" He leaned close and I realized he was trying to look down my dress.

"It's great. I love all the purple trees and pink leaves."

"Yeah." He was so focused on my cleavage he hadn't heard a word I said.

"What's your name again?" I leaned away from him a little more.

"Gregory." He licked his lips and edged forward. "I'm the Baron of Dushner."

"That's nice." I looked away from him and wondered if this guy was for real.

"You should come out sometime."

"I'll keep that in mind." I kept my response short, hoping he would catch a clue.

"Would you like another drink?"

"No, I'd rather not."

"If you're worried about getting home, you could stay at my apartment here in the city." He looked down my dress again and I felt my temper snap. I'd been polite Samantha the entire time I'd been in Lilaria, but this asshat was pushing the wrong buttons.

"Eyes up here, buddy."

"You don't wear a dress like that unless you want to be looked at." He reached out and ran a finger over my knee.

"The dress isn't for you." I slapped his hand away. "And unless you want broken fingers, you better keep your hands to yourself."

"I'm just trying to get to know the new duchess." He raised an eyebrow. "Or are you only interested in princes?"

"I'm interested in men." I stood up. "Not slugs."

I looked around for Cathy but didn't see her anywhere. Taking a deep breath, I walked toward the bar. If nothing else I could order a soda or bottled water until she showed back up. My phone vibrated in the tiny purse I was carrying and I pulled it out, thinking it might be her.

"Where are you?"

"Sam?" Patricia's voice made me freeze in place.

"Hey. It's me. I'm sorry I thought you were someone else." I put a finger in my other ear. "Are you okay?"

"Can you talk?" She sounded tired.

"Hold on." I looked around for somewhere quiet but didn't see anything. Becca wasn't standing at the stairs, so couldn't ask her either. I took the steps down and found a bathroom where the music was much more muted. "I can hear you now. What's wrong?"

"It's your dad, sweetheart." I knew it was bad for her to be calling me, but my heart still stopped.

"What's happened?" My throat tightened. "Is he—"

"No! No, but it's not good." I could hear the strain in her voice. "It's worse than we knew."

"I don't understand. Where is he?" Panic filled my chest and I saw one of the girls look at me in the mirror.

"Sam, I didn't know it was this bad. He never let us

go in with him to the appointments, remember?" Her voice choked up and she took a minute before continuing. "He's at the hospital. I couldn't wake him up."

"He's dying?" My voice came out on a sob and I covered my mouth with my free hand. I was standing in the bathroom at a club while my father was dying in a hospital.

"Yes, baby. I think he knew but didn't want us to worry."

"He knew and didn't tell us?" I whispered the words. "Why would he do that?"

"I can only guess he didn't want us to spend all our time focused on him."

"I'm coming. I'll have to get a flight, but I'll leave as soon as I can." I dragged the back of my hand across my nose, and the girl that had looked at me handed me some tissue. I mumbled a thank-you as she left but wasn't really paying attention. I needed to go.

"Okay." She sniffed. "I'm sorry, sweetheart. I just didn't know."

"It's okay, Patricia. I'll call you soon." I hung up the phone and took a couple of deep breaths. It didn't help. The tears running down my cheeks wouldn't stop. How had I not known it was this bad? Why did I leave him?

I turned on the sink and splashed water over my face. I needed to get out of here—needed to get to the airport. Rubbing my shaking, wet hands on my dress, I left the bathroom and shoved my way through the crowd. Someone elbowed me and I tripped but got right back up and kept going. The bouncer at the door said something, but I didn't hear him. There was too much noise in the club. Too much noise in my head.

I practically fell out the door and into the line of people waiting outside. Our car was gone of course, so I looked for a cab. Reporters had gathered outside, the bright flashes of their cameras blinding me as I tried to decide which way to go.

"Samantha! Duchess Rousseau!"

"Rousseau! Look here!"

"Are you upset? Did someone do something?"

"Samantha!"

"Where's Alex?"

"Where's Cathy?"

"What happened?"

"Look here!"

"Sam!"

I shoved through the people and tried to put some distance between myself and the reporters, but they kept pace. One of them reached out and grabbed my shoulder. I shrugged him off and kept walking. I had no idea where I was or where I was going. The farther I got from the club, the more my fear fed my anger.

"Tell us what happened!"

"Leave me alone!" I glared at the reporters, but they continued to snap pictures, not caring how upset I was.

"Why are you crying?"

"Samantha! Sam!"

The guy who had grabbed my shoulder reached out and tugged on my purse while pointing a camera in my face. Something inside of me snapped and fury raced down my spine. Turning around, I shoved the camera out of his hand and kicked him in the nuts as hard as I could. He went down with a groan and I turned back around and started walking away. My entire body was shaking and I couldn't stop.

"Samantha! Why did you do that?"

"What's wrong?"

"Do you miss home?"

I turned a corner and the heel of my left shoe wedged down into a grate. I couldn't regain my footing and fell.

My body slammed against a metal trash can in a loud explosion of noise. The metal was rusted and a jagged edge gashed my leg. I gasped when I hit the ground, my head slamming against the brick wall, and more tears pooled in my eyes. I tried to stand up but my feet wouldn't work; a sharp pain shot up the leg that wasn't cut while the bleeding gash on the other throbbed. A few of the photographers put down their cameras and moved to help me, but I shoved their hands away. I didn't want them touching me. These were the people who had been chasing me.

I heard scuffling in the crowd and I looked up just in time to see Alex slam his fist into a photographer's face when he wouldn't move. The man went down with a thud and his camera exploded into a hundred pieces on the concrete. A few of the photographers protested over the treatment of their colleague, but most of them just took more pictures.

"Samantha?" The panic in his voice made my tears come faster.

Alex leaned down, his eyes checking my leg quickly before he scooped me up in his arms. The photographers went wild but gave him room. I buried my face in his shirt and tried to get control of the sobs that were trying to break free. Everything was wrong. My father was dying and I was here, being chased by the paparazzi. Even with my eyes squeezed shut I could see the bright flashes of the cameras.

"I've got you," he whispered in my ear as he walked through the crowd. When someone moved to block his path, he practically growled. "Get the hell out of my way." No one argued with him. I don't know if that was because he was the prince or because he had laid a guy out.

Becca and Duvall were there, shoving reporters and

spectators away from us so we could get to the car idling at the curb. Becca had disabled a large man and he was on his knees in front of her. One of the members from the detail opened the car door.

"Call the palace." Alex slid into the seat, cradling me in his lap. "Samantha's going to need a doctor."

"There's a first-aid kit." Duvall was in the front passenger seat and began rummaging in the glove box.

The car pulled away from the curb and sped through the streets. I kept my face pressed against Alex's shirt, unable to stop the tears. When he pressed gauze against the cut on my leg, I hissed between my teeth and tried to jerk away. He mumbled reassurances but didn't let go.

"I'm sorry. I'm so sorry." I hiccupped and tried to calm down.

"What happened?"

"Patricia called." A sob broke free and I had to take a second before I could finish. "Dad's dying. I just panicked and ran out. I was going to go to the airport."

"Samantha." Alex's voice was laced with pain.

"He's dying, Alex. I left him and he's dying." I pressed my face against his shirt again. How could I live with myself? "I left him."

THIRTY-TWO

Cancer Doesn't Care Who You're Related To
—*NEW YORK REPORTS*

EVERY LIGHT IN the palace was on and there was a crew of people waiting for us when we pulled up. Alex refused to let anyone take me from him and carried me straight to his room. He laid me on his bed but refused to leave my side, telling everyone that wasn't required to get the hell out.

A petite older woman followed us, issuing orders. "Samantha, I'm Dr. Rains. We're going to get you fixed right up." She patted me on the shoulder before moving to examine my leg.

Chadwick burst into the room and ran straight for the bed. There were tears in his eyes but he didn't say a word, just reached out and squeezed the hand Alex wasn't holding.

"You're going to feel a pinch. I'm giving you a tetanus shot and one to numb the area. You need stitches." There was a sharp stick, but I didn't care. I don't know if I was in shock, but my mind felt frozen.

Someone handed me a tissue and I realized it was the queen. Her eyes were gentle as she looked at me, her calm voice reaching through the haze that had filled my head. "We'll take care of everything."

I squeezed my eyes shut and tears slid out. The one thing I cared about, no one could fix. When I opened my eyes again, everyone was gone but Alex and the doctor. He was sitting next to me, his face stone as he watched her work. I didn't look, didn't care about my leg. When she finished, she checked the ankle of the foot that had been stuck in the grate and wrapped it with a bandage.

"Take this." She handed me a pill and glass of water.

"What is it?" I opened my eyes and tried to sit up. The stitches pulled and I winced. Alex reached down and helped lift me.

"It's for the pain. You might not feel it right this second, but that was a very nasty tumble you took and your leg is going to be sore for days."

"No. I need to get to the airport." I shook my head and felt dizzy. She leaned forward and looked at my eyes.

"Did you hit your head when you fell?"

"I don't know." Nausea built in my stomach and I swallowed. "I don't feel right."

"I think you have a concussion." She dug through her bag and pulled out a flashlight. She waved it in front of my eyes and I groaned and held up a hand. With gentle fingers she felt along my head. "No cracks or blood, thankfully. You'll need to have someone wake you every hour. I don't want you flying until I've checked you in the morning."

"You don't understand. I have to leave now." I tried to move but a wave of queasiness had me lying back against Alex.

"I do understand. Wait until the morning and I'll do a quick check. Take the medicine and get some sleep." She handed me the glass of water and watched as I took the pill. Once I had, she stood up and looked at Alex. "You understand how important it is that she not leave?"

He nodded his head and I knew I was defeated. When the doctor left, Alex scooted me farther in the bed. "I'll be right back."

I lay there on my side with my fists tucked under my cheek and tried to make sense of what had happened. Alex came back with a warm washcloth, a T-shirt, and a bowl. After locking his door, he helped me slide the dress off before wiping up the blood. I hadn't realized how much there was until he had to go get another washcloth. I watched his face as he worked and reached out to wipe a smudge off his cheek. When he was done he slid the T-shirt over my head and situated me back under the blankets. I heard him slip out of his shoes before he crawled into the bed next to me.

He didn't say anything while I cried. I was riddled with guilt and grief. I was scared I wouldn't make it back in time to see my dad again. And the tears felt never-ending. Alex stroked my hair through all of it. I had no idea how long I lay there and cried, but eventually I had nothing else in me. I felt hollow, like a piece of me had been scooped out and thrown away.

"Where's Cathy?" I should have asked before now. One more thing to feel guilty over.

"She's here." He sighed. "She had gone downstairs to grab a friend and Becca had followed her. Neither of them thought you'd leave the VIP room."

"I'm not mad. I was just worried."

"You're worried about them." He snorted. "They're fine. I doubt Cathy will ever go back to a club. I've never seen her so upset."

"I'm sorry." My voice was so hoarse I had to clear my throat and say it again. "I'm sorry I caused so much trouble."

"You didn't do anything wrong." He nuzzled my hair.

"I kicked a photographer in the nuts."

He grunted a short laugh. "That's my girl."

"I really need to get to my dad." I squeezed the hand of the arm he had wrapped around me. Even though I thought I'd cried all my tears, I got choked up again. "I left him when he needed me most."

"We'll leave in the morning."

"You'll come with me?" I whispered the question.

"Samantha, you're never going anywhere without me again."

"What about the bathroom?"

"Okay. You can go some places without me." He chuckled. "I'm sorry I wasn't there."

"You were busy." I hiccupped again.

"I have something for you." Carefully, Alex dislodged me from his arm and walked across his bedroom. When he came back he was carrying a package tied in string. "I was going to bring it to you this weekend but couldn't get away like I'd intended." He placed the package on the bed next to me.

"Is this the drawing?" I shifted so I could reach the strings and tugged it open. Under the brown paper was the sketch I had waited so long to see. Tears filled my eyes and I took a deep breath. "It's me."

He reached out and tucked some hair behind my ear. "It's okay if you don't like it. I'm not really an artist."

"I love it." I ran my fingers along the handcrafted frame. It was simple and elegant; he had captured my face and all the emotion I was feeling. "This was when I got out of the car at the airport."

"There was so much going on in your eyes. You were scared and sad, but there was determination under everything else." He lifted my chin so I was looking in his eyes. "That was the moment I knew I was lost. You were so strong and beautiful."

"I'm sorry I tried to keep us a secret." I hiccupped again. His words made me want to cry, but for a new reason. "If I hadn't, this might have worked out really differently."

He took the framed picture from my hands and set it next to the bed. "I understood. I didn't like it, but I understood." He snuggled closer. "When I saw you covered in blood . . ."

"I didn't mean to scare you."

"I have never been more afraid and angry in my life." He pressed his face in my hair and took a deep breath. "I don't want to lose you and I just knew this was the end. I wanted to kill all those people standing there and taking your picture while you bled."

"I don't want to lose you either." Tears sprang to my eyes. "I lose everyone."

"Is that why you were so stubborn?" He rolled me over gently so he could see my face.

"I didn't think I would make it if you broke my heart. Not with everything else." A sob caught in my throat. "I guess a part of me always knew it was a long shot for Dad. And I just didn't think I could lose him and you."

"Why would you lose me?"

"You have to be king! You have to make little baby heirs." I sniffled again—the more I spoke, the more tears threatened. "I know I'm stupid for worrying about that, but I knew I'd end up falling in love with you. How could I not? And then you'd have to get rid of me for someone you could marry. And you can't marry me . . . I'm just an American. And I know that's really getting ahead of myself, but why start something if you know it's going to end? And, and, and—"

"I'm not getting rid of you." He framed my face in

his hands. "You're it for me. I knew it the moment I saw you tell off the maître d' at the restaurant. Do you understand? You're it. I love you. That sketch was of the moment I fell in love with you."

"You love me?" My brain was mush and I wasn't sure if it was from his words or the pain pill.

"Yes, I love you." His eyes bored into mine.

"I love you." I traced his cheek with my fingers. "Can you tell me again when I'm not on pain medicine?"

"I'll tell you every day."

"Maybe twice a day?" I felt my eyelids growing heavy.

"A hundred times a day."

THIRTY-THREE

**HRH Prince Alex and the Duchess of Rousseau
Leave for the States**
—*LILARIAN DAILY*

*T*HE NEXT MORNING came quickly. I felt like I had barely fallen asleep before the sun was streaming through the windows. The palace was bustling with activity and it felt surreal to understand the majority of it was because of my family. There was extra security around the gates, and the photographers and journalists had been pushed farther away.

While the doctor checked me out, Alex delegated his tasks to other people. Cathy took the brunt of it, her eyes red and watery whenever she looked at me. Even though I told her it wasn't her fault, I knew she blamed herself. Becca had offered to resign, which I thought was ludicrous. When I told her to shut up, she laughed weakly and promised I would never be out of her sight again. I wasn't sure if that was a good thing or a bad thing. Alex refused to leave my side and since walking was out of the question for now, we didn't leave his room until it was time to go to the airport.

The queen had arranged for their jet to take us back

to the States and it was waiting at the airport. Chadwick had gone to Rousseau overnight in the queen's helicopter to retrieve more of my clothing for the trip. Stanley and Margie had sent food, which amused the queen, but I appreciated it. That's what you did when someone was having a hard time. You fed them. It was a tradition that crossed all cultures.

I called Patricia on the way to the airport and was relieved that Dad had finally woken up. I spoke to him briefly; he was still too tired for much. Jess and Bert were with him as well, and that helped ease some of the frustration in my heart. The doctors weren't sharing much information with them because they were technically not family, but at least he wasn't alone. That seemed like such an odd thought to me. Patricia, Jess, and Bert were the closest thing I had to a real family. I did speak with one of the physicians on the way to the airport, but there were no good answers.

The cancer cells had been spreading and nothing they tried had helped. Dad had refused more chemo and had decided not to tell anyone the extent of the trouble. It was very like him to not want anyone else to worry about him, but it made me angry. I felt like he had robbed me of time with him. I confronted Dr. Bielefeld about my father's health, but his hands had been tied. He had never passed on false information, but under doctor-patient confidentiality, he had only been able to share what Dad told him he could. He apologized for not being able to do more and I believed that he was sincerely sorry.

I slept most of the flight, still miserable from everything that happened the night before. My ankle was sprained, so I had been carted around in a wheelchair and had crutches for short distances. The media had gone bat-shit crazy when we arrived at the airport, and I could feel Alex's anger like a physical force. Last night would forever be etched in our minds. I was angry too, but for the most part I just wanted to leave. The queen was dealing with the press and I trusted her to do what was best. Her first move had been to make sure there would be no assault charges pressed against Alex and me. There was photo evidence of the man I kicked touching me and grabbing my purse, which gave me the right to defend myself.

As for Alex, it seemed the reporter was at fault for blocking rescue personnel from a person in need. I had no idea how that worked, but I was saving that to tease Alex with another day. I'm pretty sure I could squeeze several knight-in-shining-armor jokes out of it.

Photographers were waiting in the States, but I chose to ignore them. In fact, our official statement was that there was no official statement at this time and we thanked everyone for respecting us during a difficult time and for giving us our space. I didn't speak or even look in their direction; Chadwick did all the talking when needed. After the debacle with the nightclub, the city had provided police escorts for us, and a security team was set up at the hospital for my father. They were taking no chances. You'd think we would need protection like this from people pointing guns at us, not cameras.

We arrived at the front entrance in a wave of sirens and flashing lights. Jess, Bert, and a man in a suit were waiting at the doors with a wheelchair. Alex helped me out of the car and into the chair.

"Your Highness. Duchess. I am in charge of the cancer ward. I'm sorry to meet you under such terrible circumstances. If I can be of any help, please don't hesitate to let me know." The man shook our hands before making way for my friends.

With tears in her eyes, Jess threw her arms around me and then patted my head like I was a sick puppy. Bert leaned down and hugged me carefully, wincing when he saw the bruise on my left temple.

"I'm fine, guys. It's just my legs. Mostly. I could walk if Alex would stop complaining about how slow I am."

"Ha ha." He pushed the chair through the doors and into the main lobby. A few patients seemed surprised to see us, but no one gave us a hard time. The doctor in charge of the cancer ward acted like an ambassador, leading us to Dad and asking if we needed anything.

"How's Dad?" I looked at Jess.

"He was awake when we came down." She sighed. "Sam, he doesn't look good. I just want you to be ready."

I nodded my head but didn't say anything. Part of me was terrified of what I'd see and the other part of me wanted to get it out of the way. Some of the staff watched us as we walked by, but it didn't bother me. They weren't going out of their way or trying to take pictures. It was more that we were interrupting their routines. It made me feel like a normal person. Who would have thought a bunch of busy, annoyed nurses would make me feel better?

When we got to the door, I made Jess stop. "I don't want to go in there in a wheelchair."

"I'll help you." Alex slid an arm around my shoulders to help me stand.

"We haven't told him much. You guys have been all over the news, but I knew you wouldn't want him to see that," Jess explained.

"Thank you."

"We'll wait out here."

Alex opened the door so I could hobble in first. He moved beside me to help support my weight on the bad ankle and we crossed the room to the hospital bed. Patricia was sitting in a chair, knitting. Her face was pale and her eyes red. I would hug her after I saw my dad. He had to come first.

"Dad?" I touched his hand, careful to not move any of the tubes or cords. Jess had been right. He barely looked like my father anymore.

He opened his eyes slowly and gave me a weak smile. "Hey, baby girl."

Alex pulled a stool over for me so I could sit down and then moved back to give us space.

"How are you?" I wrapped his fingers around mine and fought the tears that were blinding me.

"Not too bad." He squeezed my hand.

"Liar." I sniffed.

"I'm sorry I'm leaving you." His voice was so soft I had to lean forward to hear him.

"Then don't."

"I knew it was a lost cause. Can't win this one."

"Why didn't you tell me? Why did you let me go when it was this bad?" I shook my head. "I would have been here for you."

"No." His voice rose. "You needed to live life. I wasn't going to let you give up something so wonderful because of me."

"I could have gone anytime." I groaned in frustration. "You stubborn old man."

"Sam, I didn't want you to watch me die. Can you understand that? I wanted you to remember me—the real me. Not this leftover husk."

"You're still you." Tears ran down my cheeks. "I could have played crossword puzzles with you and stolen the remote for the TV after you fell asleep."

"Remember the good times, okay?" He reached up with his other hand. I leaned down so he could touch my cheek and tried not to sob. "You've lost so much in such a short time. You deserved to be part of something lasting."

"Our family is lasting." I leaned into his palm. His fingers were so cold it broke my heart. "I wish I had been here."

"No. I loved hearing about your adventures and seeing your pictures." His hand fell and he looked around the room. "Did Alex come with you?"

"I'm here, sir." Alex moved to stand behind me.

"You take care of my Sam. She's a feisty thing, but someone needs to love her in spite of it." He squeezed my fingers and I rolled my eyes.

"I do and I will." Alex dipped his head in a small bow. "You have my word."

"Good." Dad smiled at Alex. "Good."

His fingers loosened on my hand and I panicked. "Dad?"

"Just tired." He closed his eyes and took a deep breath. It rattled loudly and I bit my lip. "Love you."

"Love you too."

I didn't move from that stool until the monitors stopped beeping and the doctors made it official. I hadn't cried so much in years. The last time was when my mother died in the car accident. When they wheeled him out of the room, Alex pulled me into his arms and rocked me against his chest. I felt small and emotionally raw. I clutched at Alex, needing to know I wasn't alone.

We buried Dad next to Mom on a bright Thursday morning. Chadwick managed all the arrangements, only asking for input when he needed it. Birds chirped in the trees and it was warm enough to not wear a large coat. There were a lot of people, most of them close friends of my family, people who had served in the military with my dad, and people from school. Cops kept the report-ers as far from the funeral home as possible and I barely noticed the cameras. I was relieved to see that many of the people were very respectful of the event. There were so many flowers I'd eventually told the funeral home to start sending them to the hospital. Might as well let the living enjoy them. Rose flew in from Lilaria to attend the ceremony and laid wreaths on both of my parents' graves and said a few words on behalf of the queen.

I spent a week sorting through my parents' home. We packed away a lot of stuff to be shipped to Rousseau and got rid of things that weren't worth keeping. I gave the house to Bert and Jess as an early wedding present. They'd never have to worry about paying rent again. I liked the idea that it wouldn't just go to some stranger. Jess would brighten the place up and give it new life.

Alex and I had stayed in my childhood room. It amused me to see him walking around such a normal house, washing his hands in the kitchen sink or sitting in my dad's old chair. I was glad Dad had met him before he passed and I'm not sure I would have realized how important that was to me until it happened.

The last couple of weeks had cemented the relationship between Alex and me. There were no more questions about how we felt about each other. I'd deal with the rest of it when the time came and do my very best.

"We can stay longer," Alex told me over dinner. "Maybe we could work it out so you can finish your degree here. I could take time away and only go back for the most important functions."

"Dr. Geller got in touch with his friend in Lilaria. They're working out a way for me to finish my degree." I was actually really relieved about that. When Dr. Geller approached me after the funeral with his idea, it had made my heart lighter.

"Still, we could stay."

"No. I'm ready to go back." I shook my head.

"You can think about it." His eyebrows pulled together. "I know you miss your home."

"My home is where you are." I reached out and grabbed his hand. "Nothing else matters."

THIRTY-FOUR

Long Live the Duchess of Rousseau
—*LILARIAN POST*

TODAY WAS THE day I would officially become the Duchess of Rousseau. In light of my father's passing, the queen had pushed the ceremony back until the summer. It had worked out for the best. Not only had I been able to work on my schooling some, but my friends were here. Patricia, Jess, and Bert were representing my family and sitting in the front row.

I could hear the large crowd gathered on the other side of the doors and looked at Alex. I bit my lip and rubbed my hands together.

"You'll do fine. You can say the words in your sleep." He chuckled. "You do say them in your sleep."

I snorted and ran a hand over my gown. It was a floor-length, fitted dress, and every inch of it was covered in silver sparkles. I was wearing the deep green sash of the Rousseau family over my shoulder and the tiara with emeralds. Alex picked up my hand and brought my fingers to his lips.

"Stop fidgeting. You're breathtaking."

"This tiara weighs eighty pounds." I reached up and touched it gently.

"You wear it very well." His eyes ran over my body in appreciation. "You look like a queen."

"Please. Did you see your mother?" I patted my dress again. She was wearing a floor-length robe that trailed behind her, a sword tied around her waist, and a diadem that was older than the building we were standing in. "I'm so nervous. Where are you sitting? You never told me. Will you be up front with your mother?"

"Where would you like me to sit?" He flashed his mischievous smile.

"Where you're supposed to." I shook my head in exasperation.

"Now you sound like a queen."

"Alex? You're being weird." I reached out and touched his cheek. "Are you okay? Are you nervous too?"

"A little." He ducked his head.

"You just have to sit there." I laughed.

"Yes, but I want to sit with your family." He looked up at me and my heart stuttered. Was he saying what I thought he was saying? He wanted to be family?

"They're pretty strict about that kind of stuff." I bit my lip. "Very formal occasions like this have a rule book."

"I know." Never taking his eyes from mine, Alex moved to one knee in front of me. My heart beat so quickly I thought it would burst from my chest. There was something humbling but exciting to see him there, looking up at me. He reached into his pocket and pulled out a box. When he lifted the lid I thought I'd faint, but I didn't know how I'd get up off the floor in this dress, so I managed to stay upright.

"You want to sit with my family." My breathing had

picked up so much that I started feeling dizzy. I knew Alex loved me, knew that he saw this as our future, but never in my wildest dreams had I expected him to propose today.

"Samantha Ellen Frances, Duchess of Rousseau, will you be my wife and queen?" His bright blue eyes stared up into mine. Love and devotion shone from them.

"Yes." My voice caught. "Yes, I will."

He slid the ring onto my finger before standing up and wrapping me in his arms. His lips touched mine and I sighed. The only way this moment could have been any better would have been if we'd been naked in bed. No fuss, no big embarrassing gestures, just a guy proposing to a girl. Asking her to be his queen. I leaned back and looked into his eyes. For a moment the world faded away and we were the only two people. The excitement and relief on his face made me laugh.

"Did you think I would say no?"

"I wasn't sure how long my luck was going to hold out." Smiling, he nipped the end of my nose. "Just remember, you said yes. No taking it back."

I shook my head. "Not on your life, Prince Yummy."

"You realize this is going to make you Princess Yummy." He laughed at my expression, pulling me even closer.

"Oh no. That's your nickname." Princess? Good Lord, I was just now ready to be a duchess!

"I bet I could come up with a few good ones." His hand moved to capture mine and he brought it up so he could see the ring.

"Hey, it's not nice to call people names."

"Princess Yummy." He leaned down and kissed the ring before looking up at me with twinkling eyes.

"I'm not feeling it." I shook my head, but I couldn't stop my heart from beating so fast. Seeing the pride in his eyes as he looked at the ring on my finger made my knees weak.

"Duchess Yummy." Lifting my hand, he placed it on his chest.

"Nope." Leaning forward, I kissed him softly. "You'll have to keep trying."

"Sex Kitten?" His eyes narrowed as he leaned forward to kiss my neck.

"You're kidding, right?"

"Mm." His mouth moved down my neck to my shoulder. "Princess Sex Kitten."

"Absolutely not." I tilted my head so he could reach the spot along my jaw. "It needs to be dignified."

"And Prince Yummy is?" That special laugh he reserved for when we were alone slid over my skin.

"Of course."

"Why don't we figure it out tonight?" His hands stroked down my waist before stopping on my hips. His fingers curled around to cradle my rear as he pulled me even closer.

"I think a conference to decide a nickname is well in order." When his mouth moved back to mine, I forgot where we were and sank into his kiss. When Alex kissed you, you didn't waste time worrying about trivial things like ceremonies or who might be watching. His kiss was meant to be savored and experienced to its fullest.

"Psst! Did you do it?" Cathy's voice made me laugh and I pulled away from Alex. She was peeking out from a side door, her eyes wide.

I held up my hand and laughed when she squealed. Her arms wrapped around us and she jerked us from side to side as she jumped in excitement.

"Okay, you're squishing me." I tried to untangle myself and touched the tiara on my head. Thankfully it was still in place.

Chadwick opened the large doors that lead to the ceremonial room and stuck his head out. "It's time."

"You're going to do great!" Cathy smiled at me as she hurried to her seat.

Alex leaned forward and kissed my head. "I'll be right up front."

With a quick squeeze of my fingers he ducked through the doors to claim his seat. Which I supposed would be somewhere with Jess and Bert. I looked down at the ring on my finger and felt my smile grow. I couldn't believe he had done this right now—just before I had to go in front of hundreds of people and God knew how many video cameras. At least I wouldn't have to force my smile, the sneaky devil.

The sound of people from the other room quieted and I wondered if the queen had entered. From the hush that seemed to blanket the other room, I would guess that was the case. It was almost showtime.

I closed my eyes and pictured my parents' faces. Mom would have loved Alex, would have been so happy to see me picking up the family tradition. I had no doubts about that. And Dad would have worn his military dress suit. He would have fit in perfectly with all of the regalia and men wearing medals.

"Samantha?" Chadwick moved to my side.

"I'm ready." I opened my eyes and looked toward the doors.

"You'll do great." Chadwick stepped away from my side and nodded to the men to announce my presence. "Just don't trip. Or if you do, don't say fuck."

I couldn't help but laugh. That would be my luck. Then again, I don't think it would surprise too many people if I did do that. So far, Lilaria had seemed to embrace my rough edges.

"Samantha Ellen Frances of Rousseau." There was a

trumpet blast I hadn't been expecting and I flinched. I laughed at my reaction and several of the people sitting close to the doors followed suit.

From the back of the room, it looked like I would have to hike a mile before I reached the queen. She was a shining dot at the end of a long runway, her jewels sparkling brightly. I kept a slow and steady pace, aware of how easy it would be to trip in my heels.

Flowers lined the walkway and music from a live string ensemble filled the air. The seriousness of the ceremony seemed to roll through the crowd. Maybe it was my imagination, or the effect of the moving music, but I felt strangely connected to everyone in the room. The history that had happened in this room was impressive, overwhelming, and empowering. My family had been part of that—they'd had a hand in building this country.

Members of parliament were interspersed with people from the FBT and royals. Some of the royals I recognized and some of them I didn't. Nobility from other countries had come for the ceremony as well, which seemed weird, but I wasn't going to tell them that. There were dignitaries from the United States and even the governor of Minnesota had received an invitation.

By the time I neared the front, I could see Alex's blue eyes trained on me. He was sitting in the front row with my friends and I felt my heart swell. With the simple choice of seat, he had announced to the world that I was his and he was mine. I noticed that there was an open seat next to Cathy and Max on a platform beside the dais, but neither of them looked upset. In fact, Max was smiling, which I had learned over the last few months was a rare occurrence when in the public eye, and Cathy practically vibrated in her seat.

Her Royal Majesty waited for me in front of her throne. Her luscious robe spread out beside her, trailing down the stairs, just out of the way. As I approached the stairs, I curtsied once, lowering my head to a respectable level before taking the steps one at a time. When I reached a level with the queen, I curtsied again, but this time did not stand back up.

"Samantha Ellen Frances, please stand before your queen." Her Lilarian words carried through the room and I did as told. Having practiced so many times over the last few months, I knew to cover my heart with my right hand.

When prompted, I declared my intentions and swore to serve the crown and throne, pledged to put the people of Lilaria first in all things, and to uphold peace in all realms. I spoke the words carefully, pronouncing each one in a loud, clear voice.

The queen pinned a medal to my sash before taking my hand in hers. Pulling me forward, she kissed me on each cheek before whispering in my ear, "Welcome to the family."

I was surprised by the emotion that welled up in my chest at her words. "Thank you."

Slowly I stepped backward, curtsying once before carefully maneuvering back to the red aisle runner. I turned to face the crowd and waited as the queen announced my new title.

"Samantha Ellen Frances, Duchess of Rousseau."

Applause almost deafened me and I shook my head, surprised. Carefully, I curtsied to the queen once more before turning to the crowd and offering them one as well. This seemed to please them even more, because when I made my way out of the side door the applause increased.

"Perfection." Chadwick stood just outside of the door with a glass of water in one hand. He handed me the drink before adjusting my sash. The queen and her family entered through the door I had used, followed by the family I had made for myself.

Alex locked eyes with me as he crossed the small room. Placing a hand on either side of my face, he kissed me until I was breathless. I could hear the people from the auditorium filing out to where there would be food and dancing, but I didn't care who might see us. I kissed him like there was no one else on the planet. If someone wanted to take a picture and post it in the tabloids, let them. It wasn't the life I had planned on, but it was mine. Knowing how quickly life could change, I wasn't going to let anything pass me by. This was one of the happiest moments of my life and I was going to live it.

EPILOGUE

The Royal Wedding Guests
—*MINNESOTA REPORTS*

$\mathcal{H}$OURS OF SMALL talk, handshaking, and the unveiling of a plaque were starting to take their toll on me. I was fidgeting with the napkin I'd picked up from one of the rotating servers when Alex managed to make his way back to me across the room.

I was getting better at these types of events, but when they were as big as this one, it was hard to not feel overwhelmed. Thankfully, Chadwick was always nearby and I could count on him to extradite me from overly enthusiastic strangers. Alex was good about not leaving my side when it could be helped; unfortunately, it was quicker for us to split up to work the room when possible. And these were all people who donated to the FBT.

"You're looking antsy." Alex ducked his head down to my ear. "Ready to get me back to the hotel?"

"These shoes are killing me." Even with the heels he had me by a few inches. "And it's after four in the morning back home."

"So, you're not planning on attacking me when we get back to our room?"

"I don't know. How soon can we get out of here?" I raised an eyebrow.

"Give me five minutes and I'll have you out of that dress." He put a hand on the small of my back and guided me toward the exit. I smiled, remembering how much it used to amuse me when he did the same thing, and now I just felt special. He dipped his head down to my ear once more. "Have I mentioned how much I like this dress?" His fingers caressed the fabric and I shivered. Even now, after all this time, I couldn't fight the pull he seemed to have on me.

"Just don't tear this one. I like it too." I looked up at him and bit my lip to try and not smile. "I'm still angry about the black dress."

"Hm, that was an unfortunate casualty." His eyes ran over my body. When we neared the door, Chadwick exited ahead of us to get our car while we said our good-byes to the mayor.

When the car pulled up to the carpet, Chadwick nodded at me to let me know it was ours. Alex and I made our move to exit, smiling for the cameras that lined the ropes. I managed to trip a little on all the fabric around my legs, but Alex caught me before I went down. I laughed at my clumsiness and gave a small wave to the cameramen as they took pictures. No matter how much they annoyed me, I'd learned a lot about handling them since my father's death. Duvall opened the door while Alex helped me slide in, and I fought with the skirts to keep them out from under my shoes.

When Alex got into the car I narrowed my eyes at him. "When I agreed to your bet all those months ago, I had no idea this is how you expected me to spend my week volunteering for the FBT."

"I know." Alex leaned back in his seat but lifted my hand to his mouth. "But I had a plan."

"Oh, like your brilliant plan for getting me to fall in love with you? Stick around until I had no choice?" I snickered.

"Exactly. I was going to make you go with me to all these events as my date." He pulled me against his side as the car drove through the streets of New York. "I was going to woo you while you couldn't run away. You'd have no choice but to succumb to my charms."

"Your ego is a scary beast. It should have its own name. We could call it something frightening like Darth Yummy." He snorted at me as I snuggled under his arm. "I thought I was going to be helping with the birds. In fact, I was looking forward to it. When did you start coming up with your elaborate schemes?"

"As soon as I realized how stubborn you were."

"So, right away?"

"Pretty much." He chuckled. "Are you ready for the wedding?"

"Ugh. Don't remind me." I shivered. "The dress, the flowers, the pictures. It's going to be torture. There's so much to do and take care of!"

"C'mon, you'll look gorgeous." He kissed my temple. "And I'll be there."

"Yes, you'll be there." I glared up at him. "Laughing at me and the brown monstrosity Jess picked out for me to wear."

"Cathy thinks Jess missed her true calling in fashion."

"She would." I frowned. Those two had been like a monster with two heads when wedding-dress shopping for Jess.

"Think of it as practice." He ran his thumb over the ring on my left hand. It always gave me tingles when he did that, to know he was part of my future. That he *wanted* to be a part of my future.

"I wish. Your mother and sister have gone off the

deep end. Did you see what they want me to wear?" I shuddered as I thought about the eighteen-yard train and lace sleeves. "The dress weighed four hundred pounds."

"I'm not allowed to see the sketches, remember?" He kissed my temple. "You seem to be holding your own though. Cathy was grumbling about flowers and ribbon last week. She's horrified by your lack of concern for texture."

"Don't get me started on the ribbons. What a stupid way to spend money. I mean, what are we going to do with all of those ribbons afterward?" Technically the queen was footing a large chunk of the bill, but I didn't care. "And they're still using the whole church thing against me. I used a lot of my leverage when I insisted on getting married outside. We should've eloped."

"The wedding needs to be what you want too." He tilted my face up to look in my eyes. "In the end, no matter our titles, this wedding is about us. No one else. We could run to Vegas right now if that's what you want."

"I know." I pressed my lips to his and sighed. I loved this man. Loved him more than I ever thought possible. He'd become the stable point of my universe—part of my family. "But your mom might behead me."

"I wouldn't let her." He tilted his head to deepen the kiss and I shifted so I could run my hands through his hair. I breathed in his smell and reveled in his taste, the knowledge that he was mine like an aphrodisiac. His phone beeped and he pulled away from me with a frown. He took it out of his suit pocket and turned it off without looking, his eyes focused on mine.

"Who was that?" I sighed, trying to not be frustrated.

"I don't know." He stretched his legs out in front of him and pulled me close again. "Don't care."

"Might have been important." I turned my face up so I could kiss his jaw. He never ignored something serious, but we tried to keep normal office hours as much as possible. Otherwise we would go insane trying to keep up with everything.

"The only thing important right now is what I plan on doing to you tonight." He turned his head so he could capture my mouth in a slow, teasing kiss.

When I leaned back to slide my hands under his suit jacket I smiled up at him. "We have to be up early for our flight to Minnesota. Jess will kill me if I'm late."

"That could be a problem." He slid his hand up to grip the back of my neck and ran his lips over the pulse point below my ear. "Because I don't plan on letting you get much sleep."

"Hm. I think I can cope." I leaned forward to bring my lips back to his, but the car stopped and I realized we were at the hotel. "Can you behave yourself until we make it to our room?"

His eyes ran down my face and along my cleavage. "I can make it to the elevator, but no promises past that."

I felt my lips pull up in a grin. "I like it when you're naughty, Prince Yummy."

"Hold on to your tiara, Duchess."

ACKNOWLEDGMENTS

**Program Cuts to Commercial
During Thank-You Speech**
—*WRITER QUIRKS*

*S*UDDENLY *ROYAL* HAS been a story in my head for years and years. Without the help of some amazing people I'm not sure I would have ever been able to do this book justice. First and foremost, I must thank my family. My husband and daughter are so patient while I get lost in my head. My sister is always supportive of the random story ideas that grab hold of my imagination. She also patiently explained bird anatomy and falconry. Aren't I lucky to have someone so brilliant?

A huge thank-you to Sarah Ross for always being willing to read over my projects. She has spectacular advice and always seems to understand what I'm wanting out of the story. A big thank-you to Erika for trying to answer all the royal questions I couldn't find answers to. A massive thank-you to Elizabeth Hunter, Angie Stanton, and Nicole Williams for reading what I've written, and Liz Reinhardt and Steph Campbell for talking me down from the ledge, because every author experiences those moments of utter craziness while writing. A big thank-you to Heather Self for reading *Suddenly Royal* and for always believing in my books (a big thank-you for your keen eyes as well). Thank you to Angie Stanton for being my royal cohort. I loved having someone to talk royals with! I also need to thank Killian McRae for being so encouraging. To my writers' group—I love you guys! Thank you for always listening or offering help. I must thank all of my friends for helping spread the word about my books. Mandy from *I Read Indie* blog is always a wonder—she's one of the first people to take the time to read my books and I will forever be grateful. Globug and Hootie: Thank you for being supportive and making me laugh! Your reviews always make me smile.

A massive thank-you to my editor, Anne, who handled my self-published editing. I don't know how I managed to con her into working with me, but I'm super glad I did.

I also must thank my lovely publicist, KP Simmon from InkslingerPR, for believing in this book. Your faith in my story means a great deal. Thank you to my agent, Rebecca Friedman, for loving my story as much as I do. You've helped open new doors for me.

Thank you, Tessa from Avon, for loving my story and helping me to expand its reach! I'm so excited to be on this journey with you and the team at HarperCollins.

Thank you to everyone who takes the time to read my books. I work really hard to give you the best story possible and I'm overwhelmed by the amount of support my readers show me.

Thank you to each and every one of you.

Want more?
Keep reading for a sneak peek at

RECKLESSLY ROYAL!

ONE

THERE WOULDN'T BE more press outside of Rousseau Manor if Queen Elizabeth herself was planning to parade around in her panties while singing the British national anthem. Which, considering the penchant for royal stalking some people had, was a frightening thought. I peeked out the curtain of the top floor when the doorbell chimed—another delivery of wedding gifts for the soon-to-be married couple. I took a deep breath and let the curtain fall closed.

I wasn't sure why I was feeling antsy as my brother's wedding drew near. Turning back to the mirror in the guest room, I traced the bags under my eyes with my fingers and sighed. I brushed the stray blond hair out of my face. The blue of my eyes looked pale, almost gray in the sterile bathroom light. I hadn't slept much in the last week trying to keep the wedding stress from landing on my brother's or Samantha's shoulders. They'd been tying up loose ends at the Future Bird Trust and attending to the immediate needs of their estates and royal duties. I knew they were worried about leaving too much for me and Max to handle while they were away for their month-long honeymoon. It annoyed me; even though I knew they were doing it out of love, it felt like they didn't think I would be able to handle the responsibility.

It wasn't just the lack of sleep that had me down though. As people RSVP'd and sent in joint gifts I was constantly reminded that I had no date for the wedding; no one guaranteed to dance with me or to sneak away with me if we got bored. It bothered me. For the last few years I had all but ignored men, kept them at a distance. I hadn't kissed anyone in so long I was beginning to doubt I ever had. My cousins were having babies and I still had my V card. It was getting to be ridiculous. And as I got older it felt more like a burden than something to be proud of—an embarrassing story to have to explain to a potential lover.

Laughter from down the hall derailed my pity party. I had things to do, and the last thing I wanted to have happen was for Sam to worry about me. Practicing a smile in the mirror, I washed my hands and brushed the hair out of my face. It wasn't that I didn't love Sam or that I minded setting everything up—in fact I loved doing it all—it was just that my loneliness had been brought into sharp relief as lovebirds and cartoon hearts circled my head.

I'd scheduled a spa day for me, Sam, and Jess. It was something to help get us ready for the wedding and even more importantly, to keep Sam out of the public eye. The country was overbrimming with paparazzi, salivating for wedding pictures. Despite her increasing comfort levels with being in the public eye, I didn't want her to be stressed before the wedding. Getting married should be a happy occasion, not something burdened with strangers and roadblocks.

I made my way down the hall and peeked into the

doorway and felt my smile become real. Samantha's feet twitched and she muttered curses under her breath as the technician worked. I covered my mouth and tried to not laugh. Jess was silently filming the whole ordeal with her phone. Probably blackmail to counter the video Samantha took at Jess's bachelorette party.

"Suck it up, cupcake!" I walked in and poked one of her flailing legs. "You don't want to look like you have hairy caterpillars attached to your face on your wedding day."

"This is torture!"

"Threading is the best way to go. You're going to look amazing." I patted her knee.

"I'm going to kill you both." Sam turned her head to look at us. "Ouch!"

"My apologies, Duchess." The technician moved to the other eyebrow. "Try to stay still and it will hurt less."

I shook my head but took a couple of steps out of Sam's reach. "Stop being a big baby."

"Just think, after this you still have your bikini waxing!" Jess laughed.

A loud grunt of anger was our only answer.

When the technician finally finished she left the room to go get the wax ready. I handed Sam a bottle of water and checked our schedule on my phone. I was debating switching the times for the massage and the bikini waxing. Maybe it would be best to do the bikini wax after the massage. That way Sam would be relaxed. Of course, if I did that, it would probably ruin that after-massage-glow. Best to leave it the way it was.

"Cathy, when I said I didn't want to go to the clubs or have male strippers, that didn't mean I wanted to have my skin peeled off my body instead." Sam narrowed her eyes at me.

"You said a spa day would be great." I laughed when

she threw a pillow at me. "Relax. We're doing fun stuff tomorrow. We're just getting the torture out of the way first."

"Oh, what are we doing?" Jess leaned forward. "Tell me it's something crazy and fun."

"I'm not telling." I shook my head. "Just get through today and it will all be worth it."

"I'm not sure anything is worth what you're putting me through today." Sam mock-glared.

"Wah. Shut it and take it like a woman!" I stood up and clapped my hands together. "Ready to get waxed?"

"No. Definitely not and never will be." Sam shook her head vehemently. "No one's going to be seeing that anyway." Sam looked at me with pleading eyes. She'd gotten really good at them.

"Hello? Honeymoon, private island, your new husband?" Jess leaned back in her seat. "You don't want to look like the bride of Bigfoot."

"Hey!" Sam reached over and shoved Jess's knee.

I snorted. "Alex wouldn't notice. My brother is disgustingly besotted."

"My luck someone would get a picture of me running around in a bikini and title it something unimaginative but equally horrible, like 'America's Hairy Duchess.'" Sam drank more of her water.

"Oh! What about 'Destitute Duchess Forgoes Wax and Razors'?" Jess laughed.

"Har, har." Sam snorted.

"And that's why we're taking care of it all today." I grabbed Sam's arm. "Enough stalling."

"Let's do this!" Jess stood up and grabbed Sam's other arm.

"You two are cruel and I never should have introduced you." Sam stood up and pulled her arms away from us.

Jess and I placed bets on how Samantha would react to the waxing procedure. I felt sure that Sam would hold it together but Jess didn't agree. Thankfully, Sam didn't burst out of the room naked and half waxed at any point, which is exactly what Jess thought would happen. This meant I won the right to not help Sam if she had to go to the bathroom in the wedding dress. Being crammed in a stall, holding yards of fabric while my sister-in-law relieved herself, really wasn't something I wanted to do if it could be helped. Instead when she came out of the room she went straight to the kitchen for wine. That was something I could get behind.

Over the last year and a half I had become very comfortable with Rousseau Manor so I headed straight for the wine cellar while Sam and Jess got glasses. A couple of years ago, I wouldn't have known where the kitchen was, much less the wine. With Sam taking permanent residence at Rousseau it had meant lots of movie nights, cookouts, and shenanigans. I looked toward the cupboard for food, but didn't have to worry. Margie, the cook, had left out a tray of snacks for us to munch on.

In triumph, I held up the bottle of red I had found, while Jess cheered.

"Gimme, gimme, gimme." Sam held her hand out. "This has been a traumatic day. I need something to get me through the rest of it."

"Pansy." I handed her a glass and poured her a hefty amount. "And next is a massage. Not exactly painful."

"Pansy, my ass! Tell me again why I couldn't just get my eyebrows waxed? They feel raw." Sam touched her forehead gently before she drank some of her wine. "And don't even get me started about the torture I just went through. I would have rather been put on the rack in the Tower of London." She winced.

"Threading is the best. Your eyebrows look fantastic." I didn't mention that there would be thousands of people taking her picture or that it would be plastered across every magazine in the world. She was already antsy about the guest list and normal stuff—she didn't need to worry about the media attention.

Samantha's phone beeped and she pulled it out of her pocket. She frowned before typing quickly.

"What's wrong?" I leaned forward to peek at her screen.

"The friend I hired to work at the FBT is getting in early. Apparently he made a mistake booking his ticket and will be here tomorrow."

"Is he staying here?" I sorted through the snacks until I found a carrot stick. "We're doing the bachelorette thing tomorrow."

"I know." Sam frowned. "He was already uncomfortable about staying here. I'm worried that if I ask him to stay the night in town it'll make it worse."

"Eh. It'll work out." I smiled and shrugged. "It always does."

"So, just a massage now?" Sam looked from me to Jess. "I could use a massage."

"Massage time for everyone." I smiled and rubbed my hands together. Sam wasn't the only one that needed to relax.

"Wait a minute! Why do you guys get massages? I'm the one that's been plucked and skinned alive." Sam frowned. "I should get all three massages myself."

"No way, Princess." I laughed when her face froze. "What? That's what you'll be in a few days. Good-bye America's Duchess and hello America's Princess."

"And one day you'll be America's Que—" Jess was stopped by the look on Sam's face.

"Nope. Don't go there." Sam shook her head. "One thing at a time. That's a lot to swallow."

"You won't have to worry about that for a long time anyway." I put my hands on the counter.

"It's just a lot to take in." Sam sighed. "It's a lot of responsibility."

"Meh. It's worth it." Jess sat up a little straighter. "You've got Prince Yummy."

"And me!" I lifted my wineglass.

"And Cathy." Jess laughed. "Not to mention a ridiculous amount of money, awesome job, and fabulous friends."

"All true." Sam shook her head. "So you're saying I should stop my bitching."

"Exactly." I laughed.

"Look at us. I'm still in school, barely sleep, and poor Cathy hasn't had a boyfriend the entire time I've known her." Jess tipped her glass toward me.

Sam looked over at me and frowned, but I shrugged it off. "I'm picky."

"We get it, Cathy." Sam sighed. "It's hard to find someone worth the risk."

"What risk? I'm not talking about you finding a husband, just someone to spend a little time with." Jess wiggled her eyebrows. "Take the edge off. How long has it been?"

My cheeks heated and I took a sip of my wine. There was no mistaking what she meant. How had the conversation turned into a discussion about my sex life?

"Jess." Sam set her glass down. "Leave her alone. She has her reasons." I'd confided in Samantha once after a night of drinking when she asked about guys at school. It had been nice to talk to someone—especially my soon-to-be sister-in-law. She hadn't made me feel foolish for being scared of what could happen.

"What?" Jess looked between us before leaning forward. "Oh my God. You mean you haven't . . ."

"No." I shrugged and hoped I could pull off nonchalance, because it was the farthest thing from what I was actually feeling. "Too much at risk. How am I supposed to know if someone wants me for me? And if I just do it to get it over with, what if they try to use it against me? Or to manipulate me?" I thought about the photos of Alex that his ex had released, and shuddered. I'd never be able to understand how he had stayed so calm. I had been a wreck and the pictures weren't even of me. "It's not just my virginity. It could haunt me forever."

"What you need to do is find someone that doesn't care about your title." Jess narrowed her eyes.

"And how do you suggest I do that?" I leaned back in my seat. "Hand out surveys?"

"You need to find someone that isn't impressed by your tiara." Jess leaned forward eagerly. "Someone that maybe even hates your title."

"Oh. That's a great idea." I sat up. "Hi, I'm a princess. I heard you hate royalty. Want to go have sex?"

Sam laughed but Jess seemed unfazed.

"Why not? Take away the title and what are you left with?" Jess asked.

"A sexy blonde with a great sense of humor." Sam wiggled her eyebrows. "It could work."

"Right." I spun the wine in my glass. I had contemplated a one-night stand before, but I hadn't found anyone that inspired that kind of lust. I didn't want it to happen and not enjoy it. That seemed pointless. But I was getting tired of waiting for the right guy to wander along . . .

"I'm just saying that if someone did show up that was really hot and didn't care for royalty, you should go for it." Jess shot Sam a look.

"What?" I narrowed my eyes.

"Nothing. I'm just saying you need to live a little." Jess smiled.

"You do need to have some fun." Sam popped a piece of cheese into her mouth. "You haven't done anything spontaneous or fun since . . ."

Her voice quieted, but I knew what she meant. I hadn't been to a club or party since the night Sam found out her father was dying. It had been such a scary night for everyone. That had been over a year ago, though. I hadn't done anything but go to school and family functions in that time. Other than my movie nights with Sam, and Jess's bachelorette party. But that didn't really count.

"Okay. We need to find you a hottie." Jess leaned on the counter and pursed her lips. "I have a friend studying to be a neurologist. He's cute and driven."

"Um, no. I do not want to be set up with anyone. That's just weird." I shook my head. "No, no, no."

"Why not?" Sam poured more wine in her glass. "We're cool people. We know cool people."

"Yes, because cool people often need to tell people that." I laughed.

Sam snorted. "C'mon. A neurologist? Some people would think that was a serious catch."

"I always thought I wanted someone like Jess's friend, but I don't know anymore. I just . . ." I pursed my lips. "Maybe you're right. I should just find someone to have fun. Stop worrying about the long term."

"That's not—"

"Exactly!" Jess cut Sam off. "Have some fun! Cut loose!"

"We'll see." I took a sip of my drink before going to rinse my glass and setting it in the sink. "Ready for your massages?"

"Hell yeah!" Sam drank the rest of the wine in her glass. "Time to relax."

"Then come on!" I forced a large smile. Thinking about my love life, or rather the lack of my love life, was depressing. The chances of finding someone that would love me for me were so slim, they practically didn't exist. What Alex had found with Sam was a miracle. I'd be lucky if I found someone that didn't make me want to puke when I saw them.

TWO

"WHEN I SAID I wanted to do something crazy, I didn't mean I wanted to become a stripper." Sam stood in the large formal living room, looking at the silver poles in front of her. "Be honest. Did Alex put you up to this?"

"No, but he's going to owe me." I snickered and sat down on the floor to stretch.

"Be honest, you didn't hire a stripper, did you? That guy in the spandex, currently sitting in my kitchen is not going to shake his man-pickle in my face, right?" Sam grabbed a bottle of champagne and poured us all a glass. "Because if you did, I'm going to need a lot more to drink. He looks like Gene Simmons on steroids."

I chuckled loudly. "No. I didn't hire a stripper."

"Damn." Jess winked at me.

"I thought this would be fun! Crazy and silly, and not out at clubs or at bars where people could see us." I took my flute from Sam and had a swallow.

"This is going to be awesome. Can you imagine Bert's face when I tell him what we did tonight?" Jess bounced on her toes a little. Her new husband would probably be thrilled.

"Did you see the teacher? He could kill us with one punch! This is going to be work! And hard." Sam narrowed her eyes.

"It's a fun class, I made sure." I leaned over, touching my head to my knee. When I sat up Sam was glaring at me. "What?"

"Okay, Miss I-Can-Touch-My-Head-To-My-Leg. I'm sure this will be a blast." Sam laughed. "If I have a heart attack tell Alex I loved him."

"Will do." I stretched out over the opposite leg.

"Is it just going to be us?" Jess sat down on the floor and started her own stretches.

"Nope. We have a few more people coming." I leaned forward and brushed the floor with my fingertips.

"Who else?" Sam dropped to the floor next to me.

"Friends." The doorbell rang and I hopped up off the floor. "I'll get it."

I could hear voices and my smile grew. Yanking open the double doors I threw myself at Daniel, my face breaking into a smile. Laughing, he spun me in a circle.

"Cathy!" He kissed my cheek before setting me back on the ground. We'd become very close over the last couple of years.

"Why don't you twirl me around like that?" Chadwick asked. They'd been openly dating for a year now, and I loved seeing them both so happy.

"Because you don't have all that blond hair to spin around." Daniel made a tsking noise. "You keep cutting it too short."

"Not to mention it's red." Chadwick rolled his eyes. "And I look like a Muppet if I don't cut it." He leaned forward and kissed my cheek.

"You look great." I led them back into the house. "And dapper as always. I'm loving the tie." I flicked the pink plaid silk with my fingers. Chadwick was my favorite shopping buddy.

"I thought you were with the guys!" Sam stood up and hugged Daniel before glaring at Chadwick. "You lied!"

"I most certainly didn't. We were there and now we're here."

"Yes. Too much testosterone." Daniel laughed.

"Cathy asked us to come to this first, but there was no way I was going to be here while Sam got waxed." Chadwick shuddered. "Did she hurt anyone?"

"She was very well behaved." I winked at him.

"Oh my. So you were serious about the pole dancing." Daniel walked around one of the poles, a hand on his chin. "This could be interesting."

"Very serious. Now go change!" The doorbell rang again. "Got it."

The guest list wasn't very long, but I'd made sure the important people would be there. Sam's surrogate mother, Patricia, arrived with Lady Adriane, and Heather, the Duchess of Minsington. It might seem weird to invite Adriane, one of my brothers ex's, but she and Samantha got along well.

Opening the door, I threw my head back and laughed. All three of them were wearing feathered boas in bright colors.

"We brought one for everybody!" Patricia held up a bag.

"You have no idea just how perfect that is." I hugged them each before leading them back to the room. I pulled a bright pink boa out of the bag and wrapped it around my shoulders. Our instructor had turned up the music and was doing hip gyrations near one of the poles. He totally did look like Gene Simmons, minus the creepy face paint.

"Oh my." Patricia put a hand up to her heart.

"Oh my doesn't cover it." Heather cocked her head to the side. "I think I've been married for too long. I don't remember ever seeing a man move like that."

"You didn't go to the right places." Adriane wiggled her eyebrows before heading for the center of the room and stretching. I'd told everyone to bring workout clothes so there wouldn't be any wardrobe crisis, and it seemed that constant nagging and list making was paying off. Everyone had brought what they needed for the night.

"Let's get ready to shake this house!" The instructor clapped his hands, his French accent making it hard to understand him. "Loosen up! Get your blood pumping!"

"What did he say we're going to do to my house?" Samantha leaned toward me.

"Just move!" The music filled the room, making the windows shake. I'd forgotten how much I loved to dance. It didn't take long before I was letting go of *Princess Catherine* and dancing like Cathy—and it felt good. Free and fun. I bumped butts with Patricia, wrapped a boa around Chadwick, and laughed as Daniel did the YMCA.

I downed another glass of champagne while joking with Jess about the wedding and the new moves we were learning. Tonight was my one chance to relax and have a good time, so I wasn't going to play it safe. There were no reporters or photographers to catch me in a bad light. It was liberating. I could already feel a nice buzz from the alcohol and was enjoying myself more than I had in years. Good friends and fun would do that for a person.

Samantha was watching Patricia wiggle and shake while trying not to laugh, and almost knocked over the table with the snacks and drinks. I saved the bottle of champagne while Jess grabbed the tray of cheese. Deciding it would be better to consume the alcohol than risk it being wasted on the floor, I poured the rest of the champagne into my glass and went back to the dance floor.

Once we were loosened up, the instructor started teaching us simple swings on the pole. He made sure we put our hands in the right place and were ready to hold our weight. He adjusted my leg before rushing off to help at the pole next to mine. Giggles fought to escape my mouth as I watched Chadwick and Daniel try to push Patricia up the pole. Chadwick's normally perfectly coifed hair was mussed as he tried to coach her into wrapping her legs around the metal shaft. Daniel was making obscene faces while he propped her up with his back.

"I can't do it! I can't do it!" Her voice was high as she gripped the pole tightly. "Stop trying to bend me in *unnatural* ways!"

I couldn't help the laugh that escaped me as I watched the three of them crash back to the ground. Hurrying to their sides, I helped untangle their limbs before helping them off the ground. Patricia was red cheeked, and Daniel, who had borne the brunt of her weight, made a beeline for the drinks.

"Well, that's the first time I've been under a woman." He took a large gulp of his drink before turning to whisper loudly to Samantha. "And I think it will be the last time, too."

Patricia decided to watch the rest of the class while shouting jokes, but the instructor didn't let the rest of us escape. He wasn't a difficult instructor, but he did try to teach us some of the moves instead of letting us just swing around on the pole. I gripped the cold metal firmly in my hands and lifted myself from the ground before leaning backward and letting go so that only my legs were holding my weight.

Sam whistled and I gave her a thumbs up that was actually a thumbs down because of the way I was hanging. The thought made me laugh and my grip on the pole loosened, letting me slide down closer to the floor.

"Don't distract me! I'm upside down." I giggled.

"You're also drunk." Sam tilted a little, unsteady on her feet.

"You're just jealous that I can pole dance." I stuck my tongue out at her, which made her laugh.

I was a bit sloshed, but I wasn't going to tell Sam that. My legs slipped and I slid the rest of the way to the ground, my head stopping my fall. Maybe I was drunker than I thought. The doorbell rang as I scrambled up from my spot on the floor.

"I've got it!" Chadwick took off for the front door, his steps a little too loud.

Backing away I took a running jump and grabbed the middle of the pole. I used my momentum to swing my legs high in the air. Making sure I had a good grip on the pole I spread my legs into a split.

"Wow." A deep voice broke into my thoughts and I looked up. A man was standing next to Chadwick, wearing a backpack and carrying a large duffle bag. His dark eyes ran over my body and I shivered, which was a bad thing. My hands slipped and I fell, crashing to the floor with a loud "oof".

"Are you okay?" Sam ran over and helped me stand up, but I wasn't feeling any pain. In fact, I was feeling awesome. Looking past Sam's shoulder I smiled at the hottie and waved. He was perfection, from his messy dark hair down to his scuffed boots. And exactly what we needed to end the night with a bang.

"Heeey yooou. I don't remember hiring a stripper, but boy am I glad you showed up." I let Sam help me up to my feet and wondered why she was making a choking sound. I slapped her on the back, worried. "Are you okay?"

"I'm fine. Fine!" Sam barked a laugh. "That's not—"

"Good! Because it looks like I outdid myself!" I turned her around with a flourish to look at the delicious man standing on the stairs. His shirt strained across his chest as he shifted his feet, and I found myself thinking about tracing my fingers across those hard lines. I let my eyes run over him instead, taking in the tight plaid shirt, worn jeans, and work boots. There was nothing polished or metropolitan about him. Everything screamed outdoors. And I liked it.

"Cathy," Sam tried to stop me, but I shrugged her off and skipped up the steps.

"What are you supposed to be? A lost lumberjack?" I pulled the heavy bag out of his hands and set it on the ground. "We'll, c'mon! Someone start the music." I gyrated my hips a little and wiggled my eyebrows. "Take it off, bab-ay!"

"If you insist, gorgeous." His American accent gave me pause as a dim memory tried to fight through the fog in my brain, but it didn't last long. His eyes stayed locked on mine as his calloused fingers worked the top couple of his buttons free. I wasn't sure if it was the alcohol, or just his deep brown eyes, but I was entranced. I didn't even notice when Sam climbed the stairs.

"God, please don't, David. I'll never be able to look at you again." She covered his hands with her own and laughed, her cheeks a bright red.

"David?" I looked at him, confused before looking

over my shoulder at Jess. She was nodding her head with wide eyes like I was supposed to remember something. "David?" I said the name again, mulling over what that could mean.

I looked down at the bag I had taken from him and my eyes landed on his boots. It was then that a moment of clarity surged through my mind like a stampede of wild horses, and I covered my mouth.

"Oh God." A wave a nausea hit me. "You're Sam's friend."

I promptly turned around and threw up into a potted plant.

At Avon Books, we know your passion for romance—once you finish one of our novels, you find yourself wanting more.

May we tempt you with . . .

- **Excerpts** from our upcoming releases.

- Entertaining **extras**, including authors' personal photo albums and book lists.

- Behind-the-scenes **scoop** on your favorite characters and series.

- **Sweepstakes** for the chance to win free books, romantic getaways, and other fun prizes.

- Writing **tips** from our authors and editors.

- **Blog** with our authors and find out why they love to write romance.

- **Exclusive content** that's not contained within the pages of our novels.

Join us at
www.avonbooks.com

*G*ive in to your Impulses!

These unforgettable stories only take a second to buy and give you hours of reading pleasure!

Go to *www.AvonImpulse.com* and see what we have to offer.

Available wherever e-books are sold.

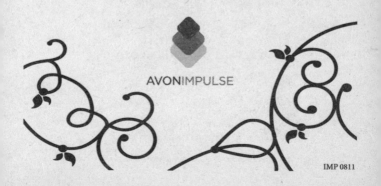

AVONIMPULSE